Usurper

A. J. Maguire

A Wings ePress, Inc.
Fantasy Romance

Wings ePress, Inc.

Edited by: Heather O'Connor
Copy Edited by: Jeanne Smith
Executive Editor: Jeanne Smith
Cover Artist: Richard Stroud

Wings ePress Books
www.wingsepress.com

Copyright © 2018 by A J. Maguire
ISBN-13: 978-1-61309-677-2
ISBN-10: 1-61309-677-1

Published In the United States Of America

Wings ePress Inc.
3000 N. Rock Road
Newton, KS 67114

Dedication

For Brendon Mann, my ideal reader.

* * *

One

Curahadh stronghold had no great hall; the centermost area of the castle was an open space bordered by four great trees rising high above a dais of marble and gold. Magic kept the trees lush and green, their wide leaves shading much of the court from any weather. Only the dais itself was not covered, its pale marble a pleasant contrast to the greenery surrounding it. Brigetta suspected there was magic at play there too, some small enchantment to keep the king from getting rained on, but she did not bother looking into the ether to see.

The eyes of the court were on her, waiting for her to speak as she knelt at the base of the dais, and she had to swallow a lump of fear that had lodged in her throat. Her tongue felt thick and dry, suddenly uncooperative, but she managed to speak at last, her voice clear as it carried through the open yard.

"The Blood Mage Noffi Elana Ordin is dead," she said. "The mage passed four nights ago in the comfort of her home on Ragamont Mountain."

Brigetta's announcement sent a roar of shock and denial through the Dyngannon court. Unrest washed through the crowd like a tide, rippling back only to push forward again as the full impact of her words settled on the people. Staring hard at the wide, elegant steps in front of her, Bree battled her own grief and tried to remain still. She kept her head bowed low, as was custom for addressing royalty, and tried to concentrate on the shimmer of quartz embedded in the stairs.

To anyone else, that glitter of quartz might have seemed inappropriate for the delivery of such tragic news, but Brigetta found a strange comfort in it, like her mentor was somewhere close by, winking at her through the very stones surrounding them.

Not dead at all, just alive in a more profound way.

"I assume she has sent you to be her replacement as Royal Blood Mage." King Porrex's voice put a stop to the din of hushed conversation building through the courtyard and Bree finally looked up.

The king seemed unruffled by the discord in his court, standing proud and regal, his ruby-tipped crown blazing in the sun, and his pointed ears looking pale against the darkness of his hair. His gray eyes squinted down at where she knelt, three scant steps away, and fear prickled at the base of her neck. For a silent moment she cursed Noffi for giving her this task, and then she bowed her head because her next words were sure to upset him and she had no desire to see his royal fury directed at her person.

"No, Great King," she heard the shakiness in her voice and paused to take a breath. "Good King," she said, sounding steadier this time, "my teacher sent me with a final message. Her instructions beyond delivering it are private."

This wasn't entirely true. Noffi hadn't specified whether or not she could tell the king of the quest she was about to take. Common sense, however, told Brigetta that informing His Royal Majesty that she was about to seek his replacement was a bad idea.

"What message has she sent?" Porrex asked.

"Simply this," Bree spread her hands before her—mostly to prove she was unarmed—and took another deep breath. The movement slid her cloak over her shoulders, revealing the intricate, swirling tattoos curling over her hands and arms. Inked into her skin in metallic golds and reds, the tattoos caught the sunlight in a delicate shimmer that caused another stir in the crowd.

Bree tried hard to ignore the sudden murmurings. She found it odd that people could be so ignorant of their own culture, and then had to remind herself that she'd been among the superstitious and terrified populace once. Noffi warned her of the fear that would come with the title of Blood Mage but she still found it unsettling, all the whispered prayers and sudden cowardice that welled up in people when she was around. She may have learned to harness magic in a way that the average Eldur couldn't, but that didn't change her core.

She was still Brigetta Isleen Chridhe, daughter of Meery and Loftson Chridhe of Grace Valley, even if her father did refuse to be alone in a room with her anymore. He looked at her with as much distrust and terror as the crowd rimming the royal dais did now, as though she might suddenly smite the whole of the court into the sea.

Noffi's voice floated through her memory. *"The people fear mages almost as much as they need them."*

Stamping down on her wayward thoughts, Bree concentrated on her purpose and addressed the king. "There is a beginning and an end to all things, Great King," she said, taking a little pride in how strong she sounded. She lowered her arms again and waited for the king's response.

Her cloak slid back into place, hiding the tattoos once more, but several in the front still stared, some in wonder and some in fear. One girl in particular shrunk closer to her father, who put a protective hand on her shoulder and drew the child even nearer. Porrex, on the other hand, did not appear moved by the sight or the message, which might have been a relief except that his cold gray eyes remained fastened on Brigetta's face. She met his gaze and knew in that instinctual, silent way that he understood her purpose.

Of course he did, she thought. One did not remain King of Dyngannon for a century without learning to interpret certain things.

Gods, Noffi, did you send me here to die?

"Cryptic and poetic." Porrex ignored the restless whispering in the crowd. "Precisely what am I to do without a Royal Blood Mage?"

She breathed a little better. This much, at least, she was prepared for.

"There are two other mages in Dyngannon, Your Majesty. I am certain either would be more than adequate for the position."

The king's mouth pursed into a grim line, displeasure ebbing out from him, and for a long moment she debated the merits of using her magic. She was not a political creature but she understood the dilemma in front of them. While there were two other blood mages in Dyngannon, she was the only mage who had practiced under Noffi's tutelage and Noffi had been the greatest mage of their time. The king would undoubtedly prefer her talents to the lesser mages of Dyngannon.

"*You are not a witless child.*" Noffi's voice chastised her from the grave. "*Quit acting like one.*"

Bree lowered her gaze to the white of the staircase and frowned, trying to anticipate the king. If he ordered her to remain as his Royal Blood Mage, she would be forced to escape the city and, quite possibly, be branded a traitor for it. But no, she thought, he would not want to ostracize the most talented blood mage in Dyngannon. The people may fear her talents but they also revered them. It would create an instability in his rule that he could not afford.

He would have to be subtler than that.

She glanced up again to find the king's gaze still fastened on her. He looked, she thought with further dread, quite calculating.

"You will remain at my pleasure," Porrex said, his gaze moving off to something or someone behind her. "We will discuss the position of Royal Mage in private."

Subtle indeed, she thought. It was time for her to disappear.

With a wave of his hand, he dismissed her at last and she slipped into the crowd. People parted to let her through, most of them shrinking away in the effort not to touch her, some going so far as to draw their expensive cloaks closer, as though Bree might contaminate the fabric of their finery. Bree pretended not to notice them, keeping her gaze focused on the path in front of her as she walked. No one stopped her, not yet, though she suspected someone would eventually.

Finding the closest doorway, she ducked inside and began heading for the outermost hallways of the keep. Gleaming obsidian floors replaced the pale marble stone of the court and labyrinthine corridors curved around the growth of many trees so seamlessly they looked as though the castle itself had grown into the land. And indeed it might have.

The fortress did not look like anything built by Eldur hands; there were no crude corners or the awkward fit of stone on stone. The walls fit snugly against each tree, the floors making way for any protruding roots that showed through without cracking, and here and there a patch of vines would crawl over the vaulted ceiling high above.

Brigetta had only visited Curahadh twice before, both times with Noffi, and her heart pinched at the memory. On each occasion Noffi had visited the hall of memory, the corridor where the names of the dead had been inscribed into the walls themselves with elegant, careful script, but Brigetta did not have the luxury of time. She imagined Noffi would have clucked her tongue at that, chastising her for being impatient and in too much of a hurry.

Still, she did not alter course. She made her way to the front gates, slipping the hood of her cloak over her head before stepping out into sunlight again. Most of the guards seemed to be in at court, leaving the dusty outer courtyard strangely vacant as she began her trek for the stable.

The courtyard itself was a wide semi-circle, ending on either side with a conical tower of white and black brick. Another testament of magic if she'd ever seen one, for the stones of the towers meshed so well that not even vine could find a place to climb. The outer wall, on the other hand, was of Eldur design: forty meters thick and housing several smaller buildings that Brigetta had never found the time or the interest to identify. Bakers or tanners or other such persons worked or dwelled there, likely both.

She cast a glance at two guards lounging on the wall.

Her companion, the Human known as Faxon Mylonas, was leaning casually against the stable wall but he seemed to spot her exit from the castle. She saw him straighten and duck inside the stable and knew he was fetching the horses as they had planned.

Praising the gods that he'd chosen to listen to her for once, she tried to relax as she closed the distance to the stable door.

They were almost out.

With any luck, the king would be too busy with all his courtiers and state affairs to notice her departure. It was a thin hope, she knew that, but she held onto it anyway, not wanting to deal with any unpleasantness.

Damn you, Noffi. Couldn't you have lived long enough to do this yourself?

She risked one glance over her shoulder and tension knotted in her stomach.

Two Dyngannon soldiers were following her, their black and green livery making them stand out against the pale stone tower. They were sturdy looking but young. Obviously Porrex did not expect her to fight a direct order. If he did, he would have sent veterans.

When they spotted that she had turned, one of them called out for her to stop, but Brigetta pretended she hadn't heard and hurried into the stable.

Of course it wouldn't be that easy. Of course the king would try to detain her. He'd read the threat in that message just as clearly as she had when Noffi told her to deliver it.

"Damn, damn, damn," she muttered to herself but the words were lost in the shuffle and whinny of several horses.

Faxon had both of their horses saddled and ready, but he hadn't mounted yet. His feral, golden eyes flicked to the stable entrance and a look of mild humor crossed his angular face. "It did not go as planned?"

"Was there supposed to be a plan?"

He flashed a wicked grin. "Can I kill them?"

Seven years with the man as her subjugate had numbed her to

his morbid humor and penchant for violence but she cast him an impatient look anyway. His grin widened, making the hollows of his cheeks deepen with shadow. He looked altogether like a madman with his thin, crooked nose and the heavy brow half hooding those golden eyes. His smile said he was just bored enough to want to kill someone and for a surreal moment she asked herself how she had come to be married to such a creature.

But she knew precisely how and why and the memory made her heart ache a little.

Some things were not worth dwelling over.

"No. Not unless we have to," she said just as the two soldiers stalked into the stable. Faxon's smile slipped a fraction but he didn't respond, turning instead to face the newcomers.

"Blood mage," one of the men said, sounding a little out of breath from the walk. She tried to gauge how old he was but Eldur were naturally prone toward elegant features and ageless appearances. Still, she was right at the fore; these two were young.

Brigetta took the reins of her horse. "That I am," she said, praying the two might be superstitious enough to let them go.

Maybe she could conjure a little magic and frighten them off.

But there was no such thing as a little blood magic. It always came with a cost and it always required the blood of an Eldur to work.

Gods, this was all so impossible. Why had she ever agreed to this?

"His Majesty demands your presence," one of the guards said, sounding firm and unyielding.

Faxon clucked his tongue. Even in her peripheral vision she could see that he was sizing up the two men. She supposed she should be grateful he hadn't already made his move, but they were in the heart of Dyngannon and he was a Human, the sworn enemy of the Eldur people. Common sense seemed to be holding him in check. Thus far his cap had kept his very round ears hidden from any scrutiny but his tanned skin and sharper features were bound to give him away at some point.

"Beloved," Faxon winked down at her, "His Majesty 'demands' your presence. Should I be jealous?"

"Do not be an idiot," she said, sliding one foot into a stirrup. The metallic sound of swords being drawn raked up her spine, forcing her to pause. Still poised to mount her horse, she closed her eyes and tried to ward off her mounting panic. Gods help her, they were really going to do this. Not turning around, she spoke again. "Gentlemen. I have no qualm with you. Do not force blood to be shed."

"The king has given you a direct order, Mage."

"Are all Eldur soldiers this annoying?" Faxon didn't move but she felt the change in him.

Violence hummed into their little space, forcing her to take a slow, calming breath. While her husband thrived on conflict, Bree abhorred bloodshed, and for the space of three heartbeats she tried to think of a way out of this situation that didn't include Faxon proving his deadlier talents.

Perhaps becoming Royal Blood Mage wouldn't be so awful. It would protect them both from execution, which was what the people would demand if they knew she'd married a Human. But to devote herself to Porrex's rule would go against Noffi's wishes and she simply could not stomach that.

"I am disobeying the king. Step aside or my lover will kill you," Bree said, lifting herself into the saddle and turning to face them.

Faxon smiled, which made him look insane again so she kept her attention on the soldiers. She could prick her finger. That action alone would give the two Eldur soldiers reason to pause, which might prevent further bloodshed.

"Only bleed when it is necessary. There are plenty of Eldur who can do it for you." Noffi's voice intruded again and Bree hissed through her teeth.

Every option she had today seemed to go against the woman.

Brigetta wondered what her great mentor would say about the unorthodox manner in which Faxon received magic, but she shoved the thought aside and tried to concentrate on the problem in front of her. Noffi had only met Faxon once in passing; she had not known

Faxon to be a subjugate at the time—thank gods—and certainly hadn't known about the marriage. She imagined the old mage would have had several things to say about the whole arrangement.

Frowning down at the indecisive soldiers, Bree looked to Faxon again. The longer they took here, the less chance they'd have to escape. Time was slipping away from them; the king would not wait long before sending more men, and court was likely nearing completion. If they were going to escape, it had to be now.

"Kill them," she said, forcing herself not to think of their youth. Gripping the reins until they creaked in her grip, she fixed her gaze on the juncture of the stable door and took a careful breath.

Faxon didn't pause; she'd known he wouldn't. The moment the order was given, he flew into action. His body swiveled to the left, unnaturally fast, as he pivoted around the closest soldier, who looked startled in spite of the weapon he'd already drawn. Bree saw Faxon's left hand drive into the gullet of the poor Eldur, spotted the spray of blood though she hadn't seen a dagger. A detached part of her mind decided that the terrifying thing about Faxon Mylonas was his proficiency at hiding blades.

The first soldier toppled to the ground as the second made his advance, swiping his sword at Faxon's shoulder so quickly she could hear the whoosh of air as the blade moved. Faxon ducked the strike and seemed to roll around the Eldur, his cloak snapping open in the quick movement. He ended up just behind the soldier, who was surprised and unprepared for the swift slide of Faxon's weapon. It sliced through the Eldur's neck, making a sudden and gory mess on the hay-scattered floor.

Blood pulsed in the air, invisible and thick and thrumming in time to Brigetta's heartbeat. Noffi was right, she thought, as she began to take measures; there were plenty of Eldur around who could bleed for her.

Bree opened her left palm and closed her eyes, allowing the steady beat of blood and heart and magic to fill her. She felt it at her center, a thrumming that needed direction, and concentrated on the horses. They couldn't afford to have someone else come and investigate. She thought for a moment about sending the mess elsewhere, but that would take more energy and time than she had. Porrex was bound to discover the deaths anyway, and given that she'd refused to meet with him, the clever king would draw the right conclusions.

Preferably after they'd boarded their boat.

The horses settled, magic having calmed them, and she sensed as magic slowly pooled around her right forearm, sinking with an unpleasant tingling sensation into a new, swirling tattoo. The tingling turned to a burning as magic inked her skin, exacting its price. She was a vessel of magic now, a storehouse, and one day—one day soon, she feared—every tattoo on her body would be stripped from her at the whim of magic itself.

When she opened her eyes again, Faxon was mounted and ready, his expression unnervingly sated. A little dazed by the transaction, she rubbed her forearm, shaking her head at the silent question in Faxon's eyes. They did not have time for her to discuss it, so he sent her a lazy wink and they spurred forward, out of the stable and away from Dyngannon court.

Two

Troy'vesk Mavon stood on the deck of the *Bitter Croften* watching his best friend untangle a fishing net for inspection, and cursed himself for being a coward. He'd rehearsed his confession a dozen times the night before, but now that the time had come, he suddenly feared what it could mean, what it could do to the friendship that had defined the whole of his life.

Kaden was going to kill him for this, he just knew it.

Hesitating, Troy frowned at the cloud-scattered horizon, thought about commenting on the weather—yet again—and finally took a deep breath of salty sea air. There was no help for it; he had to tell the man and he had to tell him now, so he turned to face his friend and said, quite a bit more loudly than he'd intended, "I kissed Evaliana."

Troy let the statement fall between them and tried not to cringe. The memory of the heated kiss intruded on him, his body suddenly torn between an aching desire to go find the woman again and the anticipation of violence from the man before him. He fully expected Kaden Dyngannon to fight him over the infraction; one did not kiss Evaliana without her brother taking offense, so Troy prepared himself for whatever Kaden might do.

Under normal circumstances, Troy would have argued that whoever Liana decided to kiss was her own business, but he wanted very badly to do it again. And again and again for the rest of his life, if he could. His fingers could still feel the slight curve of her waist and his mind was suddenly overwhelmed with the taste of her. For a dazed moment he forgot to breathe, and then remembered what he'd just said and to whom he'd said it, and he frowned, confused by the lack of violence.

"Oh?" Kaden asked and tossed an empty net onto the deck of the ship. "Did she kiss you back?"

"I beg pardon?"

Kaden chuckled and started spreading out the net, inspecting for holes and the like without looking up at him. "I asked if she kissed you back."

"You're not going to hit me?" Troy asked, a little stunned by this response and uncertain of how to process what was happening. By his estimation he should have had a broken nose by now, among other broken bits.

"Not unless you want me to," Kaden said and laughed, brighter this time, and Troy started to relax.

Cautiously, still puzzled by this reaction, Troy began to help with tending the net. Their little fishing boat swayed under the light rock of ocean waves, and every now and then he felt the knocking of the boat against the pier. Gulls squawked nearby and men from some of the larger vessels at harbor shouted orders to one another. A brisk breeze carried the scents of Big Hearth Tavern to mingle with the heavier ocean smells, confusing his senses with dead fish and sea salt and cooked onions.

Troy kept Kaden in his peripheral vision as his fingers started searching the net for weak spots, but Kaden's lean, tall form was relaxed, his thin mouth quirked up into a half-smile. Kaden had discarded his cap some time ago and sunlight gleamed off the metallic silver streaks in his black hair. The sight was always a little jarring, reminding Troy again of the differences between them.

Human and Eldur had more similarities than differences, of course, but the pointed ears and the streaked hair were hard to miss. Though not all Eldur had streaks in their hair. Evaliana didn't. Neither did Nelek. Troy was given to understand this was a matter of magic, which all Eldur inherently possessed but not all Eldur could harness. Which was confusing in its own right. But Troy had decided long ago that most things about the Eldur were complicated and odd.

If Kaden was self-conscious about his hair, he didn't show it. But then, he'd grown up on this island, surrounded by Humans who found his odd hair and pointed ears to be fascinating. Kaden was probably used to being stared at, though Troy had never bothered to ask him about it.

He wondered if it bothered Kaden at all.

"You've throttled every other man who's gotten close to Liana before," Troy said. He found a thin bit of rope and reached for the mending kit beside them.

"Bah. They were all dogs. And most of them wanted far more than a kiss."

"I'd be lying if I said I didn't want more," Troy said, his fingers still busy at work.

Gods, he hated nets.

Kaden stopped what he was doing to look at him. "Just how much more?"

And there was the violence Troy had been expecting, sudden and fierce, held under tight control. Troy met his friend's deep green eyes and fought down his momentary terror. He wasn't afraid to fight Kaden—he might even win if he tried hard enough—but he did fear losing the man's regard. The friendship they had meant more to him than he cared to admit out loud and, to be frank, it would be a hell of a lot harder to court Evaliana if her brother disapproved. And he did intend to court her properly, whether she laughed about it or not. The girl seemed to find propriety amusing and rarely followed the rules.

Which, in retrospect, was probably why she'd let him kiss her in the first place.

"Gods honest truth, Kaden, I'd marry the woman if she'd let me."

All at once Kaden relaxed and gave him a charismatic grin, his teeth flashing in the sunlight. "I thought so."

"You've been expecting this?" Troy asked, relieved again by the easy manner in which his friend was taking the news.

This wasn't turning out nearly as badly as he'd anticipated.

Kaden nodded and continued his inspection and Troy shook his head, half exasperated by his restless nature and half amused by it. The man couldn't simply hold a conversation... he had to keep moving, to divide his focus, which normally didn't bother Troy, but today they were talking about Liana and hopefully a long courtship leading to a possible marriage. Now that he thought about it, this conversation probably shouldn't have been done on the deck of the *Bitter Croften* with a bucket full of fish guts an arm's length away.

Troy heaved a sigh, chastising himself for his own timing. But there was no taking it back now, so he just shrugged and hurried to finish his work.

"The two of you have been dancing around this romance for years now," Kaden said, groaning a little as he stood to stretch. "A little advice, though?"

Troy finished with the net and followed his friend to his feet. "Of course."

"Mother won't mind the kissing but don't mention it to my father." Kaden smirked and squinted up at a low-flying gull. "Liana's his gem and all, you know? He won't like it."

Troy glanced out at the harbor, where Nelek Dyngannon was headed in their direction. The older Eldur man paused his progression over the harbor to make some laughing conversation with a fellow fisherman. He was a well-formed man, trimmed with the daily sword practices he demanded of his children, which on most days included Troy.

A beige swatch of cloth was wrapped around Nelek's head, hiding the long, pointed ears Troy knew to be there. Troy had come to understand this as a matter of safety rather than shame. Many of the Humans on Vakeshmeer were friendly with the Dyngannon family in spite of the fact that they were Eldur, but there were a select few who were not. Hiding their ears put the Humans at ease, which lessened the chance of confrontation.

It seemed unfair that the Eldur would need to hide at all.

Evaliana rarely did so. Troy had to fight back another memory as the girl's father approached. There was something distinctly wrong in thinking about her mouth, sweet and warm and supple under his own, when Nelek was so close.

"Do you think *he'll* hit me?" he asked Kaden, while the man was still out of earshot.

With a laugh and a wink, Kaden scooped up the mended net and tossed it onto the growing pile near the center mast. "He might."

"Hello, boys," Nelek said, stopping just short of the boat. His blue eyes inspected the deck once before he looked up to smile at them. "Are we ready for tomorrow?"

"Ready and clear, Father." Kaden made a limber jump from the boat to the pier.

"Excellent." Nelek paused to consider Troy, one dark eyebrow quirking upward. "You look like I just caught you with your hand in the honey pot, Troy'vesk Mavon."

Kaden's laugh bellowed over the harbor, and Troy glared at him. His glare seemed to go unheeded and Nelek glanced between them, that dark eyebrow hiking up a little higher in question. Troy leapt from the boat to the pier, trying to prepare himself for yet another confrontation, but another form jogged up to them from the harbor and the moment was lost.

Just as well, Troy thought. He didn't fancy a broken nose today.

"Oy, glad I caught ye." The familiar, grungy presence of Sessmess Kuhl, Harbormaster, stole their attention and Troy pushed thoughts of Evaliana out of his mind. "Thought as ye might like to know that some newcomer's asking about yer boy."

"Newcomer?" Nelek frowned.

"Cesper Villant brought in a boat load of visitors from the mainland." Sessmess nodded his balding head toward the Big Hearth Tavern and Inn. The building commanded the western side of Harbor Street, its girth expanding out in a massive circle. "Rumor has it there's just one asking. Male. One of those sorts you wouldn't let near your daughter at midday in public, ye know?"

"Human?"

"Aye, but I cannot be sure on his companion. She's a pretty one but her hood's stayed up since her arrival." Sessmess shuddered and wiped the sweat off the back of his neck with an already damp cloth. There was a reek to the man, stale clothes and too much alcohol, and Troy shifted on his feet, trying to find an excuse to step away without insulting him. "Wouldn't be surprised if she were Eldur, though. There's something queer about her."

"What sort of questions are they asking?" Kaden asked.

"Asked for you by name," Sessmess said. "I thought it seemed odd, beings that ye were a babe when ye got here."

"What did you tell them?" Troy asked.

Sessmess puffed his scrawny chest and shook his head gravely. "Said I'd never heard of such a boy and took my leave," he said. "As far as I'm concerned, ye are all of Vakeshmeer. No mainlander's gonna stir up trouble for ye on my watch."

"Thank you, Master Kuhl." Nelek slipped a few coins to the Harbormaster, who grinned his semi-toothless appreciation before moving off.

Troy ran his tongue over his teeth, involuntarily checking to make sure they were still in place. There were many poor souls like Sessmess around the harbor, men who preferred drink to work most days and Troy could remember his father advising him to be kind to such people. Their circumstances could easily have been reversed, his father would say. Troy wasn't certain how, but he tried to stop thinking rude thoughts about the reeking old gentleman and turned his mind to the information that had just been provided.

Vakeshmeer didn't get visitors all that often. Most ships were merchants bringing goods or taking shipments from the silver mines back to the mainland. None seemed overly interested in the town outside the harbor and certainly none had ever inquired after Kaden.

"You don't think this could be that blood mage, do you?" Troy asked.

Nelek and Trenna had warned them that a mage might come seeking Kaden, but so many years had gone by the warning had faded. Troy had imagined whatever fight was going on over on the mainland had managed to move on without Kaden, which was just as well because he didn't think his friend wanted to get involved.

Politics was not a favorite hobby for any of them.

Nelek squinted at the inn, his mouth making a firm, straight line across his face. "No, this couldn't be Noffi."

"How do you know?"

"Because Noffi is gods-awful ugly," Nelek smirked at him. "Not a soul alive would call her pretty. Her teeth alone can frighten children."

"What is wrong with her teeth?" Kaden perked with interest.

Nelek motioned to his mouth. "They're pointed."

"What? All of them?" Troy wrinkled his nose in distaste.

The idea of blood mages had always intrigued him, but Nelek and Trenna had both been reluctant to give any details before. He tried to imagine what an ugly woman with sharpened teeth must have looked like and decided semi-toothless Sessmess wasn't nearly as bad off as he'd thought.

"Hurt like hell when she bit you, too."

"Ugh. Why did she bite you?" Troy asked, giving the inn a furtive glance.

"Blood magic." Nelek gripped Kaden's shoulder. "Eldur have to bleed in order for a mage to be useful."

"So she bit people?" Troy asked, shaking his head. "That's disgusting."

"Shall we go see who they are?" Nelek grinned and waggled his eyebrows, which made him look ridiculous and Troy couldn't help grinning back. "Hate to have them come all this way for nothing."

~ * ~

"Mother will be very angry with you," Kaden told Nelek as they moved to a table.

Nelek scanned the groups of patrons in the Big Hearth, double-checking the exits of the familiar establishment. The very center of the room housed an enormous open hearth surrounded by a blackened iron railing. A large fire spit and popped, eating away at several logs and sending smoke trailing up to escape through the hole at the peak of the roof above.

It was crowded today, many of the tables full of locals that Nelek recognized, but the pathway to the entrance was clear so they could run if they needed to. And since they had frequented Big Hearth from the time Kaden could walk, Nelek knew that Barmy Friggs would usher them out through the basement if things got really bad.

Confident that he and the boys could handle the situation, Nelek relaxed in his seat. "The greatest pleasure of my life is fighting with your mother," he said to Kaden with a wink.

"I see them," Kaden said, pretending to pick at the nicked surface of their table. "Four spaces over, nearest the fire."

Nelek had spotted their targets on entry, so he just nodded. Newcomers were always easy to spot, but these two were especially noticeable. The man had a long, hooked nose and a placid expression and Nelek sensed danger there. It was likely the man could hold his own in a fight, which could prove problematic if this situation turned ugly.

There was something vaguely familiar about the woman but he couldn't risk staring at them to figure it out. Her hood draped in such a manner that her ears remained a mystery, though Nelek suspected she was Eldur. Sessmess had been right about the peculiar air that exuded from her.

"I don't like the looks of the male," Kaden said with a frown, his focus still on the table.

"Oh?" Nelek felt a swell of paternal pride that his son had recognized the threat. "Why is that?"

"He's too comfortable. Confident without arrogance, and I can't see a weapon on him. I wager he has at least two hidden, though." Kaden finally looked up from the table, but his gaze switched to the door rather than the target of their conversation. "And he smirks like Mom does when she's about to cheat."

Nelek couldn't hold back his snort of humor. "You've noticed that too?"

Kaden grinned at him and nodded. "I hope Troy is careful."

"Troy is a clever young man; he'll be smart about things." He glanced at the bar where Troy had already donned the guise of a servant and was taking orders from Barmy. The boy looked hopelessly young beside Barmy's stocky, rotund frame. He was three heads taller than Barmy, lean and trim as a swordsman should be, with bright red hair curling chaotically about his face.

Affection snagged at Nelek's heart as Troy gave Barmy a cheeky grin. Troy was almost identical to his late father with his blunt nose and crooked mouth. His hair was a touch darker than Tibitus Mavon, burnished with his mother's roan locks, but the image was clear and for a moment Nelek was overcome with grief.

Six years gone and Nelek still felt the loss of his Human friend just as acutely as the first day. Gods, he hoped he'd done right by Troy. He owed it to Tibitus to at least try to keep the boy safe and happy.

Nelek watched as Troy took drinks to several tables, weaving through the room so familiarly it looked like he really was a server for the tavern. He stopped briefly at their own table and set two monstrously large cups before them.

"Barmy says you owe him for this so you're drinking his best stock," Troy said, his mouth quirking with amusement. "And if we break anything we get to replace it."

Kaden snorted a laugh and Troy moved off to deliver more drinks. "I like that he thinks we'll break something."

"Yes, your mother would be so proud." Nelek glanced at the troublesome Human and hooded woman, saw Troy approach them with a disarming, almost goofy smile. "You know how she likes to maintain a certain reputation with the townsfolk."

The woman reached for her drink as Troy delivered it. Her arm was exposed, gold and red vines and swirls inked into her skin, looking altogether exotic and unfamiliar. Nelek tried to keep from frowning.

There was something otherly about the girl, something powerful.

Blood mage, he thought. She had to be.

Gods, why had Trenna made that bargain? They could have lived out their lives in peace and quiet.

And misery, a small voice told him, scouring his heart with names and faces of people he'd abandoned during his exile from the mainland. Brenson, he thought, his chest squeezing tight with a different sort of grief. By the gods, he prayed his brother was still alive somewhere. Alive and safe.

The woman's mouth was just visible under the hood. She spoke to her companion, too low for Nelek to hear over the teeming bar. What happened next was so fast it was almost a blur. The man grabbed Troy's collar and wrenched him downward, yanking the boy off balance and sending the serving tray clattering to the floor.

Nelek launched to his feet, Kaden beside him, as Troy's face was smashed into the surface of the table. Shoving his way forward, he gripped his hilt and met the gaze of the Human holding Troy. The man smirked at him, glancing at the scurrying crowd as everyone seemed suddenly torn about what to do. Some of the men looked ready to fight, though it was anyone's guess which side they would be on, and still others appeared more curious than anything else.

Nelek kept his sword half drawn, not wanting to attempt a real fight in such close quarters, but not willing to stand aside, either. Troy cursed in pain and tried to push back up but the unfamiliar man kept him down, pinning his collar to the table with a slender dagger. The blade sunk hard into the wooden surface, inches from Troy's face, and the boy stilled.

Swallowing hard, Nelek coached his heart into a steadier pace and glared at the man.

Troy wasn't badly hurt, not yet. There was still time for some manner of diplomacy.

"When I said we should invite them over, I had something less dramatic in mind," the woman said and leaned back in her chair.

Her companion grinned, which accented a deep scar running from the lower left corner of his mouth to the curve of his jaw.

"Release the boy; you've made your point," Nelek said and tried to calculate the odds again.

He didn't want Kaden tangling with the mage—and he was certain now that she was a mage—but he didn't want the crazy knife-fellow near his son, either. As it was, Nelek felt distinctly alarmed at the proximity of Troy to the man in question. The knife had come from nowhere, pinned the boy in half a breath, with a precision that was more than unsettling. Either the man was really that good or he hadn't cared if he'd hit the boy's nose.

"I was going to ask you to join us," the woman pushed her hood off before finishing her sentence, "Duke of Kiavana."

She was Eldur. Of course, she had to be in order to be a mage but the sight of her pointed ears was still startling. It had been over twenty-five years since he'd seen another Eldur, one who wasn't part of his immediate family, and Nelek had to settle himself before speaking. It was apparent now why she had kept the hood up. She had boyishly cropped hair, wild and curly and a deep red color like dark wine. Her features were elegantly curved, almost bewitching, but it was her eyes that struck him; they were an olive color mostly, but flecked with red enough to be noticeable.

"That's my friend, lady." Kaden's voice rumbled low and dangerous from just beside Nelek.

The woman looked at him, utterly impassive.

"I won't ask again." Nelek nodded down at Troy. "Let him up. Now."

"Release the Human, Faxon," she said with a light gesture to the table. "And let us sit for a moment."

Faxon pulled the knife from the table and hoisted Troy back onto his feet. Nelek kept his focus on the blade until it disappeared into the folds of the man's clothes. He didn't like how close Faxon kept Troy but pulled a chair over anyway, dragging it from an abandoned table nearby. Kaden did the same, though by the tense line of his son's shoulders, Nelek could tell he was having a hard time holding onto his temper. Troy was forced to sit between the mage and her companion, who'd procured a handkerchief for Troy to staunch the blood from his newly broken nose.

"Should I be alarmed or amused at how interested the public is in your affairs, Duke?" The mage nodded to the crowd, most of whom hadn't moved since the confrontation began.

"I am no longer a duke, so I ask that you not refer to me in such a way." He could sense the stirring in the crowd, hear the whispered repetition of the title "duke" as it filtered through the room, and his gut knotted.

This was getting worse by the moment.

"How should I address you, then?" the mage asked.

"By my name, which I would have given to you if you'd had the courtesy to introduce yourself before assaulting my kin," Nelek said, glancing at Troy, who was glaring at Faxon around his bloody kerchief.

Faxon snorted a laugh. "He still prattles like a duke."

"My father doesn't prattle." Kaden glared across the table at the man, who seemed amused by the verbal attack.

"My name is Brigetta Isleen Chridhe," the mage said, ignoring the rest of the table. "We met, Nelek of Kiavana, on the day your mother died."

Surprised, Nelek sat back, his hand slipping from his hilt as he stared at the woman. She looked very different now but he could see her, could remember the way she'd held his mother's hand as the life bled out of her, and felt his heart stutter in pain.

"Blood mage," he murmured, still staring.

It was an omen, it had to be, that this was the woman sent to fetch them.

Gods help them all, the time had finally come.

Three

The kettle seared through her protective cloth and right into the tender skin between her thumb and forefinger. Cursing, Trenna did an inelegant shuffle from the table toward the hearth as steam blinded her, pouring out of the spout and straight into her face. Her boot caught on the cobblestone surrounding the hearth and she gave up, tossing kettle and water onto the stones with a clatter that could wake the dead.

Cursing some more, she inspected the angry red burn making a half-moon shape in her skin before flapping her hand in a vain attempt to stop the sting.

"You could have let me do that," Liana said from her perch on the table.

"You're no more domestic than I am," Trenna said, gingerly prodding the burn. She hissed, thoroughly annoyed with herself. "Getting cut with a blade is preferable to this... this..."

"Turtle shite?" Liana's cheek dimpled into an impish grin and her blue eyes twinkled with laughter.

Trenna snorted a laugh, all her annoyance deflating. "Yes. This is absolute turtle shite. I have no idea how your father does it."

Snickering, Liana slid from the table and moved to clean up the kettle mess. Like most of the homes on Vakeshmeer, the front room shared a hearth with the two adjacent bedrooms, making a circular hut-like space sectioned off by thin walls. This helped keep centralized heating during the long winters on the island, but it meant a great deal of maintenance with the roof, making sure the chimney was clear and the shingles kept from rot.

When the children had been younger, they'd been terribly cramped, especially after Mavon passed and Troy moved in. But it had been several years since Kaden and Troy had built homes of their own and now the main house held only Nelek and Trenna and Liana. Everyone still ate there, however, conserving their food as best they could.

"Does it ever bother you that Father is better at cooking than you are?" Liana asked, pulling her mind back to the massacre on the table.

Trenna eyed the bowl of steaming water and tried to remember how Nelek had taught her to mix the gruel. She'd managed to get at least a cup's worth of water into the mixture before burning herself, which she supposed was an improvement. "Yes," she said. "And then I recall that I can best him with the sword and the world becomes right again."

Hands on her hips, Trenna continued to frown at the ingredients before her: salt, some sort of leafy herb Nelek always used, and a ground red peppery substance. She believed she was supposed to make a paste next, but there was a nagging sense in her mind that she had missed a step.

Gods, this was impossible. Why had she decided to try this again? At best she would have a table full of half-smiling family pretending her food was edible; at worst she could poison them all.

"Do you think it ever bothers Father that you're not domestic?"

Trenna tore her attention away from the table. Liana sat cross-legged beside the hearth, her hands busily drying the kettle, but Trenna could tell her daughter was waiting for an answer. Liana always kept her gaze on something else when she was really paying attention, and for a conflicted moment, Trenna wondered if the girl had managed to read her mind.

She was in the process of learning to cook again, and Trenna hadn't decided yet what had motivated this insanity.

It could be just boredom, she reasoned with herself.

But there was a lurking doubt, a niggling fear in the back of her mind, that she wasn't quite the woman Nelek needed her to be.

But how in gods had Liana read that?

Trenna frowned, trying to decide if she was being paranoid or not. Dark-haired like her father, Liana was blessed with Nelek's wide, full mouth and dramatic features. She had high cheekbones that managed to look healthy rather than gaunt, and an elegant nose that couldn't have come from either of her parents and Trenna thought, as she often did, that Liana looked more and more like her late grandmother, Auliere Dyngannon.

"I don't know, Liana," Trenna said. "Though I think if it bothered him too much he would have said so by now. Your father is rather outspoken at times."

Liana's mouth tightened into a grim line and she grunted an incoherent response.

"Why do you ask?" Trenna reached for the bowl of flour, keeping most of her attention on Evaliana.

For all that Liana took after her father in appearance, the girl was undeniably her own person and had been since she was very young. Volatile, intensely private, and terribly unpredictable, with a stubborn independence that left Trenna worried most days. Because most days, that independence ran counter to whatever Trenna wanted, and she could sense this conversation was about to take a horrible turn.

Where was Nelek when she really needed him?

"Because I am going to marry Troy and I want to make sure he'll be all right with my ...less than feminine tendencies," Liana announced, lifting her chin in an obstinate display, as though she were daring Trenna to contradict her.

Trenna could only blink at her. "Troy has proposed to you?" She managed to croak the words out and thought, *Good gods, you're just babies.*

Well, twenty years old wasn't exactly a baby. In fact, most of their peers had already married off or moved from the island or taken up responsibilities in the family trade. She realized all of a sudden that her children probably felt a little stunted here, unable to grow any further in the quiet fishing village they called home.

But still, Eldur marriage was vastly different from Human marriage. It had deep, profound consequences that she didn't believe her daughter was ready for.

"Well, no. But he will." Liana said, crossing her arms.

"You seem rather sure of yourself," Trenna said, trying to regroup.

Gods, marriage. To Troy. How had she missed this? The romance had to have been brewing for a while.

A voice hollered her name outside their little home and Trenna breathed in relief. Anything was better than this conversation. Abandoning the gruel, she hurried to the door and swung it open, scanning the surroundings before stepping out.

The air still had the bite of spring morning and the sun had reached its zenith, turning the landscape into a sea of green grass bordered by the shadow of the forest. Their house stood on the peak of a bare hill, giving her a clear view of at least seventy yards before tapering off into wilderness. And they were far enough away from any cliffs that no surf could drown out sound, a tactical decision she and Nelek had agreed upon when they'd first arrived.

A lone figure was heading toward the house, scrawny and familiar. She frowned, moving out to meet him. Sessmess Kuhl flapped his cap at her in greeting, panting from exertion as he stopped before her.

Something was wrong. Why was the harbormaster at their house? Had something happened to the boat?

"Hello, Big T," Sessmess said, and then he had to pause to take several breaths.

Poor man needed to stop drinking so much, she thought.

"Harbormaster," she said cautiously, wondering if Kaden and Troy had managed to break something in the few hours they'd been gone.

Sessmess wagged his hat in the direction he'd come from. "Trouble's brewing at the Big Hearth," he said. "Two mainlanders showed up this mornin' asking about Kaden. I told mister Nelek, and he took them boys of yours to go sort it out."

It took a moment for the words to process, and when they did she nearly wanted the awkward conversation about marriage back.

She'd been quite wrong, this was so much worse than Liana demanding to get married.

"Troy, too?" Liana asked from the doorway.

"Aye. Unless you've another gentleman livin' under this roof now." Sessmess grinned at Liana in a way that Trenna imagined he meant to be charming, but the gaps of his missing teeth only made him look creepy.

"Human or Eldur?' Trenna asked, turning back for the house, her mind already searching for a plan.

"The man's Human. Don't know about the girl."

She ducked inside the doorway and reached for the pegs mounted just inside, grabbing familiar scabbards from their hanging place. She slung the heavy belt around her waist, the words "mainlanders" and "Kaden" echoing through her, freezing her blood. She saw Liana arming herself as well and nearly argued, but there was no time and the girl would likely be safer at Trenna's side, so she began relaying instructions instead.

"Take the long sword and the cutlass but don't draw unless I do. If we must fight, stick with the cutlass while we're inside. It's a tighter space, so the smaller the blade the better. If I tell you to, take Troy and Kaden to the *Bitter Croften* and sail the island twice. Nelek and I will meet you at the practice grounds, is that understood?"

Evaliana nodded and didn't argue, which was alarming in its own right because Liana always argued when given a direct order, but Trenna didn't have time to dwell. They turned together and left the house again, armed enough that Sessmess appeared startled at the sight of them. The harbormaster's mouth dropped open and he blustered an objection, obviously not prepared to watch two women head off for battle.

"Now, Miss Trenna, you can't be meaning to use those," he said with a nod at her scabbards. "It ain't natural for womenfolk. And besides, we don't know it's that sort of trouble, now do we? I say we all just calm down and wait for your menfolk to come back with news."

Liana snorted a laugh.

"Thank you, Master Kuhl, for your help," Trenna said, snapping the purse cord from her waist and tossing the whole bag at him. There were at least twelve silver bits in it, she knew, which was more than generous for the information he'd given. Nelek would balk.

Her hands curled around her belt strap and she glared at the pathway. Nelek would balk, all right, and then she'd gut him for taking off without telling her first.

Sessmess caught the bag a little clumsily and, feeling its weight, seemed to decide it didn't matter what Trenna did because he stopped objecting. She nodded at him and started for the forest, trying to remember all the exits in Big Hearth.

So long as Nelek was still in the tavern, they had plenty of options; she just had to get there.

"Are you planning something, Mother?" Liana asked, hurrying to keep up with her.

"You mean aside from skinning your father alive?"

Liana huffed a breathless laugh. "Yes, other than that."

"I hadn't gotten that far," she said with a grunt.

And she couldn't make a real plan, not until she knew exactly what she was dealing with.

Gods damn you, Nelek Dyngannon!

They crossed the barrier into the woods and Trenna picked up speed, hopping over felled trees and familiar boulders. Her mind mapped out the lives of her children with every step, years of peaceful exile taunting her. There she saw the tree where Kaden had lost his first tooth, and they crossed the stream at the precise spot where Troy had built a dam and inadvertently angered a beaver.

She could still hear the children shrieking as they ran from the aggrieved creature and felt her heart pinch. Years and years spent trying to prepare herself for this day and now that it was here, she wanted just one more day, one more week, one more month without it.

When they hit Harbor Street, Trenna led the way to the back of Big Hearth and around the refuse gutter that drained into the ocean. A few passersby took note of them but were smart enough not to approach, hustling off on their business with furtive glances at the tavern. Trenna ignored them, knowing full well that none of the locals would want to get involved.

Trenna paused outside the door just long enough to nod to Evaliana before slipping into the servant entrance of the tavern. The heat of the kitchens assaulted her on all sides, her shirt sticking to her torso in the small moment it took for her eyes to adjust to the gloom. Three overly large cast iron ovens lined the eastern wall, each of them lit and emitting throbbing waves of heat. A heavy smell of cooked meat and spices wafted from the fire pits and Trenna's stomach growled.

Nelek could damn well cook dinner after this debacle, she thought and moved forward.

A tiny, anxious woman in an apron looked up at them in surprise and then relief. Mancy Friggs, wife to Barmy Friggs, always had a nervous disposition about her, so Trenna couldn't tell if this was her normal face or if the pinched concern on her features meant something awful had already happened.

"Gods be praised," Mancy said, wiping her hands on her apron and beckoning them forward. "Barmy's near apoplexy. He's fretting over joining them or throwing them out."

The woman wasted no time explaining further, just led them to the main room of the tavern and ushered them inside. The oppressive heat of the kitchen lessened as she moved into the main tavern but it was still warm. Liana slipped past her, sidling to the left of the doorway as Trenna followed.

She spotted the assassin first, sitting at the table nearest to the hearth and her gut clenched in reaction. Faxon Mylonas was profile to her, looking almost exactly as he had twenty-odd years prior. Fear curled in her gut at the sight of her son and husband sitting near the man, but an instant later was washed away by anger.

Trapped between the assassin and a woman whose occupation could only be that of a blood mage, Troy sat in a chair, his eyes puffed and swelling, and he was holding a bloodied handkerchief to his face.

Clenching her fists, Trenna battled her temper and made a plan.

The rest of the crowd had begun edging closer to their table, most of them blatantly listening to the conversation, which Trenna was too far away to catch. What she did know was that a crowd was good; it meant they could cause a stir and disappear quickly.

Out of the corner of her eye she saw Liana's advance, saw her daughter draw her cutlass and knew Faxon had seen it too.

Dammit, she'd told the girl to wait.

"Big T, thank gods," Barmy said, standing up with obvious relief. "I tried to warn them…"

"Thank you, Mister Friggs. May I borrow your stool?" Trenna asked, already reaching for the object in question.

"My stool?" Barmy's elderly face creased in puzzlement.

Liana shouted something about Troy, demanding to know why the boy was bleeding as she stalked toward the table, causing the already tense room to stir in surprised alarm.

"Well, yes, I suppose…" Barmy said and stopped when he spotted Liana's cutlass, gasping with further horror.

"Thank you." Trenna grabbed the stool, starting forward. She waited until Faxon stood, until he had his full focus on intercepting Liana, before she flung the chair over her shoulder with all her might.

It soared through the short space and struck the blood mage on the side of her head, startling everyone in the room. Trenna took her advantage and rushed forward as the red-headed mage fell against the table. The girl was dazed enough that she wasn't prepared for Trenna's second assault. Grabbing a fistful of spiky red hair, Trenna slammed the woman's head into the hard, pitted surface, sufficiently subduing the mage before any spells could be laid.

With the flick of her wrist, Trenna snagged the dagger from her belt loop and held it to the unconscious woman's throat in clear warning, all her focus on Faxon, who had gone quite still.

Whatever attack he'd planned against Liana had ceased and his wild, golden eyes fastened on Trenna. Nelek, Kaden, and Troy had moved during the attack, Nelek standing with the boys flanking him—not entirely out of harm's way, but at least they'd have a sporting chance. Liana's advance had been stalled as well. Trenna saw her slide toward Troy, looking concerned and Trenna thought, *Gods, marriage?*

"Hello, Trenna," Faxon said with the sort of calm a hawk might have while stalking a mouse. He still didn't move. "Nice to see you haven't lost your civilized touch."

"You know each other?" Nelek asked, giving her a meaningful look.

He was angry, she could tell, which was just fine by her, because she was furious.

This was not an overreaction, she told herself. Faxon Mylonas enjoyed killing. A lot. And she had every reason to believe the man had malicious intentions for her family. He had certainly meant to kill Liana just then, if she'd given him the chance.

"Inasmuch as one can know an assassin without meeting the business end of their blade," Trenna said, keeping her attention on Faxon.

"Well now, that's not rightly fair. We were having a polite conversation before you chose to attack." Faxon's mouth twitched in the tell-tale sign that he was suppressing himself.

In the years she had known the man, scurrying through the shadowed underbelly of Kiavana, she had never seen him react in such a way. He killed without conscience, with a brutal elegance that could give the gruffest soldier nightmares. And yet, she sensed that he was genuinely attached to the half-conscious female pinned to the table.

A woman who Trenna had just beaten with a chair and was currently holding a dagger to—an Eldur blood mage, of all things.

"Yes, I can see by Troy'vesk's face just how polite things were." She bit the words out and met Faxon's eyes.

Anger should never look cold on a man's face. It was a passionate emotion, a boiling, heated, all-consuming beast coiled in the hearts of men, waiting for a chance to be unleashed. Yet the assassin's gaze was dead cold, calculating, and she knew by instinct that he was prepared to kill her for her transgression.

Then Faxon smiled, revealing two long, opaque incisors she was certain hadn't been there before and fear coiled in her gut.

There wasn't just one blood mage at their table, there were two.

Four

He could throw his stiletto at her, the one located just under his right sleeve. It was the same weapon he'd used to pin Troy down, so it hadn't been properly reattached yet.

Was his name Troy? Faxon hadn't been paying close enough attention to their names to know for sure, but he was mostly certain he had it right. It started with a "T," that much he could remember because he'd immediately associated the boy with Trenna out of sheer laziness.

Troy and Trenna, he thought. Double Ts.

Troy and Trenna tried traipsing through town with a trembling, troublesome troupe. Terrified travelers trumpeting their...

Gods, he needed to stop.

He felt a tic in his cheek, just under his left eye, and twisted his wrist just enough to access his stiletto. The skin-warmed blade came free of its hook and slid down until he stopped it with the palm of his hand.

Keeping his body turned, he tried to gauge their faces, gingerly running his thumb along the sharp edge. None of the small family in front of him seemed to have noticed the move, or if they had they were remarkably good about hiding their alarm. He frowned at them, wondering why in gods they seemed so confident.

Oh, they were tense to be sure, but they weren't frightened. It was almost insulting.

They were a motley looking bunch, never mind that most of them were related. Troy in particular stood out with his mess of red hair and blunter features. His nose had stopped bleeding, which was a good thing, since he'd stopped blotting it with the handkerchief once the attack began. The girl, who had been advancing with her cutlass drawn, stood beside the boy, openly scowling at Faxon, so he sent her a little wink and grinned when she went to take a step toward him.

Fighter, he thought, just as Troy grabbed her arm, holding her in place. He hissed something too low for Faxon to hear but he imagined it was some kind of warning.

Nelek glanced at his daughter—there was no denying that parentage—and held tighter to the hilt of his sword. Faxon ran his tongue along his teeth and thought, that's more like it.

But Nelek was too controlled to make the first move here. If Faxon wanted action, he would have to poke at someone else.

"You used to be better company, Trenna," Faxon said and calculated the angle he would need when he threw his stiletto.

So many targets, which one should he pick?

Trenna remained poised with her dagger at Bree's throat, eyeing him with clear warning. "It's been a very long time. I've lost my sense of humor."

"Pity," he said. "Your humor was one of the things I loved best about you."

"Drop the act, Faxon. There's no love lost between us."

"You wound me!" he said with a smirk. "We were friends once, weren't we?"

"Once, yes," she conceded. "A very long time ago. But we have changed since. I have changed."

He wanted to scoff at that but couldn't. He knew full well that parenthood could change a person in a deep, inescapable way because he'd seen his sister Cahira undergo such a transformation many years before. Still, he didn't think the woman would kill Bree, changed or not.

Trenna had a certain sense of honor that hindered such an action, even back during her mercenary days, but the threat was still there and it bothered him more than he cared to admit. Studiously keeping his eyes away from his wife, Faxon debated the merits of just killing Trenna and having done with it.

"Come now, Trenna," he said, placating. He shifted on his feet, turning more toward the table, and Trenna angled her blade more precisely against Brigetta's jugular.

Faxon went still again, glaring at her.

"Don't," Trenna warned, her ivy-green eyes locking with his and he knew, could see in her gaze, that she wouldn't hesitate to kill Brigetta if he made a move.

Which, unbeknownst to her, would kill him too. Eldur marriage was funny that way, its vows sealing the fates of the bride and groom together in life and death.

Gods, please don't hurt them. Please, please don't hurt them. Bree's voice whispered through his mind and he ground his teeth to keep from snarling.

A side effect of the Eldur blood he consumed was that his mind became intimately linked with its owner, and since he was restricted to a diet of his wife, that meant he could hear her every little thought. He'd learned to block her out most of the time, concentrating on other things in the room or absorbing himself in menial tasks, and thus had learned to live with her extra voice in his mind.

It wasn't an ideal situation, but if he wanted to harness magic, it was the only option available. Bree didn't know about the side effect, of course. It was more amusing this way and, should he be granted the opportunity to sample another Eldur's blood, he did not want them hesitating to share.

We need them alive, Bree thought and Faxon twitched.

His wife had the noisiest mind, even while barely conscious.

"Liana, take Troy and Kaden out now," Trenna said, her gaze still on his face.

Faxon glanced down at where Bree remained slumped over the table. Blood smeared her mouth, running from her broken nose and Faxon skimmed the edge of his blade again.

They couldn't need all of them this badly.

"Do as your mother says." Nelek shifted to put himself in front of his son.

If he'd been in a better mood, Faxon might have smiled at that. He blinked, slowly, his mind conjuring three different ways he could get around Nelek, each of them ending with the point of Faxon's blade buried in Kaden's throat.

It would be easy, so easy.

Gods, don't let me have failed already. Bree's voice came again and Faxon hissed a breath.

"Mother, you can't expect us just to leave," Kaden said, frowning over at Trenna, who still hadn't removed the dagger from Bree's neck.

"I can and I do," Trenna said through her teeth. "Go."

Faxon chose to ignore the family byplay and focused on Trenna. "Why attack the girl, Trenna?" he asked. "The poor thing was only doing as she'd been ordered."

"And what order was that?" Trenna asked, her voice full of suspicion.

He'd expected that Trenna and her family would be wary of anyone bearing news from the mainland but he'd thought, quite wrongly, that a familiar face would have been greeted with a little more leniency. Though, if he were honest, he wouldn't have trusted himself either. He had been an assassin when she'd known him.

Technically he still was, too. He just had the luxury of being highly selective about which contracts he took these days.

"Noffi's death wish was for Brigetta to fetch Dyngannon's next king," Faxon said, deliberately looking at Kaden. "We were told we would be expected."

Kaden met his gaze with a faint, defiant smirk. He had his mother's eyes, deep green and intelligent, glinting with a fierce protectiveness for the people surrounding him. He had the strong set of his father's shoulders and the stance of a well-practiced swordsman, competent but untested, though he was dressed as a fisherman. In fact, they were all dressed as fishermen, with the exception that they were all armed with blades hanging from their belts.

Faxon imagined the local populace gossiped about them quite a bit, which reminded him of the restless crowd fringing their reunion. He sensed the murmurings of the people, saw the shocked and uncertain faces of those closest, and understood his wife's plan for what it was.

"I am sorry to hear of Noffi's death," Trenna spoke again and he looked away from the crowd. "But the mage did you a disservice. Kaden has the right to *choose* to be king. That was my agreement with the woman. There was nothing about sending an assassin to fetch him away."

"How delightfully complicated," Faxon said. He glanced at Brigetta, certain she must have known this. Why else would she seek the family out in public? She must have wanted a scene to be made, must have counted on it.

Clever little woman, he thought and then, *how did I miss it*?

"Go now," Nelek said to his son. "We will be right behind you."

The girl Liana looked about to argue but Troy took her by the shoulder, forcibly turning her to the door. Faxon watched their departure, fingering his blade once more. He owed Trenna a blow for her attack on Bree, he thought, staring at the base of Kaden's neck. He imagined the precise arch of his stiletto finding a home right there, right at that spot between the vertebrae, and had to remind himself that the boy was important.

Maybe not to him, but certainly to his wife, and he disliked upsetting her.

"That still doesn't answer why you chose to attack gentle Brigetta," Faxon said at last, when Kaden was out of sight.

"It's been over twenty years since I last saw you, Faxon Mylonas. You were over thirty then, which makes you in your mid-fifties now," Trenna said, her mouth twitching into a wry smile. "The way I figure it, the only way you can look as good as you do now is if you married an Eldur."

Faxon barked a laugh, truly startled. "You're too quick by half, Trenna. Dear gods, you never cease to surprise me. There isn't another living person who could have connected those dots."

She carefully lowered Brigetta onto the table, taking the time to make certain Bree's body wouldn't collapse to the floor when she let go. Faxon took note of that and slid his weapon back up his sleeve.

"Circumstantial," she said with a slight bow of her head. "I'm likely the only person left alive who knew you back then."

That was as much of an apology as he was likely to get, and with the crowd getting louder and more restless in his peripheral view and Kaden already gone, he opted to take it. Faxon nodded back to her, watching as Nelek moved to touch her elbow and she straightened in response.

"Kaden knows you're here now," Nelek said. "When he has decided, we'll find you."

Faxon did not acknowledge the man, just continued to watch as the two turned from the table and made their way out of the tavern. Once they were gone, he moved to his wife, carefully lifting her from the table, and headed for the stairs at the back. The crowd parted for him and he heard their gossip as he passed, heard them all whispering about Kaden being a king, wondering how they could not have known or insisting they knew all along.

He smirked and started up the stairs.

Your move, Trenna.

~ * ~

"I cannot believe you'd walk into a meeting like that without finding me first," Trenna said. Her angry stride made her move faster than normal and Nelek had to quicken his pace to keep up. "Of all the idiotic stunts you've pulled, this one goes to a whole new level. That bastard could have killed you and then played pretend tea with your dead bodies."

"That's gross, Trenna," Nelek said with a grunt.

"No, that's mild. Faxon Mylonas is absolutely insane and has been for years." She led him down the harbor, toward where the *Bitter Croften* was normally moored, never ceasing in her rant. "He once spent three days with a corpse tied to a chair, just watching it decompose."

Nelek made an involuntary sound of disgust, glancing over his shoulder at the quickly distancing tavern. He'd known the man was dangerous but this was a whole different level of insanity.

"Faxon claimed to be studying it, but I swear to gods, I caught him talking to it," Trenna said, finally stopping at the end of the pier. The *Bitter Croften* was already gone, as Nelek had suspected it would be. "So I am allowed to be furious with you for this."

"I knew Sessmess would run off and tell you. The greedy bastard is always out for more coin," Nelek said. Some ways out, already turning out of the inlet, he could see their boat. Its sail was up but it was too far away for a head count. Still, he was confident they were all there. "Where should we meet them?"

"I told her to sail the island twice and meet us at the practice grounds." Trenna strummed her left thigh in an agitated motion. "So they will ignore me completely and land in their usual place."

Nelek's mind flashed to the rocky, cliff-lined cove that their children had taken such a liking to. It was on the other side of the island, the northern shoreline that disappeared during high tide, and it was relatively safe. He relaxed a little. They had some time to come up with a plan. Though what that plan might be he was at a loss to define.

Gods, this day had been awful.

"We should move now," Trenna said and turned to glare up at him. "If we walk we can make it by sunset."

And it was about to get worse, he thought.

Nelek glared back at her. His nerves were already frayed by the afternoon's events and he was tired of this argument. "I knew Sessmess would come to you. He did, right?"

"Of course he did."

"Then by gods, I did warn you. Quit being so damned angry."

Her glare narrowed further and he knew her temper had snapped. She went to stomp on his foot and Nelek jerked it away, already prepared for the fist flying toward his face. He ducked and half turned, but her elbow caught him in the side instead, hard and unyielding. Pain blossomed in his ribs, flashing out in a wide circle at the same moment her foot came crashing down on his toes.

"Godsdammit! Are you finished?" he growled down at her. "Because I'd like to make certain our children are safe."

"I'm not nearly finished with you, you reckless bastard!"

"Then get it over with so we can go!" His voice bellowed over the harbor, sending a gull scurrying off in fright.

They stood toe to toe, glaring at each other, his nose inches from hers and he imagined any passersby were getting a good laugh from the sight. His mind flashed to Kaden's warning just before all hell had broken loose in the tavern and thought, *No, provoking Trenna is not the single greatest pleasure of my life. Why in gods can't she just shout like a normal angry person?*

After a long moment, Trenna spun on her heel and stormed away from him, heading back down the pier with so much furious energy that he saw several people swerve away from her. His ribs ached a little and his big toe was throbbing; he fumed at her, wanting desperately either to shake her or kiss her, it was difficult to decide which.

He'd known she would be upset, but he'd only intended to gather information from the mainlanders. He hadn't planned to confront them.

Not that Trenna knew that. It wasn't like she could read his mind. He supposed it did look a little bad. Still, she needed a better way of expressing her agitation. With a grimace of irritation, he finally moved to follow her, jogging a bit on his injured toe to catch up.

They cut a quick path through the small village, weaving down half muddy roads before slipping into the forest. They were well away from the village then, halfway up the west slope of Vakeshmeer Mountain. Woodland shaded them from the afternoon sun, heavy leaves making a thick canopy overhead that light could barely sneak through. Pine needles covered the forest floor, most of them brown and dead, but under the base of each tree he could see the sprinkle of green hiding there. No grass could break through the blanket of needles, leaving only the slick presence of mud underneath and his foot slipped more than once on the climb.

Vakeshmeer was never hot or humid, even in the summer. There was an ever-present chill in the northern air that kept the temperature from moving too high, which Nelek had come to prefer. He could remember the heat of Kiavanan summers and the scorch of the desert places. Inescapable dry heat that baked into the bones and dried out any moisture in its wake. Dust everywhere, he thought. No, Vakeshmeer was a good deal more pleasant, even if the winters were hard.

"There are some days, Nelek Dyngannon, when I would happily kill you myself, marriage or no marriage," Trenna said, leading the way up a steep incline.

"I didn't intend to speak with them," he said. "I only wanted information on what they looked like. You would have done the same."

"And you would be equally furious with me for doing it."

"Of course I would," he conceded, avoiding a loose rock as they continued their trek. "But I would never hit you."

"Quit whining. How long have we been married now? Twenty-six years? You know better than that."

"I know to duck when your temper starts flying, but that doesn't mean I have to like it."

"I'm not asking you to like it. In fact, I'd prefer it if you didn't."

Nelek snorted a half-laugh. "So if I start to get aroused when you strike me, does that mean you'll stop?"

She panted a laugh, stopping at the peak of the ridgeline.

From this vantage, they could see the outline of the harbor far below, its piers spiking out into the water like pikes. The inlet made a crescent of land, forming the harbor village and its scant population. Smoke from Big Hearth slithered its way into a pale sky made all the paler by the thin stretch of clouds overhead. Nelek felt his chest squeeze tight at the sight.

Home, he thought and then flinched, thinking of Brenson and Kiavana and all the people they'd left behind in their exile.

Had he ever looked at Kiavana this way? He couldn't remember feeling this warmth and longing for the mountains of Dyngannon.

He turned his gaze to the snowcapped peak of Mount Vakeshmeer and frowned.

Was it even fair to compare the two? He had known peace here. Real peace. Kiavana, the place of his birth, was a home to war and strife.

"Life is about to get complicated." Trenna's voice broke the stillness in the woods.

Hearing the regret in her words and understanding the pain she felt, he moved to stand behind her. Confident that she was finished being angry with him, Nelek gathered her close, pressing her back against his chest until he could prop his chin on the top of her head. She leaned into him with a sigh, holding his arms where they rested just above her scabbards and he breathed a little easier.

"Yes, it is," he said, gazing through the trees and up at the summit.

They'd known this day would come; they'd planned for it, trained for it, and tried to prepare their children, but now that it was here, Nelek wanted nothing more to do with it. He wanted Kaden to tell the mage to bugger off and leave them be. But he also knew his son.

Kaden was made for something more than a fisherman's life. The boy might say differently, but deep down in his soul, Kaden Dyngannon was a born leader. He just needed a people to lead.

Trenna turned in Nelek's arms and buried her face in his chest, and he heaved a sigh, pulling her as close as he could. A tremble passed through her as she clutched him tight. Nelek nuzzled her hair, trying to think of something to say, but there were no words to comfort her. She knew as well as he did what was coming. There was nothing more they could do to fend it off or delay it. So, Nelek squeezed her against him, pressed a kiss to her temple, and prayed they would be strong enough to confront the coming weeks.

Five

"We should double back home, get into the weapons deposit and catch up with Mother," Liana said, leaping into knee-deep, frigid water. She hissed a breath, wishing she'd had the foresight to wear boots instead of sandals. Her feet throbbed with the cold, her skin suddenly sensitive to every scrape of rock and pebble as they began towing their little boat to shore.

The rocky beach stretched for three miles in either direction, ending in a hooked rock formation at the west and a finger of land at the east. The cliffs cut the beach off from any travelers on foot, leaving boat or a long rope as the only access. It was a cold and unforgiving beach with no real sand to speak of, not unless one dug beneath the millions of rocks washed up here. But at sunrise and sunset it provided the most magnificent view: purples and oranges and pinks spreading unhindered for miles. It was their place of refuge and had been for as long as she could remember.

"She wanted us safe," Troy argued, splashing down beside her.

"No," Liana said with a grunt as they lifted the boat. "No, she wanted us out of the way."

"She called that man an assassin, Liana," Troy said, as he, Kaden and Liana carried the boat to a sapling at the edge of the water line.

"So that makes our leaving somehow better?" she asked.

Gods, she couldn't understand these two. Her parents were off negotiating with an assassin and neither of them appeared worried or bothered by it.

"I think they can handle themselves," Kaden said. He winked at her and turned toward the cliffs, leaving Troy to tie off the boat.

Scowling after Kaden, she fought back a shiver. The cloth of her breeches was soaked from mid-thigh down, suctioning against her legs to chill her skin. She curled her toes in her sandals, felt the soles of her feet slip over the leather and debated stopping to tighten the straps, but Troy had finished with the line. He sent her a wink of his own before turning to follow Kaden, and she would be damned if she got there last. Ignoring the discomfort of her shoes, she tramped over the rocky ground, bypassing Troy to close the gap between herself and her brother.

"You're as worried as I am and I know it," she said as she reached Kaden.

"I'm worried about a lot of things, Liana."

"Like the fact that you might actually have to become a king?" Troy volunteered with a chuckle.

Liana frowned at him over her shoulder, wishing he wouldn't make light of something so serious. But he just grinned at her, one dimple forming at the side of his mouth, and she had to stamp down hard on the urge to kiss him.

Damn dimple, she thought, some of her anger deflating.

"Yes," Kaden said. "I was just trying to think of what title to give you, Troy."

"I like where this is going," Troy said and Liana thought, Gods, they're both hopeless.

"Does Royal Chambermaid suit you?" Kaden asked, grinning as they reached the base of the cliffs.

Troy laughed. "I would build you several signs leading to the privy and then leave all the work to the servants."

They began the climb and Liana cursed her sandals again. The granite rock face was unforgiving as it scoured her toes, which were still cold from the sea, and she grumbled something incoherent about Vakeshmeer Island in general.

"Promise to make a detailed painting depicting how to properly use the privy," Kaden said from just beside her.

"A proper use of my artistic skills!" Troy exclaimed and Kaden laughed.

"Gods, I hate you both so much," Liana said, her left hand locating a handhold by instinct.

"Come now, Liana," Kaden clucked his tongue at her. "Just imagine what a painting this will be."

"I'm too busy imagining Mother and Father dead at Big Hearth," she said, grunting a little as she pulled herself up. Sliding one knee inside the cave, she managed to beat her brother inside by a hair's breadth and carefully rolled to her feet.

The entrance was wide and tall, so tall it receded into shadow high above, and it overlooked the curving beach below. No one could sneak up on them here. But then, they had nowhere to go from here either, not unless they climbed. Ocean and sky came together in the distant horizon, gray and blue and as moody as Liana seemed to be today.

But she had every right to be moody, she thought, remembering the tense fear she'd seen in her mother's face just an hour before.

"We need to go back," she said again.

"We need to be patient," Kaden countered. She watched him reach down to help Troy up and frowned.

"Kaden's right," Troy said, moving deeper into the cave as he dusted himself off. He stooped before their stash of firewood. "Just relax, would you? Nelek and Trenna have been in war. I think they can handle one assassin."

"That was years ago," Liana said. "They could be rusty."

Troy scoffed at her, pausing with an armful of firewood. "Yeah, you tell that to your mother. I dare you."

"I didn't know Mother could throw that far," Kaden said suddenly.

A flash of that chair colliding with the red-headed woman distracted her and Liana laughed in spite of herself. She did have to hand it to her mother; Trenna certainly knew how to use her environment to their advantage. Liana had taken one look at Troy with his broken nose and charged right in, no real plan in place, but Trenna had managed to take control of the situation.

Maybe they weren't so rusty after all, she thought with a sigh.

"So, what now?" she asked, finally making her way to the fire pit.

"We draw sticks to see who has to catch dinner." Kaden crouched behind the ring of stones and started rubbing his flint stone against his dagger. "We sleep and we wait for morning. Mother knows where to find us. If she gets here before high tide, she'll yell at us for the tavern debacle. If she doesn't, we'll go find her tomorrow."

"You told Mother about our cave?" Liana frowned and considered throwing her sandal at him. "This is supposed to be a place just for us. For when they're being overwhelming and irritating. This is a Mom and Dad free place!"

"No." Kaden sat back as the fire started to crawl over the wood. "Right now this is a—shite, the blood mage sent an assassin and now we have to lie low—place."

Troy snorted a laugh.

"There were three other men in the Big Hearth today who were not locals. I noticed them just before you and Mom came barreling in." Kaden expelled a harsh breath and finally looked her in the face. "So we'll lay low tonight and try to plan out what we're going to do if Mother and Father don't get here before morning."

"You planned this out with your mother, didn't you?" Troy asked, moving to crouch next to the fire. "How long ago?"

Liana crossed her arms and glared down at Kaden, already knowing the answer.

"Four years ago," Kaden said, warily watching her. "She came to me and asked for my input. Asked what I thought we should do if ever there was an emergency."

"So you told her about our place," Liana said again, feeling betrayed at the highest level.

This cave was supposed to be theirs. They'd all agreed.

"We needed a safe place to rendezvous in the event that something like this ever happened," Kaden said. "Apart from hiding in the woods, this was the only place available."

Grudgingly, Liana moved to sit beside Troy, who was cross-legged near the pit. Kaden was right, of course. This was the most logical place to lay low. Still, she hated that she'd been subverted. "She never actually came in here, did she?"

Kaden shook his head and she relaxed. "I pointed it out to her from the beach."

"Good," Liana said. She knew she sounded petulant, but she didn't care. "The point of this cave was to have a space of our own. A place where they couldn't nag us to pieces."

"Aw, c'mon, Liana." Troy nudged her with an elbow. "Your parents aren't that bad. If you were anyone else's daughter, you'd have been married off already."

"Not that there's anyone on this wretched island I'd ever want to be married to," she said, glaring at Troy until he flinched.

Low blow, she thought and immediately wanted to apologize.

Gods, why did she say things like that? She didn't mean it. Hadn't she spent the afternoon agonizing over a way to tell her mother about their relationship?

Hugging her legs, she perched her chin on her knees and frowned at the growing fire. Something was wrong with her, something deep down and undefinable and she needed to figure it out fast. Because she had a feeling if she didn't, she was going to end up old and alone.

Troy was a good man, a good friend and brother and something else she couldn't quite define. But childhood playmates made for terrible lovers, or so Liana had read. At some point, one or the other starts to crave new experiences and something fresh that their partner cannot offer. Liana had meant to ask her father about the *Ten Essentials to Arranged Marriages* she'd found in Barmy Friggs' library. It was just a little pamphlet, no more than twelve pages long, and the language was far simpler than the volumes in their own home. She was sincerely hoping her father could discredit the author, thereby freeing her to pursue Troy more fully, but even if he did manage to, there was a truth to the statement that made her uncomfortable.

"So are you going to do it or not?" Troy asked at last.

He wouldn't look at her, which meant she'd hurt him, and Liana felt her eye twitch. Why had she read that thing anyway? It was written by a Human who had no idea of her circumstances. She and Troy were meant for each other. They had to be.

"Hmm? Oh, be king, you mean?" Kaden asked, poking at the fire with his dagger. "Well, it's not just a matter of choosing, now is it? Dyngannon doesn't know I exist, for the most part. There have to be a dozen people with bloodlines to the throne. Why should mine matter more than theirs?"

"Because that blood mage said it does." Troy shifted to hook his arm around one knee. "Didn't your mother say Noffi was the most respected mage in Dyngannon? That has to count for something."

"One woman against an entire nation of people?" Liana shook her head, shoving thoughts of their relationship aside for the moment. "If you ask me, it's more trouble than it's worth. We'd have to mount an army ...an army we don't have, by the way... and force Porrex off his throne. And once Kaden is king, how would he get the people to accept him? He'd be hounded by assassins and snarky courtiers almost daily."

"Just because something is difficult doesn't mean it's not worth doing." Troy said and met her gaze, holding it.

He had hazel eyes with flecks of deep blue and for a long moment she was lost there, sensing the same spark that had led to their first kiss. She almost leaned toward him, remembering at the last moment that Kaden was here and they were having a serious conversation.

There was a double meaning to Troy's words and she knew it. At least he was admitting it would be difficult, she thought as silence took the cavern. The pops and snaps of logs in the fire pit seemed to echo off the walls as she hunted for something to say. Shadows swirled into the chamber, getting darker by the moment. Troy's firm, fine features were lit by the firelight, and his eyes remained steady on her own, pressing her for a response.

But she didn't have a response, not to him and not to her brother's plight, and she felt the walls of the cave suddenly closing in on her. For a panicked second she couldn't breathe. She needed to move, needed to hit something, needed to fight. But there was no fight to be had, not here, not without hurting Troy. She pushed herself to her feet, striding purposefully for the mouth of the cave.

"Liana...." Troy stood as well. "Where are you going?"

"Fishing," she lied. "His Majesty will want some dinner."

Kaden's rueful chuckle followed her out of the cave as she slid over the side. She heard them start talking again but resolutely ignored it. Damn Troy for putting her on the spot. He knew she hated that.

Scowling, Liana climbed back down the cliffs.

She didn't want to think about what was really bothering her. She didn't want to imagine the blood mage and the Dyngannon Kingdom and the politics. By gods, she hated politics. Father always tried to school her in the ways of courtiers, trying to give her an advantage should Kaden ever be presented with this choice. He and Mother both had shown her enough that she knew it was important, but deep down.... Deep down, she'd always hoped this day would never come.

Six

Sitting at the edge of the cave, one leg dangling over the cliffs, Kaden watched the slow leak of light into the sky and waited for the sun. He always woke early anyway, so taking the last watch of the night had been an easy choice, though he did feel a trifle guilty for Troy, who'd had his sleep interrupted for the mid watch. Kaden glanced back toward the campfire where Troy and Liana both slept, curled up on the hard cave floor; the coil of fear in his gut tightened.

They'd come. Twenty-six years later, but they'd come, just as his parents had predicted. He should have known better than to doubt his mother and father; neither were the lying type. Well, sometimes his mother would weave around the truth, but he'd never seen her tell an outright lie. Father argued that avoiding the truth was just as bad, but even Kaden could see that there were some truths best left alone.

And by the gods, how he wished this were one of them.

He turned back to the cave entrance and took a deep breath. The sun slipped up from the watery horizon, deep orange and gold, spreading talons of color across clustered clouds in vibrant pinks and reds. A storm was building in the south; clouds were gathering together, ringed with color but dark at the center. Kaden watched them for a moment, inhaling the promise of rain and sea, and his heart twisted.

What sort of pretentious, self-seeking man was he? How could he consider taking a throne?

The Dyngannon people didn't know him. They certainly wouldn't welcome him. What did it matter that a dead old woman had said he should reign? She didn't know him either. She hadn't ever visited, hadn't explained why she'd chosen him. All he had to go on were the memories his parents shared with him, and those were grim.

His father hadn't known King Porrex, but his mother had and what she'd told of him left Kaden unsettled and wary. There was always a hardness to her when she spoke of her king—her former king—and he had the feeling she generally agreed with Noffi's proclamation. Or at least she agreed the king needed to be replaced by someone, but not necessarily by him.

Kaden wasn't certain if he was insulted or relieved that his mother didn't want him to do this. He'd asked her on several occasions if she thought he should be king and he'd always had the sense she was dodging the question.

Avoiding the truth, he thought with a frown.

Dear gods, if his own mother didn't think he could do it, why was he entertaining the idea?

Kaden began plucking at the knee of his pants, noticing that the patchwork was thinning there. He would need to mend these soon. Scoffing at his own thought process, he shook his head, turning his attention to the open ocean again. Some king he was, with threadbare breeches and a skillset that revolved around fishing.

But he liked his fisherman's life. The sea was his home: a terrifying, grand, dangerously beautiful haven that had kept him safe all these years. He loved Vakeshmeer with its long winters, chilled summers and the constant taste of salt on the air. He loved hiking to the summit with Troy and practicing the blade every morning with his mother.

By the gods, why was this happening to him? Why him of all people?

Rubbing his face briskly, Kaden glanced back into the cave. Troy and Liana were starting to wake, shifting on the rocky ground beside the dying fire. He'd purposefully left it unattended for the last hour, knowing they'd need to start moving soon.

"Do you think I can weasel a bowl of porridge and a small loaf of bread off His Majesty over there?" Liana's drowsy voice was obviously directed at Troy, but Kaden snorted in response.

"I don't know, Liana," Troy mumbled, turning onto his side with a groan. "He's in that pensive state again. I'm surprised his head hasn't melted with how hard he's been thinking."

"Curses," Liana said with a heavy sigh. "I'll just have to flirt with you, then. You'll fetch me some breakfast, won't you, Troy'vesk?"

Kaden saw Troy's wide, sleepy smile and shook his head. Worry pinched in his chest but he tried very hard to ignore it. Troy looked genuinely happy. Kaden had a feeling Liana was going to move on soon. Then he'd be left trying to bridge the gap between them and everything would be awkward and painful. But he knew if he fought the relationship, Liana would only double her efforts with Troy. She was predictable like that. One did not tell Evaliana she couldn't do something.

"You'll have to flirt better than that, Liana. I've found a comfortable bit of rock here, just under my left shoulder." Troy grunted and shifted, scowling for a moment before continuing. "So you see, I'll need proper enticement."

"That's about enough of that," Kaden said, rising to his feet. "I haven't had breakfast yet and you're souring it for me."

Troy looked woundedly up at him. "But she hasn't even flirted with me yet."

Liana snickered.

"And I'd prefer it if she didn't while I'm still here." Kaden said, stretching his shoulders back.

"There you have it." Liana laughed and sat up. "His Majesty has outlawed flirting."

"No, I think His Majesty just outlawed *your* flirting, Liana." Troy paused and grinned. "How will you survive? Isn't that your customary mode of communication?"

"If I had a rock, I would throw it at you right now," Liana said.

Chuckling, Kaden glanced out of the cave again. Full daylight revealed that the storm was moving off. The clouds were distancing, still dark with the promise of rain, but at least here they would be dry. A small boat was paddling to the shore and Kaden squinted, counting two bodies on board. His mother's silver-streaked hair caught the sunlight and he smiled.

He didn't want to admit he'd been worried about them—it would give Liana something to gloat about—but he had been.

"Oh, goody," Troy said from beside him. "Here comes our verbal thrashing. I don't suppose it's too late to run and hide?"

"It won't be that bad," Kaden said and turned toward the fire. "She'll have used up most of her irritation on Father."

Liana snagged the water bucket and doused the embers in the pit, sending a hiss of steam and smoke billowing through the air. Then she sauntered to the lip of the cave and began to lower herself down. With an irreverent smile, she winked up at them, hooking the now empty bucket in the crook of her arm.

"If you say so, brother," she said. "I, for one, wouldn't be caught dead in this cave with nowhere to go."

~ * ~

Troy was surprised at Trenna's lack of anger. In point of fact, the woman seemed satisfied with the state of their little cave. She sat beside the dead fire pit, one arm hooked on her knee, armed in her customary weaponry, and surveyed the cavern with a keen gaze. Then she nodded in what he hoped was approval, and focused on her son, looking neither upset nor irritated, which Troy took as a good sign.

"Have you made a decision?" she asked Kaden.

Kaden glanced at Troy and shrugged. Troy shrugged back, just as baffled at the anti-climactic greeting. Things had been so tense yesterday he'd expected a lot more from her. They'd been found by the blood mage and her crony. Kaden was being called to be a king and by all reports it wouldn't be a peaceful transition. The situation warranted more than this, he thought.

"I'd yell if either of you was seriously hurt," Trenna snorted at them, apparently reading their expressions. "But what happens now depends solely on you, son. So I ask again, have you made a decision?"

"You can't seriously expect me to have an answer," Kaden said, crossing his arms.

"Well, the blood mage isn't going anywhere without one," Trenna said.

Kaden shook his head and frowned out at the beach. Troy could see Liana and Nelek leaning against one of the boats and suddenly wished he were down there. Trenna wasn't angry but this felt like a private conversation and for a long moment he considered leaving. But leaving now would only draw more attention to himself and anyway, Kaden might feel abandoned if he did. So Troy took a deep breath and crossed his arms too, resigning himself to staying.

"Those people don't know me," Kaden said. "And I don't know them. It makes no sense for me to be king."

Trenna drummed a light rhythm into the pommel of her sword, eyeing Kaden with an unreadable expression. Troy wasn't certain if Kaden's answer had relieved or upset her, but it did set her to moving. She stood, her shorter legs unfolding in a fluid movement. Troy watched as she moved to stand beside Kaden, her eyes searching the horizon for a long—painfully long—moment. He could sense an unspoken conversation drifting between mother and son, a gulf that seemed to widen between them the longer it took for someone to speak.

Gods help him, he should have followed Liana.

"You're right," Trenna said at last and Troy took a breath. "You don't know them and they don't know you. And you can't be expected to make such a decision without at least seeing the place first."

"I really don't like where this is going," Troy blurted, earning himself a smirk from Trenna and a raised eyebrow from Kaden. He shrugged at Kaden but didn't feel the comment needed elaboration.

The only way they could see Dyngannon was if they went there, after all. It's the only thing Trenna could mean.

"You probably shouldn't," Trenna said with a sigh. "Because it's going to be dangerous."

"Mother," Kaden said, shaking his head. "What would we really achieve by going there? Am I supposed to just take one look at the people and decide then? Because it doesn't work that way."

"Of course it doesn't work that way," she said, her gaze still on the horizon. "Nothing does."

"Then why bother?" Kaden asked.

Trenna took a long, slow breath. Troy frowned at the flicker of pain in her face. He'd seen that look before. It was the same look she gave when she was talking about his father. He felt a lump in his throat and had to look away from her as he swallowed it down.

Could it have been six years since Tibitus Mavon had died? Some days the death felt very far away from him, but other days—days like today—it was immediate, grief welling up inside him so hard and fast it was all he could do to contain it.

Good gods, how he missed the man!

"Why bother?" Trenna repeated the question, her voice a rough whisper that made Troy shiver. She turned to face Kaden and gripped his forearm, staring hard into his face. "For Ronan," she said.

Kaden straightened as though he'd been slapped, his mouth tightening into a grim line as he stared down at his mother. Ronan Dyngannon, Kaden's great-uncle, had been slain by Porrex during the Siege of Cadabyr before Kaden was born, but they all knew his story. The Prince who dared to challenge the king, who had been one of Trenna's closest friends and advisors during her youth, and who had died trying to bring peace to the nations.

Troy swallowed nervously, glancing between mother and son as silence descended on the cave. Fear lodged in his gut, firm and inescapable, as he understood that there was no choice. Even if the mage had not come, there still wouldn't have been a choice. All roads led to Dyngannon whether by honor or duty or regret. Too much blood had been spilled and none of them could ignore it, not even Troy.

He did not think his father would approve of his staying behind. Nor could he watch his friends ride off to danger without him.

"When do we leave?" Troy asked, cutting through whatever silent battle had begun between Trenna and Kaden.

Kaden frowned at him but Troy held his ground, meeting the man's green gaze without flinching.

No, he was not going to stay behind. And no, Kaden could not ignore this anymore. It was Fate and there was no fighting against it, no matter how much Troy—and he imagined Kaden himself—wanted to.

After what felt like an eternity, Kaden sighed and nodded, resigned to the situation.

Troy turned to Trenna, who was watching him with a bemused smile. She nodded to them both and hooked a thumb in her belt. "We have to go home first. Gather supplies. Then we can start hunting for passage to the mainland."

"How are we going to pay for that?" Kaden asked.

Leave it to Kaden to think of the practical, Troy thought. The man was being summoned to a throne and his first action is to think of the bill. This really was Fate.

"Who says we'll have to pay?" Trenna asked with a wicked grin.

Troy exchanged a wary glance with Kaden as Trenna slipped closer to the ledge. She began to lower herself down, climbing with ease over the cliff face.

"Oh, that can't be good," Troy said, frowning down at her.

She laughed, a bright, bubbling sound that drifted up to them as she continued down.

"No," Kaden said with a frown of his own. "No, it really can't be."

Seven

Brigetta tilted a bowl over with one finger, surveying the gooey, glumpy substance inside, and wrinkled her nose. Out of the corner of her eye she could see Faxon making quick work of the intruder, his blade flashing in the late morning light, and sighed. She let the bowl settle again, scanning the little home with a frown.

Four empty pegs lined the wall by the front door and an iron hoop hung directly above the table, holding all manner of cooking pots and utensils. Behind her stood a large pantry, well stocked by the looks of it. Several chairs circled the table, which commanded the bulk of the space, and Bree imagined many meals had been shared in this room.

It was curious thinking of Nelek and Trenna living such a simple life, given their lineage and respective histories. Nelek was the rightful Duke of Kiavana, after all. And by rights, that would make Trenna a duchess. This little home was far beneath them.

A body crashed into the table, sending it scooting across the room toward the open hearth. Bree had just enough time to withdraw her hand before Faxon threw two blades at the ill-fated Eldur man. They whizzed past her face in a blur, sinking hard and fast into their intended mark. The meaty, visceral sound of a blade sinking into skin wasn't something she thought she could ever get used to but she did her best to ignore it.

Faxon flashed her a grin, neatening his tunic as he stepped around a fallen chair and toward the gurgling man strewn over the hearth. Because she didn't want to see the killing blow, she concentrated on the blood in the air, sensed magic converging on them, and took a deep breath. She could feel it cool against her skin, could see the sharp twinkle of many little lights in the room as it waited for a command.

"We could just wait for them to come home," Faxon said with a grunt. She heard another meaty sound and had to clench her fists.

Gods, did he have to be so callous about killing?

"There will be other assassins," she said. "And we don't know that they'll come back."

"I'm fairly certain they will, but it's your eyesight, not mine. Do what you want."

Bree frowned at him. A part of her wanted to ask what made him so sure they would return here, but another part of her, a big, loud part of her, was too worried to listen. It was entirely possible that Nelek had taken his family and escaped the island already, which would leave Bree back at the beginning in her hunt for them.

And that, she couldn't stomach. Porrex already had a price out on her. If she couldn't convince the boy to fight for the throne, then she was a dead woman. Faxon was good, no doubt about it, but he couldn't contend with the might of the Dyngannon throne, not on his own.

She took a deep breath and concentrated on the spell she needed.

"Caraloomessa act all et teh," Bree whispered, closing her eyes.

Warm light filtered past her eyelids, an odd tickling sensation running over her eyelashes, and for a long moment all she could see was red-rimmed darkness. Her stomach pitched with worry, all the dangers of this action flooding her. Blood magic was always a bargain, a trade, but magic itself was fickle about the details. There was a very good chance she was about to blind herself for months.

Or forever, she thought, remembering some of the stories she'd been told.

An image began to form, blurred at first and then dizzyingly clear.

She had suddenly an aerial view of the island, treetops gliding past her so quickly she swayed. Faxon's hand clasped her own, holding her steady as she oriented herself to the view. Because she had only traded sight, the vision came with no sound. This made things even more disorienting, since she could still hear everything in the room, including Faxon's quiet breathing. His body heat warmed her left side, and his fingers tightened on her hand, but otherwise he was silent.

Battling a weird sense of vertigo, she watched as whatever bird she was sharing sight with turned in a wide circle, scanning the forest floor in search of food. Unfortunately for the hawk, its hunting grounds were being intruded upon. Bree counted five bodies making a steady trek through the woods, and breathed in relief. Sun shimmered off the streaks in Kaden's hair, making him easy to identify.

They were all right, thank gods.

They were on the other side of the island, but they were all right.

"They are moving this way," she said, glad she couldn't see Faxon's smug smirk. She knew he was doing it, though. He always did when proven right. "But it will be a while before they get here."

"They'll have a weapons cache somewhere nearby," Faxon said. "Trenna will want to arm up before they depart the island."

Bree held back a remark. She didn't like that he called the general by her bastardized name. Tray'Lana Delphinium Silvanus was a hero among the Eldur, or she had been before Porrex slandered her as a murderer. Now the people were a mix of defiant disbelief or hateful acceptance of the propaganda.

Noffi had never fully divulged what had happened at Castle Cadabyr all those years ago, but Bree didn't think Tray'Lana could have murdered the prince. For one, Noffi would not have helped the woman get away if she had, and for another, Porrex didn't push hard enough to find the girl. If Tray'Lana had truly murdered Prince Ronan as Porrex insisted she had, then why hadn't more sentries been sent? Why hadn't a full-scale war against the Human borderlands been started?

No, something was missing here; Bree could feel it.

"How long do we have?" Faxon asked.

Brigetta concentrated on the bird's view, estimating the distance between the cabin and the approaching family. "Several hours at the least."

"Beautiful. Be a dear and don't move from this spot." Faxon lifted her by the elbows and set her down somewhere, helping her into a chair.

Releasing magic, Bree found the expected blindness and sighed. She really had hoped that magic would swap her vision back immediately, but there was only blackness before her. She didn't ask the obvious question of what Faxon was doing. The table scuffed across the floor, then a chair plunked down, and finally she heard the creak of wood as he sat down.

Undoubtedly, he had a view of all windows and entrances, as well as her person, and was prepared to wait and watch. Bree took a deep breath and settled in her own chair, wishing she'd just asked him how he'd known the family would be back.

~ * ~

"Well damn," Trenna said with a sigh. "The door is open."

Kaden looked at his mother, though none of them paused. They made a steady, slow progression through the field toward their home, each of them keeping low to the ground. It seemed a moot point to him to keep crouching, what with all the noise they were making, but it was what Nelek and Trenna were doing, so the rest followed suit.

A hawk flew by overhead, screeching a warning call, and Kaden glanced at it before focusing on the main house. Squinting hard, he tried to make out if there was any movement inside the place, but there were too many shadows. As they neared the building, his mother gave signals, sending Troy and Liana to the west and his father to the east, and Kaden guessed at her plan.

Troy and Liana would have access to the west-facing window at the back of the house. Father, on the other hand, was headed for the only window in the main room. He would act as the second line of defense, cutting off their intruders from any obvious escape routes. That left the front door—which they were rapidly approaching—for Trenna and himself.

He cast a quick glance at his own home, several yards away from the main house, and frowned. They would need to check there later if they meant to stay the night.

Trenna slipped in front of him, stepping up to the doorway with her sword drawn. She stopped on the threshold and Kaden could see the tip of her blade lower a fraction.

"I might have known you'd be here, Faxon," Trenna said.

Kaden easily saw over her shoulder and into the main room. There were two dead men on the floor, one by the hearth and the other at the bedroom door. The blood mage sat with her back to a wall, her head bowed, and the assassin lounged in Troy's favorite chair, both feet propped on the table.

"Indeed," Faxon said without moving. "We've been here quite some time. As you can see, I took care of some nasty business for you."

"And I imagine your services come at a cost."

Kaden couldn't tell if Trenna was amused, irritated, or worried. She sounded flippant, but her body was still poised for battle, and her attention remained fixed on Faxon. She didn't signal for anyone to stand down, so the danger hadn't passed yet.

Faxon grinned. "You remember me well, Trenna. Everything has a price."

"These men were a nuisance, nothing more. I was expecting them and we could have easily taken them down," Trenna said, shifting on her feet. "I'd say you bought yourself an hour of my time, nothing more."

"There were two men here. Two hours."

"They wouldn't have been here if they hadn't followed you to Vakeshmeer. You'll get one hour and my apology to the mage for the incident with the chair."

Kaden followed this exchange with a dark sense of humor but said nothing. Two dead men equaled two hours; he'd known his mother could be ruthless, but good gods!

The red-headed woman snorted her amusement. "One hour," the mage said. "But I will choose when and where I spend it and the boy's presence is required."

Trenna glanced back at him. Kaden shrugged, honestly not caring. Nothing the mage could say would sway him, nor did he think it should. If he were going to agree to be king, he was going to need a lot more than words. He'd need a lot more than a family visit to the old lands too, but that seemed beyond the point now.

"Done," Trenna said and then, more loudly, "It's safe."

The edges of the room came to life, his father climbing through the window, agile and quick, and Liana and Troy stepping in from the back. Unnervingly enough, Faxon remained seated. He didn't seem the least surprised that he'd been surrounded. Though, in Kaden's estimation, the man couldn't have been a good assassin without becoming accustomed to being surrounded.

He reminded himself to ask his mother how she had come to know this man.

"What's your next move then, Trenna?" Faxon asked.

Stepping into the house, Trenna made her way for the hearth. Kaden followed, not entirely certain what they were doing, but preferring to be on the move as opposed to standing in the open door. He glanced at the mage as he passed her, startled to find her eyes milky and pale. Her head was cocked in an awkward sort of way, as though she were listening intently, and he feared that his mother had somehow knocked the sight out of the poor girl. The chair had hit the mage very hard. He could remember the clatter it had made when it connected with her head.

"We agreed you'd have an hour of our time," Nelek said, moving to help Trenna drag one of the bodies off the hearth. "I don't believe that means we have to share our plans with you."

"That seems a bit petty." Faxon frowned.

"We're not friends," Liana said, crossing her arms and glaring at him. "The boundary is clear. One hour. I'd suggest your little mage chooses her hour quickly."

Kaden felt an uncomfortable flush burning his ears and began helping to clear the hearth. Gods, he hated all this attention. He wanted to get on a boat and just sail for days, preferably alone.

"Your daughter is quite charming," Faxon said after a long moment. "It's a pity you didn't stay in Kiavana. She would have made an impressive duchess."

Trenna snorted a laugh and knelt beside the hearth. Pulling a dagger from her belt loop, she began to scrape at the cobblestone in the floor. Nelek did the same, several feet opposite her, and Kaden frowned. He glanced at Liana and Troy, who seemed to share his bafflement, as his parents unearthed two long metal hooks. Nelek and Trenna nodded to each other and then lifted, straining against the hooks with equal grunts of effort.

Kaden moved to Trenna, leaning down to help hoist the heavy stone up and away from the hearth. Stone scraped across stone, grinding along until it finally encountered the wooden floor, revealing a deep hole hidden under the hearth. A large trunk lay within, long and thick, and Kaden began to suspect what would be inside.

He helped his parents lift the trunk out, shuffling over to the table to drop it. Faxon finally moved his feet, leaning forward as Nelek produced a key for the heavy iron lock mounted on the trunk. Inside was an assortment of weapons, oilskins, and pouches, and Kaden felt the ever-present knot in his chest tighten.

This was really happening. They were really leaving.

"By gods," Faxon said. "I could love you, Trenna."

The blood mage made an annoyed sound.

"Sorry, darling." Faxon grinned at his wife, who turned her head toward the door.

"When we made this cache we were expecting Mavon to accompany us." Trenna began distributing supplies, ignoring Faxon completely. She looked up at Troy, who stood beside Liana. "I won't do you the dishonor of trying to talk you out of coming, Troy. But you must understand that we don't know the current state of politics within Dyngannon or the borderlands. It's quite possible that Human and Eldur alike will try to kill you."

Troy grinned and winked at her. "Sounds like a lot of fun."

Kaden straightened and frowned at his friend. While he didn't want to leave Troy behind, he didn't want to be the cause of his death either. Kaden opened his mouth to speak, prepared to argue the man off, but Nelek stopped him, shoving a pouch and scabbard in his hands. Meeting his father's eyes, he saw the warning there and closed his mouth.

Scowling, Kaden took the pouch and scabbard, wondering what the hell was wrong with the man. He couldn't possibly want Troy hurt.

But then, he couldn't leave Troy behind either. Other assassins would come. No, his father was right. Troy was safer with them.

Trenna reached the bottom of the trunk, efficiently tossing scabbards and leather chest pieces to each member of their family— Troy included. There was one satchel left, a small, brownish and tattered thing that she retrieved with a shaky hand. She stared at it, grief etched into her features, until Nelek gripped her shoulder. Kaden saw the look his parents shared, a remorseful and resigned expression that made the hair on Kaden's neck stand on end. Then she tucked the satchel away, as though hiding it from view, and faced the room again.

"From this point forward, we all wear layers," Trenna said. "Undershirt, the leather chest piece, and a tunic. We want to be protected but we don't want to go announcing that we're trouble before we've even opened our mouths."

"So you *do* have a plan?" Faxon asked, though by his tone Kaden knew he was mocking them.

"Of course." Trenna looked at Faxon and smiled, all venom and insincerity. "Only now that you're here, you get to be the bait."

Eight

Nelek leaned against the railing near the bow of the *Bitter Croften* and frowned out at the ocean. The dark blue of deep water slid around their little fishing vessel with ease, curling and dipping in the distance, and Nelek took a long breath. Their ship wasn't made for long voyages—it just didn't have the storage space—but it could get them to the next island over. They'd have to sell it when they got to port, and then their last tie to Vakeshmeer would be severed.

He swallowed hard, trying to resolve himself to what had to be done.

They needed to distance themselves. They needed all traces of their presence to vanish so that any assassins or informants sent looking for them would come up dry. This was a matter of safety, dammit.

And yet, all he could think about was what they were leaving behind.

His memory flooded with images of his children: Kaden learning how to read from one of Trenna's novels, and Liana crawling through the front room, trying desperately to keep up with her big brother. He remembered Tibitus Mavon on the day Troy was born, pacing back and forth at Big Hearth because Human custom would not allow him in the birthing room.

Nelek had always thought that silly, but he wouldn't say so to his friend, at least not then. He was fairly certain he'd mentioned something of that nature when the man had tried to keep him away during Evaliana's birth.

"You look sad," Liana said, startling him.

He glanced at her as she leaned against the railing beside him, and tried for a smile that felt wobbly at best. "Reflective," he said.

"Yeah," Liana said with a sigh. "I'm going to miss it too."

"Really?" Nelek turned to face her better, surveying her expression curiously. But Liana was a difficult woman to read and after a moment he gave up. "Of all of us, I had expected you would be pleased to leave. Vakeshmeer is very confined."

"You can want to see new things and still love your home," Liana said with a smirk. "I always dreamed I would travel the world and come home again after a year or so."

"Travel doing what?" He tried to hide the humor from his voice, but she must have heard it because she fixed him with an icy blue glare.

"I hadn't worked that out yet."

"Ah," he said and tried to think of something to say that wouldn't anger her further.

Gods, she could be so touchy sometimes.

He glanced over the deck of their small fishing boat, spotted Kaden and Troy at the helm, both looking amused about something. Brigetta and Faxon were likely in the little cabin below deck, sequestered away and doing blood magicky things. Nelek didn't care as long as they stayed away from his children. He didn't see Trenna anywhere, which was a little odd, so he checked again.

When he still couldn't find her, he asked Liana. "Where's your mother?"

Liana nodded to the closed cabin door. It was built under the helm, deep into the ship, and had three short steps leading down to it. "She had business with the blood mage. Apparently the woman can see shapes now, so that's progress, I guess."

"What sort of business would Trenna have with her?" Nelek asked, frowning because Trenna hadn't mentioned anything to him.

"She didn't say."

He pushed away from the railing and started for the cabin, a new suspicion forming in his gut. What was his wife hiding from him?

The boat rocked suddenly, lurching to the left as though it had been struck by a large wave, and he lost his footing. Kaden shouted in surprise and Nelek heard Liana's echo of alarm just before his left hip smacked into the deck. He grabbed at the first available rope, a line leading up the main mast, as his body began to slide over the deck.

"What was that?" Troy asked, loudly enough that Nelek could hear him from his place near the mast.

Nelek glanced at the calm sea and felt the hair on the back of his neck prickle. Shoving himself back to his feet, he hurried for the cabin door. The latch lifted but the door was locked and wouldn't budge.

"Trenna!" he called and struck the wooden surface with his fist. "Trenna, open this door!"

"What's going on?" Liana asked from behind him.

"Hell if I know," Nelek growled and then pounded on the door again. "Open this door or so help me, I will kill everyone inside!"

"Everyone except Mother, of course," Liana suggested, though he could hear the worry in her voice.

"That's debatable," Nelek said and shoved his shoulder against the door. It rattled and shook under his weight and he felt the impact rocket pain down his arm. "Godsdammit!"

A high, agonized scream sliced through the air, barely hindered by the wooden cabin door and the knot in his gut tightened in response. He'd heard that scream before; he knew that voice like it was his own, and every instinct he had seemed to fly into action. He stepped back, braced himself on the short walls beside him, and surged forward with a hard kick.

His foot hit the door with so much force the wood splintered and the lock loosened. He leaned back and did it again and the cabin door flew inward, its lock snapping out of place to hit the floor.

Nelek rushed inside and stopped abruptly. He felt Liana skid to a halt just behind him too, but his attention riveted on Trenna. She was in the center of the small space, curled up on the floor with silver fire licking all around her. He saw her hands clasped tight against her ears and felt his mouth go dry.

He knew what this was. He'd seen it before, years ago when they'd first met.

"Gods, Trenna," he whispered. "What have you done?"

And then, because she was still screaming and in pain, he went to her. Crossing the room in two quick strides he knelt beside her, pulling her writhing form onto his lap as the spell continued its work. The fire did not scorch him; he'd known it wouldn't. Just as he'd known it would hurt. But he was prepared this time, gritting his teeth and burying his face in Trenna's hair as the unnatural fire raged around them, bone-jarring pain slamming into him.

Transformation spell.

By gods, she'd undergone the transformation spell.

Why hadn't she talked to him first?

Little by little the fires receded, sinking back into Trenna's body, taking the pain with it. Trenna slumped in his arms and he stayed there, panting in pain and anger as he stared down into her freckled face. Normally her skin was fair, not freckled. And the streaks in her hair were gone.

In fact, her hair had completely changed color, going from light blonde to a reddish color, like the fur on a fawn. And, lastly, her ears were no longer pointed but round like a Human's.

"Fascinating," Faxon said from the corner of the room, and Nelek had to force himself not to charge the man.

"What the hell?" Liana asked and Nelek gripped Trenna more tightly.

Trenna was unconscious, her body too strained from the ordeal, and it would be some time before she woke. Which was a good thing, because if she were conscious at this moment, he would likely be strangling her.

They hadn't discussed disguises for when they arrived at the mainland and now he knew why. She must have been planning this for some time, waiting for the right moment to test if this mage was a powerful as Noffi.

Gods, she was such a reckless, irritating woman!

"Dad, what's going on?" Liana asked again.

Nelek ignored her. He had to ignore everyone or he might explode at them all. Instead he stood, lifting Trenna off the floor to deposit her limp form into one of the bunks lining the walls. The move brought him closer to the blood mage, who looked weak and spent, her eyes no longer white but fixed on the general direction of the door.

He tucked Trenna into the bed, carefully fixing the blanket around her shoulders, and took a long, deep breath. This was how she'd looked when they'd first met, he remembered. He'd almost forgotten the freckles running chaotically across the bridge of her nose. The shape of her face was the same, high cheeks and crooked mouth, too thin to be called pretty. But when she smiled it was wide and true, hitting him in the gut every time, and he wondered again why she hadn't told him.

She should have told him.

"Dad..." Liana tried again, but he lifted his hand to stop her.

"Get out," he said quietly. "Everyone. Get out."

Liana looked hurt at the command but after a moment she straightened her shoulders and glared at Faxon and Brigetta. "You heard him," she said and gestured to the door.

After a brief hesitation, Brigetta and Faxon moved, Faxon gripping the mage's elbow to help her out of the cabin. Liana followed a heartbeat later, shutting the broken door behind her. It swung open a crack and then beat back against the frame, smacking in time with the rock of the boat. Nelek stared at it and then turned back to his wife.

She looked peaceful, her face lax in sleep, blissfully unaware of the havoc she'd wreaked on him. Listening to the creak and rock of the boat, he tried to reason through what she'd done.

What she'd done behind his back.

"Godsdammit woman," he muttered and pressed his forehead against the wooden wall. "What am I to do with you?"

~ * ~

Trenna woke slowly, every inch of her body aching and sore. She tried to remind herself if it had hurt this much when Noffi did the spell. But that was over thirty years ago and the details were hard to pinpoint. Porrex had been there that first time, passively observing as the fires turned her from Eldur to Human, and she imagined, much as she had back then, that the king had hoped she would die in the ritual.

It was known to happen from time to time, if the blood mage wasn't strong enough to conduct the spell, or if their mastery of magic wasn't quite what it should be. So he was probably disappointed when Trenna had survived the ordeal, but as it was, her mission had taken her out of the political picture for over a decade, which meant he won in the end.

Her mission, she thought. Gods, it had been so long since she'd worn a uniform she could barely recall how it had felt. Duty and honor, once her very lifeblood, were a haunting echo to her now, a faded memory she could barely touch.

She remembered now, remembered the thunder of her own heartbeat as she'd realized Porrex's plan to get her out of Dyngannon, remembered the agony of that first transformation as it had come over her. She'd been a fool back then, knowingly walking into that ritual, walking into Porrex's plan. He had felt the sway of the Eldur people, had sensed her popularity as a threat, and dealt with it.

A secret mission of utmost importance, he'd said.

You're the only one I can trust to do it, he'd said.

And she had known, deep down she had always known, that he never meant for her to succeed. But she had succeeded, in a sense. She'd returned to Dyngannon with Nelek and they had all fought to rescue Auliere, Nelek's mother and Porrex's daughter, and Trenna had undergone this godsawful spell for what she'd hoped would be the last time, reclaiming her Eldur form.

Gods, this was such a bad decision, she thought, fighting to open her eyes. She became quickly aware of the rock of the ship because her stomach pitched. Swallowing back the need to vomit, she coached herself into breathing, staring up at the wooden ceiling. Someone had put her in bed, which she was grateful for, because the last thing she could remember was lying on the floor.

Nelek. It had to have been Nelek.

He'd been there at the end, she was sure of it.

She turned her head, cringing when the movement made the little cabin spin in her vision. Trenna hissed a breath through her teeth and forced herself to focus. It was difficult because the room continued to tilt and sway, but she was still able to spot Nelek in the bunk across the room.

He had his elbows on his knees and he was staring at the floor, his shoulders tense. Trenna grimaced for a whole new reason, recognizing just how upset he was before he even spoke.

"Are you all right?" he asked.

She grunted in answer, ever so carefully shifting onto her side so she could see him better. "I'm alive," she said, wishing he would look at her.

He grunted back, his jaw going tense but he kept his gaze on the floor. Her stomach pitched again, but this time with worry. She'd seen Nelek angry before but this was different. This was deeper somehow, a gulf yawning wide between them and she panicked, fearing it might be irreparable.

"Nelek, I..." she began but he cut her off.

"Are we even now?"

"Even?" she asked, scrambling to catch his meaning.

"I run off and confront the blood mage without you, and you conduct a ritual that could have cost us our lives," he said, weighing the two scenarios with his hands. "Is that how this works?"

"No," she said, forcing herself to sit up. The movement cost her, every muscle in her body flaring with pain, and she nearly lost her control. But she managed not to wretch in front of him, coaching herself into short, shallow breaths until the nausea passed. "It's not like that," she managed to wheeze between breaths.

"No?" Nelek asked, finally looking at her.

His blue eyes blazed fever bright and his wide mouth was set in such a hard line that Trenna flinched, wishing he'd look away. But he didn't and she couldn't either, some instinct in her refusing to back down.

"Look, that's not what I intended," she said at last.

"Exactly what did you intend, Trenna?" He got to his feet, his fists clenched so hard she could see the strain in his forearms. "Because I'm having a difficult time understanding it."

Gods, why had she done it in private? She couldn't quite remember now.

"I wanted to make sure the mage could do it before suggesting everyone undergo this," Trenna said, thinking, *and I didn't want to tell you what it would cost.*

Damn Faxon and his negotiations.

"And you didn't think I needed to know?" Nelek asked, his voice rising.

"That's not... no. I just..." Trenna frowned, trying to organize her thoughts into something more coherent.

"You thought, hey, I can do this with no problem. I've been through it twice now," Nelek continued, his rant gaining momentum. "Never mind the fact that I could die, which will kill my husband too, thanks to Eldur marriage. Leave my children as orphans with a blood mage and an assassin on board. It'll be perfect."

"That's not what happened," she said through her teeth.

"Then what did happen?" He exploded and she shouted back, "I knew you would argue about it!"

"Damn right I would!"

"And we don't have the luxury of a lot of choices right now."

"So you thought to force our hand? You do it first so the rest of us have to? Is that it?"

"No!" Her anger was quickly shoving all the side effects of the spell aside, but she didn't quite have the strength to stand up.

"Then what in gods would possess you to sneak behind my back and set up a ritual that could have killed us?"

She flinched, recognizing just how bad this really looked. Taking a deep breath, Trenna found a calmer mindset, a calmer tone of voice, and tried to explain. "I trusted that the mage was powerful enough that our lives were never in danger," she said. "Noffi wouldn't have chosen her otherwise."

Some of the tension went out of his shoulders and she continued, not wanting him to interrupt until she'd gotten out the pertinent bits.

"I was afraid she might change me into a hag or that some odd deformity might overtake me. In which case, I would have demanded to be returned to normal immediately. A disguise is worthless if it leaves you defenseless at the same time."

"All of this could have been discussed with me," Nelek said.

His anger wasn't abating, not that she'd imagined it would quite yet. Or ever, if she were honest. But he was at least becoming relatively calm. Trenna watched him, weighing her next words.

"The main reason I wanted to test it first," she said, holding his gaze. Gods, his eyes were so blue and so angry. Part of her wanted to apologize and beg forgiveness and kiss him until they were both naked and breathless, but that wouldn't resolve anything. He needed to hear it all. "I wanted to know if the pain would be the same. I thought maybe it could vary between blood mages. Maybe Brigetta could make it less... awful."

He frowned, his fists clenching and unclenching as he watched her. She saw the fury and the conflict and the hurt in him, and swallowed back her fear. She'd done some monumentally stupid things in her time but this one seemed to be the worst. She'd alienated her husband, something she'd promised herself she would never do, not to him. She alienated enough people in her life; she couldn't bear it if she lost him.

"You knew I wouldn't let you walk into that pain without a fight," Nelek said. "You knew I would have taken that risk rather than let you do it. So you left me behind to do it on your own."

She exhaled slowly and nodded. "Yes," she said quietly. "I knew you wouldn't have let me do it at all. You would have cut the conversation off, made some attempt to forbid it..."

"Because it's reckless and crazy and I don't want to see *my wife* suffer like that, let alone my children," he snapped at her and she closed her eyes.

"The pain passes, Nelek."

"You think that makes it all right?" he shouted and she heard him hit something.

Trenna flinched at the sound but didn't open her eyes, not yet. "Nelek..."

"You know, after twenty-three years married I really thought you would have figured it out by now," he said and she opened her eyes, frowning at him.

"Figured it out?" she asked, gripping the bunk to hold herself steady as the ship rocked.

"That it's not just about you anymore," he said, shaking his head in exasperation. "We're supposed to be a team, Trenna. You and me, back to back, fighting whatever comes our way."

"We are..." she started but he cut her off.

"No, we're not," he said, furious again. "How can we be when you run off and do something like this without me? You knew I wouldn't agree with it. You knew I wouldn't let you do this. And you did it anyway." He started for the door and then stopped, one hand on the doorframe as he looked back at her. "No, it's worse than that. You did it *because* you knew I wouldn't want it."

"I did it because it's the best option we have and I knew you wouldn't listen!"

She felt her face flush and debated getting out of the bed, but she knew her legs wouldn't be ready to work yet and she didn't want him to see that. She knew him, knew he wouldn't be able to stand aside while she was in need no matter how angry he was, and didn't want to put him in that position.

His fingers tightened on the doorframe, his jaw clenched, and then he shook his head, pulling the door open to stalk out. She watched him go, watched the door clatter loosely against the frame, and fell back against the bed with a groan.

"Well that couldn't have gone worse," she muttered to the ceiling.

Nine

"You're barking mad," Troy said.

He couldn't look away from Trenna, even though the rest of their party was staring at him. He didn't know why he was fighting the issue either.

The magic had done a good job at transforming Trenna into Human, but seeing her without the silver streaks and pointed ears just felt wrong. She was right, of course. If they were heading into the borderlands, then they needed a better means of hiding the fact that they were Eldur. Still, his mind was caught on the warning she had given to her children.

"It's going to be very painful," she'd said. "And it won't be brief."

He looked to Evaliana. She stood beside him, curly black hair smudging into the gloomy shadows of the tiny cabin. She'd gone a little pale at the announcement and he knew she was frightened, but she gave him a strained smile and leaned against the wall. He frowned at her, trying not to think of her screaming the way Trenna had just an hour or so before.

No, that hadn't been brief.

"Mother is right," Liana said. "It will be better this way."

"When will we do this?" Kaden asked, putting an end to Troy's argument.

Scowling, Troy glanced at where Faxon leaned against the wall beside Liana. The assassin was picking his fingernails with a slender dagger. Faxon winked at him, his mouth twitching into a sly smile, and Troy had to quell the desire to grip his hilt.

Troy sincerely disliked Faxon. He tried to tell himself this had more to do with the man's profession than with the fact that he'd broken his nose, but even Troy knew it was a close call. Still, he imagined his vanity would recover at some point. Faxon could have just killed him, after all, so there were worse fates than a broken nose.

"We will find a place on the next island," Trenna said. "Sackersbee is normally crowded this time of year. We should be able to slip away unnoticed."

"We will need to find a new ship anyway," Faxon said, glancing at the blood mage, who was silent beside him. "I can guarantee we're being hunted. Bree didn't exactly leave Dyngannon Court on the best of terms."

Troy crossed his arms and was about to ask what he meant but Trenna beat him to it.

"How many did you kill?" she asked, eyeing Faxon.

Faxon grinned. "Only two, and I swear it was in defense. They seemed to think they could detain my wife against her will."

"Porrex only sent two men to detain a blood mage?" Trenna asked, though by the sound of her voice Troy could tell she was driving at something.

Faxon nodded, obviously not caring that there were two men dead by his own hand. Troy tried hard to stop scowling. What made a man so cold? Had Faxon's parents been particularly twisted or something? Did the man even *have* parents?

Gods, what could they be like?

"I doubt Porrex meant for them to survive. With the murders on top of her refusal to stay at Court, the king has ample reason to chase her down." Trenna rolled her shoulder slowly, frowning at the floor as she worked through everything.

"You think Porrex sent them to die?" Faxon asked. "How disappointing."

Liana scoffed in disgust and Troy couldn't help making a grunt of agreement. This man was insane.

"Blood mages hold a certain kind of political power," Trenna said. "They are tied to Eldur history in such a way that the people would have protested if he attempted to keep her against her will."

"Let her kill a couple of men and the protest turns against her," Kaden said. "Gods, that's a fine pickle. We can't count on her opinion swaying anyone at Court now either."

"Not unless someone else admits to the murders," Liana said, looking at Faxon.

"Yes, child," Faxon responded dryly, "because I am just the sort of man who would confess to something like that."

"Do you have any soul at all?" Troy blurted, unable to stand the man's careless attitude anymore.

"Not since last I checked," Faxon said, finally lowering his dagger. "Besides, there seems little use to my sacrificing myself for my wife's good name. Not only did she allow me to do it, but my execution would also be her death. The word of a dead woman hardly seems helpful."

"You know, I don't even understand why we're listening to you," Troy said. "How the hell did you even get on board this ship?"

"Troy," Kaden raised his hand, beseeching him to stop but he just couldn't.

"First you show up and announce yourselves by assaulting one of us..." Troy straightened from his corner, stepping toward Faxon as he spoke.

"How is your nose, by the way?" Faxon asked.

Troy overrode him. "Then you break into our house and try blackmailing Kaden into talking to you. And then you do gods knows what to make Trenna look like that and now you're saying you want everyone else to undergo this excruciatingly painful spell..."

"Well, not you," Faxon said with a sharp grin. "You're already Human."

What little resolve Troy had left broke and he drew back his fist, prepared to deliver a solid blow to Faxon's left eye, but something firm caught his arm before it could fly. Kaden was at his side, grunting in an effort to keep him from hitting the man.

"Let it go," Kaden said lowly. "Come on. Let it go."

"Why are you protecting him?" Troy asked.

Faxon was smirking at him, the bastard. Troy glared back but let Kaden pull him away.

"Hell if I know," Kaden said. "But I am. So let's just calm down."

"What does Father say?" Liana asked, bringing them back to the conversation at hand.

Trenna glanced at the wooden ceiling, a look of intense remorse crossing her face. Nelek was at the helm. He hadn't spoken to anyone but Trenna since the spell had been conducted and was, justifiably, furious.

"You can ask him yourself," Trenna said quietly. "But we will need a decision before we reach port."

"Well I say no," Troy grumbled, folding his arms. "You shouldn't have to."

"When we come to port in Cadabyr it will be behind Human lines," Trenna said. "Brigetta says that Brenson has created peace between Kiavana and Cadabyr, but it is a major thoroughfare for trade. There will be spies there. Anonymity is our greatest defense."

"What exactly does this spell do?" Kaden asked.

Troy rolled his eyes. "Gods, I can't believe this."

"It takes your physical form and replaces it with a Human form," Brigetta said, her voice flat. "Your true form goes into the ether, where it waits to be summoned again."

"And how long does it last?" Kaden asked.

"Until your true form is summoned again," Brigetta said. "Any Eldur can undo a transformation spell. But it takes a mage to perform the original rites."

"So, we do this and we can change back any time?" Liana asked.

"With the proper words, yes," Brigetta said. "And yes, I will teach them to you. Should anything happen to me, you will be able to fix yourselves."

"Does it hurt both times?" Troy asked, glaring at the mage.

Brigetta seemed to be able to locate him, but her eyes were just slightly off from his form. "I have never undergone a spell such as this. Until today, I'd never performed it either."

"Yes," Trenna said. She was looking at Kaden, sobering honesty on her face as she confirmed it. "Yes, it hurts both times."

"Hats," Troy suggested, but Liana shook her head.

"A hat or a cloak can only do so much," she said. "Like it or not, Mother is right. This is the best way for us to hide."

Kaden's face wore the same resignation. Troy scowled at them all. "Fine," he said, turning to the door. "But I'm sure as hell not watching you all do it."

~ * ~

Faxon lounged in the crook of three branches, high enough in the tree to be shrouded from view. The dirt path below made a wide semi-circle around the base of a hill, leading to the shack that Bree had chosen for the transformation ritual. He probably could have been a help during the ritual, but he'd already seen it once and really, someone other than Troy'vesk needed to be on watch. The boy was too angry to be much good out here, and for the dozenth time, Faxon wondered why they were letting him tag along.

He could hear the boy shuffling about on top of the hill and wondered how much of a fuss would be made if he just killed Troy. Likely a big one, he thought with a sigh.

Giving up on that daydream, Faxon reached into his cloak and pulled out one of the slender vials of blood he'd stored there. This one was labeled with a small "T" on the side and he stared at it, turning the glass in his fingers so the blood left a light coating on the side.

Trenna's blood, donated reluctantly on board the *Bitter Croften* when Faxon had demanded some kind of payment for his wife's services in the ritual. He had a vial of Nelek's and Kaden's as well, but they'd drawn the line at Liana.

Pity, he thought, uncorking the vial. He could always use more.

Raising the vial to his mouth, he drained its contents, letting the thick, coppery substance linger on his tongue a moment before swallowing. Closing his eyes, Faxon concentrated on the thrum of blood magic in his veins. He wondered, as he often did, if this was how Brigetta felt magic, or if his Humanness brought the pulsing hum through his body.

If he allowed the blood to fade from his system, then it would try to kill him when he took another dose, so he'd learned to maintain a minimum amount of Eldur blood, using Brigetta as a donor every morning and evening. Eldur law prohibited such a transaction, of course, but Bree had never complained about it.

Just as well. If she ever did, he would just take what he needed while she was asleep.

Blood magic was not a stationary thing. He could see it in his mind's eye, running through him like liquid silver. This was the first difference between Trenna's blood and Brigetta's. Bree's blood was always tinted a deep red color and magic filtered everything through his vision to mimic the shade, painting his sight with crimson. He'd lived with this for so long that he was startled when the tint shifted from red to silver.

It wasn't a gray or steel color, either, but a true, glinting silver— the same metallic shade as the streaks that had been so prominent in Trenna's hair.

Was this a difference in family lines, he wondered?

Bree never spoke of colors, so Faxon assumed his vision was another matter of his Humanness. He would need to collect different kinds of blood in the future to see. In the meantime, he thought with an indulgent smile, he wanted to see what the blood of Tray'Lana Silvanus could do.

Faxon gave magic a vague request; he wanted to hear as much as possible.

Magic complied immediately, the sounds of the surrounding forest suddenly blaring in his ears, and Faxon nearly fell out of the tree. His own heart pounded so loud that it was painful, his eardrums popping as the onslaught of sound continued. He could hear the market a mile away, a chaotic hum underneath the sharp whistle of wind through the trees. Closer by, Kaden shouted in anguish, obviously undergoing the ritual, and Faxon nearly screamed as well, wanting the noise to end.

Pick something, he told himself; pick one thing.

He heard Bree's heartbeat, heard the tell-tale flutter every fourth beat. That broken little heart had stayed his hand the night he'd gone to assassinate her. In her drugged state she hadn't felt his hand on her wrist, hadn't known how close his dagger had been to her throat. But he'd felt that flutter, that irregular beat, and stopped himself.

He still wasn't certain why.

He concentrated on her heartbeat, forcing himself to ignore all other sounds until at last the pain began to recede. Exhaling slowly, he loosened his grip on the tree and decided that yes, this was a matter of family lines. Noble blood held a great deal more power than the average Eldur, which was likely why they were considered nobility in the first place.

What would royalty be like, he wondered.

He could feel the tingle of magic under his skin, could sense the intelligence of it as it coursed through him.

What are you? he asked it.

This wasn't the first time he had posed the question. He knew it could hear him, knew it was listening, but the strange entity that existed in Eldur blood had never answered him before. He didn't expect it to answer now, but he caught a flicker in his vision. Holding perfectly still, Faxon asked the question again, this time whispering out loud.

"What are you?"

The flash came again, closer this time, and he made out the shape of an abnormally large dragonfly—silver-bodied with opaque wings flapping rapidly. It hovered just in front of the branch he was seated on, steady enough that he knew it was deliberate.

He didn't precisely hear a voice, be he felt the words come back to him.

"No," it said. "The question is, what are you?"

Uncertain how to answer and curious at the response, Faxon chose to remain motionless in the tree. The dragonfly mimicked his stillness, its round head facing forward. Though Faxon couldn't see any eyes, he knew it to be staring back at him. He had a sense that it was equally curious about him and, he recognized with a small jolt of alarm, equally—if not more—dangerous than he was.

The dragonfly itself wasn't the danger. This was merely a manifestation of something far greater, a physical symbol for the magic still in his body.

It had been a very long time since Faxon had felt like a fool, but he felt so now. Whatever else this entity might be, he knew it was ancient and powerful.

"Oh, thank gods." Troy's voice boomed in Faxon's overly-sensitive ears and he cringed, glancing down at the path.

Trenna stood at the edge of the forest, signaling for them to move. She squinted up at him through the branches, her eyebrow quirked in silent question, but Faxon didn't move.

The dragonfly darted down toward her, morphing as it flew into something Faxon was quite certain he had never seen before. Serpentine in shape, but with four legs ending in clawed feet and dramatic, scaled wings. Each folding joint of the wings had a vicious hook, adding to a sense of predatory danger that was only amplified as the creature wove its way around Trenna's form.

Trenna didn't seem to notice her visitor. She kept standing there, one hand on the pommel of her sword and the other on her hip, watching him with interest. The creature curled itself around her, its long, spiked tail wrapping around her left leg, its torso making a loop of her waist, and then finally its head coming up over her shoulder to stare back at him. The face was mostly a long muzzle. It opened its gaping mouth of many pointed teeth and let out a tremendous roar that pierced Faxon's magic-enhanced hearing so that he had to grit his teeth to keep from crying out.

Faxon gripped tight to a branch to keep from falling. His foot slipped and his knee banged into the trunk of the tree. Cursing, he caught himself and looked back at Trenna.

"Are you all right, Faxon?" she asked.

The creature was gone. He scanned the surrounding area just to be sure, but he could feel that it had left.

"Faxon?"

Or it had not quite left, he realized. He could hear it in her voice, could sense it in her person as she made her way to his tree.

"Fascinating," he said.

"What?"

He didn't answer her, concentrating instead on his descent. Dropping from the lowest branch, he landed just in front of her, surreptitiously checking her shoulders for any signs of the creature. It was obvious that Trenna was unaware of what had just transpired, or if she were aware, then it was on some subconscious level. Faxon tucked that knowledge away, determined to investigate it all later, when he had more information on the history of the Eldur people.

"Did it all go according to plan?" he asked.

"Yes. We're all happily Human now."

Faxon scoffed at her. "Well, you're Human in appearance, but I rather doubt you're all happy about it."

Ten

Trenna watched Evaliana and Nelek leave and tried to quell the anxiety growling at her. She didn't like splitting up. She wanted her family together, all of them, including Troy. It was easier to protect them that way. And yet, she knew this was the right plan. An assassin could hunt a group of seven far easier than pairs.

Still, she couldn't shake her apprehension as her husband and daughter disappeared into the forest. As altered as they might be, with Human ears and lighter hair, she still knew them for who they were. Both were tall and lean, and both carried the confidence of swordsmen. Someone was bound to notice that, especially in Evaliana.

"They'll be all right, Mother," Kaden said and put a hand on her shoulder.

She forced herself to turn away from the road and tried to smile up at him. "I am sure they will be."

"Liana listens to Dad."

"Most of the time."

Kaden grinned. "Yes, most of the time."

Trenna looked back at the path and sighed. "Gods help the man."

They both turned to move back toward the shelter. For safety they would wait an hour before trekking back to town. By then, Nelek and Liana should have found lodging for the night. Brigetta, Troy, and Faxon were likely already settled and at some point Faxon would bring news of the available ships leaving port.

If all went according to plan, they would each find different means to barter passage on board the same ship.

If, she thought with a deep sense of foreboding, everything worked out right. She didn't know what she'd do if they had to take different ships.

"Is Evaliana a lot like you were when you were younger?" Kaden asked.

Startled, Trenna blinked up at him. "Yes and no," she said, stopping short of the lean-to.

The little shelter was made of driftwood, all of it piled up around standing pines, with a roof of thrush and no door to speak of. Too nervous to be cooped up, Trenna turned to the footpath leading to the beach. Kaden, either sensing or sharing her disquiet, turned with her. They picked their way over fallen trees and prickly bushes until the tree line broke onto a startlingly wide, rocky beach.

The tide was coming in, clamoring up the shoreline with frothy determination. It was just after midday and the sky was gray, melting off into the distance where ocean and clouds seemed to mold together. Trenna took a deep breath of salty air and smiled. She felt altogether small and powerful, like she was both threatened by and an integral part of the sea.

"I've always been opinionated and stubborn," she said after a moment. "When I was younger I was reckless, but I cannot remember being as angry as your sister is."

"No?" Kaden sounded surprised.

Trenna laughed. "I'm passionate, to be sure. And I've a quick temper. But when it comes down to it, my passion is fueled by my love for life. Evaliana... she has a smoldering anger at what she perceives as injustice. Or I think she does anyway. I could be wrong."

Kaden laughed and they began a slow walk down the beach. "I didn't think you were ever wrong," he said.

"The trademark of a leader, Ronan taught me that," Trenna said. Rocks squished into the sand under her boots and she looked down to watch her feet. "Even if disaster strikes, it was a disaster you intended to have happen, he told me. Soldiers have to believe their commander has control over all situations."

"He sounds like a great man."

"Ronan was probably the greatest Eldur ever to have lived," Trenna said quietly. The words were hauntingly familiar. Even more unsettling was a sense that her Prince was nearby. She could swear she could hear his laughter just under the crash of the surf, and if she looked over her shoulder she might see him standing there beside her.

She stopped without meaning to and turned. Though she'd known he wouldn't be there, Trenna felt a pang of sadness at the empty beach scene. A part of her wanted to imagine him there, standing proud and dark, with his regal boots getting wet from the waves. But instead, her mind conjured the last moment she'd seen him, his sword locked with the blade of another Eldur, and his own father stabbing him in the back.

"He would have been a good king," she said.

Trenna closed her eyes and tried to shove against the wall of grief that hit her. Ronan hadn't just been the Crown Prince to her; he'd been a mentor and an intimate friend. All of her hopes for the Eldur race had resided in him and when he'd died, Trenna had thought Dyngannon died with him.

"Is that why you don't think I can be king?" Kaden asked. "Because I'm not like Ronan?"

Trenna opened her eyes and looked at him. To anyone else, Kaden's face was unreadable, his thoughts hidden under a stony mask of patience. But Trenna knew her son. She saw the hurt, the echoing self-doubt, and the conflict in him.

"No, Kaden." She met his eyes and tried to smile. "On the contrary, I think you're the only person who *should* be king."

"Why?"

He sounded truly puzzled and she managed a real smile, gesturing for them to continue their walk.

"Because you ask the right questions," she said. "Many men in your position would focus on the throne itself. They would ask how to get the throne for themselves. You, on the other hand, ask why you should take it. Your immediate thoughts go to the people that are under the throne. That is why you should be king."

"Then why don't you want me to do it?"

Trenna found it disconcerting to realize her son knew her just as well as she knew him. She hadn't told him she didn't want this for him, but he'd surmised it anyway. Trenna sighed and glanced out at the horizon, trying to find the right words.

"Ronan was a great man, son. But he was a lonely one. His every action was a sacrifice for his people." She frowned and stopped walking again, turning to face the ocean fully. "Forgive me, Kaden, but I wanted you to have a life of your own choosing. I want love and happiness and laughter for you. These are things a crown can never buy you."

Kaden was silent for a while and Trenna didn't impose. She couldn't imagine facing the choice he had. How does someone choose to be a king, she wondered. There were many who would grasp at the throne, striving for the perceived power they might have, and there were a few who would succeed in taking that power. But, she thought with a troubled sigh, power wasn't the choice she had presented to her son. Sacrifice was the choice she'd given him—to live the life he wanted or to live for the betterment of their people.

Either way, a price would be paid. If Kaden chose to be king, then he would bear the bulk of the pain, denying himself for the sake of the people. If he chose to walk away, the people would be subject to a wrathful, greedy King Porrex.

"I don't think I can do this, Mother."

His voice was so quiet she almost didn't hear him. Trenna looked up at him. Wind flipped his dark hair back, giving her a clear view of his profile. Strong features like his father, she thought. A slightly cleft chin, hard cheek bones and broad forehead, but he had her mouth—thin and quirky. His eyes were undeniably like her own: deep green as ivy in the summer. Her heart swelled at the sight of him and for a wistful moment she considered telling him he couldn't.

She could feed his doubt and let him run off to pursue whatever would make him happiest.

But that, she knew, would be the worst betrayal of all. Not just to the people he might lead someday, but also to Kaden himself, and the potential he had to be great.

"You asked me once, a long time ago, how to lead men in battle," Trenna said. "Do you remember what I told you?"

Kaden looked down at her. "You said the secret was in knowing who the good men are."

She smiled and nodded. "I imagine running a country would be much the same. Know who the good men are, empower them to do what is right, and all should work out."

"And what about my enemies?"

"Oh, you'll want to know who they are, too," she said wryly. "But your focus should stay on the good. Dwelling on the bad men will give them power over you. Fear will dictate your actions instead of generosity and peace. Do you understand?"

Kaden took a deep breath and nodded. "Yes, Mother. I believe I do."

~ * ~

Kaden led his mother up the gangplank of the *Penelope-Anne*, thinking what a colossal mistake this whole thing was and wishing he could somehow convince everyone to stop. But everything was already prepared. They'd already separated into their smaller groups and his mother had that look again. It was the look she always got when her mind was made up and there was no dissuading her. Kaden sighed and glanced at her.

"I don't suppose that magic could have turned you into a boy, could it?" he asked her.

Trenna smirked at him. "Varren and Ronan used to say I was half boy as it is," she said.

"Varren?" he asked, stopping just short of boarding the boat.

The *Penelope-Anne* was a four-masted, full-rigged ship, and if Kaden were fully honest with himself, just the sight of her intimidated him. Even with the sails rolled up, the lines and rigging made chaotic spider webs across the deck.

He missed the *Bitter Croften* already.

"My older brother," Trenna reminded him.

She rarely spoke of her family, so it took a moment before Kaden remembered: Varren Silvanus, eldest child of Count Jamson and Countess Valaranna Silvanus, a soldier but long since retired. Aside from Varren, she had another brother by blood named Navell, who had tried to kill her on the day Kaden was born, and one oath brother named Brockley Croften, who was deceased. Kaden frowned down at his mother, wondering what she must be feeling, heading back into all that pain and turmoil.

"Mom," he whispered and she shook her head at him.

"I'm your sister from this point out, Kirkwell," she said, deliberately using his fake name.

He frowned some more, wanting desperately to argue with her, but she was right. If they were discovered, it would put the others in danger, particularly Troy, who was acting as decoy. He and the blood mage had already booked passage on this ship, along with Nelek and Liana, though they were supposed to pretend not to know one another.

Gods only knew how Faxon was getting on board, but Kaden and Trenna had been hired on.

"What are you going to do when they figure out you can't cook?" Kaden muttered to his mother, who flashed a bright grin.

"Best you go find Master Regmond," she said with a wink. "I'll just go find the galley."

"Good of you to join us, Mister Clarkson," a booming voice called over the fray of men working and gulls squawking, and it took Kaden a moment to realize he was being spoken to.

Kirkwell Clarkson. Next time, he was going to come up with the fake names.

Kaden almost flinched at the mocking tone, but kept his composure as he turned to Regmond. His first day as a crewman and it appeared he was late.

"Afraid I wasn't aware..." Kaden started to explain, but Regmond cut him off.

"Never mind that. Roll up your sleeves and pass your gear to your sister. She can see it to the proper place." Regmond nodded to Trenna, who bobbed an awkward curtsy in heavy skirts. "Miss, you'll be needed at the galley as soon as you're sorted."

Kaden quickly passed his sack and coat to his mother and moved to follow Regmond across the deck. A large winch was lowering a net full of cargo into what Kaden assumed to be the main cargo area. He squinted at the pile of crates as they passed, trying to determine what it was they might be carrying to the mainland, but each crate was hidden under the massive knotwork in the netting and he couldn't make out any distinguishing marks.

It was really none of his business, either, but Kaden couldn't quell his curiosity.

"Am I correct in assuming this is your first voyage to the mainland, Mister Clarkson?"

"Yes, sir."

Regmond made a displeased sound that reminded him so much of his mother, Kaden almost laughed. He smashed the instinct down as they made their way to a nook full of fishing nets just beside a stairway leading to the helm. The abandoned nets were tangled, but on cursory glance appeared to be in good repair.

"You're at a distinct disadvantage, then." Regmond stopped before the pile and turned to face him. "Fishing ain't the same as crossing the deep, Mister Clarkson. Most of these boys have been at it their whole lives. Right now you'll only get in the way."

Kaden frowned and looked down at the nets. "If you don't mind my asking, sir, why did you agree to take me on then?"

Regmond's pockmarked face twisted into a sort of half-smile and he rubbed the back of his neck with a sigh. "Captain's request, actually. Three of our passengers are to be ladies, at least two of them with genteel breeding. Captain said that they might need a female to serve them proper."

Kaden rocked back on his heels, understanding immediately. "My sister," he said.

"Too right," Regmond nodded down at the nets. "But the two of you are a package deal—or so Miss Delphy made sure to note—so we're stuck with your green-gillied arse for the crossing. No offense."

"None taken," Kaden grumbled, feeling deeply offended, but not wanting to get thrown off the ship.

"So," Regmond made a sweeping gesture to the nets. "You stay here, out of the way. Inspect the nets, which I imagine you're familiar with, and don't cause no trouble. We'll give you a squick of training once we've set sail and settled."

"Yes, sir."

Kaden watched the boatswain walk away and took a deep breath. He wasn't certain if he should be amused by Regmond's partial disdain, or insulted, but as he settled in to inspect the nets he decided not to care. He still had no intention of taking the throne, but things were in motion now that he had no control over. The safety of their family—of Liana and Troy—was threatened. If it appeased the blood mage for Kaden just to step foot on Dyngannon soil, then he would do it.

Maybe then she'd go away.

Even as he began sorting the nets, Kaden knew it was a vain hope. This was about more than the throne. Nelek and Trenna had family in Dyngannon, and a history that couldn't be forgotten. He slid his first net through his fingers, frowning out at the enormous pile.

No, this wasn't about the throne, not really. This was about family.

Eleven

"I daresay that boy Trevor is quite handsome, don't you think, Miss Eve?"

Evaliana kept her gaze fastened on the hole in her spare stockings, knowing full well that Miss Gloria Deppenshire was asking her a direct question. They were in their cramped little cabin on board the *Penelope-Anne* with little more than a week's worth of travel behind them, and little less than a week's worth of travel ahead of them, if the captain was to be believed.

The boat rocked with the swell of the deep sea and Liana had to nestle into the tight corner at the head of her bunk to keep steady. A brass lantern fixed to the wall gave them very little light, making the task of mending her stockings even more aggravating than normal. But if Liana went above deck, she would be forced to watch Miss Gloria ogle Troy, ostensibly known as Trevor Lovelace in their guises.

Gloria seemed to be made of porcelain, her skin was that fine, with features set at soft angles and a mouth that made a perfect bud right in her face. Rich auburn hair, too—damn her hide. The colorful locks spiraled over her shoulders, stopping at the center of her back, and Liana often fantasized about shaving them all off.

"I say, Eve, haven't you finished with that yet?"

"No, and I'll thank you not to talk to me while I have a needle in my hand," Liana said. "As you've already observed, I am less than talented at sewing."

Gloria tittered at this, which only served to annoy Liana further. Shoving the needle through one section of the stocking, Liana stabbed the meaty part of her thumb—which had been steadying the cursed fabric. Biting back several unsavory words, Liana hissed in pain and promptly began sucking the blood off her thumb.

Miss Gloria, in all her girlish delight, set to giggling uncontrollably at the sight.

Searching desperately for her patience, Liana inspected her bruised and bleeding thumb and prayed for a good, strong wind to push them closer to the mainland. Or a nice, blunt object to bludgeon Gloria with; either would do.

There had been a part of Liana that was excited to be Human, even if only in appearance, but ever since the ritual she'd felt odd, like something was missing, and she itched for her real skin. Which seemed terribly unfair.

Growing up surrounded by Humans who found her either fascinating or terrifying or both, she'd yearned to be normal. Or at least normal by Vakeshmeer standards. And now that she looked normal, she felt stranger than ever.

Gods, magic was annoying.

"You should give that to Delphy," Gloria said. "The servant is supposed to handle things like that."

Liana held back a wayward comment about her mother's less than domestic nature and prepared to sew again. It was difficult remembering all the pseudonyms and pretenses. It took every ounce of her concentration to remember that Kaden was now called Kirkwell, Troy called Trevor, Father Norand, and the eerie blood mage was called Lady Isleen. Mother's name wasn't hard. She'd taken half of her middle name—Delphinium—and seemed to answer to it like second nature.

Liana wondered if Trenna had gone by Delphy before; perhaps when she was younger—even before she'd led the Dyngannon Army. But it was difficult to imagine her mother as a child. In fact, Liana sometimes thought Trenna had just manifested to life, swords in hand and all that unbending, unseeing stubbornness clinging to her.

Infallible, perfect Trenna, Liana thought with a scowl. One of these days the woman would wake up and realize her way wasn't the only right way to do things.

Hopefully right in front of Liana, too.

"Really now, Eve." Gloria moved to sit on the bunk across from her. "Young ladies such as ourselves should embroider things, not patch up holes."

"I fear I left my embroidery in the trunk below decks," Liana said, barely masking her sarcasm. "And I'm bored. So I will tend to my own stockings for now."

"Bored?" Gloria's bright golden eyes widened in disbelief. "But how can you be bored? Just think of the grand adventure we're on! How many ladies our age have sailed the divide? I tell you, I have not met a single one. We are privileged, you and I."

Liana glanced at their cramped room, scanning the too-short bunks built into the walls, the slanted roof where they could hear many feet pounding overhead, and eyed her companion again. "Yes, privileged," she said, not bothering to hide her sarcasm this time.

The little door to their room opened abruptly and Trenna came in, balancing a tray of food in her hands. Trenna, looking flushed and a little winded, bustled into the small room, kicking the door closed behind her. Liana bit the inside of her cheek to hide her smile. It was gratifying to see her mother in a dress, and even more amusing to watch the look of irritation on her face as she remembered to bob a curtsy.

"Do you know how to knock?" Gloria said and scowled at Trenna. "I swear, you must be the most incompetent maidservant I have ever been forced to handle."

Liana spotted the violent tic in her mother's left cheek and decided she should diffuse the situation. "Come now, Miss Gloria.

The ship is tilting every which way and the woman has her hands full. I prefer my breakfast still on the plate as opposed to hearing a knock on the door."

Trenna glanced at her, flashing a faint, appreciative smile, but made no comment to defend herself. It was just as well, since the imperious Miss Gloria continued to stare down her nose at the tray of food in Trenna's hands.

Gloria huffed dramatically. "I suppose you are right, Eve." Then, with an air of disdain, she fluttered her fingers at Trenna. "Well, come in then. What nonsense have the cooks dredged up for us this morning?"

"Porridge and toast, miss. With blueberry preserves," Trenna said, her voice a monotone. Liana suppressed another smile as her mother moved to set the tray on the table that separated their bunks.

Thank gods I'm not the only one who hates Gloria, Liana thought.

"What? No butter?" Gloria asked in a whining voice that made Liana cringe.

"The daily butter ration is being reserved for a special dinner tonight. Today is the captain's birthday and the cook is working hard at making an appropriate meal," Trenna said, and by the way she clenched her fists, Liana knew her mother wanted to hit the woman.

She had a brief, pleasant daydream about that before Gloria gasped with delight. "His birthday, you say?"

Trenna nodded and stepped back from the table, and Liana realized she was watching her mother too much. Glancing away quickly, she kicked herself for a fool. They were supposed to be strangers. They were supposed to maintain an aloof distance. No hints that they might recognize each other.

"Quick, Eve, how old do you think the captain to be?"

Liana returned her attention to the hole in her stocking. "I'm sure it's quite rude to speculate."

"Oh, posh! We must think of something appropriate to do for him tonight." Gloria stood and snatched the stocking out of her hands, thrusting it toward Trenna.

Her mother took the garment slowly, sharing an uneasy glance with Liana. "Do?" she asked.

"Not you," Gloria said, eyeing Trenna with contempt. "The captain wouldn't want anything from a silly little maid, girl. Now go and mend Miss Eve's things while we conspire something spectacular for him."

"Such as?" Liana asked, almost fearing the answer. She saw Trenna fold the stocking in her hand, her eyebrows quirked up with unbridled curiosity.

"What songs can you sing?" Gloria asked, and Liana felt the blood drain from her face.

Trenna coughed into her arm, hurrying back for the door again. But Liana heard the small, choked laugh and caught the wicked grin on Trenna's face. Liana glared at her for a moment before focusing on Gloria, who didn't seem to notice the byplay. She was too engrossed in her own thoughts, naming off songs as prospects.

"'Blue Melody,' do you know that one?" Gloria asked.

"No."

Liana curled her fingers into fists as the door closed behind Trenna. By gods, she needed out of this room before she strangled her roommate.

"I quite agree, that maid is a complete scandal," Gloria said, obviously misinterpreting Liana's expression. "Do you know, she doesn't wear petticoats! I saw! She wears men's trousers under that skirt of hers."

Liana feigned surprise.

"Oh, it's true!" Gloria went on. "And boots that reach to her knees. Oh... when I tell my mother, she will be all abluster. Who ever heard of a woman behaving in such a manner?"

Liana nodded gravely, as though she agreed, and wondered what it meant to be "all abluster." It didn't sound good and Liana tried to imagine what the girl would do if she ever saw Liana's trousers. They were packed deep in a trunk somewhere, but now that she knew her mother was wearing some, she'd be certain to find them. Then maybe Gloria would be too scandalized to talk to her anymore.

It was a cheery enough thought that she couldn't help smiling.

"I'm afraid I don't sing," Liana said. "Leastways, not any songs that would be familiar to the captain."

~ * ~

Trenna chuckled all the way back to the galley, squashing up against the walls here and there as men passed her. She hated being in such a tight space with so many people. All around was the smell of men and sweat and fish and sea, bodies too close together for too long. One of the crew gave her a lecherous wink as she passed and she ignored it, imagining what her daughter was going to do about Gloria and her duet. It would be a marvelous disaster—and hopefully a harmless one.

Maybe she could get word to Kaden that he should volunteer as a server for the meal. He wouldn't want to miss this.

She slipped inside the galley, her good humor waning when she found it occupied solely by Mister Parsens, the captain's cook. The greasy, pale fellow had a reckless habit of touching her whenever he found an opportunity, but normally there were too many other people around for him to make any real advances. Thus far she had managed to keep her temper in check, but she could tell by his deep smirk that he'd planned this chance meeting. It didn't seem to matter to the beady-eyed, sallow-cheeked cretin that she was supposedly a sister to one of the crew.

"Did the young misses appreciate their blueberry preserves?" Parsens asked.

"They seemed to," Trenna said and pocketed Liana's stocking.

"Of course they did," Parsens said, tossing something into a big pot on the table. "I knows how women like their sweets, heh heh."

Trenna ground her teeth together to keep from responding to the creepy man's wheezy little laugh and moved to fill a tray for Brigetta. He leered at her from across the table and she saw him lick his cracked lips from the corner of her eye. She put a bread knife on the tray, close enough to her left hand should she need it.

"I been watching you," he said.

"Truly?" Trenna said, placing a bowl of porridge on the tray. "What a terribly shallow form of entertainment."

"Yeah, you think you're clever," Parsens said with another leer at the front of her blouse. "But them fancy words is what gives you away."

"Fancy?" Trenna asked, divvying out a portion of blueberries. "Tell me, Mister Parsens, which word was fancy for you? Shallow? Or entertainment? Or was it perhaps the whole of them put together that stumped you?"

"You think you're so much better than me, you little twit…" Parsens took a step toward her but stopped when another figure entered the galley.

Trenna glanced at the doorway and suppressed a smile. It was Nelek, and by the tightness in his jaw she knew he'd been watching them before entering. She met his eyes briefly before returning to her task, loading the tray with a biscuit and spoon.

"What do ye want?" Parsens demanded, glowering at Nelek.

"The captain was saying he had some final instructions for the dinner tonight," Nelek said calmly. "Something to do with a ship-shaped cake. I apologize but I've forgotten the details."

"Ship-shaped cake?" Parsens fairly exploded. From the corner of her eye, Trenna saw him draw up, his short, meaty frame somehow looking rounder in the dim light. "A ship-shaped cake? What does he think I am? A magician?"

Nelek merely shrugged at this outburst, stepping aside as the old cook stalked out the door. When he was safely away, Trenna snorted a laugh and grinned.

"Did you make that up, or is the captain really wanting a cake that looks like a ship?" she asked.

"Oh, it's real," Nelek said. He closed the door and moved deeper into the galley. "I don't like the way he looks at you."

Her heart pinched with satisfaction. They'd left things too uneasy after the ritual. Time and space had stretched the matter thin between them and she hadn't been given the opportunity to apologize. She glanced at the empty galley and decided it was time. "Parsens is harmless. I'll put him in his place if I have to."

He made a disgruntled sound and she giggled, unable to help herself. "Are you jealous, Mister Norand?"

"Jealous isn't the word I'd use. That man could be dangerous," Nelek said and the coil of fear in her center loosened. There was hope yet. They could fix this.

"Only dangerous to himself," she said. "Trust me, I've handled worse."

Nelek glanced at the closed door and stepped closer to her. She stopped with the tray mostly full, her hands braced on the table. Trenna's heart quickened at what she read on his face. His eyes shone so bright a blue that she swore they could almost be glowing. It was silly, she thought as she watched him. Feeling this way was girlish and silly, but she wanted him to kiss her so badly she could already taste him.

Twenty-odd years married to him and she still wanted his kiss.

"I owe you the most profound apology," she murmured to him as his arm slid around her waist, pulling her back against his chest.

"That you do," he said quietly.

She closed her eyes, so grateful to have him holding her that she forgot where they were. He was solid and warm against her back, his breath stirring the hair at her temple, and her heart ached for the last weeks.

"Gods, I was so stupid," she whispered.

"Yes, you were," he murmured and kissed her temple. "And you were right. It was the best move. But you should have found another way to tell me."

"I know," she said. His thumb was making a gentle stroking motion over her belly and it was all she could do to breathe.

The ship rocked and groaned around them, the sound of feet thumping overhead drowning out the hiss of steaming water on the stove. It smelled of onions and cooking meat and Nelek, and Trenna wished fervently that they could be themselves. Be damned with disguises, she wanted him to keep touching her.

"Don't ever do that to me again," he whispered and she murmured back, "Never."

"I mean it," he said. "I don't think I could survive it if you did."

She turned in his arms so their gazes could meet. She knew it was him despite the changes magic had made, rounding out his features and dulling the shine of his hair. It seemed that magic could not alter a person's eyes, though. His were as blue and clear as the day she'd met him.

Touching the stubble on his cheek, she promised, "Never again."

He leaned forward, their mouths grazing, but movement outside the door forced them apart. Feeling a little dazed and tremendously disappointed, she scowled at the door. Nelek frowned too, then turned to whisper in her ear, "Second watch of the night, meet me in my room."

He paused to give her a wink, then turned for the door and left. Trenna watched the door where he'd gone and sighed, trying to calculate how many hours before the second watch.

Too many, she thought and finished loading Brigetta's tray.

Twelve

Nelek held his wooden goblet lest it slide off the captain's dinner table and tried to ignore the constant groan of the ship around them. Even after years as a fisherman, he still hated sailing, especially deep sea sailing, and it was everything he could do to keep from drumming a restless beat onto the table with his fingers. But fidgeting like that would give away his unease and if there was one thing he'd learned in life it was to hide such feelings away. His youth at court taught him the value of an inscrutable expression, so he flexed his fingers once and held a little tighter to his goblet.

Captain Horace burst out laughing at the far end of the table; something his first mate said had that whole end of the table roaring, to include Troy. Nelek spared them all a brief smile and watched as Trenna served Liana a piece of the infamous ship-shaped cake. It was rare to see Trenna in skirts and the sight delighted him more than he could let on. For one, they were still in disguise and weren't supposed to know each other, and for another, Trenna quite obviously disliked the dress. He didn't want her thinking he preferred her this way, even if the sight did have his imagination running rampant.

Gods, he hoped she wore that to their meeting tonight.

They had some business to discuss, but after, once she knew of the pirate sails that had been spotted and the captain's idiotic decision to keep the crew hushed about it, then he was going to enjoy her. Ruck those skirts up around her thighs and pin her to the nearest wall, finally touch her the way he'd been wanting to for over a week. He could almost hear that sultry little moan she always made when he nuzzled her neck, could remember the track of her fingernails along his back and had to coach himself into breathing properly.

Maybe he could get a message to her and make sure she wore the skirt.

She caught him staring and met his gaze, one arched eyebrow quirking up in question. Realizing at last that there was still conversation going on around him, he concentrated on the room.

Master Regmond was smirking at him, the man apparently having guessed at his train of thought, and Nelek cleared his throat, shifting in his seat so that he could focus more on Troy. It was difficult, but he managed to banish thoughts of his wife, watching as Troy played the part of Brigetta's young charge. Much to his surprise, it was Troy who seemed to take to the deception with ease.

For some reason he'd expected Kaden to be better at this sort of thing, but by all appearances his son was awkward and uncertain, stumbling over his answers whenever someone asked about his life. Liana too was left stuttering every now and then, and hers was a much easier lie. She was, after all, in disguise and in truth, traveling with her father for the mainland.

Nelek wished he'd taken the time to teach his children the finer points of subterfuge.

"Oh, Mister Trevor, you are beastly!" Miss Gloria giggled, drawing Nelek back into the conversation.

Troy appeared baffled and turned a bright shade of red, which earned him a good deal of ribbing from the men around the table. Deciding it best to join the conversation, Nelek took a sip of his mead and forced himself not to scowl. He truly hated the honey-based drink but it was apparently the captain's favorite.

"Miss Eve doesn't sing, but I was so hoping to perform for you, Captain." Gloria said and smiled brightly at the captain, who smiled back immediately.

Horace was a strangely full-figured man, very tall with a barrel chest and a neck almost as thick as his arms. Nelek always felt small and short when standing near the man. He imagined Trenna might feel the same way when standing next to him, but she had lived all her life as short and spry, so the feeling for her would be commonplace.

"Perform a song?" Horace asked, dark eyes glittering. His face was flushed from drinking and his large apple cheeks splotched crimson in the dim light.

Gloria nodded excitedly.

"My dear, I would be honored," the captain said.

Liana hissed something low and under her breath. She lifted her goblet and took three long gulps. Nelek thought to caution her on drinking too much, but just then Miss Gloria began to sing, her remarkably clear voice filling the little room.

Nelek didn't recognize the melody, but it was precise and pretty, and talked of the ocean depths. The table hushed to listen, all three of the captain's closest lieutenants staring at Miss Gloria. Horace himself watched Brigetta, who sat poised and unperturbed with a large ribbon hiding her ears. Her face was visible and she gazed, transfixed, at her uneaten bread roll.

Nelek didn't like the intensity of the captain's gaze. Brigetta normally took her meals in her room, keeping the need for a ribbon or any other sort of deception unnecessary, but apparently the captain had insisted enough to get "Lady Isleen" to join them all for the night. Thus far, only Horace had tried to carry on a conversation with her. Nelek hoped it remained that way.

Troy shifted in his seat, still blushing. It took Nelek a moment but he realized at last what was making Troy so uncomfortable. Miss Gloria, hitting the apex of her song, was steadily watching Troy.

Nelek took another drink and finally met Liana's gaze. She gave him a tight smile and it was then that Nelek realized there was something romantic going on between his daughter and Troy'vesk

Mavon. He glanced between them, fighting the irrational desire to punch Troy in the face, and the need to remain nonchalant.

Just how long had this been going on?

He looked back at Trenna, who was filling another goblet for the captain. She met his eyes and gave him a compassionate smile, obviously having noticed the same thing. He gave her a flat, questioning look and her mouth twitched at the corners.

Curse that woman, he thought. She'd known. She'd known all about Troy and Liana and she hadn't told him. His fingers tightened on his goblet. They were going to have a long talk about communication in their marriage when they came to port.

The song ended and Nelek applauded Gloria with the rest of the table.

"I tried to convince Miss Eve to do a duet with me, Captain. But as I said, she doesn't sing." Miss Gloria smiled at Liana and even Nelek could see the condescension in her face.

"It's not that I don't sing," Liana said, fiddling with her spoon. "I said I don't know any songs that the good captain would be familiar with."

"That's quite all right, my dear," Captain Horace said.

"Nonsense," Gloria said with a giggle. "Until I hear her sing I will believe she simply cannot."

Liana's fingers stilled. Very carefully, she set down her spoon and turned to face the head of the table. Nelek sensed the danger and cleared his throat, hoping to distract her before she hurt Miss Gloria somehow. But to his astonishment, Liana started to sing.

It was a soft, melancholy song about war and pride and Nelek immediately knew it. This was the song Trenna had sung when the children were babes. It brought him back to Vakeshmeer, to their little home on the hill. He could see Trenna by the hearth, rocking Liana in her arms, with Kaden settled at her feet. His heart swelled at the memory and he smiled.

Liana's voice was hushed and warm, and he noticed belatedly that the room seemed to hold its breath for her. She wasn't as practiced as Miss Gloria, but she brought a soft sort of passion to the song that couldn't be overlooked. It was only when she finished, beseeching her loved one to come home from the borderland wars, that he realized she'd sung a song of Dyngannon.

He glanced at the very Human audience and prayed these men wouldn't notice. They all looked enraptured, heartily applauding Liana for the sweetest song they'd heard in ages. They didn't seem to notice Miss Gloria's unhappy huff. Only Captain Horace looked perplexed, but Nelek realized that the captain was, once again, staring at Brigetta. The only thing different now was that Brigetta was smiling at Liana.

"Well done, Miss Eve," Troy said.

Liana smiled at him. Nelek felt his eye twitch at the way they watched each other, but throttled his irritation. This was Troy'vesk. His daughter could do much worse.

"What an interesting song," Gloria said primly. "I do confess, I have never heard it before. Wherever did you learn it?"

"From my mother," Liana said.

"But I thought you never knew your mother."

Nelek cleared his throat as Liana looked at him, her eyes widening. "She didn't," Nelek said, as calmly as possible. "But her mother sang it to her when she was a babe, before she died. I fear you've had a poor rendition. I couldn't remember all the words when Eve asked me about it."

"Not at all, not at all," Horace said. "It was perfectly splendid."

The conversation moved on to the uncommonly good weather they were experiencing and Nelek relaxed. None of the other officers seemed to take special notice of the situation and the captain didn't look back at Brigetta. Only Miss Gloria showed any signs of outward distress, suddenly claiming to be too tired for any more fun.

"Would you escort me back to my quarters, Mister Trevor?" Gloria asked.

Troy blinked once. "Of course, Miss Gloria."

He glanced in Nelek's direction with an embarrassed smile and excused himself from the table. Nelek watched the pair go and frowned. Troy was a handsome youth, but his red hair normally put women off. And he was a good man. There should be no reason why he felt so irritated about the attraction between Liana and Troy.

Trenna slipped out of the room just behind them, ostensibly to keep watch as a chaperone. When Nelek looked back to Liana, he thought maybe Trenna's true purpose was to act as a bodyguard. Liana had the tell-tale tic in her left cheek that threatened violence.

With a deep sigh, he settled into his chair and took another drink. As if this journey couldn't get any worse, now he had to worry about his daughter murdering her bunkmate.

~ * ~

"This meeting seems unwise," Brigetta said. "Your daughter's singing debut already has the captain curious."

Trenna ignored her, focusing instead on stripping off her skirt. She was still wearing her pants so it didn't take very long to prepare for her clandestine outing. Tucking a blade into her left boot, she pulled her hair into a bun and then stuffed it under a cap. She debated bringing her sword, pausing to stare at her bed. It was safely hidden under the mattress but she knew it would only hinder her so she left it.

"General, I must protest," Brigetta said again. "The captain may not seem like he knows much, but he has a hidden bite."

"The captain is curious because of you," Trenna said and moved to the door. "He's taken a fancy to you. I'm sure you've noticed. It doesn't help that you decided to call yourself a lady."

"The song your daughter sang was clearly from Dyngannon."

"Yes, it was. Though I doubt they took as much notice of it as we did. We were raised with it. They were not. I'm sure it won't be given a second thought."

Trenna hoped not, anyway.

"And what do you expect to do if you are caught tonight?" Brigetta asked. "General, you cannot kill anyone."

Trenna peeked out the door, then closed it again. Everything looked clear but she waited a moment longer.

"First of all," Trenna said, glancing away from the door, "stop calling me 'General.' That life is so far behind me it's laughable. Second, I don't plan on killing anyone. I'm surprised you think I would. If I run into trouble, I'll improvise."

Grinning, Trenna winked at the mage and slipped out the door. Pressing close to the wall, she stood still for a moment, listening to the sounds of the ship. Timber creaked and groaned around her and she could feel the swell of the sea underfoot. One person was pacing on the main deck directly above her. She knew by the sounds of his boots that it was an officer because a common sailor would be barefoot.

Her room was positioned just before the half deck above, near the main mast on the leeward side. Nelek's room was closer to the aft of the ship, which meant she would have to sneak past several of the officers' doors to get to him. She'd been surprised at the number of officers on board, but with a crew of sixty-plus she imagined twelve officers was a little on the trim side.

Slowly creeping down the corridor, Trenna eyed which doors still had light seeping through the cracks. The second watch had just begun, so those still awake were likely trying to prepare for bed. She just hoped none of them felt nature's call while she was still in the hall.

Nearing Nelek's door, she paused to listen again. She counted doors, making certain she was at the right one. The officers were bunked four to a room, so if she had the wrong door there was likely to be a kerfuffle. She could take on four men if she had to, but the greater threat was earning the ire of the captain.

Taking a deep breath, she gingerly scratched on the door. It opened and in the gloom she could just make out Nelek's smile. He pulled her into the room and closed them in, leading her by the hand to the back wall. A lantern standing on the table at the far wall dimly lit his features. Troy, she noticed, was absent. She worried about where he'd gone, but her thoughts went to static as Nelek's mouth closed on hers. He gave a throaty groan and pulled her tight against him.

Trenna moved closer still, wanting to feel every lean inch of him. His hand gripped the back of her neck, tilting her head so he could deepen the kiss. She shivered in reaction, grabbing fistfuls of his nightshirt.

Gods! She didn't want to stop.

His teeth scraped her lower lip and he pulled back just enough to whisper, "Trouble is coming."

"Trouble?" She whispered back, but he was kissing her again, his hands roaming over her sides.

"Pirates are following." His hands settled on her hips and he kissed her three more times before resting his forehead against hers. Panting, he continued their hushed conversation. "The ship is barely armed. If they catch us, there will be a fight. The officers are a little green."

If her head hadn't been buzzing from all the kissing she might have been more alarmed. As it was, Trenna could barely keep her mind on his words instead of the way his lips were moving.

"Why hasn't the captain warned us?"

"He warned the crew. I think he wants to save you females from fretting."

Trenna wrinkled her nose. "This female is going to kick him in the delicates."

Nelek snickered, running his palms over her ribs and back down to her hips. "Kick him when we get to port. I don't think the crew would take kindly to the action right now. It's his birthday and all."

Trenna smiled and nuzzled the side of his neck, holding him as close as she could. "Very well. But at port he's getting a good, solid kick."

"I've warned Troy and Liana, but I thought you could tell Brigetta. Faxon was adamant that she be made aware of the problem."

"I will." Trenna closed her eyes and listened to the steady beat of his heart. "Where is Troy now?"

"On deck. He'll come down in an hour."

"An hour?"

Nelek drew the cap off her head, carefully pulling her hair out of its bun, and smiled down at her. "One glorious hour, my wife," he whispered.

Trenna smiled back, rising to her tiptoes so she could kiss him again.

Thirteen

Kaden yawned behind his fist and headed for the aft of the ship, squinting against the morning fog. The air was damp from more than the sea—the scent of rain heavy in the air—and he quelled the natural fear of a storm in his mind. Oil lanterns became soft glowing orbs around the ship, catching the moisture and dulling their shine. It made an eerie sight as he continued his trek across the deck and he shivered, doing his best not to imagine every ghost story and superstition he'd heard.

Master Regmond had put him on early watch, which suited him just fine. His bunkmates each had serious snoring problems and the small slab of padding meant to act as his mattress did little to protect him from the wooden floor. He didn't think he'd had a full night's sleep since boarding the *Penelope-Anne.*

Other areas of the ship had hammocks, but Kaden's lack of importance had relegated him to a small space on the outskirts of the main cargo hold—which he had learned held several tons of raw ore. The ore was a special order for one Master Bixaltries, who was meant to meet the ship at Cadabyr port. Every sailor had their own theory on what a man would want with so much raw material.

Nedry, a young, tow-headed boy and one of Kaden's bunkmates, swore it was for sorcery. Max, also a bunkmate, but with dark hair and a constant smirk on his face, thought this suggestion silly and insisted there was silver hidden in the ore. Kaden, however, was certain the main element was copper.

This led to several unsavory discussions, but Kaden imagined it wouldn't matter to Nedry or Max that the ore's origin was from a prime copper mine. Nor could he feasibly explain how a common fisherman could be educated enough to know trade lines and geography, so he just let the matter drop whenever it came up.

Halfway across the deck he spotted something on the horizon and frowned, stopping to peer into the mists. Nedry would be angry if he didn't relieve him soon, but Kaden waited anyway, certain he had seen something. It took several minutes but he spotted the shape again and his gut clenched in warning.

There were sails on the horizon.

A ship. A large ship on the starboard side and getting closer.

Pirates, he thought. Gods alive, they really were being pursued by pirates.

Turning on his heel, Kaden ran for the aft, bounding up the steep stairs two at a time. Nedry scowled at him. "About time, you ninny."

"Go wake Master Regmond," Kaden said, glancing out into the mists again. "The cursed ship is here!"

"What?" Nedry blinked and turned to the railing. "I dun see anything."

Kaden glared out at the foggy ocean, searching for it again.

"It's there, dammit, now go wake him!" Kaden said, thinking, *It is there. I saw it. Twice.*

"I'm not waking Master Regmond without some proof, Kirkwell." Nedry shook his head.

"There!" Kaden pointed at the distant shadow of a sail just as it slipped behind the fog again.

"I still don't see anything," Nedry said, peering out at the starboard side.

"It's there, I'm telling you! Now who's the ninny, you bastard!" Kaden said and Nedry scowled at him, looking as obstinate as ever.

Kaden spun away and ran for the nearest scuttle. He knew what he'd seen, and he knew it was danger. His gut knotted tightly at the prospect of battle and he thought of sounding the alarm on his own.

But the other ship would hear it too, and they needed whatever time they had to prepare.

He slid down the scuttle ladder, thumped to the ground and ran for Regmond's room, weaving past the slowly waking crew as he went. Pausing in the middle of the corridor he stopped. His mother's room was adjacent to the Master's. Not sure if he'd have the chance later, he opened her door and slipped inside.

Trenna was remarkably good at waking up when she needed to. She sat bolt upright the moment he closed the door, and in the gloom he could see her blinking back sleep to frown up at him.

"Pirates?" she asked, her voice flat.

He nodded, breathless and grateful that she seemed to be a step ahead. Gods knew they would need it.

"Go tell Regmond," she said and flew out of bed.

She flipped back her mattress and reached for her weapons. Nodding once to a drowsy looking Brigetta, Kaden slid back out the door. He almost forgot to knock—Regmond was particularly grouchy when his quarters were invaded—but Kaden managed two raps on the door before stumbling inside.

Regmond was already awake and preparing for his morning rounds. Kaden caught a hard glare from the man as he stopped with his coat half buttoned.

"Well?" Regmond asked when Kaden didn't immediately explain himself.

"The ship, sir. I saw it in the mists. Starboard side and very close."

"How close?"

"Close enough I wasn't confused about its intentions, sir. It's headed straight for us."

Regmond resumed the task of buttoning his coat. "You seem rather familiar with pirates' intentions for a fisherman, Mister Clarkson."

Kaden almost blushed. "I'm many things, sir, but certainly not an idiot. I may never have seen a pirate ship before, but I can recognize danger when I see it."

"Did anyone else see the ship?"

"No sir, just me."

Kaden frowned. He wanted to get back on deck. If it came to a fight he'd be better use up there. And he knew that would be where his parents would go. But Regmond was taking his time with his shoes, quietly and precisely measuring his movements. Kaden shifted on his feet, frowning at the lack of urgency in his superior.

"Your orders, sir?" Kaden asked, hoping to spur the man on.

"We will calmly return to the deck, where you are to point out this ship, Mister Clarkson."

"But sir, there isn't time. We should wake the captain now."

Kaden almost bit off his tongue at the glare Regmond sent him. He knew he'd overstepped his bounds but the circumstances seemed to warrant it. They were about to be attacked, he just knew it, and over three quarters of the men were still sleeping. Flat-footed, his father would call it, unprepared and surprised.

"I will not be rousing the captain because a little fisherman got spooked," Regmond said.

"You're a blathering idiot!" Kaden hissed, pivoting on his heel to leave.

"Mister Clarkson!"

Regmond's voice was drowned out by the sudden, shrill whistle call on deck. An instant later the gong of the alarm bell reverberated through the ship. Kaden turned his own glare on the boatswain as though to say, "I told you so," and then hurried out of the room. Several of the officers came staggering out of their rooms, rushing half-dressed for the main deck.

Liana's door opened and his sister poked her head into the corridor. Kaden met her wide blue gaze with a grim look. He was about to warn her when Regmond shoved his way between them.

"Stay in your room, Miss Eve. Nothing to fret about, I'm sure," Regmond said, then grabbed Kaden gruffly by the collar. "Come along, Mister Clarkson."

Kaden thought to pull away, to go and warn Father, but Regmond dragged him to the end of the corridor and up the steps before he could try. On deck, Regmond immediately let him go, the boatswain's focus switching to the other ship. Crewmen ran across the deck, fetching weapons or following commands shouted from the helm. Nedry was at the alarm bell, pounding at it with all his might.

The pirate ship was easily visible now, closing in fast. He gauged that they had only a few moments before the enemy would be on them. Their trajectory was too sharp and the *Penelope-Anne* was at an angle that gave the pirates all the advantage.

Gods alive, there was nothing they could do. The *Penelope-Anne* was too large to outrun them.

Kaden reached for his side, his hand searching for his weapon, but he was met with air. He glanced down, remembering he'd left his sword behind a crate in his room. Weapons were a sign of wealth, Faxon had said, and told everyone to hide theirs unless they were needed.

"Blast!" Kaden turned back to the scuttle, pushing past men heading for the deck.

"Clarkson!" Max, who had just stumbled onto the deck, grabbed Kaden's arm before he could pass. "Where the bloody hell are you going?"

"I need a weapon," Kaden said and tore away from the younger man's grip.

"And you have one?" Max shouted after him.

Kaden heard him start to follow. He wanted to wave the boy off but knew it was too late. He could think up some clever lie about how he'd come up with a sword later. At present, he had to get armed and get to the deck. Father would likely already be alerted and heading there. Troy, too. Liana, for appearances' sake, should stay in her room, but Kaden doubted she would. The stubborn pixie would be up and fighting in her skirts if she had to.

Taking the last passageway, Kaden skidded into the open compartment he'd been living in for two weeks. There was no door, but two partitioned walls sectioned off the space. On either side were crates and storage, some for crew rations and others for paid transport. The large crate in the center of his quarters was one of the copper crates, easily identifiable by the branded "B" on each side.

Kaden rushed for the crate and began to slide it away from the hull wall.

"Where'd the likes of you get a blooming weapon, eh?" Max asked from the doorway.

"Family heirloom," Kaden said, straining against the crate.

It was sort of true, too. He had gotten it from his mother.

"Heirloom?" Max said. "What sort of loony fisherman are you?"

The crate came away from the wall with a great screech and Kaden reached behind it. His hand met with air.

"What?" he said out loud, peering behind the crate.

His sword was gone.

"I asked what sort of loony..."

"No," Kaden began frantically tossing back his bed roll, ignoring Max completely. "No, no, no!"

"You're right barmy is what you are," Max said. "For a tick I actually..."

A meaty thump cut Max short and Kaden looked up. Faxon stood in the entry, gazing down at an unconscious Max in a deeply unsettling way. He looked, Kaden thought, as though he were deliberating whether to kill young Max. Kaden spotted his own sword in Faxon's hand and scowled.

"Assassin, stowaway, thief. Your talents know no bounds," he said.

Faxon looked up from Max and smiled. "To be sure, Your Majesty."

Kaden moved from the crate, snatching his sword away from Faxon. "Don't call me that," he said.

"As you wish," Faxon glanced out into the passage. "Follow me, Your Grace."

"Faxon..." He tried to find another argument but the man was already moving.

Kaden scowled and followed. Faxon led him down several passages to the scuttle again. Footsteps banged overhead, men's shouted orders coming muffled through the ceiling, and Kaden swallowed tightly. Battle was coming, he thought. Real battle.

What sort of pirates would these be? All were detestable, to be sure, but some were bloodier than others.

Faxon went down the scuttle instead of up.

"Where are you going?" Kaden shouted after him.

"This way, sire."

"Faxon, I swear..." Torn, Kaden glanced up the scuttle at the distant gray sky.

"Hurry, if you please."

Scowling, Kaden leapt down the scuttle ladder. No sooner had his feet hit the floor than Faxon was off again, leading him toward the prow. Large crates took up most of the space, making the walkway cramped and barely maneuverable, but he followed Faxon anyway.

What in blazes was the man doing?

They finally stopped at the second-most bulkhead. Faxon started inspecting the bulkhead walls, humming to himself, and Kaden looked up at the woodwork above. Timber sealed so tightly together here that it almost looked seamless and he knew himself to be far below the water line. He couldn't hear what was happening above anymore, and had to battle his worry aside.

They would be all right, he told himself. They would all be all right; they were far better trained than any pirate.

"Yes, this will do." Faxon said at last.

"Do for what?" Kaden asked. He looked down just in time to catch Faxon's fist with the center of his face.

White-hot pain bloomed and he heard his nose crack. Staggering backward, he had just enough time to worry that Faxon had been sent to kill him. Then something solid struck the back of his head and he fell.

~ * ~

Faxon debated just leaving him as he was. Kaden made a rough sight, what with his broken nose bleeding everywhere. There might be some questions as to why he was down here instead of topside, but the boy could easily say he didn't remember. People didn't take a whack to the head like that without some adverse effects, after all.

However, he couldn't leave the boy unarmed, either. Should things turn sour and the ship be overrun, Kaden might need protection. Faxon reached down and shifted Kaden's sword until the boy was lying half on top of it. Faxon doubted the future king of Dyngannon was smart enough to find it anywhere else.

With a smirk, Faxon reached inside his shirt and pulled out a vial of Brigetta's blood, its stopper marked with a "B." He only had two vials left of Trenna's blood, but he was curious to see it in action.

A loud crash hit overhead and the ship tilted.

Scowling, Faxon opened the vial and downed its contents. Running back for the scuttle, his vision flared fiery red, tinting everything in sight. By the time he reached the main deck magic was pumping through him.

A hatchet blade swooshed over his head as soon as he emerged, its owner just as startled to see him as he was for nearly being beheaded. Another blade thrust just beside him, burying itself in the chest of his would-be executioner, and Faxon glanced over his shoulder to find Nelek, who swiftly retracted his blade and nodded to him.

The deck surged with combat. Berserk shouts called from both ships, men locked at the starboard side where the enemy had tethered the *Penelope-Anne* during his absence. It was remarkable how fast the enemy had reached them but he had little time to dwell on it. Most of the *Penelope's* crew had only bludgeoning weapons and their fists to fight with, giving them a distinct disadvantage.

Faxon scowled at the sight and shouted to Nelek, "Where is your wife?"

"There," Nelek said, pointing off to the side with his sword.

He seemed to be assessing the danger in their current circumstances because he frowned at the starboard side, where Trenna was currently engaged. Faxon watched as a bulky man lifted her by the lapels and threw her back. She hit the deck and rolled, sliding to a crouch near the scuttle beside him. Nelek remained where he was, armed and glaring at the line of men holding back the pirates.

They had very little time.

Trenna glanced between Faxon and the scuttle opening.

"Where's Kaden?" she asked, pressing a knuckle to her bloody lip.

"It seemed best that His Majesty remain safe below," Faxon said.

Trenna frowned. "My son would never agree to that."

"I persuaded him," Faxon said and smiled when she narrowed her eyes at him. "With my fist, of course."

"Faxon..." Her words were cut short as the ship lurched leeward.

Faxon had to grab hold of the scuttle edge to keep from sliding. Trenna reflexively snagged his boot to keep upright and searched the ship to see what had happened. Her face was set in grim lines and he followed her gaze up the main mast. He spotted her concern immediately: the *Penelope's* rigging had tangled with the enemy ship. A deep groan resonated from the masts as they both began a slow bend under pressure.

He looked down at the fighting. No one was attempting to cut them free of the boarding hooks. At least not yet they weren't. Faxon was sure they meant to if they could suppress the steady stream of invading pirates, but if they tried cutting the hooks while the two masts were still tangled they risked tearing their own ship apart.

"Oh, godsdamnitalltobloodyhell," Trenna said. "Can't one thing go right?"

Nelek shook his head. "Not today," he said. "The line is breaking. We're about to be overrun." He glanced down at his wife and winked. "I'll go free the boarding lines."

Trenna nodded at him, her mouth twitching into a small smile. "I'll get us untangled," she said and looked to Faxon. "The moment we are free you need to separate the ships. I don't care how you do it, just do it."

Faxon grinned. "Yes, General."

She smirked at him and pushed to her feet again. With one last shared smile at her husband, she charged off for the main mast, dodging crew that was hurrying to the fight.

"I never saw her appeal before," Faxon said to Nelek, "but I have to admit there is something stirring about a woman who takes charge."

Nelek eyed him. "As long as what is stirring is above your belt-line."

Faxon laughed as Nelek moved into the fray, fighting his way toward the starboard side. The boat rocked, sending several men swaying over the deck. Up at the helm, Captain Horace was engrossed in battle. Every order he bellowed was lost in the crash of blades and screams of combat, but Faxon imagined it had something to do with the masts.

He looked up at where Trenna was climbing.

"Separate the ships, hmm?"

Under the craze of fighting he could hear the splash of waves colliding with the hull. Waves, he thought, and smiled as an idea started to form.

Fourteen

"You cannot possibly mean to go out there," Miss Gloria said.

Liana ignored the girl, shimmying out of her dress and reaching for her sack. She could keep the corset on—tight as it was, Liana was confident she could still fight in it—but the skirts had to go. The commotion overhead continued, spurring her to grab her trousers and leap into them. She didn't bother removing her pantalets—there just wasn't time—so the trousers fit more snugly than usual.

Then she reached under her mattress and pulled out her shortsword, and was immediately comforted by the familiar grip. Unsheathing it, she charged for the door, not bothering to look at Gloria or even answer the girl.

Something slammed into the back of her shoulder before she could open the door, and an instant later she was pinned against creaky wood. She managed to turn her head and avoid breaking her nose on impact, feeling the rough door scrape across her cheek instead. Confused, Liana blinked back sparks of pain and tried to push away. Cold steel pressed just under her chin and she froze. Miss Gloria pushed against her, holding her down with more strength than Liana would ever have guessed she owned, and by the knife at her throat Liana could surmise the situation.

She wasn't certain which made her angrier, being kept in her room while everyone else was fighting above, or the fact that she'd been sleeping right next to an assassin for several weeks. Either way, they were all in a lot of trouble. But there was no way Gloria could know who she really was. That's why they'd undergone that horrible transformation.

"Gloria, what are you doing?" Liana squirmed but the knife dug deeper into her chin. She stopped and held her breath, trying to figure out what her mother would do in this situation.

"I'm asking myself that exact same question right now," Gloria said. "Try not to struggle. I'd rather not pierce your skin just yet."

"Can't you hear the pirates? I can fight. I can help get them off the ship."

"And where would a pretty thing like you learn to fight, hmm?" Gloria's mouth was close to Liana's ear.

"It runs in the family," Liana said through her teeth. "Why are you doing this?"

"In the family, you say?" Gloria tsked. "Much like the song you sang for the captain?"

Liana frowned, even more confused than before, and then realized her mistake. Gods help them, she'd given them all away with a stupid song. Closing her eyes, she fought off a wave of guilt. Kaden, Troy, Father, Mother, they were all going to die because she'd given in to petty jealousy. What had possessed her to sing that song? It was so clearly Eldur and she'd known it.

"Who are you?" Liana asked, battling for calm.

She still had a good grip on her sword. If she could shove Gloria off without getting sliced open, she had a chance here.

"Oh, I think the more interesting question in this situation is who you are, Miss Eve. You look Human but you sing Eldur songs. You hold to Eldur ethics. You're far too independent to be a real Human female. No," Gloria tapped the knife against Liana's skin. "No, you're something else."

Liana was relieved to hear the indecision in Gloria's voice. Maybe she hadn't messed everything up after all.

"Were you raised by the Eldur?"

"Yes," Liana said through her teeth.

"Interesting," Gloria said. "The boy who travels with Lady Isleen, was he also raised Eldur?"

That, she thought, was dangerous ground.

"How should I know?" Liana asked, shifting her feet for better balance.

Gloria's demeanor changed abruptly. "Do not trifle with me," she hissed. "I will kill you."

Someone pounded on the door. It rattled under Liana's cheek and she praised the gods that be for the timing. Gloria cursed and Liana launched herself backward, pushing off the door. She collided with Gloria, who fell into the table, which promptly collapsed under their combined weight.

They toppled to the floor in a tangle of limbs and broken wood. Liana shoved her elbow into Gloria's face, felt the impact numb her arm right down to her fingers. Gloria's head snapped back, striking the edge of the bed with a meaty thwack.

Scrambling to her feet, Liana rushed for the door. Gloria shouted behind her and white hot agony stabbed through her left leg as Gloria's blade buried itself just behind her knee. Stumbling to the door, she fumbled with the lock but the latch smeared in her vision and she missed. Disoriented, Liana swiped at the latch again but her fingers felt heavy and thick, uncooperative. She fell against the door, sweating, and looked back at Gloria.

"Poison, I'm afraid," Gloria said as she stood up. "It's what I'm best known for. This one in particular works very fast."

Liana released a breath. Whoever was on the other side of the door was getting impatient. They'd moved from pounding to kicking, she could tell by the force behind it. She wanted to reach up and unlatch it, but nothing would move for her anymore.

Gloria crouched beside her. "Who are you, really?"

Liana tried to smile. Her pulse was slowing, the rapid tha-thump, tha-thump growing sluggish in her chest, getting so heavy she could feel every contraction of her heart. The room swirled in her vision, blurring the sight of the hated little cabin room.

Gods, not here. Please don't let me die here.

"Pity," Gloria said and stood up again.

~ * ~

Troy kicked the door again. Something was wrong—very wrong—when Evaliana Dyngannon chose to hide behind a locked door. He'd come here for her, knowing she would be preparing to fight and wanting to be at her side when she did it, but the door was latched and he'd heard someone shout in pain. Rearing back, he kicked the door again. The impact rattled through its hinges, but it remained latched and closed.

Gods dammit, the carpenters on this ship had done too good a job.

Brigetta stepped into the corridor from her room just beside Liana's, one dark eyebrow lifted in question. She glanced between him and the door and frowned, moving into the hall.

"Something is happening in there," Troy said by way of explanation.

"So I gathered." Brigetta turned to face the door in question. She glanced up and down the corridor. Everyone else was already above deck, fighting or preparing to fight, leaving them a small amount of privacy.

Troy watched as Brigetta lifted a hand, palm out, and started murmuring something under her breath. He fidgeted on his feet, trying not to think about the fact that she was calling on magic because the whole business unnerved him.

Didn't Eldur have to bleed for this to work?

The hair on the back of his neck prickled.

Who was bleeding?

The door shimmered a bluish white, wobbling in his vision for the space of three breaths. No, blood magic did more than unnerve him; it was terrifying.

A heartbeat later the door disappeared and a large sheet of water went splashing to the ground at their feet. He jerked back, startled, and then saw beyond the doorway and into the room. Liana was prone on the threshold, looking pale and clammy, and an equally surprised Gloria gaped at him. Her pretty mouth opened in shock at their appearance, but the surprise was short lived. She drew back and threw something at him.

It blurred in his vision as he ducked, swiveling out of its path so that it buried itself in the wall nearest Brigetta. A dagger, he realized, and then leapt over Liana, caging Gloria in the room.

"What have you done to her?" he asked, drawing his sword. He couldn't look at Liana. Not yet. Not until the threat was subdued.

Gloria smiled. "Oh, Trevor. You never lose your charm."

He spotted Brigetta as she moved to kneel beside Liana and prayed they weren't too late.

"But then," Gloria glanced at Brigetta, "Trevor isn't really your name, is it, Kaden? You could save me some trouble and tell me where your parents are."

Troy frowned and gripped his hilt. "Go to hell."

Gloria clucked her tongue at him. "And here I thought we were friends."

Troy kept his eyes on her, but checked on Liana. "Is she all right?"

"No," Brigetta said from behind him. "She's been poisoned."

The words slammed into Troy's chest and he gripped his hilt tighter. He leveled his blade at the cornered woman. "I don't imagine Gloria is your name, either."

She smiled and didn't respond, spreading her hands out deprecatingly as she took a step backward. Her wide, flowery patterned skirt brushed over the floor, its deep purples and pinks somehow menacing in the gloomy light.

"Where is the antidote?" he demanded.

Gloria grinned wider but said nothing. Troy advanced on her, forcing her to retreat until her back was against the wall. He settled his sword point at her neck, glaring at her grinning face, and debated killing her. She deserved it. All that flirting and girlish behavior, all the lies she'd given to try and draw him in; he felt a fool for not noticing sooner.

Brigetta began murmuring something but he ignored it.

"Antidote. Now," he said through his teeth.

Gloria's eyes widened in surprise, but she wasn't looking at him. Her gaze was riveted just past his shoulder, at where Brigetta and Liana were. A lick of flame flashed in his peripheral vision and he cautiously turned to look. Brigetta had one hand on Liana's shoulder and the other pointing at him. Or rather, pointing at Miss Gloria, whose wide-eyed gaze filled with terror.

He heard her breathe a soft, "Oh gods!" just before fire encircled them.

Startled, Troy stood immobile, his sword at Gloria's neck as the deep, unnaturally red flame swirled around them. He flinched, expecting to be burnt but felt no heat. Fire normally had some orange in it, he was sure. And yellow, definitely some yellow.

"No!" Gloria shouted, launching forward.

She sliced herself open on his blade, a red gash opening on the side of her neck, but she didn't seem to notice. She swiveled past him in a crazed effort to reach Brigetta. Troy turned with her, swiping a hand at her back. His fingers snagged on the collar of her dress, jerking her to a halt. The fire followed her, curling around and sinking into her skin on all sides.

Gloria gasped in sudden pain, grabbing her leg as she toppled forward. Her dress ripped from Troy's hand and he nearly stumbled over her, his gaze locked on her leg, on the blood soaking her stocking. Gloria hit the wooden floor inches from Liana, one hand still reaching for Brigetta. But there was no strength to it and in the next moment, Gloria went still.

Straightening, Troy watched as the flames withdrew, pouring back into Brigetta's skin. He swallowed his unease, still trying to understand what he had just witnessed. Brigetta's hair seemed brighter somehow, redder, and the gleam in her eyes was unsettling.

Liana groaned and shifted on the floor, reclaiming his attention. He stepped around Gloria to kneel beside her, running a shaking hand over her hair. She looked pale and confused, but otherwise unharmed, her blue eyes focusing on him with some effort.

"Troy?" she whispered and flung her arms around him. Troy squeezed her against his chest, feeling the warmth of her and the solid grip she had on him, and breathed his relief.

"What happened?" she asked into his shoulder.

"I'm not altogether certain myself," he said, looking to Brigetta.

The mage slowly pushed herself to her feet, swaying a little with the movement. She looked unsteady and a trifle dazed and Troy wondered what magic must cost her. Liana pulled back from him and peered up at Brigetta.

"I was dying," Liana said quietly. "I could feel it."

"Yes, you were," Brigetta said matter-of-factly. "I transferred the wound and the poison to Gloria."

"But… doesn't a person have to agree to a transfer?" Liana asked.

"Only Eldur have the power of choice in such matters," Brigetta said. "It is our blood that is the source of magic. Humans do not have that privilege."

Troy glanced at Gloria's body. The woman's printed skirt fanned out over the ground, showing the tangle of her legs and the bright splotch of blood soaking through the ivory of her stockings. He shuddered in spite of himself. The girl hadn't a chance the moment Brigetta started her spell, which alarmed him on many levels. "But… if that's the case, why haven't the mages done that sort of transfer on the battlefield?" he asked.

"Because Porrex does not know it is possible." Brigetta's voice sharpened. "He would seek to use it to obliterate the Human race and I, for one, will not allow it. My actions just now were morally questionable at best, but Porrex is unethical to the core."

"Oh," Troy said, feeling somewhat relieved that this blood mage had a moral compass.

But there were others like her who might not.

"Morally questionable?" Liana asked. "You saved my life. Thank you."

He shoved that debate from his mind to concentrate on more important issues. Liana was alive. He would take that and the rest be damned.

"How are we going to explain this?" Troy asked, nodding down at Gloria.

Brigetta blinked at him, then frowned at Gloria's body. She looked puzzled for a moment, then started to hum something under her breath. Troy glanced out at the corridor. Thus far the fighting was limited to the deck but he could hear it intensifying. He looked to Liana, who caught his gaze and seemed to understand. They were out of time. They needed to get up on the deck.

A wet splash drew his attention back to Brigetta. Where Gloria's body had been was now a large, flopping fish, its mouth gaping and closing as it slowly began to suffocate. Its form beat a frantic rhythm into the floor and Troy had to fight back an ominous, dark fear from his mind.

Good gods, blood mages were terrifying.

"Somehow," Liana said as she got to her feet, "that's not any easier to explain."

"So don't explain it," Brigetta said, breathless as she turned for the door. "Now go help the fight. Pirates would try ransoming or selling us and we don't want either."

Troy stiffened, watching the empty doorway where Brigetta had disappeared.

Ransom or slavery, he thought—or just execution if they weren't worth anything.

Sharing a grim look with Liana, he started for the door.

Fifteen

The deck was a swarm of bodies. Several pirates had made it across the starboard side and were spreading out over the ship, engaging the *Penelope's* crew with indiscriminate force. The irritating part was that Nelek couldn't quite differentiate between friend and foe. Both were in various states of slummery with sweat patched, threadbare garb and no shoes in sight. The only ones he could identify were the officers of the *Penelope*, who continued to shout orders that were either ineffectual or unheeded.

He shoved his way to the next anchoring rope and cursed Faxon Mylonas for this mess. The man obviously hadn't paid attention to the state of the crew when he'd chosen this ship.

Nelek cut through the anchoring rope and turned just in time to spot a fist heading for his face. He ducked, catching the fist with his shoulder instead, and thrust his sword into the man's gut, pushing forward until the man toppled away. Nelek panted and glanced up at where Trenna was still climbing the shrouds. She was midway up, nearing the crow's nest, but someone was following her. Nelek squinted, recognizing the greasy hair and broad shoulders: Parsens.

Remembering the leering cook from the day before, Nelek tried to determine if Parsens was on his way to help or if he had more nefarious thoughts in mind. In all the chaos, the cook might believe Trenna to be an easy target. Nelek clenched his fists.

"Dad!" Liana's voice yanked him back to the fight.

He spotted her at the hatchway and then had to move as a sword cleaved down at him from the right. Swiveling left, he avoided the blade as it chunked into the railing, splintering the wood near one of the hooked lines. His new opponent abandoned the sword after one attempt at yanking it from the railing. Nelek swung his elbow, catching the man in the ribs.

The pirate grunted, jabbing a quick fist into Nelek's nose. He felt and heard the crunch of bone breaking as pain burst in the center of his face. Nelek staggered backward. Through the haze of pain and blood, Nelek felt hands grab him and in his confusion he grabbed back. His body slammed into the railing, agony piercing his lower back and down his left leg. For a breathless moment, Nelek thought something important had snapped.

An instant later that worry vanished, when his opponent seized him by the chin and started pushing, trying to shove him overboard. Nelek snagged hold of the railing with one hand and tried to push the man away with the other. His feet slipped and his body started to teeter on the rail. His left foot lost purchase with the deck and he caught a glimpse of churning sea far below. There was barely a foot between the two ships, he saw. If he fell he'd be crushed.

Grunting, Nelek pushed back with all his might, trying to regain his footing. He heard a meaty crunch and the pressure suddenly released, his opponent falling to the side as Troy grabbed him by the lapels. Disoriented, Nelek had to rely on the younger man until he caught his footing. The pirate was dead, skewered from behind, lying horizontal just inches away.

Troy grinned at him. "Abandoning ship already?"

Nelek coughed and laughed, more relieved than he wanted to let on. "Not hardly."

Beyond Troy he spotted Liana's run for the shrouds. The girl had obviously seen Trenna and was determined to help. Higher up, Trenna was engaged with Parsens, who was grinning like an idiot down at her. Nelek's eye twitched. Parsens swung, his blade whipping past Trenna's head far too close for comfort. Her leg was stuck and she was having trouble avoiding the man's swings.

"Gods above," Troy said, staring up at the scene. "We're in a fine pickle."

Nelek scanned the deck. There were pockets of fighting everywhere, but he could sense that the battle was not in their favor. If they didn't break free soon they would be at the pirates' mercy. He looked back up at Trenna.

"Crossbow," he said.

"What?"

"I need a bloody crossbow!" He ignored Troy, searching for the weapon.

He spotted a discarded one at the helm, near the captain's feet. Charging forward, Nelek avoided the fighting, weaving this way and that as men from both ships got in his way. He sprinted up onto the half deck until he reached the crossbow and snatched it up. But the blasted thing wasn't loaded. Nelek cursed and began a frantic hunt, scanning the deck for any loose bolts.

"Here!" Troy shouted.

Nelek turned as the boy shoved a bolt in his hand. Then he went to work. He slid his foot into the stirrup, pointing it down as he drew back on the string with both hands. There was a loud click as the cocking mechanism took hold and he lifted the crossbow, sliding the bolt into its groove quickly. He peered down the length of the bow, locating Trenna's position.

Liana had just reached the fight. She swung her sword, slashing Parsens in the leg. The cook screamed, his voice mingling with the clamor or combat all around them. Nelek squinted down the crossbow, focusing on his breathing, on the snarl Parsens gave Liana. Parsens sliced down at her, knocking her sword from her hand.

Nelek tugged back on the trigger. The bolt flew out of the bow, burying itself in Parsens' side. The man arched in sudden pain and toppled backward, rolling down the netting until his left arm got tangled. There he stopped, limp and lifeless. Nelek lowered the crossbow.

"You have got to teach me how to do that," Troy said with a whoop.

"I wasn't aiming for his side," Nelek muttered and thought, *I was aiming for his throat.*

Nelek watched as Trenna untangled her leg and prepared to climb again. She paused just long enough to wave her thanks down at him before heading for the mess of lines above. Nelek breathed in relief and dropped the crossbow.

"It'll do though," Troy said and handed him his sword.

"Yes, it will," Nelek said. "Now let's go free this ship."

~ * ~

Trenna scrambled up to the crow's nest and surveyed the mess. The horizontal beams of both masts were crossed over each other, their rigging tangled in no less than five places. She glanced down at the battle below and scowled. They were losing. Troy and Nelek were both fighting to cut the boarding lines and the rest of the *Penelope's* crew was charging about with no clue about what to do.

What the hell was wrong with this ship? Sailors should have more experience than this, shouldn't they?

"What happens if the pirates win?" Liana asked, scurrying up beside her.

"Nothing good," Trenna said and frowned over at the enemy ship.

More men were preparing to cross, pushing their way onto the *Penelope* with brute force. Three men were climbing the shrouds, either to try boarding from there or to begin separating the rigging on their own—which wouldn't be in the *Penelope's* favor either way. Trenna grunted in displeasure and handed Liana her shortsword. Liana took the weapon with a sheepish smile but made no comment on how she had lost her own.

It didn't matter, not now, so Trenna ignored it and snagged the knife from her boot.

"Cut those two lines there," Trenna pointed to the closest tangles. "I'll get the others."

The ships lurched and they had to grab the nest to keep steady. Trenna felt the groan of wood as the two masts rubbed against each other and took a deep breath.

"When the ships separate, there's going to be a backlash," she said, looking away from the cross of timber and back to her daughter. "Hold on tight."

Liana nodded, her black hair slashing across her face with the wind. It had come loose at some point in the battle but the girl didn't seem to notice. Trenna hesitated. Fear lodged hard in her chest and for a breathless moment she had to coach herself into a steadier heartbeat.

Gods, why had she let them come on this insane venture? Kaden didn't even want to be here, dammit.

The ships rocked again and she nearly went over, but she found her footing and nodded to her daughter before climbing out on the beam. Scurrying across the mast as quickly as she could, she bypassed the first two knotted riggings, leaving them for Liana. At the third tangle she straddled the beam and set her knife to the line, sawing through it as hard as she could. Moments later the line snapped away from the beam and jerked the ship so that she had to steady herself.

She glanced back at the enemy ship. The three men were more than halfway up the shrouds, moving fast. Trenna crawled her way to the fourth knot, feeling the beam jerk under her as Liana cut a line. Reaching the cross of beams, Trenna held her blade with her teeth, tasting cold metal and salt and something dirty as she climbed onto the confusion of lines and riggings. She had to lean hard to the left and strain to snag the fourth set of tangles.

Not really caring which ship they belonged to anymore, she sawed through them, cutting everything connected to the two riggings that were jumbled together. There was another jerk through the beams as the lines fell away, and in her peripheral view she saw one of the three approaching pirates fall, catching himself on the shrouds far below.

Another snap from Liana's end and Trenna started to move again.

One more, she thought; just one more.

The fifth knot was higher on the enemy ship, just near its own crow's nest. She surged forward, clamoring up the beam as fast as she could, praying she could get there before the enemy.

Faster. Must be faster, she thought, half climbing and half crawling her way towards the rigging. Something grabbed her foot and yanked her to a stop. Trenna kicked without looking, recognizing the firm grip of a hand around her ankle. Her free leg swung through the air, missing the pirate completely.

"No!" Liana shouted from further down the beam just as the pirate's blade sunk into the back of Trenna's leg.

Pain seared through her calf muscle and Trenna lost her grip on the beam. She fell back, twisting around far enough to see her attacker just before she landed on him. The lean, bearded man grunted in surprise as they collided, but managed to keep his hold on the line. Her left cheek smacked into his collarbone and she scrambled to grab hold of him, stopping her descent.

Trenna didn't wait. She struck out with her dagger, hitting him just under the right armpit, angling the blade like she meant to climb with it. He shouted in a mix of pain and outrage and finally let go of the mast, taking her with him. Pushing away from the pirate, Trenna breathed a curse and reached for the line again, abandoning her dagger.

The line slipped through her palm, burning and cutting into her skin. Instinct wanted her to let go but with the rapidly approaching deck she managed to grip harder, letting the rope slice into her until she finally jolted to a stop. Dangling there for a breathless moment, Trenna glanced down, watched as her opponent missed the shrouds completely and smacked into the deck below, going silent and still.

One of his compatriots, having seen his body land, glanced up at her with a scowl. Trenna ignored him, ignored whatever he shouted to the rest of his crew, and turned to start climbing again. She'd lost a lot of ground in her descent and had to push herself to hurry. But her right calf throbbed and her hands were slick with blood, making the climb agonizingly slow.

Gritting her teeth, she pulled herself upward, sensing her body's growing weakness.

Gods, how deep had that bastard stabbed her?

Reaching the knot, Trenna tried to determine which end would keep her with the *Penelope-Anne* and which would land her stranded on the enemy ship, but Liana cried out in pain and she looked up again. Liana had taken a cut in her arm and was dangling from the mast, that last cursed pirate hovering over her, prepared to strike again.

Trenna grabbed any line, no longer caring where she ended up, and sawed through the knot. The rope whipped away from the beam and the two masts slipped free with a deep, reverberating groan. Trenna held onto her line as the ships separated, realizing an instant later that she was being carried back with the enemy ship.

Gods dammit all to hell. Could nothing go right?

The pirate who had sliced Liana teetered on the beam and fell screaming between the two ships and she thought, well, at least that much was good. The ship rocked back into a more natural position, throwing Trenna against the main mast. She slammed full-length against unforgiving wood and lost her hold on the line.

Flailing, she managed to snag another line and slowed her descent, swinging out wide over the deck of the enemy ship. Agony burned through her palms but she held on, swinging out and then back into the mast again. Her left side struck the post but she didn't dare let go of the rope. Dazed, she hung there for a moment before realizing the deck was close enough to drop.

Letting go of the rope, she hit the deck, shouting in protest as her calf flared up with a sharp, throbbing pain. Panting, she looked up at one very startled pirate whose sallow face showed such a comical expression of surprise that she huffed a laugh. He continued to gape at her as she rolled to the left and up to her feet.

Giving him a wink, she half limped and half ran toward the *Penelope-Anne*, praying she could get there before she was stabbed again. She couldn't see Nelek in the mass of fighters but she knew he would be there somewhere. He probably even knew where she was. He was good like that.

Nearing the railing, she slowed, trying to pick her first target. There was still a teeming mass of men trying to shove their way onto the *Penelope* and she would need to get through them.

A wall of water shot up between the two ships, cutting them off from the *Penelope*, and she stopped short and stared. The water was twice as high as the ship and curling in their direction, all frothy and dangerous, and she knew precisely what was coming next.

"Faxon Mylonas, you clever bastard," she muttered and then pivoted on her heel, ignoring her wound for the more important aspect of survival.

She ran for the aft of the ship, disregarding the surprised looks of men as she passed and the pulsing pain jabbing through her leg with every step. Sprinting up to the poop deck, Trenna ran for the railing, got one foot on the ledge of the ship and pushed off.

She was airborne for a long time. Long enough to hear the screams of the men on the enemy ship and the crash of water into wood. There was a sharp, booming crack as the main mast broke and then she was submerged, cold water roaring around her. Her body was towed by a strong current and she swam with it, coaching herself to remain calm. Her chest squeezed tight with the need for air and she pushed for the surface, breaking through several seconds later to cough and sputter.

She treaded water for a moment, scanning the area for the *Penelope-Anne*. She found it a moment later, impossibly far away and growing more distant. If she could reach it before the sails were loosed she had a chance.

Trenna started swimming.

Her leg hurt and her body ached from the fight, making her swim far more labored than it should have been. She looked up to find the ship still ages away and choked on a sob. Despair lodged in her chest; the sails were unfurling.

"Wait!" she shouted, coughing on salt water. "Wait, curse you!"

It was no use. They couldn't hear her, not this far out. Exhausted, Trenna watched as the sea continued to drag her away from the ship.

To her left she spotted a large bit of wood floating in the water and diverted for it. She grabbed the edge and hoisted herself up, flopping onto the hard wood with a curse. It was a section of hull, she could tell by the curve, and it was just big enough to keep her out of the water.

Well, she thought, there are some advantages to being small.

Glancing up at the *Penelope-Anne*, she prayed Captain Horace would turn about for survivors. Nelek would make sure of it, she knew. She just needed to be patient.

She lowered her head to the wood and shivered. "Gods alive, I am too old for this turtle shite."

Sixteen

Liana hurried down the shrouds, her hands and feet missing their marks often as she tried to keep the distancing wreckage in sight. Trenna was back there, in the ocean, without a boat to protect her.

"Oh gods, oh gods," she muttered to herself, dropping the last three feet to hit the deck hard.

A wave of giddiness rolled over her, making her sway, and pain prickled through her left arm. She ground her teeth and shook her head, blinking twice to get her bearings. Then, she ran for the starboard railing, passing Troy in her frantic pace.

"Hey!" Troy called after and she heard him take chase.

"Mother!" she shouted, forgetting all pretenses and danger as she came to a stop before the railing.

Troy stopped at her side. "Liana?"

She ignored him and shouted again. He seemed to realize what was wrong because he cursed and started hurrying along the railing with her, squinting down at the deep, fathomless blue churning just below the ship. The rest of the crew was busy setting sail or subduing their would-be captors. Several of them glanced in her direction, but

Liana couldn't give a damn what they thought about a woman in pants.

Her father met them near the aft of the ship. A long, shallow scratch cut from his left cheek and led up into his hairline. She took in his blood-spattered clothes and the angry puff of skin around his eye and breathed in relief. He was alive, which meant Trenna was alive. She blessed the complexities of Eldur marriage for that small comfort.

"Have you lost your mind?" Nelek hissed at her, drawing her up short. "Stop calling for your mother, Eve."

He stressed her fake name and she shook her head at him. "You don't understand," she said, pointing out at the sea. "She was on the other ship when we separated!"

Nelek looked stunned. He glanced out at the watery horizon and clenched his jaw so tightly she could swear she heard his teeth crack. The mix of pain and fear in his face made her heart ache. He closed his eyes for a conflicted moment and Liana thought he might be praying. Then he opened his eyes, nodded once as though confirming something for himself, and gathered her wounded arm with both hands.

Pain flared through the limb, making her dizzy.

"Troy... Trevor... take her to see the surgeon. Or Lady Isleen," he said quietly. "Isleen might be better."

"But..."

"Liana," Nelek said in the tone of voice that meant she was not allowed to fight, "she isn't dead. We would know by now. Go take care of yourself. I'll see the captain about a rescue."

"I want to go with you," Liana said. "I can help ..."

"Evaliana Auliere Dyngannon," he said and one of the crew glanced at them. "Do as I say."

She shut her mouth and turned stiffly to Troy, who took her by the elbow. The crewman who'd been staring turned back to his work as Liana allowed Troy to lead her across the bloodied deck. Little rivers and lakes of blood formed around fallen men and she realized someone was already scrubbing it away. The captain was off to the leeward side, eyeing a small crowd of men subdued on their knees, and she realized them to be the stranded pirate crew.

Gods, what would the captain do with them?

Her arm felt heavier the further they walked, the needling pain morphing into a heavy, insistent throb that pulsed through the whole limb. Troy's grip on her changed, pulling her closer as they reached the scuttle. They had to go single file down into the ship, Troy forcing her in front of him so that she was leaning back against him as they descended. By the time they reached the bottom she was panting. A fine sweat had broken out over her face and neck and she feared she would be sick.

Troy seemed to fear it too, because he slowed the pace, murmuring a gentle word of encouragement to her as they made their way back through the corridor. They passed her own doorless room but she didn't bother to look inside. The events that had transpired with Gloria felt somewhere far away and all that was in Liana's mind was her mother.

She replayed the battle, the moment when the ships had separated and Trenna had been whisked back with the enemy. Trenna hadn't seemed surprised in the least.

Troy knocked twice on Brigetta's door and it opened. "Liana's hurt," he said and promptly dragged her inside, straight past a mildly annoyed Brigetta.

"I'll be all right," Liana said, but her protest sounded strained even to her.

"No, you won't," Faxon said, emerging from the corner like an apparition. He nodded to Troy, who promptly ignored him.

"Sit her down," Brigetta instructed, gesturing to the beds.

Troy brought Liana to the nearest bed and she sat, groaning a little because her elbow bumped something that rocketed pain all the way through her shoulder.

"Trenna was on the other ship when we separated," Troy said, frowning. "Nelek is working on a rescue."

"Mr. Norand," Brigetta said pointedly, "will be most persuasive, I'm sure."

"I don't suppose I can get a vial of the girl's blood..." Faxon said but was cut off.

"No." Troy eyed the man. "Why the blazes are you here?"

"Visiting my wife, of course." Faxon smiled lazily at him.

Brigetta tore open Liana's bloody sleeve, revealing a four-inch gash running diagonally across her arm. It was deep but not life-threatening. At least Liana didn't think it was life threatening. She shivered and leaned back, trying to gauge how much blood she'd already lost.

Troy crouched beside her, looking unhappy and worried.

"Alas, my wife is busy," Faxon said with a sigh. "I will go see how Nelek's negotiations with the captain go. We'll need him here if there's to be no rescue."

"But there has to be a rescue," Liana protested. "The captain wouldn't leave her behind."

"Wouldn't he?" Faxon said and slipped out the door.

~ * ~

Kaden woke with a thundering headache. Groaning, he shifted and felt something sharp slice into the back of his thigh. He cursed and rolled to the other side, revealing the sword he'd been lying on. For a confused moment he stared at it and then he remembered.

The ship was under attack.

Only, the sounds outside his little corner were not of combat. He heard sailors complaining, people shuffling about, but no shouts of agony or clash of metal. He frowned and pushed to his feet. His head swam and he swayed, catching himself on the nearest wall before he could fall again.

Blast that Faxon Mylonas! The demented man had assaulted him and run off to battle.

"You'll want to stay here, Your Majesty," Faxon whispered from beside him.

Kaden whirled to face him, intent on shouting something obscene to let the man know how furious he was, but the movement only enhanced his dizziness and he had to swallow back bile instead.

Rapidly approaching footsteps stole his attention and he glanced at Faxon, who shook his head once and remained silent.

Oh, gods, had they lost the ship?

What were they going to do with a ship full of pirates?

He'd heard stories of pirates before and none of them were good. People were either killed, conscripted, or sold into slavery. Gods only knew what port they might end up at. This was a disaster.

Frowning, he tried to think of how to take the ship back. He'd need his parents first. They'd know what to do.

The footsteps stopped abruptly and a hushed conversation came into his hiding space.

"You're telling me Mister Clarkson had a weapon hidden in your room?" Regmond's voice rumbled on the other side of the bulkhead and Kaden nearly sighed in relief.

"Yes," that was Max, Kaden could swear by it. "He said it was an heirloom or something, sir. Which I thought was right strange as he's supposed to be a fisherman and all."

"And you actually saw this weapon?"

Why was this important?

"Well, no, sir. But as you said the passengers pulled out weapons to defend the ship, I thought it best to tell you. What with the plans getting botched as they were."

Plans?

He glanced at Faxon, who put a finger to his lips, signaling for him to stay quiet. Kaden scowled back at him. He wasn't stupid enough to give away their position. Faxon grinned arrogantly, his eyes glittering in the dim light, and Kaden had the distinct feeling the man knew what he was thinking.

"What are we supposed to do, sir?" Max went on after a minute. "That woman cut us free and the *Contessa* was destroyed!"

"I don't know," Regmond said, sounding truly annoyed.

"But sir, if we get to port and the real…"

"Quiet, you fool!" Regmond hissed.

Kaden's mind flashed to the moment he'd run to warn Master Regmond of the other ship, to the way the man had brushed him off. He'd gotten up, but slowly, and refused to warn the captain. Any sane sailor would have roused the captain immediately. Kaden closed his eyes and berated himself as a fool. That was how the other ship had closed in on them so fast. Regmond had been on duty all night. He'd likely kept people away from the deck, further shielding the enemy's approach.

"Where is Mister Clarkson now?" Regmond asked.

"I don't rightly know, sir. Someone hit me from behind. I didn't see them leave."

"Blast it all!" Regmond said. "It was likely that confounded woman. Sister indeed. Ha!"

Kaden smiled. Of course, it had actually been Faxon who hit Max but it was still funny to hear how annoyed Regmond was at his mother. The man was probably wishing he'd never laid eyes on the pair of them.

"Find Mister Clarkson," Regmond said. "We can't get any answers from the passengers but we can certainly interrogate *him*."

"Do you think they know, sir? About us?"

"No, not likely. But they obviously have some secrets of their own." Regmond's voice started to distance, as though he were moving away. "And with the *Contessa* gone, let's hope those secrets can make up for what we lost today."

Kaden listened to them leave, heard the scuttle door shut and released his breath. Faxon moved to the bulkhead and peered around it. In the gloom of the place, Kaden could only make out the paleness of his cheekbone and the sharp angle of his jaw; the rest of him was consumed by shadow, as though the darkness itself were draped around the man.

"You will need to stay hidden, Your Grace."

"Call me that one more time and I will nail you to the hull of this ship," Kaden said through his teeth.

Faxon flashed him an irreverent grin. "So you do have some of your mother's fight in you. I was worried for a moment that you took more after your father," he said. "Ever the diplomat, your father. Always walking the line between peace and war and never capable of fully committing to either."

"You know nothing about my father."

"Don't I?" Faxon clucked his tongue at him. "For shame, Kaden. I was a subject in Kiavana for a good portion of my life. I saw your father's rise to power. He was naïve back then, but time seems to have cleansed him of that."

"Watching his rise to power does not mean you know him," Kaden said curtly. "Now, how are we going to warn the others about Regmond and Max?"

"*We* aren't going to do anything," Faxon said. "You are going to stay here. I've put up a barrier that makes this look like the last bulkhead. No one will know you're here unless you speak, so try not to talk to yourself."

"I am not a child in need of safe-keeping…"

"No. You're the last hope for peace in Dyngannon."

Something in the way Faxon said it brought Kaden up short. It was almost as if the man truly meant it. But he was a Human assassin, not an Eldur patriot. It made no sense. Kaden stared at him, wondering what the hell his game was.

"You will stay here, Kaden Dyngannon. It is what your mother would have wanted."

"My mother would have wanted me at her side today, fighting off those pirates." Kaden almost went on, intent on letting his full fury out, but stopped. "Why did you say that in the past tense?"

Faxon held his gaze but said nothing. Kaden's chest squeezed tight but he didn't look away.

Mom, he thought.

"Where is my mother?" he asked.

"Trenna was on board the *Contessa* when it was destroyed," Faxon said at last. "They have not found her yet."

"But they are looking?"

Fear crawled up his spine and cinched tight around the base of his neck. He was a man of the sea; he didn't need to hear Faxon say it. Under his feet he could feel the steady push of the ship through water, the constant bob and bump of a fast cut across the ocean. They weren't searching for survivors; they were at full sail, running away from the event.

"Is my father still alive?"

"Yes."

Kaden closed his eyes and took a deep breath. She was still alive. And as long as she was alive she would fight to return to them. He had no idea how, but she would.

Opening his eyes again, he looked at Faxon. "Go warn the others. And ask Brigetta if there is anything you can do for my mother."

Faxon quirked an eyebrow at him in wry amusement and gave him a mocking bow. "Yes, sire."

Kaden didn't laugh and he didn't balk at the title. He just watched the man leave and prayed that somehow, some way, he would see his mother again. Because Faxon was wrong. Without her, Kaden didn't give a damn about the plight of the Eldur people. All they were to him was a bedtime story and some distant relations. Trenna was the link.

Nelek could tie him to Kiavana, but with Uncle Brenson leading the people there, Kaden imagined he wasn't needed. He would not interfere with Kiavana or Dyngannon without his parents. That was his decision.

He moved to collect the sword from the ground and stared down at the open blade. His blood stained the tip but he didn't move to clean it. Turning the blade to see the smudge of blood on the other side, his mind was suddenly miles away, transported quite against his will. He could hear battle, chaos and screams of pain, but above that he heard the steady thumping of his own heart.

He felt as though something else were in the room with him. Something ancient, passionate, watching him from everywhere. He could sense its observation, feel it urging him toward some unspecified goal, but when he looked up he was still alone.

With a shaking hand, he wiped the blood on his shirt and frowned.

So now I am going crazy too, he thought.

Seventeen

"You must search for her," Nelek said.

He was doing his best to hold onto his composure but even he could tell he was failing. His left eye twitched as he watched Captain Horace move to sit at the large desk in the center of the room. Panic swelled in Nelek's chest and he took a moment to breathe, desperately trying to ignore visions of Trenna floating half-dead in the ocean.

Horace continued to shuffle through manifests and charts, arranging them into some sort of order. The captain wouldn't look at him. Nelek could sense the anger in the man, see the stiff way he moved, but it appeared the captain was keeping a tighter rein on his emotions than Nelek was.

"Captain, she saved the ship. We must find her. We owe it to her to try!" Nelek said again.

Horace looked up. "I am eternally grateful to Miss Clarkson for her actions today, Mister Norand. However, I did not ask her to risk herself in such a fashion."

"No one else was taking action."

That wasn't entirely true. Everyone was fighting by that point. It just took the pair of them to get the ships separated and safe. Gods, what was wrong with this crew? Surely at least some of the officers should have known what to do.

"If you won't go after her, then give me a boat and I'll go myself," Nelek said.

"And leave your daughter here alone?" Horace eyed him suspiciously. "You're very quick to run off after some woman you barely know, sir."

"None of us would be here if not for her. Captain, I am begging you. Please turn the ship about."

"The girl is likely dead, Mister Norand."

"No. Not this one. I swear to you, she is alive."

"And how do you know that, sir?"

Nelek stopped just short of answering. *Because she's my wife. Because we are Eldur and if she were dead, I would be too. Because I refuse to let her die.*

He clenched his fists and looked away, fighting for the right decision. The creak and sway of the ship only intensified Nelek's desperation. He could imagine her out there, swallowed by waves in the watery expanse, completely alone. They were meant to die together. That was the purpose of Eldur marriage, to live and love and laugh side by side until the day they left for the After.

Gods, he should have dived in after her the moment Liana told him what had happened.

"I am not a fool, sir," Horace said. "People do not cross from the islands to the mainland on a whim. Normally I don't care about your secrets. I just ferry you lot across the ocean and enjoy my payment on the other side. But this time... this time there are games afoot that put my entire ship at risk."

Nelek looked back to the captain. The ferocity that flashed in Horace's eyes might have quelled a younger man, but Nelek had too much at stake. His children needed whatever protection he could give them. If he died in the next few minutes, anonymity might be the only thing he could give Kaden and Evaliana. So he stared back at the captain, unwilling to answer any more.

"I am tempted to shove you and your daughter in with the pirates," Horace said and stood to his feet. "But by all accounts you helped rescue my ship. Even your daughter was seen fighting, which shocked a good number of my men. For your efforts I will allow you to keep to your rooms."

By the way he stressed the word "allow," Nelek knew this was a forced confinement. They would be locked away until they came to port, and after that, Horace likely meant to turn them over to whatever passed for authority in Cadabyr harbor. It would be one more headache on this godsawful journey, but he suspected Faxon would free them eventually.

"Unless, of course, you would like to elaborate on who you really are?" the captain asked.

"I cannot tell you without risking the life of my daughter," Nelek said, still clenching his fists.

How far from the wreckage were they now?

"So she is your daughter?"

"Yes," Nelek said, thinking he might be able to steal a lifeboat. But even if he did and managed to reach Trenna, neither of them was a magnificent sailor. Their chances of survival would still be slim.

"But Eve and Norand aren't really your names, are they?" Horace asked.

Nelek stayed silent. Maybe he should just break the man's face and force him into turning the ship around.

"No, I didn't think so," Horace said and nodded to the door.

Nelek stood there, debating the merits of outright mutiny until at last, recognizing defeat, he turned and left the room. Master Regmond met him on the other side of the door and began escorting him back to his room. Captain Horace was nothing if not efficient; there was already a sentry posted in the hallway, barring him from contacting Evaliana. Nelek glanced at his daughter's room and was startled to see it had no door. She wasn't inside, but he imagined she was still with Brigetta, which was good.

The door shut behind him and he growled low in his throat. He would have to leave. Soon. The longer he waited, the farther away she would be. But how was he to reach a boat and steal it in broad daylight with so many men wandering about? And could he leave Kaden and Liana behind?

His gaze caught on his unmade bed and his mind swerved to Trenna, to what they had done in here just a few short hours ago.

He closed his eyes and remembered the taste of her—minty from the tea they'd shared. He could feel the smooth contours of her body under his hands and the rough scrape of her callouses as she'd held on to him. The scents of the day were in her hair; salty sea air and onions from the galley.

Nelek staggered to his bed and reached for her cap. They had lingered too long and she'd had to hurry away. She'd left the cap on the table and he'd meant to tease her about it later. He lifted the coarse material to his face and breathed her in again. She was there, barely, with all the onions and sea he had held in his arms last night.

"You know she's not dead yet."

Nelek whirled back to the door. Faxon stood there, dressed as the sentry and smirking in a highly annoying way.

"She can't be dead because you're still alive."

"I know that," Nelek said.

"Then quit grieving and let's get to work."

"You mean," he lowered the cap and frowned. "You mean there's something you can do?"

"Well, there's always something we can do. It's blood magic, after all. We just can't guarantee that it will be helpful." Faxon cracked the door open and peered outside. "It's clear. Come along."

Nelek followed, stuffing Trenna's cap inside his shirt. Another sentry was on duty, his back turned to them, but Faxon didn't seem to care. They hurried to Brigetta's room and slipped inside. Liana looked up from where she sat on a bed. Her arm was bandaged and strapped to her chest with a sling but she looked healthy.

"What did the captain say?" she asked as soon as the door shut.

Nelek shook his head in answer. Because he couldn't stomach the fear in his daughter's face, he looked away. Brigetta stood beside her own bed, carefully arranging a wig on her head. It covered her ears and was nearly the same color as her own deep red hair. She looked completely at ease with herself, pinning the curly thing down until she was certain it would stay. Nelek watched, both out of confusion and a desire to avoid Liana's gaze.

"Where is Troy?" he asked.

"He's our guard," Faxon said, gesturing at the door. "Give a man a hat and a new uniform and you'd be surprised how many people won't recognize him. Very few actually look at the face these days."

"The captain will call for me very soon," Brigetta said. "He's been far too curious about me and your stunt on deck with the water will have him suspicious."

"Stunt?" Faxon asked, feigning disappointment. "I thought it was quite inspired."

"It was effective, to be sure," Liana said. "But waves don't normally shoot straight up between two ships."

Faxon grinned and winked at Liana. "As I live and breathe! Evaliana Dyngannon just complimented me."

"It was an observation, not a compliment," Liana said.

Faxon clucked his tongue twice at the girl and then turned his attention back to Brigetta. "You really think this is going to work?" he asked, eyeing Brigetta's wig.

"As long as he doesn't touch it, yes," Brigetta said.

Faxon made a noncommittal noise in the back of his throat and crossed his arms. Nelek glanced between them. For half a tick, he saw what appeared to be a flash of possessiveness in Faxon's eyes, but it was gone in an instant. Nelek frowned. He wasn't certain he wanted to believe the man capable of such an emotion, let alone have anything in common with him.

"His Majesty has given us an order, wife," Faxon said. "He is justifiably concerned for his mother's welfare."

"Majesty?" Nelek asked, feeling lost.

"He means Kaden," Brigetta said.

"Where is Kaden?" Liana asked.

"Safe," Faxon said. "I'm afraid we have traitors on board this ship. They were suspicious of him and now he needs to stay hidden."

"Hidden where?" Liana asked, but Faxon merely winked at her.

Nelek's eye twitched at the idea of Faxon being the only one to know where Kaden was, but they had bigger problems. Kaden would be all right. In fact, Kaden was probably safer than the rest of their group, given the captain's irritation at present.

And Kaden wasn't alone in the ocean, quickly distancing from them.

"Who are the traitors?" Brigetta asked, picking up her cloak and swinging it over her shoulders. "It might help me in my negotiations with the captain."

"There's no telling how many are here," Faxon said. "But the two we found include the boatswain and one crewman named Max. Apparently there's something valuable on this ship besides the would-be king."

"He's not going to be your king," Liana said with a scowl.

"How are we to help Trenna?" Nelek asked, putting an end to the fight before his daughter could become fully engaged.

Brigetta met his gaze. The angles of her face softened with compassion and she gestured to her bed, where several candles and a sundry of unfamiliar items lay scattered on the blankets.

"It will take some preparation," she explained. "Faxon will show you what to do while I am gone. When I get back, we will see what we can do for your wife."

"Why not do it now?" Nelek asked, eyeing the bed of candles. "We don't know how much time she has left."

"Because the captain is demanding a meeting with me," Brigetta said, lifting her hood to cover the wig. "And if I don't go now, they will interrupt us."

"Interrupted magic is always bad," Faxon said, managing to sound bored.

"What do we do if someone comes knocking?" Nelek asked.

Brigetta walked to the door. She opened it a crack and moved to leave, but paused. Half out of the room, she looked back at him and smiled.

"Pray, Duke of Kiavana. If anyone knocks, pray."

Then she slipped out and latched the door behind her.

~ * ~

Captain Horace was remarkably blunt when angry. Brigetta had no sooner stepped into his office than he was demanding what she could tell him about blood magic. He really had been watching her too closely, she realized. The man circled her twice and both times she knew he was searching her hair, trying to locate her pointed Eldur ears. His sense of propriety kept him from all-out assaulting her person, which she imagined was the only thing keeping her identity a mystery.

"Blood magic?" Brigetta asked calmly. "You mean like the Eldur use in battle?"

"Do not play games with me, woman."

"Woman?" She frowned at him. "Whatever happened to 'my Lady?'"

"It crawled out the door when a bloody great wall of water destroyed the enemy ship!" he roared. "You know more than you're saying."

"Of course I do. I'm a woman, such is my nature."

He glared at her and Bree worried that she'd gone too far. For all intents and purposes, Horace was harmless, but it would be better for them if he remained in charge. Especially if Master Regmond was a traitor, as Faxon suggested.

"More to the point, I think, is the question why the *Penelope-Anne* was targeted," Bree said. "What have we got on board that could be worthy of so much effort?"

"It's a big sea," Horace said, gesturing flippantly to the side. "Pirates will take whatever they find."

His movements were too animated, she thought. *He knows something.*

"Pirates do not usually keep spies on board a potential target," she said, testing the waters a bit.

Horace looked at her sharply. "What did you say?"

"Well, unless the watch was blind, someone ought to have seen the danger before it was too late to act," she said, watching his face from the corner of her eye.

His mouth tightened at the corners and the vein near his left temple bulged a bit.

"There was fog," he said.

Oh yes, he knew something.

"And sailors are not trained to watch harder in a fog?" Bree asked and shook her head. "No, Captain. You have far more troubles than an errant blood mage on board your ship."

He scowled at her. "So you do know something about blood magic."

"I know enough to never want to cross a mage."

Horace smirked, apparently reading the implied threat. He knew what she was. Her eccentricities had drawn his attention and he was quite convinced that she was the cause of the wave that took the other ship. Never mind the fact that she'd been in her room for the entirety of the battle, or that Liana had run amuck on deck.

Or that Miss Gloria was missing.

Bree wondered why he hadn't questioned her about the lost woman. She still wasn't certain what she would say about it, but his preoccupation with blood magic showed a gross oversight on his part. Or perhaps he wasn't asking because he didn't want to know. Bree suddenly had the worst feeling that Horace was somehow playing with her.

"What is on board this ship?" she asked.

Horace sat down at his desk. "Return to your room, Lady Isleen. I'm sure you need to recover from the traumatic events of the day."

She frowned and debated arguing, but he began scrutinizing several charts and ignored her presence. Sensing there was nothing more she could do, Brigetta turned and left the captain's rooms. She walked out on deck, escorted by Master Regmond, and passed Troy where he stood on guard at the front of their corridor. The boy didn't so much as blink at her and Regmond didn't seem to notice the bloodied uniform. But then, there were a lot of bloodied uniforms today.

Regmond delivered her to her door and she slipped back inside without looking at him. Faxon could deal with the traitors as he saw fit; there was no need for her to bother with the man.

Inside, Nelek and Liana were both using strange smoldering sticks to light candles arranged throughout the room. The sticks were one of Faxon's many alchemy experiments put to practical use, and she inwardly blessed her husband's foresight in bringing them. It looked like the Dyngannon family had used their time well, because everything was ready.

Behind her the door opened and she had to move for Troy to enter. He latched the door and then leaned against it, nodding that they were in the clear. The crew should be busy with cleanup and Horace had already conducted his interviews. They had maybe an hour before someone suggested the guests needed to be fed.

That would have to be enough time.

Bree stepped into the middle of the room and double-checked the candles. They were set in four circles, one in the center with the others ringing it. Troy could stay where he was, just outside the furthest ring, guarding the door. She pointed Liana to the ring closest the center and the girl moved to oblige. Faxon stood behind Liana, quickly drinking a vial so he could be useful during the spell.

"Nelek," Bree said quietly. "I need you beside me, here in the middle."

Nelek stepped over a line of candles, moving to stand beside her in the center ring.

"Hold out your hand, please."

He held his right hand flat in front of her, his palm down. She was a little surprised that he knew the ritual position for drawing blood, but decided to ask him about it later. The boat was getting farther away from Trenna, which would limit what she could do for the general. With a quick move, Bree drew the dagger from her belt and stabbed him through the hand.

Liana gasped and went to step forward but Faxon grabbed her shoulder, keeping the girl in place. Bree glanced at them, making sure the child wouldn't move further, and was relieved by the nod Faxon gave her.

Nelek's blood fell from the dagger's point, splattering against the wooden floor and magic grew thick in the air. The candles changed from orange-red to copper, flaring to unnatural heights. Power pulsed into the room, swirling around Bree, waiting for a command. She released the dagger's hilt, concentrating on the quick thrum of Nelek's heartbeat.

Bree listened hard, hunting for that other heartbeat, the evidence of his wife. She found it a moment later, strong but distant. Closing her eyes, she called out on magic for a creature nearby—anything that could see Trenna—and swapped her vision again.

It was a gull this time, not flying but floating in the water, which was a little better because it allowed Bree to orient herself more easily to the sight. She spotted Trenna lying on a bit of wreckage several feet away. The woman was either asleep or passed out, but clearly alive. She'd tied something around her right calf and seemed to have taken great pains to keep the leg out of the water.

Bree encouraged the gull to move closer. It did so, flapping into the air with a dizzying show of speed. It landed on the very edge of the wreckage and Trenna turned her head to look at it. Bree could see the beginnings of fever in Trenna's glassy green gaze.

That was not good news.

"Are you going to replace her with a fish?" Liana asked quietly. "Just like Gloria?"

"She's too far away for that," Bree said.

"Then what are we going to do?" Nelek asked.

Bree exhaled. She really didn't have a clue how to help the woman. If she tried the transporting swap, Trenna could end up further away or deeper down. There was no way to control the magic from this distance.

"There's another ship coming," Faxon said. "South by southwest and only three leagues or so behind."

Brigetta straightened. There were moments when she truly loved that man. She urged the bird to fly and watched as it headed south by southwest. She trusted Faxon's report, even if she didn't understand how magic could work so differently for him. What she needed now was for the wind to guide the other ship to Trenna.

Faxon seemed to read her mind. "They're heading in a slightly different direction. I'll give them a push the right way."

Bree let the bird return to Trenna. She heard Faxon grunt, knew he was doing something with magic, but still couldn't see him. She felt the push of it, though. Magic passed over her skin like a sudden, cool breeze. A moment later, the waves began to change and she knew he had succeeded.

"Now what?" Liana asked.

"Now we wait," Faxon said.

Eighteen

Trenna knew she was sick. She only ever had dreams when she was seriously ill and she was having a bizarre dream now. There was an ugly white bird sitting next to her on her bit of wreckage and it was talking. The bird, not the wreckage. More than that, it was talking in Liana's voice, and sounded quite irate.

"What do you mean we wait? How long do we wait? What are we waiting for?"

Trenna smiled and closed her eyes. "I don't know, baby girl," she said and tried to let the bob of the makeshift raft assuage her. But her leg was on fire where the pirate had stabbed her and she had a sinking suspicion it was infected. And despite the high sun she was deeply cold, the kind of cold that made joints ache and limbs stiff, which made it difficult to find a comfortable spot to sleep.

She had a feeling she was going to die soon, which irked her.

Funnily enough, Trenna had never thought about dying. She'd known she would die one day, but assumed it was better to concentrate on every minute given to her rather than wallow in the despair of mortality. There was something more after this life and she knew it, so it didn't make sense to dwell on things she couldn't control.

The thought of leaving Kaden and Evaliana and Troy behind was painful, of course. But Nelek and Trenna had raised their children well. She believed they had a chance to be something marvelous on their own, even if it grieved her that she wouldn't be able to see what they chose to become. Kaden might actually be a king one day. Troy would stick with Kaden forever, helping to forge peace between Human and Eldur. And Liana... well, gods only knew what was in store for Liana.

She felt a little bad that Nelek was going to die too. Still, dying together guaranteed that their souls would greet the After in good company. She didn't care how nice the After was; if she didn't have Nelek beside her she wouldn't want to stay.

Trenna drifted in and out of sleep. Or perhaps she just stayed asleep because the cursed bird was still there whenever she opened her eyes. It stood at the edge of her little raft, watching her, its head canted to the left or right at random intervals. It didn't talk again but the intent stare was disconcerting. Around the third or fourth waking time she got angry at it.

"You are not pecking out my eyeballs," she said hoarsely.

She reached for her dagger, surprised at how weak she was.

How long had she been floating?

Her dagger wasn't at her belt. Trenna frowned and tried to sit up. The raft rocked with the movement, teetering so far she was afraid she'd tip over. The bird squawked and flew away as she lay back down.

Head spinning, she closed her eyes and forced herself to breathe.

Yes, I am very sick.

"Gotta be the leg," she mumbled.

Dirty pirate weapon makes for a quick and easy infection, she thought. And then, *Good gods, I really am going to die.*

Strange voices caught her attention. Trenna turned her heavy head to the left and was greeted by a large vessel headed her way: two masted, with the bust of a serenely naked woman on the prow. Her gaze caught on the round cheeks of the sculpture, the demure smile that was depicted there, and she wondered if that was what a classic beauty was supposed to look like.

One man jumped from the ship with a line in tow and she knew he was coming to her rescue. If she'd had more strength she would have laughed. She looked back at where the bird had returned, perching in its same spot on her raft.

"Like I said," she told it, "you're not getting my eyeballs."

The bird tilted its head, squawked, and took off again as her rescuer swam up to the raft. He was a ruddy man with a full beard and hazel eyes that peered at her in concern.

"Blimey," the man said, then called over his shoulder. "She's alive!"

Darkly tanned face, she noted as he began pulling her off the raft. Given how weak she was and that she had nowhere else to go, she let him. There was a pungent smell of onions on him that hadn't quite washed off during his plunge and she was reminded of Parsens and the galley.

"You have a very pretty ship," she told her rescuer just before her body plunged into the ocean again.

She shuddered and shivered as her feverish skin reacted to the water. It was an effort to link her arms around his neck as instructed, and he had to hold onto her with one hand as his comrades began pulling them toward the ship. She let her head rest on his shoulder and closed her eyes, feeling herself glide through the water with relative ease.

Several moments later they were both towed out of the water and lifted high, swinging onto the deck with quick efficiency. Many hands helped lower her to the deck and she was so relieved that she didn't care who pinched her where during the movement.

Her legs wouldn't hold her upright, so she sagged down, her head pressing against firm wooden deck. Not dead yet, she thought as a shadow covered her. She squinted up at another sailor who wore brightly buckled boots. His face hid the sun and she couldn't make out his features, which was just as well.

"Alive, eh?" he said. "Well, get her below and call the captain. He'll be wanting words."

"She's injured, sir," her rescuer said, crouching near her head.

"Yes, I can see that." The man nudged her bandaged leg with one shiny boot, sending a rocket of pain through her that woke her up.

"Bloody bastard," she said through clenched teeth.

Someone nearby laughed.

"Best get her to Master Kort then." He waved a hand at the small crowd gathered around them. "Get to it."

Men scattered in a flurry of movement and she was lifted again, carried quickly toward the aft. She tried to stay awake as they deposited her into a hammock, but the fever had taken hold and everything seemed to swirl in her vision. A new man took charge of her, ushering everyone out within moments of her arrival, and she assumed this to be none other than Master Kort.

Master Kort was a tall, curiously well-groomed man in a blood-stained linen shirt and trousers. Despite the ominous blood on his garb, he seemed far cleaner than the average sailor and he smelled of lye soap when he brought her a cup of water.

This he helped her drink by holding her head, wordlessly tilting the cup and assuming she had enough faculties to swallow. She did, but her throat felt raw and she grimaced as it went down. He hummed at her reaction and moved off to start gathering things she presumed were for her leg. She spotted a bandage, coarse thread and a needle. Her stomach turned and she wished she could pass out. She had a strong constitution, but she truly hated needles. Especially if said needle was meant to pierce her skin.

"What have we got, Kort?" a new voice said from the door.

"I'm not entirely certain, Captain. But I'm guessing an infection."

Trenna squinted at the door, but her vision blurred with fever and the shadows in the room hid the captain from view.

"I need the swelling to go down before I can sew her up."

"How long before she's capable of talking?"

"Remarkably, she's awake now," Kort said. "Would you like me to do an awareness check?"

"How long will it take?"

"Oh, no time at all," Kort said and threw something at her.

Trenna jerked in surprise and raised her hands in defense, but the fever made her slow and she missed. A copper coin thumped onto her chest and she peered at it for a hazy moment. The hammock swayed in response to her sudden movement and she nearly vomited, but somehow managed not to.

"She looks a little green, Captain. I wouldn't stand too close," Kort said. "But otherwise she's awake enough for conversation."

"Right then," the captain said and walked to her hammock.

His eyes were sunk so deep in his face they looked like large circles of shadow. Only the hint of gray seemed to squint down at her. The rest of his face looked like it was stretched thin across his skull, making his jaw and teeth jut out at her. He had a pinched nose comically small for his face and Trenna had to blink several times to make sure she was seeing him right.

"What's your name, lass?" he asked.

Lass? No one had called her that since she was a child.

Then she remembered she looked Human, which reminded her of assassins, and she had the coherency of mind to make up a fake name.

"Milli," she said. "Milli Drake."

She wasn't certain if Drake was a common Human name or not, but it was all she could think of. The captain didn't seem bothered by it, just nodded and looked down at where Kort had begun removing her makeshift bandage. If he was a clever man, he would recognize the wound as martial in nature, so she couldn't risk lying about that.

No, she thought as he squinted at her leg. It was best to stick to the truth as much as possible.

A wave of dizziness threatened to take her, but she closed her eyes and focused on breathing until it passed. When she opened them again, the captain was watching her face, frowning indecisively.

"What happened, Miss Drake? How'd you come to be floating in the ocean?"

She told him most of it, leaving out the truth about her family and Liana's exploits on the mast. It was shocking enough that one woman had fought; Trenna doubted they could handle two.

Humans, she thought with some asperity.

She tried to make the wave sound natural, too. A rogue wave had hit them during the fight and that was the last she'd seen of either ship. The story was more believable that way, or at least she hoped it was. When she finished, the captain hummed and scratched his chin.

"Seems like you've had quite the adventure, Miss Drake," he said after a moment. "Can't see why Horace'd let a girl fight, but it doesn't sound like there was much choice in the matter."

"He ran afoul of my temper, sir," she said with a hiss. Kort had begun scrubbing something into her wound and it hurt like the devil. "Happens to the best of men."

The captain chuckled. "So I can see," he said. "Kort will take good care of you. Soon as he says you're able to move, we'll get you someplace more accommodating."

Trenna finally had the common sense to worry about her new predicament. She was no longer a castaway, but she was now on board an unfamiliar ship with unfamiliar men. She didn't want to think poorly of her new captain, but he did have the face of a skull and if there'd been other women on board, she was certain they would have presented themselves already.

Kort dumped what could only be alcohol into her wound and her leg flared in vivid pain. Trenna cursed and gritted her teeth, gripping the hammock sides in an effort to restrain herself.

"Good gods," Kort said. "I've never heard a woman talk like that."

"Maybe a little warning next time, Master Kort." The captain chuckled as he turned away. "When she gets stronger, I think she might actually hurt you."

She was too busy trying to breathe to respond.

~ * ~

"Brought you some food, Your Grace," Faxon announced as he sauntered into the space. He was carrying a large box and a broadcloth sack.

Kaden scowled at him. "Tell me about my mother."

"Oh, she's relatively safe," Faxon said and dropped the sack beside Kaden's bedroll. "As safe as we could make her, anyway."

"What does that mean?" Kaden asked, shifting to sit up and take the bag. He hadn't eaten in a day and a half, so he was glad for the food; he just couldn't get himself to thank the bastard for bringing it.

"Well, she's not going to drown, if that's what you're worried about. She got picked up by another vessel about two days behind us." Faxon moved to set the box on the floor. "Knowing your mother, however, it's only a matter of time before she charms her way onto the gangplank."

"You don't know my mother at all," Kaden groused.

He didn't know why he kept fighting the man. He was just tired of being patronized and he missed his family. He wanted to be up top with Troy and the others, but he knew Faxon was right about the need to stay out of sight.

"On the contrary, I know your mother a mite better than you do, son." Faxon grinned at him. "Or did you already know she was good friends with a family of criminals?"

"With enough drink, my mother can be friends with anybody," Kaden said.

"Good point." Faxon turned his attention to the box.

Kaden pulled a bread roll from the sack and tore into it. He spotted dried meat and several boiled eggs in the sack as well and tried not to grimace. He had a sudden longing for his father's meat pie, for the scent and savor of onions mixed with carrots and flaky crust. As he chewed on stale bread, he let his mind be transported to the cottage on Vakeshmeer. Late afternoon sunlight lanced through the western windows, a cool summer breeze stirred a house already in motion. His heart ached, remembering the comforting routines of a life they were sailing away from.

Nelek would be by the cast iron stove, teasing Mother about his choice in wives because she couldn't cook to save her life. Liana snickering in the corner, a book open in her lap. Troy lounging beside Liana with a book of his own as he waited for dinner. And by the fireplace, Kaden would be helping Trenna sharpen weapons.

He lingered on that memory for so long he swore he could hear the grind of stone against metal as Trenna made long, sure strokes over her blade. That sound should have warned him, he thought. That purposeful, relentless scrape had been present all his life. It was not the sound of a normal fisherman's life. It was a harbinger of violence, a taunting reminder that his life there was temporary.

A loud crack brought his attention back to the present. Faxon had broken into the box, prying it open with his dagger. Kaden watched the lid splinter and lift but couldn't see what was inside. Faxon's eyebrow lifted, his usually passive features going blank for a surprised moment. Kaden swallowed his bread and stood, moving to Faxon's side out of curiosity.

The box was filled with large, round coins that glinted golden in the dim torchlight. Kaden blinked twice, half expecting the sight to change right in front of him. When it didn't, he knelt beside Faxon and drew out one of the coins. It was heavy in his hand and had a familiar symbol on the face: two lions squared off with a blooming rose in the center. Kaden ran his thumb over the depiction and tried to remember where he'd seen it before.

"Where did you get this?" he asked.

"Captain's room," Faxon said absently. "Next to two other identical boxes."

"Three?" Kaden glanced down at the box again. "Gods above, how much do you think is in there?"

"Enough to warrant a pair of pirates sneaking on board," Faxon said.

Kaden grunted in agreement. Just one box would have been enough to capture attention; three was begging for someone to try to steal them. Why would Horace keep them on his ship? Were they his, or was he transporting them for someone else?

He frowned at the smooth contours of the center rose. He knew this symbol. It wasn't Human, at least not belonging to any Human lord he'd heard of. The islands off the mainland weren't beholden to any of the border lords that ringed Dyngannon, but many sailors brought money through taverns like Big Hearth. He was certain this one was different.

Faxon took a coin and flipped it into the air, catching it deftly a second later. Kaden looked at him, startled by the gleam of amusement in the assassin's eyes.

"What I'd really like to know," he said, shifting to his feet, "is what old Horace has to do with the Duchy of Kiavana."

Kaden faltered and looked back at his coin. That was where he knew this symbol. His father had a silver clasp with the same image on it. He remembered a winter where his parents had argued over selling it. They'd been short on food and Liana had fallen ill enough to make them all worry. He could still feel the tension as he'd spied on their argument. Nelek insisted it was no more than a bauble; Trenna was adamant that they had left enough of their home behind and would not see it sold. Nelek sold it anyway and Trenna didn't speak to him for at least a week.

As soon as Liana was better, Trenna left the house and didn't come back for several days. When she returned she had the clasp. She never did explain how she'd gotten it back. Glancing at Faxon, Kaden had the sudden, uneasy feeling she'd stolen it.

Friends with a family of criminals, he thought.

Kaden stood slowly and turned the coin over in his hand. "Has Kiavana made an alliance with the borderlands?"

Faxon gave him a considering look and pocketed his own coin. "I forget sometimes how sheltered you've been, Your Majesty."

Kaden ground his teeth but made no comment. He watched Faxon replace the lid on the box and slide it behind Kaden's makeshift bed. The haphazard pile of blankets and crates hid the box easily, but Faxon threw a torn bit of blanket over it anyway. Kaden frowned at it, wondering again where Faxon slept because it was never here.

Maybe assassins didn't sleep.

"Kiavana and its two closest neighboring lands, Cadabyr and Mavon, have been allies since your parents went into hiding," Faxon said. "Your esteemed uncle has been working very hard at peace negotiations with Dyngannon, but to no avail. In fact, I wouldn't be surprised if Porrex had declared war on Kiavana by now. He was a heartbeat away from it when we left."

"I didn't think Porrex would openly attack family," Kaden said. "I thought he'd gone to a lot of trouble to frame my mother for Prince Ronan's death."

Faxon moved to the gap separating his hidden room from the rest of the ship. He grimaced, the scar on his face twisting with the expression. Kaden shivered as he watched the man, wondering what ghastly wound had created such a scar.

It seemed odd to him that Faxon kept abreast of political issues. He imagined much of Faxon's interest came from his profession; assassins thrived on political hold, after all. But there was something else here: a bone-deep feeling that Faxon cared about the Dyngannon throne.

"It's been a long twenty years on the mainland, Kaden. Your grandfather no longer cares about subtlety," Faxon said. "If he hasn't declared war on Kiavana by now, he will very soon."

"And you think this money has something to do with it?"

"I think your Uncle Brenson is a very clever man. He'll be looking to secure safety for his people."

Nineteen

Nelek gazed at the golden lions on the coin. They faced each other, their mouths open in a roar and their claws raking at the space between them. The blooming rose kept them from actually touching, but Nelek imagined the two would rip each other apart if they could. If, of course, they weren't just pieces of heraldry.

He'd often thought Kiavana's standard was a horribly accurate metaphor. As he was growing up he'd cast the role of the lions to himself and his father. The rose in the center could be none other than his mother, whose life depended on King Goddard's survival. He rubbed the rose with his thumb, remembering how small and frail she had looked in Brenson's arms.

Nearly thirty years in prison had taken its toll, wasting her down to a thin slip of nothing, all bones and fragile angles. His heart ached, his memory tracing back to the black veins webbing beneath her nearly translucent skin, the price of her magic to save him. Swallowing tightly, he palmed the small coin and stared at his feet.

"Well, now we know why the pirates came," Troy said from the corner.

They were in their room, each of them squashed against a wall as the ship rocked violently. Wind and waves beat the hull of the ship and though Nelek hadn't been permitted out of his room for several days, he'd lived with the sea long enough to recognize a squall. Faxon crouched by the door, one strong hand braced against the frame. Nelek glanced at him, forcing memories of his mother away.

"Three such boxes?" he asked.

Faxon nodded.

"So you think..." Nelek furrowed his brow and regarded the coin again. "You think Horace is an agent of Kiavana?"

"Not this Horace," Faxon said.

"What do you mean, 'not this Horace?'" Troy asked.

"I mean, I don't think the man acting as captain is the real Horace," Faxon said patiently. "It's just a suspicion, and I can't prove it yet."

Nelek frowned. That would complicate matters.

"And you hid one of the boxes?" Nelek asked.

Faxon nodded again.

Curling his fingers around the coin, Nelek felt its solid, cool surface against his skin and took a deep breath. Hope flared through him... things he hadn't considered in a long time came crashing into his mind. He'd held his concerns at bay for so many years it was a relief to face them now.

What was it Trenna had said?

"You can't live in tomorrow and you can't turn back time. You must focus on living here and now. And when it's time to return to Kiavana, you will be ready for it."

Nelek smiled faintly, catching the sound of her voice in his memory. She was right. Somewhere in the middle of his worry for Kaden and the daily struggle to keep Liana tame, he'd managed to forget he was sailing home. Living in exile, even for the safety of his children, had left a burning hole in the center of his chest.

His brother was alive and well and fighting against Porrex. His home was still standing amid all the turmoil and it was time, finally time, to help.

"So you think the captain is one of the pirates who snuck on board?" Troy asked.

"I cannot prove it yet," Faxon said again.

"Which means waltzing in to ask him about Kiavana would be a bad idea," Nelek said. "Horace is bound to notice the missing box eventually. We'll wait for him to come to us."

"And why would he come to us?" Troy asked. "We've been stuck in our rooms all this time."

"He'll go to Brigetta first. He already suspects her of using magic," Nelek said. "But Brigetta will send him to us."

He turned to look at Faxon, who snorted a laugh.

"There's the old duke I know," Faxon said. "That's the happiest I've seen you since the attack."

Nelek faltered, thinking of Trenna in the hands of an unfamiliar and possibly unfriendly crew. They knew she was on another ship, but Faxon and Brigetta had been unable to glean any information about it. He imagined he should be grateful she wasn't drowning, but they also knew she was injured. A healthy Trenna on board a ship of miscreants was nothing to worry about. She could probably drink them all under the table. An unhealthy Trenna, on the other hand, was more worrisome.

He pushed his fear away.

"You can't live in tomorrow," he muttered under his breath. Then he shook his head and refocused on the room. "We have work to do now. Faxon, tell Brigetta to expect Horace's call shortly after the storm has ended. Tell her only to direct him to me."

"Yes, Duke," Faxon said dryly. "Shall I get you some tea while I'm out?"

Nelek met his look of tempered distaste with one of bland tolerance. There were moments when he forgot the assassin was likely insane. Then there were other moments when he couldn't shake the feeling that something else was looking back at him through Faxon's feral golden eyes, something dark and dangerous that made him feel cold. It wasn't a matter of the day, either. It happened frequently, with the abrupt switch of topics or the sudden decision to go right instead of left. One moment Faxon was for them, the next Nelek believed the man would happily slaughter them in their sleep.

It was bizarre and unsettling, but Nelek knew better than to back down. As swiftly as the man turned violent, he also abandoned such attitudes. Faxon grinned suddenly at him, then lifted to his feet and disappeared through the door.

"That man," Troy said after a long moment, "is not right in the head."

~ * ~

"I'm seriously considering taking the leg off," Kort said with a deep sigh.

Trenna heard him and forced her eyes open. Fever raged through her body to the point she feared her bones would melt. They certainly ached, throbbing in time with her heartbeat. Or maybe that was the headache; she couldn't quite differentiate between them anymore.

The dim lantern light pierced her vision and made her head throb. It took several seconds for her to concentrate on the figure hunched over her hammock. Kort was positioned just beside the offending limb. He scowled and stroked his chin, glaring between her leg and the instrument cabinet just beside them.

It seemed to be his custom to talk to himself. She wasn't certain how long she'd been lying in the hammock, but she'd woken several times to the sound of Kort's rich, cultured voice. He had a northern accent, very distinct with its roll of the *r*'s and the enunciation of certain vowels. It was oddly comforting to her. Combined with his cleanliness and his position as ship's surgeon, she chose to believe he was an educated man.

She liked educated men. They almost always sided with peace.

Trenna swallowed hard and tried to work up the strength to speak. Her tongue was a thick, dry obstacle in her mouth and her voice was strained and hoarse.

"Before you go chopping bits off," she said, exhaustion forcing her to pant, "there's one more thing we could try."

Kort started, glancing at her as though he'd forgotten she was there. His sharp gray eyes rounded in surprise and then squinted in humor. He chuckled and moved closer to her head.

"I should have known you wouldn't be asleep."

Trenna wanted to tell him she *had* been asleep and he'd woken her, but took a slow breath instead. She would need what strength she had left if she was going to survive. Kort levered her up to drink some water. Her skin stung where he touched her, the coolness of his fingers biting into her fever. She grimaced and forced herself to swallow.

"I know you don't want to go about as one-legged Milli," Kort said gently, "but the alternative is that I let you die."

"My name isn't Milli," she rasped.

Kort froze, a burnished eyebrow quirking up in mild surprise. "Oh?"

Under normal circumstances, Trenna would have made some remark about the range of intelligence it takes for a woman to tell the truth while surrounded by unfamiliar men. But she was very sick. She could feel herself fading, the life blood in her slowing down, running thick and hot through her veins. Soon it would stop, her heart too taxed to pump anymore, and she would die.

Stupid pirate weapons, she thought miserably.

"I'm not Human, either," she whispered.

At this Kort straightened, both eyebrows lifting. "I think I would have noticed if you were Eldur, miss."

"I am enchanted. This is not my true form." Trenna exhaled shakily. "There is a chance… if we break the enchantment … my leg will heal on its own."

That was only half the truth. What would really happen was her true form would replace the fake one. She just prayed the injury was replaced at the same time. She wasn't a blood mage, so she didn't know for sure. What she did know was that amputation would definitely kill her. Without a mage there to stem the flow, she would bleed out.

"You're delirious," Kort said. "There is no such enchantment."

She met his eyes, willing him to listen. He stopped, his concern growing more pronounced by whatever he could read in her face.

"My name is Trenna Dyngannon. My son is great grandson to King Porrex Dyngannon of the Eldur people. If you do not help me now, Porrex will uncover my son's identity very soon and kill him."

Kort stared at her and she could see him fighting through her words. It sounded ludicrous, she knew, but time was short. Her hammock swayed, tilting the room in her peripheral vision, but she kept her gaze fixed on Kort.

A small part of her wavered. She wasn't a blood mage. She knew this ritual, had gone through it three separate times, and hoped her familiarity with the words would grant her success. But it was risky. Gods above, it was risky, but her options had run out.

"I'm going to get you something to help you sleep," Kort said.

He made to turn away and she summoned every ounce of her strength into grabbing the dagger at his belt. Her fingers curled around the wooden hilt, each joint aching with the movement, but she managed to grip hold and drew it partway from the sheath. Kort whirled in surprise, knocking it from her hand and sending the dagger clattering to the floor. Trenna groaned.

"Miss Milli!"

"My name is Trenna. Please listen to me..."

"What in gods did you mean to do with my dagger?" He crouched down to pick up the fallen weapon and stood again.

She held up her left hand, felt and saw it shake and tremble as she held it aloft. It was far heavier than normal. Kort eyed her open hand with a frown and tapped his blade against his thigh.

"Stab it right through the center," she said.

"What?" Kort asked incredulously. "You want me to stab you?"

"Be precise, Master Kort." Trenna fought a wave of dizziness and blinked hard. "Try not to skid off the bones."

"This is ridiculous. I'm not stabbing you, Miss Milli."

She ground her teeth and shut her eyes. The heavy thud of her heart struck in her ears and she counted three ticks before it came again. Gods help her, she needed to do this now before it was too late.

"What is your first name, Master Kort?"

"Walerian."

"Walerian," she said and opened her eyes again. "If you try to take the leg I will die. I will bleed and bleed and nothing you do will stop it. It is likely that the transformation process will kill me too."

"Milli..."

She cut him off. "You've felt my pulse. You know it is different."

He frowned, unable to contradict her.

"Eldur are different. My body may look Human but the blood is still mine," she said. "It is the key of our magic, Walerian. I cannot do this ritual without it. Please."

She stretched her fingers open, baring her palm for him. For a long, indecisive moment he stared at her. Trenna watched him, silently pleading with him just to do it. The ritual words rolled through her mind, ready for the moment the blade hit her. Walerian exhaled softly, lifted his dagger and thrust it into her hand with startling precision.

The blade slipped through, grazing past small bones in its passage until the tip tore past the skin on the other side. She breathed in mingled pain and relief.

"Lorenessana et all acht tae," she murmured.

A distant roaring sounded in her ears like a thousand horses charging down a hill, moving closer and closer to her. She tried to prepare herself for the impact. It hit her, a full-body smack as though she'd fallen a great distance and suddenly landed on unyielding rock. Her ears tore upward, stretching and peaking into their natural shape, and Walerian Kort gasped.

She tried not to scream.

Silver flame burst from her center, licking around the hammock. Kort took several hasty steps back and pressed against the nearest wall. Trenna saw him from the corner of her eye. He looked terrified and fascinated all at once.

Yes, she thought, an educated man.

The flames seared into her skin, burning it away and replacing it with another form. Hopefully her form.

Her strength waned. Trenna felt it sputter out, felt her heart finally stop, and exhaled. The flames did not stop. She saw them, knew she shouldn't be able to see anything because she was dead, and then, in the flicker of fire, she saw something else.

It took her a moment to realize it was Nelek. He was in his room with Troy on board the *Penelope-Anne*. Troy said something and Nelek smiled, then doubled over in sudden agony. Trenna flinched. She wanted to rush to him, to help, but she knew she couldn't.

So this was what it meant to die with your spouse. How utterly cruel magic was to make her watch.

Nelek grasped Troy's shoulder in an effort to sit upright.

"Trenna," he said, and she heard him clearly.

"I am so sorry, Nelek," she whispered. "I can't..."

"You can," he said fiercely.

Trenna faltered. He could *hear* her. How could he hear her?

"Nelek?"

"Trenna, listen to me," he said, panting as another wave of pain took them both. "You can do this. You can fight through this. It's not our time yet."

"Isn't it?" she asked sadly.

"No," Nelek growled the word. "Because I'm not with you. We will die side by side, do you hear me? It's not going to happen like this."

"I have no strength."

"Then take mine."

No sooner had the words left him than the image disappeared. Her heart struck again and she pulled in a long, gasping breath. Silver flames danced around her, swirling and shifting as they poured back into her center. She lay there for a long while, bewildered and breathing, until she finally lifted her hand and drew the dagger from her skin.

The fever was gone.

Kort made a choking sound and she turned her head to see him. He'd gone an unhealthy pale color and was squashed against the wall in terror. She reached up and touched her pointed ear, confirming she was back in her normal body. Kort's alarmed expression could have told her as much, but Trenna still wanted to feel it for herself.

"I had not thought it would actually work," Kort said in a strangled voice.

Trenna carefully sat up and checked her leg. It didn't feel injured anymore, so she began to unravel the bandages covering it.

"What would you have done if it hadn't worked?" she asked with some amusement. "After having stabbed me in the hand, that is."

She flexed her fingers on the wounded hand, felt torn muscle and cartilage flare to life, and grimaced. The last time she'd done a transformation spell, Noffi had been there to remove the hand wound. She pulled the bandages from her leg, revealing the smooth, unmarred flesh beneath.

Trenna breathed in relief. A wounded hand she could deal with. An infected leg ready for amputation she could not. She only hoped Nelek would not pay too high a price for his sacrifice. She knew blood magic well enough to understand what had just occurred. Magic had swapped their strength, giving her what she needed to complete the transformation.

Gods, please don't have given Nelek the wounded leg, she prayed.

"To be honest," Kort said, "I didn't have high hopes for your survival. A little wound in the hand seemed silly to worry about."

He appeared to have collected his wits. His face was returning to a more natural pallor and much of the fear she'd read in him was gone. He looked more intrigued than anything else as he moved forward to examine her leg. Trenna watched him as he touched the skin where her injury used to be with careful fingers.

With the fever gone she could see him more clearly. He was lean, almost on the thin side, with straight, narrow shoulders and a long neck. His dusky brown hair was tied back, but several strands had come loose and curled around his face. He was young, early thirties at best, and had a goatee that was precisely trimmed. When he looked back at her, his gray eyes glinted with keen excitement.

"Good gods, is your son really a threat to King Porrex?" he asked.

Trenna paused. That wasn't the first question she'd imagined he would ask. She'd been relying on the idea that any Human would want Porrex ousted, but now that she could think coherently she worried she was wrong. Most Humans, after all, would prefer not to deal with anything Eldur. Some could be outright hostile toward her race.

"Yes," she said and checked the room for weaponry.

Walerian hooted with joy, startling her enough that she nearly toppled out of the hammock.

"The captain will be very pleased to meet you, Miss Trenna."

He moved to help her out of the hammock and she became aware of her clothing. She'd gone into battle in her trousers and Kort had cut away much of her right pant leg for easier access to the wound. With a quarter of her trousers missing and her shirt bloodied and ripped, she knew she made for a distressing sight. He seemed to notice the problem as well because he frowned down at her.

"Well, we can't be presenting you to the captain like this, now can we?" he said and clucked his tongue.

He left her to crouch beside a trunk at the side of the room. Lifting the lid, he began rummaging inside, drawing out spare pants and a clean linen shirt that seemed far too nice for a mere ship's surgeon. He started rambling about how it was all going to be too big on her but that the alternatives were worse. She almost agreed with him but forced herself to remember his earlier comment.

"Why will the captain be happy to see me?" she asked, suspicious.

Walerian stopped with his hands full of clothes and blinked up at her. "Well, because we're agents of Kiavana of course."

The breath left her in a rush. Brenson Andreas Dyngannon, Duke of Kiavana, was her brother-in-law. The last time she'd seen him, he was waving them off as they left Kiavana for peace talks with the border lords. Their talks had ultimately failed and they'd been forced to live in exile, but Brenson, it seemed, had managed to organize peace with the Humans. Peace enough to have Human agents sailing the seas anyway.

Trenna laughed.

Walerian stood, his face concerned. "You are a friend of Kiavana, are you not?"

Trenna smiled and took the garments from him. "I'm more than a friend to Kiavana," she assured him. "I'm family."

Twenty

Faxon waited in the shadowy corner of Horace's private room. He stood patient and still, exercising his considerable amount of self-control. He'd already rifled through Horace's personal effects and knew there wasn't anything incriminating there. Not to the untrained eye, at least. Aside from gut instinct the only evidence Faxon had against the captain was a slight change in handwriting on the ship's logs.

Combined with the Kiavanan gold and the sad state of the ship's defenses, Faxon knew Horace had to be a turncoat. If Faxon were right, then this even explained Horace's lack of investigation regarding the spies. He knew Bree had warned the man of it, but nothing had been done.

Before Nelek went and made a fool of himself, exposing them all as Eldur, Faxon needed to make sure he was right. He considered it pure luck that Nelek had suddenly fallen ill. Bree explained it as a marital blood magic, that Nelek and Trenna were bound in such a way that blood mages were not always necessary to conduct a trade.

Given what he understood of blood magic, Faxon wasn't altogether surprised at this. In his mind was the memory of a silver creature with claws and great teeth, its serpentine body curled possessively around Trenna's torso.

Blood magic was powered by something ancient and unique, completely independent of the Eldur people. Independent and, if he wasn't mistaken, intelligent.

He felt the last vial of Trenna's blood under his shirt, pressing into the skin above his collarbone. He'd bled Kaden while the boy was unconscious and his vial lay directly beside his mother's. Faxon wondered what kind of power lay in the would-be king's blood but didn't have time to investigate. They were still on board a ship of traitors, after all.

Observation told him that most of the crew was oblivious. Only Max, Regmond and Horace had displayed any nefarious traits, which gave him some hope that the situation could be quietly handled.

The door opened and Horace stormed inside. Behind him Regmond followed, quickly shutting them in the room. Faxon watched, motionless, in the corner as Horace stalked to the desk and slammed his fist into its nicked, unpolished surface.

Horace must have discovered the missing chest. How very gratifying it was to hear his suspicions confirmed.

"This is a ship, Master Regmond," Horace said, practically vibrating with fury. "There are only so many places a box and a boy could hide."

"We've checked everywhere, Captain. Mister Clarkson is gone," Regmond said. "Why not ask your passengers what is going on? You know they aren't who they say they are."

"Because one of them is a blood mage and I'd prefer to keep my skin from being flayed off in pieces, you cursed fool!" Horace moved to sit in his chair.

Now there was a creative use of magic, Faxon thought, and stored the sentiment away for future use. He'd never tried that before but it sounded fun.

Regmond scowled and looked away. Faxon twisted his wrist, unlatching the blade hidden at his forearm. It slid down until he caught the hilt.

"You really think Lady Isleen turned Gloria into a fish?" Regmond asked.

Faxon scowled. While he was pleased his wife had been able to deal with the assassin, he was also alarmed that he hadn't noticed anything odd about the girl. That rankled his pride.

He held his blade lightly and began to calculate distances. Horace was closer, but Regmond was a better target. They needed Horace at the helm for now.

"I don't know," Horace said. "There's no other way a fish that size could get into Gloria's room. Certainly no one was fishing during the battle."

Faxon flicked his wrist and sent the blade soaring through the air. It breezed past Horace's head, making him stiffen in surprise, just before the dagger buried itself in Regmond's neck. Regmond made a startled choking sound, his eyes bulging. He took one staggering step forward and collapsed face-first into the desk, sending several papers fluttering to the ground.

Horace leapt to his feet, turning around and unsheathing a dagger from his belt. Faxon eyed the bulky man for a moment before slowly emerging from the corner. He shifted his left wrist, unfastening his secondary weapon and letting it slide down to his open palm.

"Sound the alarm and you will be dead before help can reach you," Faxon said, calm and quiet.

"Who are you?" Horace demanded, his gaze flicking to the door.

"That hardly matters," Faxon said, moving enough to give him a clear shot at the man should he try anything. "What does matter is who *you* are. Because you certainly aren't Captain Horace."

Horace blanched, eyes going round in shock, and Faxon smirked.

He loved it when he was right.

"I'd ask you why you would impersonate an officer, but with the gold and the attack on the ship it's fairly obvious," Faxon continued. "It is a trifle disappointing that you're just a thief... an elaborate thief, but still just a thief. But then, I'm just an assassin."

"What do you want?" Horace asked. He licked dry lips and glanced at the cabinet in the far corner. The cabinet where Faxon had found the boxes of gold. "I have money."

"If I wanted money, I would have taken it already," Faxon said, bored by this conversation already.

"Then what?"

"Be quiet, you old fool, and listen carefully." Faxon thumbed the edge of his knife and smiled at the indignant glower Horace sent him. "You are going to cease searching for Mister Clarkson and your missing case. You will leave your passengers alone. Most especially Lady Isleen."

"Why would I do that?" Horace asked, his fists clenching and unclenching at his sides.

"Self-preservation," Faxon said. "If we come to port unmolested I will give you back your case of Kiavanan gold."

Horace blinked at him in disbelief. "And why would you do that?"

"Simply put, I don't care about you. I don't care for money, either," Faxon said comfortably. "But I also don't have a problem killing you. So I feel obliged to make a bargain. Get us to Cadabyr, leave us alone, and you'll have your money."

Faxon walked to the door, steering around the mess on the desk as he did so. Horace turned to watch but made no move to stop him. Faxon glanced at the growing pool of blood under Regmond's body and debated retrieving his blade. He had several more so he didn't really need it, and he imagined the Eldur designs inscribed on the blade would instill further fear into their fake captain.

Pausing at the door, Faxon lifted a finger. "It goes without saying, but if any of your lackeys should cause trouble, you'll lose another box. I know you've at least one other on board. Starts with an M? Mark? No, no. Max."

"How can I trust the word of an assassin?"

He paused with one hand on the door latch. "Normally you buy an assassin's loyalty," Faxon said thoughtfully, "but in this case, you're going to have to rest assured by the fact that I have no interest in who you are."

He looked back at Horace, who stood unmoving behind his desk. Regmond lay heaped over the desk's surface, his legs dragging awkwardly across the floor as the ship tilted in a swell. Faxon considered the mess of dead body and blood for a moment before opening the door.

"Good luck with him," Faxon said cheerfully. "I'm sure you'll be creative."

He slipped out of the captain's room and hurried away, ducking into the closest scuttle he could find. He thought of visiting Bree but opted instead to check on Kaden. He was confident the Horace-Impostor would do as he was told but wanted to make sure Kaden was aware of the situation. The boy was nigh to useless as it was; he didn't need to be caught by surprise.

Twenty-one

"You're certain he's all right?" Kaden asked as he helped Nelek to his feet.

His father grunted and grabbed the ship's railing to stay upright. They'd managed to get him onto the deck, but Nelek was still too weak to stay upright for very long, and Kaden found it quite startling to see his otherwise healthy father so unsteady. There was no wound on him, no signs of fever or illness, but Nelek had no strength. It was like something had reached inside the man and yanked out all his vitality.

Kaden shuddered, wondering just how close to death his mother had to have been in order for magic to do this. It must have been very, very close.

"You could try not to talk about me as though I weren't right here," Nelek said.

Kaden smiled at the irritation in Nelek's voice. "Trust me, Father. If you weren't here I could say a lot worse."

Troy snorted a laugh and offered his arm to Nelek. Liana and Brigetta hovered behind them, waiting to disembark the ship. Kaden watched Nelek eye Troy's arm like it was something venomous.

Then, growling several choice words, he allowed Troy to help him towards the gangplank.

He knew Faxon was waiting to deliver the gold to Horace until after they'd left the ship, but Kaden kept checking for danger anyway. Most of the crew were busy with the tasks of coming to port and unloading, but Max continued to glare at them. Kaden wasn't certain how he felt about paying off the fake captain and his lackey, especially in light of his mother's absence. It was, after all, the fault of the imposters that they'd been attacked at all. Trenna could be right here with them if these fools hadn't attempted to take the ship.

At first Kaden hadn't understood why the imposter had gone about it this way, but he believed he'd figured it out. The pirates needed Kiavana to believe the ship was sunk to avoid any investigations as to the whereabouts of their gold. At least, they needed Kiavana not to look for it long enough for them to melt the coins down and reshape them.

Unfortunately for the pirates, they'd tried swiping the money right in front of the real Duke of Kiavana. Kaden imagined Nelek would have people sent to find these pirates as soon as possible, and there would be nowhere for them to hide.

Kaden glanced at Brigetta and Liana, both of whom were watching Nelek with identical frowns. Nelek was swaying, each step unsteady, making him look almost like he was drunk. Kaden moved forward to take his father's other arm and help him down to the dock, ignoring the man's grunt of protest. Still, Nelek let him help, and they made a labored progression down the plank and onto the dock.

After weeks at sea, the transition from boat to solid ground was startling. It took several steps before Kaden felt at ease again. Gulls squawked and fought over gutted bits of fish along the harbor, mingling with the hum of people in various conversations. A bright blue sky cast the harbor in an almost cheery light, but in the distance Kaden could see the makings of a storm clouding the horizon. He took a deep breath and prayed the storm would be mild. Trenna was still out there, after all.

Brigetta directed them to a small tavern on the far side of the dock and Kaden continued to lead his father, straining every so often as more weight leaned into him.

Nelek was tiring far too quickly.

They moved into the tavern. fishy, salty air transitioning to the closed, smoky scents of a well-used hearth. Many unwashed men crowded the front room and Kaden worried they wouldn't be able to find any lodging. He pushed forward on his own, leaving Troy to handle Nelek. Kaden bumped into several bodies as he headed for the bar, not bothering to apologize. Speaking to one of the men, even to be polite, could land him in an altercation and he wanted to avoid a fight.

They'd made it to the mainland, and while they may still look Human, Cadabyr was a port town. Not everything was friendly at port, and men with hot tempers often sought an outlet, regardless of the shape of one's ears.

Something prickled the hair at the base of his neck as Kaden leaned against the bar. It was strange to think that this was his birthplace and curiosity gnawed at him. Cadabyr stood on the threshold of Eldur lands, just a few days' journey from Kiavana. He wondered who stood as the lord here now. The last reports his parents had received said Lord Willmont Cadabyr died during the siege against Porrex. Human politics were much like Eldur politics; there were lords and knights and serfs and tenants, and titles were kept within the family line. The one thing Humans lacked, or just chose not to conform to, was a king.

Catching the eyes of the bartender, Kaden nodded once and the large, curly-haired man nodded back. After delivering a pitcher of something frothy to another customer, the bartender made his way down the bar, lifting an eyebrow in question.

"A room," Kaden said in answer. "Two if you have them."

The bartender shook his head. "I've only got one left. What with the militia coming through."

"We'll take it," Kaden said and pulled out several silver coins to prove it.

The money caught the bartender's attention. He moved closer to Kaden to inspect it and Kaden laid the coins on the bar. With a satisfied grunt, the bartender scooped them up, storing them away under his tunic.

"Second door on the left," he said, jerking his head toward a back hallway. "Kitchen closes at eight."

"Thank you," Kaden said and turned to help Nelek again.

They squeezed their way out of the crowded room and into the back hall. He heard Liana hiss something but couldn't make it out and glanced back to check on her. Bree slipped closer to the girl's side, nodding once at Kaden to keep moving, which only served to annoy him further.

Gods, that woman was a nuisance. He needed to find a way to get rid of her.

Opening the door to their rented room, Kaden held back a groan. After so many weeks at sea he'd been hoping for a little more space. There were two beds taking up the majority of the room and nothing else, not even a chair. Though, to be fair, he didn't think a chair would have fit. With a sigh he helped Nelek to the closest bed, ignoring several stains on the floor.

Nelek sunk onto the creaky bed, sighing in relief.

"How long until this wears off?" Nelek asked grouchily.

"I don't know," Brigetta said. "I'm afraid that's entirely up to magic."

"Great," Nelek muttered.

"Well we can't go anywhere until Mother gets here," Kaden said. "So you've got some time to rest."

"Oh, I doubt that," Brigetta said, moving to sit on the other bed. She settled with a whoosh of skirts and folder her hands in her lap. "The front room is full of militia. I'd wager they're stopped here for the night and intend to march for Kiavana in the morning."

"What makes you say that?" Kaden asked.

He glanced at the door where Liana and Troy lingered, both of them looking annoyed and uncomfortable. He'd missed something, he could tell, but their body language seemed to suggest they weren't upset with each other at least. Kaden focused on Brigetta again.

"Let's look at the facts, shall we?" Brigetta said. "Duke Brenson is known to support peace between Humans and Eldur. Porrex doesn't like this on the best of days. Add the fact that Duke Brenson happens to consider me both a friend and an ally, and that I escaped from Dyngannon without permission…"

"Porrex would go to war with Kiavana," Troy said.

"Not would, young man. Is. Porrex *is* at war with Kiavana. And this militia is heading to Duke Brenson's aid," Brigetta said, looking fairly proud of herself.

Her eyes were laughing, Kaden thought, a sinking sensation in his gut.

"Oh, gods," Nelek breathed and closed his eyes.

Kaden rubbed his forehead. An ache had settled itself right between his eyes and it seemed to be growing. He suspected the blood mage had known this would happen. The moment she'd set out to find him, the trap had been laid. She couldn't be blamed for Porrex's bloodthirsty nature, but she had to have known this would happen.

There was no way they could leave until Kiavana was safe. Kaden knew his father would need to be there, would need to see his brother alive and secure.

Brigetta had brought them right into the war.

He looked at her, fighting several emotions. They'd been played. Even if Trenna hadn't made the suggestion that they come to the mainland on their own, Brigetta would have mentioned the precarious position Duke Brenson was in and they still would have come.

Gods dammit, he thought, wanting very much to punch the woman in the face.

She watched him so passively, so quietly, that it became an effort for him to stand still. But he did stand still. He stood rigid by his ailing father and stared back at her.

She would not win.

He was the son of Nelek Vronat Dyngannon and Tray'Lana Delphinium Silvanus. He would not let his temper break in front of this woman and he would not fall prey to her schemes. Not ever again.

"Go buy us horses," Nelek said, pulling out his money purse. "We will ride with them tomorrow."

"You really think you can ride?" Troy asked and Liana, almost overriding him asked, "What about Mother?"

"The blood mages can wait for Mother," Kaden said.

Brigetta's eyes flickered. "We've a bargain, you and I, Kaden. I'll not be leaving until it is met."

Kaden clenched his teeth. "You get one hour of my time. Take it now."

She considered him for a long, tense moment, her head tilted just-so, her pale features glowing in the dim room. He could see flecks of red in her eyes and sensed a presence in her that made his hair stand stiff. It was that same presence he'd felt in his hiding place on the ship; he'd recognize it anywhere: that restless, purposeful growling in his gut.

What the hell was it?

"No," she said at last. "You are not ready yet."

Kaden scowled. "You are not welcome in our party, Mage."

"Then I will simply follow you," she said with a shrug. "But I will have Faxon wait for your mother."

Brigetta stood, the movement bringing her intimately close, and she gazed up at him. He forced himself not to look away. It may have been her intention to get him involved in Dyngannon politics, but by the gods! He would decide what that involvement meant.

"I am not your enemy, Kaden Dyngannon," she said. "You might try remembering that in the future."

"Well, you're sure as hell not a friend," Kaden said, glaring down at her. "Now get out."

Brigetta sighed and turned to slip past Liana and Troy, who closed the door behind her. Kaden shifted to the tiny fireplace set in the wall and reached for the striking stones, not wanting to comment further. Out of the corner of his eye he saw his father and realized with some surprise that the man was asleep.

Gods, how long had he been out? And how in hell was Kaden supposed to manage all this with his father so ill?

Rubbing at the throb in his temple, Kaden frowned into the dead fireplace, feeling altogether inadequate and unprepared. Then, with a deep sigh, he began to build a fire.

One thing at a time, he thought.

~ * ~

Liana scowled at the door. Some man had groped her on the way through the tavern and she wanted to go throttle him. Were it not for Troy's quiet intervention she would have done it already, which was annoying her considerably. But Troy was right; they had to see to Father.

She forced her attention back down to where Nelek was sleeping. Troy and Kaden were both snoring in the other bed, sleeping in an upright position each with a leg dangling over the side of the bed and their backs against the wall. She could see the pale outline of Troy's cheek through the gloom and sighed. He looked so peaceful that she almost wanted to curl up there, as though that peace could somehow soak into her through proximity.

He was handsome in an unconventional way, with deep set eyes and a prominent nose. His mouth was lax in sleep, but when he was awake it was nearly always smiling, quirked up at the sides in wicked humor. And he had that wavy red hair mussed about his head, looking rakish and somehow charming, and she smiled at him.

Crossing her arms, she leaned against the door. Guard duty was nothing new to them. Both Nelek and Trenna had insisted they stand guard whenever they were in town or anywhere away from home, but staying awake in the middle of the night was just irritating. She wished she had a book or something. Anything to keep her from dwelling on the danger they were in.

She thought of the way Kaden had stared down the blood mage and her heart ached. He'd looked so commanding, so sharp and composed, and for one tick she'd seen why Brigetta wanted him as king. Liana didn't want to admit it, but her big brother probably would be king someday. He'd get into the heat of battle, rally men to his side, and dethrone Porrex with all the focused skill their parents had taught him.

And when the dust had settled and all was done, he'd slowly fade out of her life. He'd try to keep contact. He might even try to keep her at court with him, but even Liana knew she wasn't made for that sort of life. She was a wild creature, meant for the country and adventure, not some pampered courtier.

No, if Kaden became king, then he would eventually leave her. Maybe he wouldn't forget her, but life as a king would consume his time.

Liana took a shaky breath and looked back at Troy.

Troy'vesk Mavon, the boy she wanted to love with all her might.

She bit her lower lip, remembering the way he had kissed her. He'd been tentative at first, like he was afraid she might hit him, but as the kiss continued it grew more focused. She blushed and looked at the floor. He wasn't the first boy to take an interest in her, but most of the others had been more intrigued by her ears than anything else. She was an oddity to them, and when they grew bored with her they moved on to some other, Human girl.

She found it highly amusing that she looked Human now. All her life she'd been fighting to fit in, to be like all the other girls on Vakeshmeer, and now she finally looked like them. But her strangeness was still apparent. Her spirit was not that of a typical Human female and she could sense it. It was like trying to bottle up sunshine, she thought. No matter what she looked like on the outside, Eldur blood pulsed through her, making her more restless than usual.

Nelek shifted in his sleep, muttering something incoherent under his breath. Liana wondered if he was dreaming of mother. His eyebrows were pinched in concern, but after a moment they smoothed out. She hadn't noticed it before, but her father didn't look the same without Trenna nearby. It was like they fit together in such a way that neither could fully be themselves without the other standing near.

She wondered if that was a trait of Eldur marriage or something unique to her parents. She wanted to believe it was unique, just as Nelek and Trenna were unique as people, but that was likely romantic fancy.

Her gaze turned back to Troy and she swallowed hard.

She didn't love him the way her parents loved each other. Gods, she wanted to, but she just didn't. She wasn't even certain she could love him like that, or that she even wanted to, for that matter—which made her behavior these past months unforgiveable.

How could she explain to him that she couldn't need anyone the way her parents needed each other? The very idea terrified her. She wasn't completely certain why, either. She just knew, down in her core, that a love like that could destroy her.

But she did love Troy. She did. She felt it in her gut every time he grinned at her. And yet, she would survive if he chose another above her.

Gods, what did that say about her?

Exhaling through her teeth, Liana moved to wake Kaden. It was his turn to stand watch and she needed to try sleeping. They were meant to ride for Kiavana in the morning and this would be her last chance at a bed for several days.

Twenty-two

Rain pattered against the wooden pier, thumping on Trenna's hood in a purely obnoxious manner and she pinched her cloak tight. She surveyed the miserable port town, trying to convince herself that it would look better in sunlight. Gray clouds hung heavy in the sky, blotting out the sun, and where the pier ended at the muddy road she could see several large puddles.

Gods alive, how she hated the rain!

Apart from the crew of the *Rosalie*, which had just made port an hour or so ago, the harbor town seemed thinly populated. One or two people rushed between buildings, running from shelter to shelter in whatever quest had called them out of doors. But for the most part the streets were empty. It had the feel of being recently deserted, like a great mass of people had drifted through the town not long ago, their spirits having left some kind of ghostly fingerprint on the place.

She'd bet her best shirt that an army had been through. She'd seen it enough in her lifetime to recognize the signs of recent, heavy use on a place.

"The *Penelope-Anne* is still moored," Kort said as he hurried up to her, looking frazzled but collected all at once. It was a stranger manner she'd learned about him early on, like he was comfortable in his skin but out of sorts with the world at large. "But Horace and all the passengers are gone."

"Gone?" she asked with surprise.

Why would Nelek leave her? He had to know she was coming.

The hair on the nape of her neck prickled and she eyed the town again.

"I don't know about Horace, but the word is that every able-bodied man was heading for Kiavana." Kort glanced at the ship. "Lord Cadabyr rallied everyone in response to Kiavana's distress call. Good man, that Cadabyr."

"So there is an alliance between Cadabyr and Kiavana?" she asked.

"Oh, yes. Ten years strong."

Trenna exhaled and bit her lower lip. So that was the army. Her heart pinched a little, jealousy knocking at her pride. She and Nelek had tried to forge such an alliance twenty years ago and Porrex had botched it all to hell. While she was gratified to think peace was possible at all, a part of her wished she and Nelek had more of a hand in it. They'd bled and sacrificed for this; they deserved to be here.

Nelek deserved to be here.

"I need to go tell the captain," Kort said, adjusting his hood for better protection against the drizzle. "He'll want to know."

"Yes, of course," Trenna said, turning to smile at him. "Please give him my thanks. If ever I need to sail again, I'll know who to look for."

"Do you know what you're going to do?"

She laughed, amused at his concern. Kort had a knack for worrying. This probably made him a better physician, but it also made him ask some ridiculous questions. Questions like how she was going to find her family, if they'd have a spare set of clothes for her, or what she would do if some brute tried to make off with her person.

That last one was her favorite. He'd gone several shades of white when she listed all the ways she might convince such a brute to leave her alone.

Humans, she thought, always assuming a woman alone was a woman in distress. It would be their undoing one day.

"As a matter of fact, I do," she said. "If Kiavana has called for aid, then Gideon Mavon should be marching. I intend to intercept him."

Kort blanched and wiped water off his face. It was a futile move because the rain kept coming, but that didn't seem to matter.

"What? On your own?" he asked.

"Not quite on her own," a familiar voice said.

Trenna looked to where Faxon was wandering up to join them, looking as miserable as she felt, his cloak sodden with rainwater and his shoulders hunched from the wind. Perhaps Nelek hadn't left after all.

Faxon scowled at her, stopping just beside Kort in a clearly dangerous way. She was mostly certain he wouldn't kill the Human but decided it best to get Kort away from them.

"There now, Walerian," she said. "I've an escort. You needn't worry anymore."

"So it would seem," Kort said, eying Faxon with frank distrust. "You're quite certain you'll be all right?"

"Absolutely," Trenna said. "Now go before the captain starts to wonder where you've been."

Kort nodded agreeably and hurried off for the ship. Trenna turned back to Faxon, who grunted in annoyance and began leading her down the pier. She followed, wondering what might have caused the man's mood beyond the rain. She hadn't thought anyone hated the rain as much as she did.

He didn't speak until they'd made it into a small, questionable inn and he'd locked them into a private room. Removing her hood, she glanced at the single bed and chair that occupied the space, registering that Nelek was not here.

Her heart squeezed a little in disappointment.

"I see you've your ears back," Faxon said.

"A necessary transition," Trenna said, spotting a familiar bag beside the chair. Nelek had left her personal items with Faxon. She sighed. "They were going to take my leg."

He made a noise in the back of his throat but she didn't bother explaining further. If Brigetta hadn't already told him what such a thing could do to an Eldur, then Trenna wasn't about to.

"Why Mavon?" Faxon demanded from the doorway. "Our spouses are marching into battle without us. Why would you detour?"

So that was the reason he was upset. He'd been spying on her before announcing himself. How typical.

Trenna removed her cloak and hung it on a peg near the door. The room was cold, the effects of the storm seeping through many cracks in its wooden walls. She thought about wrapping the bed's blanket around her, but it looked in desperate need of a good washing. So, she headed for the fireplace instead, kneeling to start stacking firewood into its mouth.

"Trenna," he said, a warning note in his voice. "I will not ask again."

"I didn't think you would," she said, stuffing several bits of straw under the larger logs. "And in answer... I never said you had to come."

"Do you have any idea what happened to Nelek because of your 'necessary transition?'"

Her hands froze on the striking stones.

"I imagine," she said slowly, "he was sapped of strength for quite some time."

"He still hadn't fully recovered when he rode off for Kiavana."

She closed her eyes, cringing from the thought of her weakened husband. "Nelek is very stubborn, but also intelligent. He won't push himself beyond his breaking point."

"Not like you would, you mean."

She opened her eyes again and refocused on the fireplace. "Well, I suppose he is smarter than me in some ways."

"I know you love him, Trenna. How can you leave him vulnerable like this?"

"Because he'll be vulnerable if I don't do this," she said.

Faxon frowned. "What do you mean?"

She sighed again, frowning at the fireplace before her. She didn't like explaining herself to this man but it seemed necessary.

"Gideon Mavon is marching from the west, but he has to pass through a section of Dyngannon lands to reach Kiavana," Trenna said, working as she spoke. "And right in the middle of this patch of Dyngannon is an Eldur outpost. I know because I built it. If Gideon is not warned, he will march right into a trap, and whatever help Nelek might have gotten will be lost."

"How do you know Gideon is marching?" Faxon asked.

"Because the very large shipment of steel that the *Rosalie* just delivered is meant to be transported by road to Kiavana, where it is supposed to be met by Gideon himself," she said.

"But Gideon won't make it through this pass without intervention," Faxon said.

"Exactly."

"So get someone else to warn him. It doesn't have to be you."

"I repeat... you don't have to come," she said and took up the striking stones.

She could feel Faxon glaring at her, but continued to beat the stones together until a spark finally lit in the straw. Trenna leaned forward and blew on the small flame until it ignited with a healthy whoosh and heat flared through the fireplace. She sat back with a satisfied smile.

"I know you, Trenna Croften. You would not detour like this just because one man might fall into a trap."

She lost her smile. No one had called her Croften since she'd married. That was her adoptive name, the name she'd shared with her oath brother Brockley, and it carried the weight of loss with it. She tensed, remembering a tight tunnel with gloomy light, heavy with the scent of blood. She could still feel the dead cold of Brock's skin under her hand as she'd been forced to say farewell.

Twenty years gone and the grief was still fresh, sharp like the bite of steel in her gut. Trenna clenched her hands and forced the memory away.

"You're right," she said. "I have several reasons for warning Gideon. But as I said before, I'm not asking you to come with me."

"No, you're not asking, but that doesn't mean you don't expect me to follow."

"Oh, trust me, Faxon, I'd prefer it if you didn't," she said, sliding her boots off. She placed both before the fireplace to dry and rubbed at a sore spot on her shoulder.

"But you know I will."

"Unfortunately, yes." She stretched her legs out, letting her bare feet get nearer to the blazing fire.

She wiggled her toes as warmth seeped into her skin, relaxing for the first time in several weeks. For however small and nasty this room was, it at least had the benefit of staying still. It might not be as clean as she'd like it to be, but it would do for the night.

"I could tie you to my horse and drag you to Kiavana," Faxon said lowly.

Trenna sensed a real threat in his voice and looked up to where he hadn't moved from the doorway. His shoulders were tense and his fists were in tight balls at his sides and his glower made the scar on his face vivid white.

"You could try," she said, slow and calm. "But I wouldn't suggest it."

She'd lost her weapons in the ocean, but Kort had given her a saber. She felt the scabbard pressing into her right hip and calculated distances. Faxon was fast, and he could use blood magic. She would have to roll back or to the side if he came at her. Maybe she could grab the blanket and throw it at him, give her a minute to get to her feet. And only if she absolutely had to would she draw the weapon.

Faxon was a crazy bastard, but he was a crazy bastard currently working on her side. And she had fond memories of his Uncle Pendaron that made it difficult to stomach his death.

They stared at each other for a long, strained moment before he cursed and looked away. Trenna was a trifle surprised to have won that stare-down but tried not to let it show. Faxon almost always got his way.

Or cheated his way out of people.

She would have to watch what she ate around him. He liked herbs and things that could make people more complacent.

"My wife is not a warrior," he said.

"No, but she's surrounded by highly trained swordsmen," Trenna said, watching him closely. "And while we're on the subject... how does a man like you get married?"

"Blackmail," he said with a smirk. "And she's not surrounded by your family, she's trailing them. Kaden threw her out of the entourage."

Trenna winced and clucked her tongue. "Figured out he'd been played, did he?"

She felt a spurt of parental pride that her son had worked through the mage's machinations. Eventually he'd piece together that Trenna had known where this was going and she imagined he would be furious. He didn't have quite the temper Liana did, but he could still get worked up. He would demand to know why she hadn't warned him and she would have to remind him that she *had*, every day of his life. Maybe not about Bree specifically, but certainly about Dyngannon.

They were bound to end up here, marching toward a war none of them had started. Better for it to be now, while she and Nelek were still of some use to them.

"You don't seem surprised," Faxon said, dragging her out of her thoughts.

"That you had to blackmail your way into a marriage?" she asked and winked up at him. "I'm not. I've told you before and I'll tell you again, you don't get enough sun. You skulk in the shadows so much you look like a ghost."

He snorted a half-laugh and moved to sit on the bed. Much of the violence seemed to seep out of him as he shook his head and sighed. He looked more Human and vulnerable than she'd ever seen him in her life, and she almost regretted teasing him.

"There are times, Trenna, when I hate you so much it makes me like you again."

~ * ~

After three days' hard travel, they finally found the road. Trenna made them ride cross country, which Faxon was all right with since he'd never cared for taking the main road anywhere. Main roads were common. It was in the side paths that you could find the truly interesting things in life. On the main road people were predictable, staying in oft-used camping spots and holding tight to traditional hospitality and polite conversation. Off the beaten path, it was anyone's guess what you might find.

Like a Human assassin addicted to Eldur blood and an exiled Eldur general.

Well, "addicted" was too strong a word for it. He could stop drinking it whenever he pleased; it just meant giving up magic at the same time. And he wasn't ready to give up magic.

Trenna urged her horse onto the road and dismounted. He watched her crouch, gloved fingers gingerly touching the ground as she inspected it. Summer sun lit off her blonde hair, setting the silver streaks into a faint shimmer and Faxon remembered the silver tint from his vision. Trenna had never mentioned seeing anything through a silver haze, so he imagined this was unique to consuming blood.

"Good," she said. "They haven't been through yet."

"Eventually you're going to tell me what this is all about, right?" Faxon asked, idly picking at his saddle horn.

She stayed on her haunches and looked up at the mountain pass. The Ffrey Mountains climbed high to their right, a natural border separating Dyngannon from Human lands. Midday heat baked the land, giving them an expanse of dry, brown desert until the more distant peaks shadowed the horizon. Faxon rubbed his shoulder and followed her gaze, imagining several more days of travel through waterless desert.

"Reinforcements," Trenna said and pushed to her feet again. "I hope."

He frowned. "Gideon is already marching this way. We could wait here and intercept him but I can tell by the way you're moving that isn't your plan."

"Gideon isn't who I'm talking about," she said, moving to her horse again.

Faxon glared down at her, seriously considering ramming a blade into her throat. It'd serve her right for dragging him in the opposite direction of the fight.

She patted the dapple-gray mare he'd managed to steal for her and began rifling through the saddle bag. She hadn't asked him how he'd acquired their horses but he imagined she'd guessed it. He wasn't exactly known for his law-abiding tendencies, after all. Bree would have given him a sour look by now for the action.

"Then who?" he asked, battling down his temper.

"Porrex is a snake," Trenna said as she pulled a small, leather-bound book from the saddle. "But he's a clever snake. He'll have sent most of my regiment to the outpost on the other side of this pass. It's remote and so far away from Dyngannon's heartland to be considered exile."

"Your regiment?"

"Yes." She took a sealed envelope from the book and stared at it for a moment.

"Why wouldn't he have just executed all of your men?"

"You're thinking like an assassin again, Faxon," she said. "Name me a better way to lose the confidence of your subjects than to mass execute the very people who have been awarded for keeping the borders safe." She paused and turned to walk towards him. "No, at least some of my men are alive. And it's time I returned to them."

He could read a new, determined set to her shoulders as she approached him. Sometimes it was hard for him to remember that she was several years his elder, but the way she looked at him now brought those years into focus.

"This was never about warning Mavon, was it," Faxon said, squinting down at her.

"It was partly about warning Mavon," she said and held up the envelope for him. "This is from Lord Tibitus Mavon for his son, Gideon. When they arrive you must insist on handing this directly to His Lordship."

"What? No. I'm not staying here." Faxon eyed the envelope in her hands.

She really had gone insane.

"Gods help me, Faxon. I am trusting you with a matter of honor." A muscle jumped in her jaw and she kept the envelope between them. "I know that's outside your range of expertise but you're the only one I've got at the moment. Once he's read it, tell him General Lana Silvanus has gone ahead to clear the path for him."

He leaned forward in the saddle, bringing his face closer to hers. "Do I look like a scrubby urchin you can lose in an alley? I'm not a messenger, Trenna. And even if I were, I'd have to be out of my mind to accept such a thing. You think Gideon is going to thank the person who delivers a death letter from his father?"

"No, probably not. But he's not going to kill you either," she said, sounding reasonably sure of herself.

"And how do you know that?"

"Because I knew his father," she said. "And if Gideon is half the man his father was, he'll respect your life regardless of the sad tidings you bring."

Faxon scowled down at her. She was as unmovable as a fortress wall, ivy-green eyes hard and sharp on his face. For the briefest of moments, he felt fear in the pit of his stomach. She reminded him of the serpent creature from before. The silvery streaks in her hair exactly matched the shade of its scales, and her lithe, trim body looked coiled, prepared to pounce.

He reached out and took the envelope.

Trenna glanced between his face and the parchment before turning. She walked to her horse and mounted again in one smooth movement.

"I wouldn't be surprised if they were here by nightfall," she said. "Try not to kill anyone. While I can guarantee he won't harm you for the letter, he is still a commander and won't take kindly to losing a soldier."

"It's not like I constantly kill people, Trenna," he said, tucking the envelope into his vest. "Give me some credit."

She gave him a flat, dubious look, then clucked her tongue and spurred her horse forward. They shot up the path, headed for Dyngannon, and Faxon let go of a breath. Dust curled in the wake of her passing and for one tick he actually admired her. She was somehow methodically reckless.

He touched the crinkled envelope in his vest and shook his head, searching the area for a good place to make camp.

Twenty-three

Nelek woke to the sound of hushed conversation just outside his tent. The rain had lessened, but he could still hear the light patter of water on the tent overhead and the smell of wet dirt and grass permeated the place. He opened his eyes, examining the shadows of his small space, and realized it was still dark outside. Dark but early, he thought, recognizing other sounds from beyond his thin walls.

The army was breaking camp, preparing for the final march to Kiavana.

His gut tightened, thinking of Kiavana under siege and his brother in danger. Gods, they'd been gone too long. He should have insisted on coming back the moment Kaden and Liana were of age.

Wiping a hand over his face, he held back a groan and scowled up at the tent's flimsy roof.

"He's not ready," Liana's voice carried from somewhere close by. "We should wait and let the army go ahead without us. Maybe a full day of rest will help him recover his strength."

Nelek frowned, knowing exactly who "he" was. His children had been fighting him on this since they'd left Cadabyr harbor, and while he wasn't fully recovered, he was getting better by the day. Even with all the riding they'd been doing, he could feel his muscles gaining strength, returning to normal.

"You know he won't go for that," Kaden said. "This is his brother. Would you stay away if I were in trouble?"

"Well… no, but maybe we can convince him to wait for Mother. I mean, what good is he if he's half dead before we get there?"

Nelek grunted and sat up. Joints popped and muscles ached with the sudden movement, reminding him of the hard ground he'd been sleeping on for four days. Five days riding, four nights camping and he was ready for a real bed and solid walls. He was ready, he thought as he crawled out of the tent, for his wife to return to him, dammit. The brisk chill of high mountain air assaulted him from all sides but he ignored it to focus on his children, carefully rising to his feet.

Gods, his body hurt. He was getting too old for sleeping on the ground.

"That's quite enough of that," he said. "I'm hardly half dead, Liana."

Kaden and Liana jolted in surprise, exchanging guilty looks before turning to face him. Liana crossed her arms and frowned at him.

"But you're not at full strength either," she argued. "What if we charge into battle and you die? Mother would come back from the dead just to beat us all senseless!"

"You have to admit," Kaden said, "that an undead version of Mother is a trifle alarming."

"It's not up for discussion, Evaliana. Now, start breaking camp," Nelek said, ignoring the levity in his son's voice.

He would not have his children conspiring against him, so he stared hard at his daughter, waiting for the stubborn flash in her eyes to fade. There were times when he wondered if Trenna had been like Liana at this age, full of fire and restlessness but without wisdom to guide her. Time had tempered Trenna; he'd seen it especially after Kaden was born, but Liana was too young and had none of those experiences to quiet her. And he thought there was more to his daughter's restlessness than a simple call for adventure.

There was a line of bitterness running straight through her, a lonely ache Nelek had sensed in her since childhood. He'd done everything he could to help her, but Liana was far too independent to tell him the root of the problem.

Sometimes he wondered if she even knew herself.

Liana finally looked away and moved off for the other tents, her shoulders stiff with anger. He watched her tall, lean form disappear into the shadows and shook his head. Gods help him, but he wished he understood the girl better. He turned back to Kaden, who was watching him with an unsettling intensity.

"Where's Troy?" Nelek asked, just to change the subject.

"He went to listen to Captain Targyll's battle plans," Kaden said. "We thought it was best to know what they were planning."

"Good idea," Nelek said.

"You did teach me that knowledge could mean the difference between victory and defeat, Dad."

"Well, I'm glad something stuck," Nelek said and stretched his back.

Kaden chuckled, glancing out at the shadowy forest. For a moment he looked so much like his mother that Nelek felt his heart squeeze tight. Something in the set of his jaw, the resigned expression on his face was so much like Trenna, it was uncanny.

"You know you'll be a liability," Kaden said. "I understand why you have to go, but we need to be realistic about this."

Nelek gave his son an unamused look. "I'll be fine."

"If you're not up to regular strength before we get there, you'll need to stay close to Liana," Kaden continued, ignoring him completely. "She's better than Troy and me, combined. She can keep you safe."

"Keep me safe?" Nelek asked, bristling under the very idea. "Kaden Andreas," he said, lowering his voice in case someone walked by. "I may be your father but I am also the rightful Duke of Kiavana and I will not be..."

"Mollycoddled?" Liana asked from behind him. She was carrying a heavy bag, which she dropped beside the tree next to Kaden.

"Usurped?" Kaden suggested.

Nelek glanced between his children, disliking the banter more and more. They were impossible, absolutely impossible.

Liana wrinkled her nose and started pulling the pegs from his tent. "Too much irony, brother. After all, what have we come here to do again?"

"Oh, right," Kaden said, pushing away from the tree. He walked up to Nelek, that same expression on his face, and stopped just before him. They were the same height, bringing Nelek face to face with his son. "This isn't up for debate, Dad. You die, so does Mom. You can't ask us to watch as we become orphans for an uncle we've never met."

"Brenson..." Nelek started to say but was cut off.

"Is your brother. I know. And I'm your son."

They stared at each other, Kaden calm and Nelek less so. He did see their point, of course. Neither of them knew Brenson and they had no real ties to Kiavana but still... Still, Nelek couldn't stomach sitting this out.

"I'm not asking, Dad. I'm telling you. Either we do this my way or we don't do it at all," Kaden said, dead serious.

Nelek felt his heart pick up speed as he fought for a reply. For one aching second he saw the king in his little boy, a king that Noffi had managed to recognize before he'd even been born. But this was Kaden. Kaden who used to sneak into bed with him and Trenna during thunderstorms and who would giggle at fish because of their funny "fwippers" when he was a babe.

"All right," Nelek said at last, desperate to push the memories aside. Something about them was heartbreaking today and it made his chest squeeze tight.

Kaden relaxed and sent him a roguish wink. "Good, then," he said. "Now, let's go meet Uncle Brenson."

~ * ~

Brigetta kept pace several yards away from Kaden and his family. Rain drizzled around her, soaking her horse and making her hood droop so low over her face that she kept having to push it up. She caught Troy glancing back at her several times but he offered no apology for her displacement, which was fine. She could serve them better at a distance anyway.

Kaden's hood whipped off his head in a sudden gust of wind, and for a split second, she saw a glimmer of silver around him. It seemed to pulse twice, shimmering in the gloomy rain, and then faded from her view. Bree frowned.

Magic did not often display itself like that, not even in royalty.

She dug her nails into her palm, drawing blood so that she could see Kaden more clearly. His false Human form blurred out of view, leaving her with the true visage of the boy to inspect. It was unnatural for him to have the silver streaks in his hair. Normally that trait was passed on by the father, not the mother, and Evaliana had no such distinguishing mark to her. There was no denying Kaden's parentage, either. While he had Trenna's eyes, his bone structure more closely matched Nelek's.

How, then, was it possible for Kaden to have the silver in him when his father did not?

Glittering, clear silver ensconced the boy with bits of gold flashing in chaotic rhythm. She had to reach through her memory for family trees.

The silver came from Tray'Lana, there was no doubt, but the gold was from somewhere else.

She changed her focus to Nelek and wasn't at all surprised to see the former duke shrouded in blue and gold. And there was the difference, she realized, as she focused on Kaden again. All Eldur had a line of blue in them, a trace of family lines watered down through time, a taint of commoner blood running through every noble house.

All Eldur save one: Kaden Andreas Vronat Dyngannon. For whatever reason, magic had pooled together in this one boy.

Bree sat straighter in her saddle. Noffi must have seen it. Even before the boy was born, Noffi must have seen the difference. That was why she'd sent Bree to fetch him, why she'd kept silent all those years—because Kaden was powerfully different.

If Porrex had known, the boy would have been dead inside of a year.

Bree shuddered, pulling her cloak closer. She hoped Faxon hadn't been arrogant enough to bleed the boy. Gods only knew what would happen to her husband if he tried consuming it. And now that she knew how special he was, Brigetta resolved herself to the task of seeing Kaden on the throne.

Before, it had been duty alone that took her to Kaden, but now it was something more, something built into the fabric of her being.

The Eldur people needed Kaden and she would see that need met.

Her horse slipped on the muddy ground and she had to direct it to the side. She felt the powerful push of the creature's flanks as it found steady terrain and climbed the hill. Everyone had stopped at the crest of the mountain, so Brigetta found herself side-by-side with Troy. He flashed her a faint smile, before looking down at what had stopped their progression.

Kiavana sprawled through the valley below and Brigetta became grateful for the view magic gave her. She could see masses of soldiers converged on Kiavana Fortress, all of them blazing Eldur blue. What Humans she could spot on the battlements appeared like shadows, their dark forms scurrying between cover as they returned fire on the invading army. Even under siege the fortress looked defiant and formidable. Bree saw a streak of fiery arrows as they soared from the battlements and into the swarm of soldiers below.

"Gods above," Troy said.

"Targyll's taking his men to the southeast," Kaden said. "I don't suppose you've got any suggestions, Father?"

Bree looked over at where Nelek was mounted beside his son. His hood hid most of his face, but she could see the grim line of his mouth as he surveyed the action below. She would have preferred General Lana to be with them, but Nelek knew Kiavana, had grown up in this valley, and might prove more competent than she imagined.

At least she hoped he would.

"Targyll is assuming reinforcements from Mavon's lands will be here soon," Nelek said. "He'll be leaving his flank open. We should guard them until help arrives. Kiavana doesn't have enough men to help drive this army off, and Targyll's forces are mostly militia. We need to get into the castle without being noticed."

"Right," Liana said with an unladylike snort. "Just how do we go unnoticed through that?"

They all stared down the mountainside. The place was surrounded by chaos and violence, a teeming mass of shadow and movement. From their vantage they could see the surge of bodies as they clashed against the castle walls.

Bree's heart fluttered in her chest as she imagined Kaden down there being cut at left and right. No, they couldn't go that way.

Clearing her throat, she waited until everyone in their little group turned to look at her and tried for a confident smile. Kaden appeared annoyed by her nearness and she felt her smile slip, rushing to explain herself before he could banish her again.

"I know you don't particularly like me," Bree said, holding out a placating hand. "But I am married to one of the more notorious criminals of Kiavana. It should go without saying that there are other ways of getting inside the castle."

"You can get us in?" Troy asked.

"I know a way," she said, nodding once.

"What way?" Kaden asked. He sounded impatient, so she turned her focus on Nelek.

"There are tunnels beneath the castle," Bree said to Nelek. She knew he would catch her meaning. His mother had built them, after all. "My husband showed me one or two. Most notably he showed me the passage Trenna used when she was avoiding you, Duke."

Nelek stiffened in his saddle and scowled. "That was a long time ago. How do you know it's still functional? It could have collapsed."

"It could have," she conceded. "But it's either that or we try knocking on the front gate."

Nelek eyed her for a long moment before he turned to his son. She watched as the two conferred for a moment and pulled her hood a little lower on her head. Icy flecks of rain still managed to pelt her chin and neck and she suppressed a shudder. She caught Troy staring at her and smiled at him. The boy didn't smile back.

"All right," Nelek said, bringing her attention back to the conversation. "We'll follow you to the tunnel."

Twenty-four

Trenna found the outpost in better repair than she'd remembered: four wooden towers, four wooden walls, two gates positioned at the north and south. There was a ditch at the south wall that was full of spikes and pitch.

It was far more than a watch post now. It looked more like a first line of defense, which alarmed her to some degree. If she failed here, then Gideon's forces would have to fight their way through, delaying the advance on Kiavana.

If, of course, they could get through.

Trenna frowned down at the structure and shifted on her rocky perch. The small outcropping in the mountainside gave a perfect vantage of the fort and the road through the pass, which was why she had been forced to subdue a watchman before moving in for a better look. She glanced back at the unconscious soldier and silently apologized to him.

He was familiar, but it took a moment for her to remember his name.

Gus, she thought. Rimaford Gus, but he hated his first name.

He was one of her best scouts and she was gratified to see him still alive. His being here also meant she'd been right and the rest of her men were here as well. But that didn't mean she could just waltz into the outpost uninvited.

She left the ledge and moved to start stripping Gus of his gear.

"I'm sorry about this," she said to the comatose man, "but I need a word with your boss."

Gus was lean and trim, so his uniform mostly fit. Like just about everyone else, he was taller than she, so she had to roll the pants at the waist and tuck the excess fabric into her boots. She donned the standard issue Dyngannon armor: padded leather chest guard and thick pants in familiar browns and brackish greens. She kept her own boots, but made a point of stowing the soldier's cavalry footwear high up in the tree. She wanted him delayed as long as possible, after all.

Then she tied her hair up into a tight bun and grabbed his helmet. The helmet itself had a flat, wide nose guard that hindered her view, and it took a moment for her to adjust to it. Satisfied that she looked remotely like a soldier again, she started down the mountain, sliding through steep shale, and keeping close to trees as much as possible until she reached the bottom.

Above her, dark, heavy clouds were coming in from the east and the wind was pushing through the pines at an increasing rate. The chill bit through her newly donned armor and she shivered, sending another silent apology to unconscious, unprotected Rimaford.

Trenna paused long enough to scowl up at the sky, more problems snagging her attention. Rain could delay Gideon and a delay could cause the collapse of Kiavana. If Kiavana fell, they would be forced to seek refuge in the borderlands, maybe even retreat back to Vakeshmeer and into hiding again. If Kaden chose to fight for the throne, his position of strength would be diminished almost beyond repair.

They would have to start over, and all the sacrifices that had already been made toward the peace process would have been for nothing.

Tibitus Mavon would have lived in exile for nothing.

Brock would have died for nothing.

She tripped on a rock and nearly fell over, but caught her balance and stood still for a moment.

Battling down a swell of grief, Trenna took a long, slow breath and started walking again, ducking several branches as she went. Crushed pine wafted from the loam underfoot and the ground was soft enough she knew she should be concerned about footprints, but she brushed that aside in favor of speed.

Reaching the main road, she stopped and ducked low, peering out to ascertain the normalcy of the soldiers milling through the fort gates. They all looked purposeful, their minds set to their tasks, and she could sense that they weren't expecting anything out of the ordinary today. They certainly didn't expect their former general to sneak past their defenses, she thought with a smirk.

A returning hunting party carrying a large buck approached the gates and she left her hiding space to join them. Blending into the small group, she ducked her head and began counting steps, praying the group wouldn't suddenly notice the new addition. Keeping close enough to the group to appear part of it, she crossed through the gates unnoticed and then veered off before someone could get curious.

Things were orderly inside the fort. She spotted one group of men training in a section near the east wall and another group sorting through weapons at the smithy. High up on the battlements she counted three patrols and at least two of them kept glancing down into the yard. Still, most of the soldiers seemed relaxed and she got the feeling they'd been stationed there a while.

Locating the northeast tower, Trenna walked toward it with her head low. If she were remembering correctly, the captain's office would be inside, and she needed to see exactly who was in charge and have a brief word. Maybe she could convince them to just let Gideon pass through, no harm and no bloodshed. It was a long shot, but she had to try.

Glancing up, she caught the eyes of a passing soldier and quickly looked away. He was familiar, too familiar, and by the frown on his face she had the feeling he felt the same way about her. She heard him stop behind her but kept moving, ducking inside the tower door just as he called for her to halt. She closed the door, shutting him out.

His name flashed into her memory as she lowered the heavy wooden bar to seal the tower closed: Sergeant Covin, third platoon, fourth squad. But he'd been wearing different cords of office now and it appeared he'd been promoted.

A good choice for sergeant major, she thought, but what had happened to Fennily?

"What the hell are you doing?" someone said from behind her.

Trenna ignored the nagging question of her former sergeant major and turned to face the tower. Light played off the wooden walls, setting the space into a warm glow and showing the indolent drift of dust in the air. Cleaning obviously wasn't a priority for this captain. A ladder led up into the tower proper, connecting with the outer wall and the battlements. Depending on how close a patrol was, she had all of two minutes to explain herself before the entire fortress was alerted.

Three people stood in the room, two at the far end, hovering over a desk. One was at the ladder and it looked like he'd just come down. She recognized all three of them.

Lieutenants Bervam and Holster, both good men and among those she counted as friends, stared at her with growing agitation. She saw Bervam slide a knife from his belt.

Captain Malory Levat, on the other hand, watched the proceedings with a great deal of humor on her face. Trenna wasn't certain if she was proud or annoyed that Malory stood as captain. The woman had been ambitious when Trenna knew her, and that ambition had never counted how many men she lost on the battlefield. As long as the objective was met, Malory felt vindicated. That was why Trenna had never promoted the woman.

Annoyed, Trenna thought as she glanced over their faces. *I'm definitely annoyed.*

Malory of all people would resent being stationed here. Things were not going to go as smoothly as she'd hoped.

"Give your name and rank, soldier," Holster demanded.

Trenna hesitated a moment longer, debating the pros and cons of giving them a fake name, but there seemed to be no reason for it. She reached up and removed her helmet, knowing the streaks in her hair would be answer enough—there were only so many Silvanuses to go around, after all. But she spoke anyway, overriding the audible intake of breath that pulled through the room.

"General Tray'Lana Silvanus," she said. "But I go by Trenna now and I think I'm still technically a duchess."

"Lana?" Bervam asked, shock thick in his voice.

Trenna focused her attention on Malory, who bleated an absurd laugh. Trenna shifted her weight on her feet, let her knuckles graze the scabbard at her side just to remind herself the weapon was there. She watched as Malory leaned her arms on the table and continued to chuckle, her shoulders shaking with her mirth. The dim light made her auburn hair shine, and Trenna had a brief memory of the day they had met.

Porrex had ordered Malory's placement under Trenna's command. The king had rightly assumed that many in the army, and particularly in Trenna's favored unit, held more loyalty to her than to the throne. Trenna could remember the full, wide smirk Malory had given her after receiving her first order. Trenna didn't know what that order had been anymore, but she'd felt a foreboding even then.

This woman was trouble.

"You have no idea how long I've waited to say this," Malory said. She looked up and met Trenna's eyes. There was that smirk again. "Arrest her."

Holster and Bervam exchanged glances but didn't move. Trenna calculated the distance between her position and the ladder. Bervam was in the way, but she was confident she could get by him. It was a straight shot from the ladder to the top of the wall. She wasn't certain what she would do once she got there, but her main problem was just getting out of the room.

Gods, she'd been so stupid. She should have known Porrex would put someone like Malory in charge.

When nobody moved, Malory's round face twisted into a scowl. She eyed Holster in particular and straightened. Trenna heard the squeak of the woman's gloves as she bunched her fists and coached herself to remain calm. Malory's infamous temper was about to surface again. Trenna felt a pinch of guilt that her men had been subjected to this woman's rule.

"Lieutenant Holster," Malory said curtly. "Need I remind you what will happen to your sister and that lovely niece of yours should you disobey me?"

The full extent of the problem became terribly clear to Trenna. Holster's tortured expression told her everything she needed to know, and Trenna felt a surge of rage well up inside her.

Blackmail. Her men were being held hostage here.

She rolled her left shoulder slowly and took a deep breath, cursing Porrex to every layer of hell. Holster turned and walked toward her, drawing his sword at the same time. Out of respect for the man he was and the family he was protecting, Trenna kept her hands away from her weapons. She still had the helmet in her right hand and as he neared her she began beating it lightly against her thigh, feeling the cool, solid metal smack into her leg.

"Bervam, call the master at arms and tell him to prepare for a prisoner," Malory said. "His Majesty will be quite pleased to know we have apprehended his son's murderer."

Trenna gripped the helmet so tightly the metal edge bit into her skin. She remembered Ronan the day he died, the sound of his voice shouting for her to get to safety, and for a long, aching moment she saw the arch of Porrex's blade as it came down. She had to fight to breathe again as Holster stopped in front of her. He had his sword to the side and in striking distance but he made no move to touch her.

She met his blue-gray eyes and battled her grief down. Malory was trying to upset her, trying to pick a fight, and she knew it.

"It's all right, Holster," Trenna said. "I understand."

"General," Bervam started, but Malory cut him off.

"She's not a general anymore, Lieutenant. And I gave you an order."

Trenna glanced at Bervam, who looked as though he'd swallowed something particularly sour. He was older than Holster but not by much, and she could see by the tense line of his shoulders that he was ready for action. All she had to do was make her move and he would support her. Trenna met his gaze and held it. She searched her memory for family relations, trying to see who he was willing to risk on her account.

"I am so sorry, Lana," Holster said.

Trenna turned her attention back to the lieutenant in front of her and gave him her most compassionate smile. "I know, Holster. So am I."

Trenna swung her helmet up, smashing it into the side of Holster's head before he could move. He grunted in pain and half turned, leaving his left side wide open for her attack. She kicked him in the hip, high enough to know she hadn't permanently damaged him but still solidly enough that he staggered away, collapsing against the nearest wall.

Malory cursed and drew her weapon, advancing quickly through the room. Trenna met her halfway, dodging the first three strikes Malory sent without grabbing her own sword. She saw Bervam close the upper hatchway, shutting out any patrols that might happen by and hear the fight. Trenna made a mental note to kiss that man, and finally slid her sword from its sheath.

Trenna caught a high strike with her sword and quickly deflected it to the side. The strike was disconcertingly slow and Trenna wondered if Malory was playing some sort of game, or if the captain had simply stopped with her daily practices.

"Why did you come back?" Malory asked and swung again.

Trenna leapt back, sliding behind the desk to keep a barrier between them.

"Oh, you know, I missed the food," she said. "I tried making my own gruel but it just didn't taste the same."

Malory thrust her sword at Trenna's midsection, reaching over the desk and over-extending herself. The woman was relying on her longer reach, but hadn't factored in speed. Trenna avoided the strike and nearly took the advantage, but she wanted some answers before she put the woman down.

"Where's my brother Varren these days?" Trenna asked.

She believed she knew the answer to this one. Her youngest brother, Navell, was general of the Dyngannon army now. He was a staunch Porrex supporter and had been highly rewarded for his service. It didn't hurt that he was also the illegitimate son of the king. There was no hope for Navell; she knew that.

But her older brother, Varren, was another story entirely.

"Last I heard, he was laying siege to Kiavana Fortress," Malory said with a sneer.

Trenna's heart skittered in her chest, but she nodded. Her suspicions were confirmed. If Porrex was holding the families of her soldiers under threat of death, she could only imagine what he would do to Varren's children.

Malory rushed around the desk and Trenna retreated, blocking several strikes until she felt the back of her heel touch the wall. She saw Bervam restlessly shifting on his feet, watching the fight with half-lidded eyes as though he'd already figured out what she was doing. The rest of what Trenna wanted to know she could get from Bervam, so she determined to end things.

"You'll never get the throne," Malory said. She was panting and had a wild, unsettled look in her eyes.

"Well, that's good," Trenna said with a smirk. "Because I don't want the throne."

"Then what do you want?" Malory asked, launching forward before Trenna could answer.

Trenna stepped to the left and let Malory's sword bury itself into the wall. She turned quickly, grabbing Malory's wrist and slamming her elbow into Malory's nose at the same moment. The shock of the strike sent tingles into Trenna's fingers but she held firm to her weapon. She felt bone crush and saw blood spurt over Malory's mouth and chin but she didn't stop there.

She wrenched Malory's hand away from her weapon, twisting her arm into an awkward position, before kicking the woman in the knee. The crack of bone snapped into the room and Malory cried out. Trenna released her arm and let the captain topple to the ground. Dazed, Malory stared up at her as Trenna finally leveled her sword at Malory's throat.

"I have one more question for you, Captain," Trenna said quietly. Part of her recoiled at what she was about to do, but she tightened her grip on her sword and focused. She searched for that dead place inside her, the place that held all of her anger and pain, and let it come to the surface as she posed her final question. "Just how many of my men did you get killed while I was away?"

Fear flickered in Malory's eyes.

"I want a number, Captain," Trenna growled down at her.

"I…"

"Do you even know?" Trenna asked. "Or have you been so focused on your own advancement that you couldn't be bothered to record it?"

Malory glared up at her. "They're not your men anymore."

"They will always be my men," Trenna said, lowering the sword and ramming it down into Malory's chest. She kept her gaze locked on Malory's face, watched as the woman passed from shock to pain to nothing within the space of three breaths. The captain slumped and went still, her last breath hissing out into the quiet room.

Trenna withdrew her sword and silently cleaned the blade on Malory's shirt.

"Two hundred forty-three and a quarter," Bervam said after a moment.

Trenna looked up at him. "I'm sorry?"

"The number of men who died under her command," Bervam said. "Two hundred forty-three and a quarter."

"You're going to have to explain the quarter bit."

He smiled without humor and nodded down at Malory. "She cut off Ruskin's hand when he made a supportive comment about you during a briefing."

Trenna closed her eyes and sighed, no longer sorry for the dead woman and more enraged at the pain Ruskin must have suffered.

She couldn't really remember who Ruskin was, but he'd stood up for her and that counted for something in her book. Once Kiavana was secure, she would have to find the man and see if she could repay him somehow. She couldn't replace his hand, but she could do something.

"Did you come alone?" Bervam asked.

She opened her eyes and smiled grimly at him. "Did you think I would try marching into my own men?"

Bervam snorted a laugh and shook his head. He took his helmet off, revealing a tattoo-laden bald head that he began to rub in thought. He stared alternatingly between Malory's body and Holster, obviously trying to map out what his next move should be.

"I don't imagine you came here just to check on us," he said.

Trenna looked at Holster. He was unmoving by the barred door and she felt a surge of guilt for taking the man down. "You know me," she said. "Everything I do has more than one purpose."

"So you did come to check on us."

She smiled and winked up at him. "Don't tell the others. They might be insulted that I did. You're the best of the best, after all."

"Not a word," Bervam promised with a grin of his own. "But what should I tell them?"

Trenna sheathed her sword and crouched beside Malory. The blue and white cord dangling from the woman's shoulder signified her as captain. Trenna reached out and yanked it off her uniform before standing again. She turned to Bervam, who had moved to her side, and held out the cords.

"I can't ask for their help, Bervam. Not with their families in danger," Trenna said. "Tell them I'm going to save Kiavana and then I'm marching on Dyngannon. I *will* save their families. They just need to stay here and follow orders."

"Orders from Porrex," Bervam said with a scowl. He shook his head and stepped away from the cords. "He'll send us straight after you and you know it."

"Yes, I do," she said and moved forward. Taking his hand, she pressed the cords into his palm, closing his fingers tightly around it.

It wouldn't be official, not inside Porrex's army, but her men would know. "With any luck he'll attach your unit to Varren's battalion. He'll suspect that I won't want to fight my brother and my own men. You'll have to go to war with me."

"Lana..."

"Captain Bervam," she said firmly, emphasizing his new title until he clamped his mouth shut. She saw a muscle jump in his jaw as he held back another protest, and met his gaze. "Go to war with me, Captain. Keep these men and their families safe."

"And just how am I supposed to do that if we're going to war against you?"

Trenna grinned at him and winked. She turned and moved to Holster again. Taking her helmet back, she put it on her head and started for the ladder. She was going to have to run if she wanted to stop Gideon from marching straight into the fort. Her horse was half a mile away and it would be dark soon.

"General Lana, I'm serious," Bervam said from behind her. "War isn't exactly a safe place. You've tasked me with the impossible."

"I have every confidence in you, Captain," she said without turning. She gripped the ladder and started to climb, pausing when she reached the top. "There's going to be a large army marching for Kiavana. I'll lead it away from the fort, but I'd prefer it if your scouts conveniently stayed out of the west forest range."

"Right," Bervam said with a note of bewilderment. "Stay out of the west."

Trenna smiled down at him, nodded and pushed the hatchway open.

Twenty-five

It might have been a manor once, but age and weather had crumbled the walls to an almost unrecognizable state. The dilapidated building was situated on a small inlet with a wide, undisturbed lake surrounding it. The forest seemed to be doing its best to overtake the half-collapsed conical towers. Vines and weeds crawled over pale stone, and peppered throughout what he could only assume had once been the courtyard were small trees sprouting between bits of rock.

Troy dismounted his horse and frowned at the ruins. They'd ridden most of the night, resting the horses just long enough to eat, and this was what they were looking for?

He didn't know whether to be sad that a manor could be reduced to such a state or amazed at the relentless growth eating away at it.

"What is this place?" Liana asked.

Her voice was quiet, almost reverent, and when Troy looked at her he saw her shiver. She kept hold of her horse's reins, but her blue gaze was fixed on the highest wall. She looked unsettled, maybe even frightened, and Troy frowned some more. He looked back at the ruins, trying to see what she saw, but could only find rough rock and greenery. He wondered if something in her Eldur blood was speaking to her, but was afraid to ask. Everything dealing with magic troubled him and he wasn't certain he wanted to know.

"This was my mother's home," Nelek said.

"Grandmother Auliere?" Kaden asked as he dismounted.

Troy moved to tie his horse to the nearest tree. He felt painfully out of place and needed to do something, so he busied himself with unloading his saddle bags. He knew Kaden would scoff at him for thinking it, but when it came to Dyngannon family history, he knew he didn't quite fit. He was Human, the son of their mother's rival, and while Trenna had always called him a sign of peace for the future, his love and involvement in their family could not blot out the past.

Pulling his sword from the saddle, he started strapping it on, barely listening to the conversation behind him.

"Brenson and I used to spend hours swimming in the lake," Nelek said. "There's a river that runs just past Kiavana fortress and ends right here. In fact, one of my earliest memories of your mother is in that river. Our camp was overrun and we had to flee."

"I know this story," Liana said, tying her own horse just beside Troy. "You both nearly drowned, didn't you?"

"Yes," Nelek said with a smirk. "We took turns dragging each other out of the water."

Brigetta stepped into Troy's view and he lost track of the conversation. The mage gave him a smile that he imagined she meant to be compassionate, but the pale light caught in the red flecks of her eyes and for a second all he could see was the glint of ruby. It made her look frightening and almost demonic, and Troy had to suppress the impulse to step away.

"So, where is this tunnel?" Kaden asked.

Brigetta tied her horse nearby and began rifling through her own bags. "It's underneath us, young Kaden," she said.

"I searched for nearly twenty years to try to find the tunnel connecting mother's manor to Kiavana," Nelek said. "Are you telling me you've found it?"

Troy heard the disbelieving tone in Nelek's voice and watched Brigetta. The fine bones of the woman's face lay in elegant curves, perfectly symmetrical and without flaw. They'd been traveling together for weeks now and Troy had yet to find a freckle on the woman. Though now that he thought about it, Liana and Trenna were the same in Eldur form. That seemed a trifle unfair to him.

"You are forgetting that I have something you do not," Brigetta said and unclasped her cloak. With one fluid motion, she removed the garment and swished it up onto her horse's flanks.

She rolled her sleeves up, exposing the intricate twine of tattoos running over her arms. Then she pulled a dagger from a sheath at her thigh and pressed the edge to the base of her thumb. She looked up at Troy and winked before turning to face Nelek. Thus far, Nelek had not asked the obvious question and Troy applauded the man for his patience. Troy himself was wondering what Brigetta had that Nelek did not, but in the next instant the answer became obvious.

Brigetta cut her palm open and murmured something under her breath. Troy was standing so close to her that he could see the moment the blood turned to flame. It seemed to leap out of her skin, a crimson color so deep it was unnatural. Mesmerized, Troy stared as the flame rolled over her hand and ignited her tattoos. All at once the woman lit up, each line of her tattoos smoldering against the pale backdrop of her skin.

Troy took an involuntary step back. He heard Liana breathe a curse and felt gratified he wasn't the only one shocked. Kaden's eyes grew round and startled and he gripped his hilt as though in reflex. The only one unmoved by the display was Nelek, who simply grunted and watched the mage.

Brigetta took three steps forward and knelt. For a second, Troy swore he saw her tattoos begin to move, curling around her arms as she pressed her palms into the ground. A hollow sound growled through the courtyard. The moss-laden stones in front of Brigetta seemed to roll away, each one grinding against the next as it lowered and disappeared into shadow.

A moment later, Troy saw what was happening. The stones were reforming into a staircase leading down. An archway built itself at the bottom, rock and dirt all moving at once, until finally the growling stopped. He could see a long tunnel beyond the archway, and the sudden blaze of torch light puffing to life along the walls.

Brigetta slumped forward, shaking. Her tattoos slowly faded to their normal gold and for a moment they all stood in stunned silence.

"Well, that explains why I could never find it," Nelek said at last.

"Indeed," Brigetta panted and carefully got to her feet. "Shall we proceed?"

Nelek glanced at Kaden, who shrugged and then nodded.

If his friend was worried about walking through a magical tunnel that defied all known engineering, Troy couldn't tell. And under normal circumstances, Troy would have balked at the action himself, but these were not normal circumstances. They were in Dyngannon, Trenna was still missing, and there was a siege going on at the end of this tunnel.

No, he thought, there was nothing normal in his life anymore.

So he stepped past Brigetta and started down.

~ * ~

Kaden kept pace with Troy. Torches lined the stone walls, giving light to the low, arched ceiling and the briny green lichen that covered it. The place was permeated by a rich, earthy smell and something sweet like crushed leaves in the autumn. The cold seemed to reach out from the stones themselves, slipping past his cloak and tunic as though he were bare from the waist up.

But that wasn't the worst of it.

Something was here. Some presence lived here, he could feel it. It was there at the edges of his awareness, moving quickly through the shadows, taunting him.

"So, how long are you going to keep your Human skin?" Troy asked.

The words were hushed, but they'd been walking in silence so long it startled Kaden to hear his friend's voice. He glanced at Troy, who met his gaze briefly and gave a roguish wink. Nelek and Liana were behind them and the mage was up front, but none was close enough to hear them.

"I hadn't decided," Kaden said. He was grateful for the distraction, so he concentrated on Troy. "Why do you ask?"

"Oh, you know," Troy said with a wink in his direction. "I miss your ears."

Liana snorted somewhere in the dark behind them. "Got a thing for Eldur ears now, do you?"

"Well, I'm rather fond of yours..." Troy said, lowering his voice.

Kaden prayed his father was preoccupied at present, not wanting to deal with *that* argument today. "I thought we'd stay Human at least until we reach Kiavana," he said. "Then, we can change back if we need or want."

"Ah, but how will Brenson recognize Nelek if he's still... you know... looking like a Human?" Troy asked.

"His wit and charm should do it," Liana said.

Kaden pinched the bridge of his nose and sighed. He hadn't actually thought beyond the need to reach Kiavana and now, well, now they were almost there. Maybe they should stop and undergo the ritual, he thought.

An unpleasant prickle crawled up his neck as he remembered the pain from the spell. Trenna had said that returning to Eldur form would be equally unpleasant, and he wondered if maybe they could just stay Human forever. Surely that could keep them safe when they finally left Kiavana and all this war behind.

Not that his father would leave.

There was just no getting around it; Nelek wouldn't abandon Kiavana or his brother, not again. And where Nelek was, Trenna would be.

Gods dammit all to hell, he thought and clenched his fists.

He didn't know how long they'd been trudging through the dank corridor, but he imagined it must have been a while. The walls started to change, becoming tighter and more twisted. After several turns he noticed another tunnel leading off to the left. It was shadowy and unlit, and he realized it was the first crossroad he had seen since entering.

He was curious and wanted to ask about it, but that would require speaking to Brigetta and he didn't want the woman to get the wrong idea. He was still annoyed that they'd been forced to rely on her help. He'd been manipulated before, mostly by Liana trying to get something she wanted, but Brigetta had deliberately withheld vital information. She had known Porrex would march on Kiavana the moment she left Dyngannon and she'd meant to dangle that fact in front of his parents, forcing them into action. He couldn't stomach the idea that anyone would play with people in such a manner; it was detestable.

They came around another corner and stopped. The tunnel branched off in three directions, each of them dark. Kaden realized a moment later he really shouldn't have been able to see anything because the torches weren't lit here. He glanced at Brigetta, who stood three paces in front with her hood back. Her arms were bare again and the thin, spidery tattoos looping over her were glowing a soft white, illuminating their path.

He frowned.

He still didn't like the mage, but he had to admit she was useful.

"You can come out now," Brigetta said. Her voice had a soft lilt to it, mellow enough to feel almost comforting.

Kaden was about to ask who she was talking to, when he spotted movement in the tunnel to his left. He gripped his hilt in surprise and shifted to face the danger. He sensed more than saw Nelek and Liana move up behind him for support.

"Brennie thought you might be coming," a new voice said from the shadows. Whoever it was sounded male and young.

"Duke Brenson," Brigetta emphasized the title with a tinge of asperity, "is a very wise man. Now come out of there before you spook the guests."

"The guests are already spooked," the man said, but he emerged anyway.

Kaden watched as a shadowy form detached from the wall and stepped into view. He almost thought it was Faxon, but on closer view realized it couldn't be. This man was tall and bony, but not in an unhealthy way. He had the look of a boy fighting into manhood, all clumsy limbs and awkward angles, but when he moved there was a practiced stealth to him, as though he had spent hours and hours learning to move without being noticed. It was the same sort of silky movement he'd seen Faxon use, and Kaden wondered for a moment if this was the assassin's son.

"Nelek, meet Lodas Mylonas," Brigetta said without looking at them. "He's the son of Cahira and Sprague Mylonas, who you might remember from before your exile."

Nelek grunted and Kaden knew by experience that his father was unsettled. He almost looked over his shoulder to see if he could read anything in Nelek's expression, but stopped when he noticed Lodas's attention on Liana. Kaden tightened his grip on his hilt and eyed the man. Lodas didn't seem to care about the warning. His mouth twitched into a half-smile and his amber gaze stayed on Liana. Kaden fought down the urge to strangle the twit.

"Nelek, you say?" Lodas grinned at Brigetta. "My, my, Auntie Bree, aren't you winning points with the duke today."

"We need to get into Kiavana," Troy said.

Kaden felt gratified that Troy was as annoyed with this fellow as he was.

"Well yes, that would be why you're skulking about in the tunnels, wouldn't it?" Lodas said. He turned and gestured toward the middle tunnel. "Follow me, then."

Kaden scowled as they started to move again, thinking that if Lodas continued to look at Liana that way, he was going to throttle the man.

Twenty-six

Faxon leaned against the dry, cold boulder that was acting as the back of his tent. The rain had mostly stopped but he could still hear the light drip-drop of water against his fabric shelter and imagined it was coming off the branches of a nearby tree. Trenna's prediction that Gideon would be there by nightfall had proven false, which gratified him to no end. It seemed the girl wasn't as clairvoyant as she pretended to be.

The mighty Trenna Croften had been wrong about something.

But he did not ride after her to gloat, dearly as he wanted to.

Sadly, he found himself following her instructions, huddled in his little shelter with a small fire hissing just outside of the cover. He'd managed to keep the fire during the storm only because of magic. The logs and ground circling his fire were drenched and yet the flames danced on, impervious to the rain. Faxon stared hard into the twisting fire, watching the shimmer of crimson at its heart.

Reaching into his tunic, he pulled out a vial of Trenna's blood from his hidden pouch and hesitated. That cursed serpent creature hadn't shown itself since the last time he'd utilized her blood, but he could still sense something lingering inside him. He'd walked blindly into that encounter and it had left him a little shaken.

He turned the vial in his hand, watching the thick red substance smear across the inner glass.

There was something in her blood, something powerful. Whether Trenna was aware of her connection to this creature remained to be seen, but Faxon had the distinct impression that it didn't want Trenna to know. Or maybe it didn't care if she knew. He really wasn't sure.

What he did know was that this entity was interested in him almost as much as he was interested in it. So he pulled the stopper from the vial, took a deep breath, and drank.

He was prepared for the shift in color this time. He blinked once, watching as Brigetta's red tinge was overcome by Trenna's silver. When he finally managed to get home, Faxon would have to start annotating which family lines bred what colors. The colors weren't an accident; they meant something, he just didn't know what. He thought maybe nobility had a play here. Trenna was, according to Bree, from old Eldur nobility. Perhaps magic was more prominent in such families precisely because they were noble.

"You're on the right path," a familiar voice said.

Again, the voice was more inside him than out, but this time the creature manifested itself as a great silver owl. It perched near his feet and Faxon noticed that the red glow of his unnatural fire still shone in his vision. He could see the flicker of scarlet reflecting off the owl's shiny surface. If he didn't know better, he would say the creature was made of metal, but its feathers ruffled up and it shook its massive wings and there was no denying it was made of softer stuff.

Faxon looked back to the fire and frowned. The change in colors had not been able to affect the heart of the flame. That seemed significant.

"You conjured that fire using the red," the owl told him. "Why would it change?"

Faxon wasn't quite certain how to respond. He knew he hadn't asked about the fire out loud, which led him to the disconcerting conclusion that this creature could hear his thoughts.

"Of course I can, I'm inside you," the owl spoke again. "Really now, I thought you were clever."

He grunted, annoyed.

Great, he thought. *Magic is a cheeky bastard.*

"The arrogance of mortals never ceases to amaze," came the reply. "Tell me, creature. You are not Eldur and yet you've mastered the blood. Have you paused to consider the ramifications?"

"Ramifications?"

"You did not think a steady diet of Eldur blood would go without consequence, did you? Even now it is changing you, pulsing through your veins with single-minded purpose."

Faxon glared at the bird. Its head tilted to the side and its large, opaque eyes blinked once. He had the sense it was laughing at him, and for good reason. If he were forced to be honest with himself, he had not really considered what the blood might be doing to him. It had always been something he harnessed, something he was in control of. Only now did he realize that the blood itself was equally harnessing him.

But to what end?

The owl did not respond. Faxon stared at it, willing it to answer, but the creature did not move, didn't even blink. It just gazed at him in silence, the pop and hiss of his campfire mingling with the constant drip of water against his tent. A cold, crawling sensation slid up his spine as he gazed at the creature, remembering with vivid clarity their first encounter and the question it had posed.

"No, the question is, what are you?"

Only now when he heard it did he notice the mocking tone of the creature and the question took on new meaning.

What have I become? he thought. And then he remembered it was still changing him, at that moment was coursing through him, altering him from the inside out.

"Good gods," he whispered. "What will I be?"

The owl spread its wings and with a great flurry of movement launched into the air. Faxon had to lean forward to see around the shelter roof, but he caught sight of it flying away. It swooped low to the ground, passing across the road before disappearing into the forest. Faxon pressed his hand against the vials under his shirt. He felt the smooth contours of each slender vial through his tunic and tried to quell the spark of fear in his chest.

It had been a long time since Faxon had been afraid. The emotion was almost foreign to him, but he recognized it now, recognized it and immediately smothered it with fury.

Perhaps the blood was changing him, but it would be a change *he* chose, not it.

Movement on the road caught his attention and he forced those worries away. Riders were coming, and lots of them. Faxon scooted out of his shelter and began to tear it down. He yanked the blanket he'd chosen for a roof away from the boulder, feeling the edges tear where he'd anchored them, and quickly rolled it up. It was wet and made his hands ache with cold, but he ignored the sensation and focused on the company of men heading toward him.

He tied the rolled-up fabric to his saddle, which was spread out in the dry spot of his camp, and glanced over at where his horse was tethered. The large brown gelding flicked its ears and pawed restlessly at the ground, no doubt reacting to the approaching men and their horses. Faxon willed the horse to calm down, murmuring the incantation Bree had taught him at the beginning of his training. He felt the magic go to work like a buzzing under his skin, saw the glow of silver seep into the horse until it relaxed.

Faxon pulled the envelope Trenna had left him from his inside pocket and moved to stand at the side of the road. He did a mental tally of his weapons just in case Gideon Mavon proved less honorable than Trenna had supposed. He had two knives strapped to his forearms, hidden under his sleeves, and one more tucked inside his boot. His sword was in the open, dangling at his left leg in a well-worn scabbard that used to belong to his Uncle Pendaron.

Three men on horseback spurred ahead of the company and headed directly for Faxon's position. Faxon crossed his arms and waited, hearing the light rumple of parchment in his left hand. He decided he could use magic to replace their hearts with some inanimate object if he needed to. He'd always wanted to try that but refrained because of Brigetta. She always got cross with him when he killed using magic. She didn't seem to like him killing with swords or poisons either, but when he used magic she got particularly angry.

But Bree wasn't here today.

"What is your name, sir?" The centermost man on horseback sounded civil enough and looked to be in charge. He stopped his horse two paces from Faxon and frowned at his sword.

He was brawny, with wild brown hair running to his shoulders and a full beard that even Faxon felt envious of. Even if Faxon hadn't known the politics surrounding the four border lords, he would have known this man to be a member of Gideon Mavon's force. He was dressed in a red and gold uniform with the heraldry of a phoenix embossed on his chest in black—the signature of the house of Mavon.

"Sir," the bearded man said again, "your name."

"Mylonas," Faxon said, eying the other two men.

Both were stout, uniformed, and kept checking the surrounding trees. Faxon imagined they were searching for signs of an ambush and made sure not to move. He wouldn't give them an excuse to try to kill him.

"And what are you doing out here?" Beard asked.

"Waiting for you, actually."

Beard's eyebrow lifted. "Oh? And how did you know we would be out this way?"

"You're marching toward Kiavana," Faxon said, trying hard not to sound bored. "There are only so many ways you can go."

"Well, you found us, so what is your business?"

Faxon almost liked the bearded fellow. He was a no-nonsense, get to the heart of the matter sort of man. So, Faxon held up the envelope with Mavon's seal in full view. Beard tensed and his dark eyes narrowed at the parchment. Faxon thought about saying something more but there didn't seem to be a need. Beard ordered the man on his right to ride back and fetch "His Lordship." Faxon watched and waited as man and horse galloped back toward the approaching army.

"Where did you come by this?" Beard asked.

Faxon debated telling him about Trenna, but decided it best not to mention her yet. She was once the general of Dyngannon and many of these men probably lost loved ones because of her. Now that he thought about it, Faxon wasn't certain what would happen when Trenna returned.

"I was told it was a matter of honor," Faxon said instead. "You can see the seal is unbroken. I've kept my end of the bargain."

"A matter of honor?" Gideon Mavon asked as he rode up.

There was no mistaking that red hair and towering figure. Even on horseback Gideon seemed a head taller than the rest of his men. And now that Faxon was getting a good look at him, he could see the similarities to the boy, Troy'vesk. They each had long, sharp noses and eyes that mixed between green and blue. Their mouths were different. Troy had a smaller, thinner mouth where Gideon's was wide and full. And where Troy still clung to youth, all lean muscle and lanky legs, Gideon was a man in his prime.

"Yes," Faxon said.

"Yes, my lord," Beard corrected him.

Faxon merely eyed the soldier and held out the envelope again. Gideon moved his horse in close and reached down to take it. He leaned back in his saddle and stared at the seal for a long moment, his face creased into a deep frown. Then he cracked the seal and slid the parchment open. Faxon watched as Gideon read, hunting for any sign of aggression.

It would be easier if Gideon simply attacked. Then he could kill a couple of men, leap on his horse and speed away before the army could catch him.

But Gideon did not attack.

"Where is General Lana Silvanus?" Gideon asked without looking up from the paper.

"She went ahead to clear a path for you."

Faxon wasn't certain if he was amazed or annoyed that Trenna had been right. Just because the woman knew his father didn't mean she could know how the son would react. And yet, by all appearances,

Gideon seemed to be doing exactly as she had predicted. Gideon ordered Beard to alert the men there might be trouble ahead and prepared to take his troops into the mountains.

"Are you friends with Lana Silvanus?" Gideon asked him as Beard spurred away.

There was a deceptive civility in Gideon's voice and Faxon smiled up at the man, pleased to see there was more to him than Trenna could have guessed.

"As a matter of fact, no," Faxon said. "She tolerates me because she has to, but I'm fairly certain she would have my head on a stick if she could."

That was exaggerating things a bit. He didn't think Trenna wanted him dead, but he knew she didn't appreciate his meddling with her children.

Gideon considered him for a long minute. Faxon twisted his left wrist, unhooking the clasp holding his blade in place. He caught the dagger with his fingers, keeping his hand out of view as he waited. Gideon frowned down at him, then grunted in displeasure and shook his head.

"Very well," Gideon said. Then he turned to the remaining soldier. "Put him in irons."

Twenty-seven

Nelek held the hilt of his sword so tightly his fingers ached. He kept pace just beside Liana and watched Brigetta and their guide with intense focus. He knew Lodas's parents, knew the part they had played in the fight against Goddard, but found no comfort in it. The entire Mylonas family seemed to have criminality bred into them; there was no telling what this Lodas was capable of. So, Nelek watched him and prayed he could protect his children if needed.

The tunnel grew smaller and he had the sense they were moving uphill. Rough, familiar walls tightened around them until they had to walk single file. He let Liana pass him, squinting in the dark so he could make out the shape of her shoulder as they continued to walk. Brigetta still acted as a light source, but with so many bodies between him and the mage, Nelek felt almost completely swallowed by shadows. He knocked his head against the low ceiling more than once and had to feel his way with his feet.

He heard a thump in front of him and Liana cursed.

"Is everyone all right back there?" Lodas asked.

Nelek frowned, disliking the special attention Lodas seemed to be giving his daughter. He almost said something, but Liana beat him to it.

"Everyone will be just fine once we're out of this blasted place," she said.

"You have an aversion to tunnels, my dear?" Lodas asked with a chuckle.

"No, not really. I just prefer being able to see when I'm in one," Liana said. "And I am not 'your dear.'"

"Oh? Then whose 'dear' are you?"

"Mine," Troy said and the word came out like a growl.

Nelek nearly tripped at the fiercely possessive sound in Troy's voice. There was no mistaking the intent behind the statement. Nelek squinted at Liana. She turned to look back at him and caught his gaze. Her face was mostly in shadow, but he could see the apology in her eyes and realized suddenly how much he had missed.

He'd seen Troy and Liana together. They'd shared furtive gazes and awkward smiles, but never once had Nelek suspected anything was going on.

Gods alive, he was a fool.

"Forgive me," Lodas said, sounding altogether too amused by the situation. "I didn't think the lady needed defending."

Troy and Liana spoke at the same time. "She doesn't." "I don't."

And Nelek thought, *like hell she doesn't.*

In his mind was a little girl in pigtails dashing toward him on the pier in Vakeshmeer, laughing and calling for him. But as he looked at her now, nimbly maneuvering through the tunnel, he could see the woman she was struggling to be. Young still—gods, so young—but a woman just the same. Sighing, he shook his head and continued his trek, resigning himself to the situation. If Troy was her choice, then he couldn't fight her on it. He wasn't even sure he wanted to.

Brigetta stopped at the foot of a narrow staircase, her tattoos fading down, leaving them in a darkness so deep it was disorienting. Nelek touched the wall at his left and tried to concentrate. His eyes adjusted slowly and he began to see a shaft of light coming from the top of the staircase. He heard Lodas and Brigetta start to move, and then everyone else followed. Nelek used the wall to help guide him, carefully picking his way up the rough stairs.

The source of light became apparent as he neared the top. There were several arrow loops cut deep into the stone and he began to realize where they were. The tunnel had led them straight into the inner bailey of Kiavana, to the southwest tower. The last time Nelek had been in this tower he'd been rushing to his brother's aid.

Much like he was now.

Only this time Brenson wasn't about to be executed. This time Brenson was under siege.

But that tunnel had never been there before; he was sure of it.

Nelek looked back just as he emerged from the stairs and into the tower proper. Behind him the stairs ended in solid rock, making him blink in surprise. He reached out to touch the wall, wondering if it was a trick of the light, but his palm flattened against cold stone and he frowned.

"Your mother built that entrance to be used only by those who can manage blood magic," Brigetta said, answering his unasked question. "I found it a year or so after you went missing."

Nelek turned away from the wall. "I imagine Brenson has found it most useful," he said.

"Oh yes," a new voice said from the doorway. "We've been using it to spy on the army outside."

Nelek found Sir Faolan just inside the tower. He was covered in grease and sweat, and there was a cut near his left temple that had been mended at least once. Faolan scanned the room with a frown. He looked much older now; deep lines formed around his mouth as he frowned and there were traces of white in his dark hair, but Nelek knew him.

Nelek saw the leak of blood through the man's bandage and felt his chest squeeze tight with worry. If this was how his brother's bodyguard looked, he was terrified of what injuries Brenson might already have suffered.

Faolan's gaze settled on Brigetta and a strange flicker of emotion crossed his face. It was only there for an instant, but Nelek saw it.

He glanced between the knight and the mage as an uncomfortable silence overtook the room, but then Faolan turned away from her and focused on Nelek.

"And who is this?" Faolan asked.

"Nelek Dyngannon and his family," Brigetta said matter-of-factly. "We must see Duke Brenson."

Faolan's eyebrow hiked upward in surprise. "They're Human," he said.

"Yes," Bree said. "Much like Trenna was when you first knew her."

"So this is a spell?" Faolan asked, eyeing them all in turn. "Is Trenna with you?"

"No," Kaden said. "But she will be here soon."

Faolan's gaze fell on Nelek and after a moment the man's eyes flickered with recognition. Nelek smirked, glad that he was at least recognizable to the old knight in his Human form. It seemed that anyone who'd known him before wouldn't mistake him in this disguise, which was heartening. He didn't want to undergo the transformation spell until it was absolutely necessary.

"Take me to my brother," Nelek said to the knight.

Faolan was quiet for a moment and then nodded, turning to escort them out of the tower. Nelek followed, confident that his children would be right behind him. Bree and Lodas stayed behind as they left the tower and stepped into a blur of movement. The inner courtyard, normally reserved for courtiers and the like, was filled with soldiers. Four large fire pits roared near the center, each of them heating massive cauldrons. He smelled pitch in the air, a sharp, pungent odor that brought home the reality of their situation.

Kiavana was under siege.

Nelek gripped his hilt and scowled. He'd felt it ever since Brigetta had shown up in Vakeshmeer—the undeniable link he had to Kiavana—but now it hit him full force. These were his people; this was his home. He was rooted here in ways that went beyond even the connection to his brother.

In his arrogance, he'd thought Brenson would be safest with him gone. Porrex's ire rested mostly on Trenna, after all.

Nelek had underestimated the king's paranoia.

Halfway through the yard, they were stopped by several men reporting to Faolan. Nelek listened, determined to save his home and his people from this new threat. He may have been gone for twenty years, but he was returning, and gods help the man who tried to stop him.

"They've got a new engineer," one man told Faolan. "He's already begun construction on the trebuchet. He's guarded by six men."

Faolan grunted in displeasure. "Six? I guess they're finally tired of us assassinating them."

"Aye, sir," the soldier said. He glanced at Kaden and Nelek got a profile view, surprised to find the man was Eldur. While he and Brenson were Eldur, most of Kiavana was Human. The man stared at Kaden for a moment before continuing his report. "Our spy says there's a large force coming in from the southeast mountains. The king's bastard son apparently isn't worried about them, though. Porrex already has a unit in the pass that will cut off any reinforcements from the borderlands."

Faolan tensed, looking truly alarmed. "Are you certain?"

"Mavon's leading the forces, sir," the Eldur said with a crooked smile. "If he's half the man his father was, we shouldn't need to worry. He'll find a way around that pass. Even if he has to move the mountains themselves."

"Mavon?" Troy asked, sounding surprised.

"Lord Gideon Mavon," the soldier supplied, eyeing Troy with frank curiosity. "He commands the largest Human army outside of Kiavana."

"Thank you, Lieutenant Kesseck," Faolan said. "Hopefully our friends on the outside will have as much luck with this new engineer as they did with the last three."

Kesseck pulled his gaze from Troy and nodded at Faolan. With another glance in Kaden's direction, he shoved his helmet onto his head and left. Nelek watched him go, torn between pride that

Brenson had managed to keep a bridge of peace among some Eldur and Humans, and the unsettled feeling that he'd met that man before.

Faolan resumed their walk toward the northeastern tower, gesturing to the other soldiers for them to give their reports as they went. Apparently, several civilians had been relocated from the outer bailey to the main hall and most of them had resumed work on aiding the wounded. Faolan nodded in acknowledgement and the soldier ran off.

The final report was given by a slip of a boy whose uniform was strapped down by many belts and scabbards. There were so many weapons on him that Nelek lost count and gave up, watching instead as the boy took up pace directly beside Faolan. He removed his helmet, revealing a long black braid and feminine features, and Nelek blinked, amending his first assumption: girl, not boy.

"We lost four more archers in the southmost tower," she said brusquely. "Varren's forces are converging just outside. If we don't get more archers up there, you won't have to worry about a trebuchet, because Varren's going to climb right up our walls."

"Dell, I've given you all the archers I can spare," Faolan said. "Any more and we risk exposing all other towers to the enemy. You're going to have to make do."

Nelek noticed immediately the lack of formality between these two. Still, he was surprised when Dell grabbed Faolan's arm and stopped them all in their tracks. They were just outside the main hall now, its massive structure rising tall and defiant beside them.

For all her slight form and fierce youth, Nelek thought Dell looked quite a bit like that tower: unshakeable and firm.

"Faolan, I *can't* make do," Dell said. "I've got fires sprouting with every volley they shoot at us and ladders I have to shove off our walls in between that. I know you think Navell is the greater threat but you're wrong. It's Varren Silvanus who is flanking us and he will succeed if you don't listen to me now."

Faolan scowled, obviously torn. After a moment, he looked back at Nelek.

"I don't suppose any of you can handle a crossbow?" he asked.

"Yes," Kaden said. "I can."

Faolan met Nelek's eyes, silently questioning him. Nelek hesitated a moment, worried over sending his son into danger, but nodded once. They were all in danger here and their fates would be no different from Kiavana's.

"Troy, go with him," Nelek said. "See if you can't help manage the fires long enough for the archers to do their work."

Dell eyed Kaden and Troy but didn't object. When Faolan deferred them to her she just nodded, pivoted on her heel and started away.

"That's your cue, boys," Faolan said.

Kaden and Troy glanced at each other and hurried to catch up with their new commander. Nelek watched them go and swallowed back the impulse to chase after them. He stayed where he was, frowning at Dell's back and praying the girl had as much wisdom as Faolan seemed to believe.

"Adelle Croften," Faolan said, nodding after her. "She's a pain in the arse, but she can get the job done. Your boys will be safe enough."

"Croften?" Liana asked.

Nelek felt the name like a barb deep in his skin. He clenched his fists, his gut suddenly roiling in surprise. His memory flared to life, bringing him to a dark tunnel saturated in blood and death. An infant's wail pierced the tight confines of the tunnel and Brockley Croften stood at his side, congratulating him on his son's birth. The awed relief Nelek had felt at the sound of his child's arrival was quickly washed away by grief. He could still feel Brock's hand on his shoulder, see the flash of Brock's teeth as he smiled in the torchlight.

"Aye," Faolan said. He was looking hard at Nelek, as though trying to read into whatever visions Nelek was seeing. "Daughter to Sir Brockley Croften and Lady Adelyte."

"Brock had a daughter," Nelek murmured, feeling cold dread in his center.

"And a son," Faolan supplied, turning toward the door again. "Twins. Brenson took them in after their mother died."

Orphans, Nelek thought as Faolan pushed open the doors leading to the main hall. For a dizzy moment, he almost couldn't breathe, but Liana's hand on his shoulder steadied him. She stared at him with a grim expression and nodded once, firm and confident. The movement was so much like her mother that renewed guilt and pain swelled up in his chest.

Twenty years hiding in safety while Brock's children had lost their mother. His heart tore. He hadn't known Adelyte was pregnant.

"Father," Liana said.

He shook his head and focused. Sir Faolan had already left them. Gripping Liana's hand where it rested on his shoulder, Nelek took a steadying breath and forced regret out of his mind. There would be time enough for that later, if they survived the siege. He stepped forward, walking into the main hall without looking back.

~ * ~

Liana followed her father through Kiavana's main hall, frowning at the tense set of his shoulders. They'd been in trouble since the moment they left Vakeshmeer, but the news of Dell's parentage had hit him hard. She remembered stories of Sir Brockley Croften, and the mournful look on Trenna's face whenever his name was mentioned, so she knew Brock was important. She wondered how her mother would react to the twins.

The hall was crowded with people: women and children and old men tending the wounded. Sweat and blood mingled in the air and Liana fought the urge to hide her nose in her shirt. The hot, musky press of bodies seemed to swarm around them as Faolan led the way to the back. She heard several gasps of surprise as people began to recognize Nelek, which concerned her because they were still in disguise.

How could they tell?

"The duke," they said. "The duke has come."

Some moved toward him, touching his arms as he passed, and Liana was struck by the intense hope that flared in their faces. She looked at her father again, saw him pause to cover an old man's hand where it had found purchase on his elbow. The man was stooped, with a wide balding patch at the crown of his head and one eye that wouldn't open. She caught a glimpse of gnarled fingers clutching Nelek's arm before her father's hand covered them.

"I knew you'd come, milord," the man half-wheezed the words. "I knew you would never let Kiavana fall."

"Not while I still have breath," Nelek said in reply.

Liana heard the fierceness in the quiet promise and a chill shot down her spine. She'd known he was a duke but somehow had never seen it. All the stories of her childhood flooded back to her, stories that had never felt real before. Stories about Nelek living as a prince, and the plots he'd been forced to make with his little brother, Brenson. Or the one about the way her parents had met: Trenna foiling an assassination attempt on Nelek and getting knighted for her pains.

But this was all surface knowledge, the sort of knowing that resembled the shallow bits of the sea. One could look into the shallows and catch glimpses of things beneath, but beyond that it turned to murky blue. A fisherman could spend his whole life on the ocean and never fully know it, just as Liana suddenly didn't know her father.

Nelek parted from the old man, who smiled after him, revealing several missing teeth. Liana ducked her head and hurried to catch up, unsettled by this new understanding of Nelek.

Faolan brought them to a small stone staircase that curved upward. The smells of the hall disappeared as they climbed, replaced instead by the stale, cold scent of a room too long closed off. Voices reached them as they neared the top of the stairs, both men and both serious. Liana shivered and reached for her hilt.

Soon, she thought, *very, very soon we shall have to go to battle.*

She remembered the fight on the *Penelope-Anne*, the chaos and terrible sounds that had come with men pressed into combat. It had been her first real engagement, short as it was, and she couldn't help feeling that she had failed somehow. Trenna had trained them all from the moment they could walk, showing the best means of holding a blade, the spots to aim for, but there was something different about actually hurting a man.

They emerged into a surprisingly ornate room. Liana scanned the space twice just to catch all of the contradictions. A fireplace embedded into the rightmost wall was empty, which explained the chill draft. Nearby was the largest bed Liana had ever seen, piled high with fur-lined blankets in various shades of green. Three tapestries hung on the walls and each of them was so complex that she couldn't rightly make them out at first glance.

At the far corner a young boy with dirty brown hair worked diligently at cleaning a breastplate. He was perhaps eight years old and his clothing was covered in soot. He looked so out of place there that Liana stared. The boy didn't look up, not even when Faolan began to cross the room. Liana forced her attention away from the boy and to the men surrounding the center table.

It wasn't hard to recognize Brenson. His eyes were different, more cat-like in shape, and his hair reflected a deep auburn color in the candlelight, but his other features so closely resembled Nelek's that she almost smiled.

The other gentleman was also Eldur. His pointed ears peaked beside a head of copper-streaked brown hair. Liana had only ever seen the streaks on Kaden and Trenna, so she was surprised that they came in different colors.

Brenson looked up from the table just as Faolan began to speak.

"I found something interesting in the tunnels, my lord."

Brenson's brow drew into a tight furrow, and then lifted in shock as he spotted Nelek. He abandoned the table, striding toward Nelek as Nelek moved forward. They stopped in front of each other and for a moment Liana wasn't certain what to expect. Neither man was smiling, but they weren't scowling either. And then Brenson exhaled a sharp laugh, grabbed Nelek by the arms and drew him into a tight embrace.

Liana relaxed, hearing the muffled sound of Nelek's laughter as he held onto his brother.

"I was beginning to think I'd seen the last of you," Brenson said, pulling away just enough to clasp Nelek's shoulder.

"Never," Nelek said with a grin. "I'm like a pebble in your boot."

"Where'd your ears go?" Brenson laughed and Nelek touched one rounded ear with a faint scowl.

"Precaution," he said. "We weren't sure what we were walking into."

Brenson's eyes caught on where Liana still lingered in the doorway. She could see the clear intelligence in Brenson's gaze, and sensed the mischief in him. Were they not under siege, she imagined he was one of those courtiers Mother had often spoken of, men and women whose true motives could never be seen on the surface. It didn't matter that he was dressed in padded armor, or that his left arm was wrapped in a thick bandage, Brenson still managed to look just shy of aloof.

"And who is this?" Brenson asked.

Nelek turned and beckoned for her. She hesitated, but walked toward them. The boy in the corner glanced up at her, hooded brown eyes surveying her person for a moment before he went back to work. The Eldur, on the other hand, gazed straight at her in utter passivity. She felt her cheeks flush and fought down the urge to hide under the bed.

Nobility, she thought, feeling overwhelmed.

"This is your niece." Nelek introduced her as she made her way to his side. His hand clamped onto her shoulder, firm and reassuring. "Evaliana Auliere Dyngannon."

"Niece?" Brenson asked, clearly surprised. "What happened to my nephew?"

"He's in the southwest tower, my lord," Faolan said. "Dell made off with him."

"Ah, Dell," Brenson said and nodded as if this explained everything. Then he turned back to Nelek, his expression suddenly serious. "Where is your wife?"

Nelek's eyebrow lifted. "She's on the way," he said. Glancing at Faolan he added, "Why does everyone keep asking me that?"

"You mean aside from the fact that if she dies out there we'll have the joy of cleaning up your corpse?" the Eldur man said dryly.

Liana held tight to her hilt and forced the image of a dead Nelek from her mind. Trenna would not die out there. She just wouldn't.

Brenson half turned, frowning at the Eldur for a heartbeat before speaking to Nelek. "I believe you already know Commander Ledeiv."

"Yes," Nelek said, sounding grim. "I see you took my advice, Levatto."

The commander inclined his head just-so, a smirk playing at the corners of his wide mouth. "My men and I have come to respect Duke Brenson."

"And Ronan?"

Something flickered across Levatto's face and the smirk disappeared. "He was properly cared for."

"Trenna will be glad to hear it," Nelek said before he turned back to Brenson. "Now, why are you looking for her?"

Brenson shared a look with Faolan and Liana felt the tension in the room rise a notch. She watched silently as Brenson returned to the table, Nelek trailing him.

"General Navell Silvanus has issued a statement that all hostilities against Kiavana will cease if we relinquish 'Lana' to his authority," Brenson said with a heavy sigh. "The man is convinced she is here."

Liana bristled, suddenly not so intimidated anymore. Nobility or not, there was no way these men would be "relinquishing" her mother to anybody.

"You can't possibly mean to turn my mother over to them," she said. She strode to the little table, half pleased that she'd managed to startle Brenson and completely annoyed that her father had not said it first.

"Well, she's as fiery as her mother, I'll give her that," Faolan said with amusement.

Liana's cheeks burned and she glared at the knight. She almost spoke again, but Nelek gripped her shoulder. She met his steady blue gaze and swallowed back whatever response she'd meant to give, scowling instead.

"No," Brenson told her calmly. "But I was hoping she could give some insight. Both men attacking my home are her brothers, after all."

"Dell is quite adamant that our focus should be on Varren," Faolan said.

Brenson looked to Nelek and Liana could read the question in his face. For a tense moment, Liana tried to remember any stories from her childhood that might help. Trenna spoke often of her home in Verburrge and the time she'd spent with Varren and Prince Ronan. There had to be something that might clue them in on what to do, but for the life of her Liana couldn't think of anything.

Apparently neither could her father, because he shrugged and shook his head.

"I really don't know," he said. "But if Varren suspects she is in here, then he'll be planning his actions based on what she would do."

"So, our best bet is to defend ourselves in exactly the opposite manner," Brenson said with a scowl. He sighed down at the maps on the table. "Now... what *wouldn't* Trenna do?"

Twenty-eight

Trenna's horse shifted under her, snorting in protest at the oncoming army. She reached down and patted the speckled mare, silently counting Gideon's force as it made its way up the mountain pass. Mavon's stark red standard fluttered in a high breeze, snapping and curling itself in an unsettling way. Trenna's chest went tight, every instinct she had urging her to turn and flee.

It was a strange warning and she couldn't quite decipher it. Gideon didn't know her and shouldn't have cause to harm her, yet she feared he would. Squinting at the haze of dust closing in on her, she frowned. The line of men snaked through the pass, curving behind the nearest hill only to appear again further down the road.

Seven hundred, or near to it, she guessed. Mavon had been busy the last few years. His father had only ever commanded half that many.

Three men broke off from the main company, spurring their horses up the hillside in her direction. Trenna watched them come, her gaze fastening on the red-headed man in the middle. Gideon was as big as his father with a dusting of freckles on his face and a clearly hostile gleam to his greenish eyes. Trenna held her horse steady as the riders came to a stop three paces from her position, and wondered what stories Tibitus might have told his eldest before they'd forged peace.

"Lana Silvanus?" Gideon asked, though there was little question in his voice.

Her hair and ears likely gave her away.

"They call me Trenna these days," she said.

Gideon's two men shuffled to the right and left, moving to surround her. Trenna relaxed her fingers on the reins and took a deep breath. This was not how she'd envisioned their meeting. She hadn't expected a grateful embrace or anything of the sort, but respect and civility might have been nice. She had delivered Tibitus Mavon's final letter, after all, and in her saddle she had Mavon's ashes. She'd promised the man that his ashes would be returned to Mavon lands and she had every intention of seeing that through.

Unless, of course, Gideon killed her. That would certainly put a hiccup in her plans.

"Where is Faxon Mylonas?" Trenna asked. "The man I left for you."

"Was he important?"

Trenna stiffened, gritting her teeth at Gideon's antagonistic tone. For a horrible moment, she thought Gideon might have killed Faxon, which would mean Brigetta was dead, which would put her family in even more danger. She met Gideon's gaze and held it, suppressing the urge to draw her sword and be done with pretenses.

"Not overly important, no," she said. "But I did tell him you were a man of honor like your father. I would hate to be in error."

Gideon's mouth contorted, the bristle of his three-day beard glistening in the dying light of day. He looked so much like Tibitus that Trenna's heart ached, memories of Vakeshmeer and a friendship she'd never predicted flaunting through her mind. Ten years he'd survived with them, helped them build a life amongst the Human community, only to be taken by fever in his old age.

Gods alive, she missed him.

Gideon nodded once to the bearded man on his left, who promptly spurred off toward the slowly approaching army. Trenna kept her attention on Gideon, who eyed her with grudging interest. He must have expected something else from her, something to give him reason enough to kill her, because she could see the twist of his scowl as he continued to survey her.

It occurred to her then that Gideon had never been afforded an explanation as to his father's disappearance twenty years ago; he couldn't have been more than fifteen years old at the time of the peace talks in Cadabyr. Tibitus must have warned the boy that there would be danger but still, losing his father, even to exile, could not have been easy.

Suddenly understanding the animosity aimed at her, Trenna took another long breath and decided to mend bridges. If, of course, this bridge was mendable.

"Your father spoke of you often," she said. "He loved you very much."

Gideon's shoulders tensed. His jaw flex twice before he responded. "Not enough to return."

"Returning would have alerted Porrex to our survival," Trenna said. "It would have placed you in danger. So in point of fact, he loved you too much to return."

Gideon's expression turned hard, either in defense or anger, and Trenna worried she'd somehow overstepped. "I am a grown man, Duchess of Kiavana," he said curtly. "Speaking to me of my father's overabundant love is not going to impress me."

In her peripheral view, she saw two riders approaching, but kept her gaze on Mavon. The pity she felt for the man warred with the sense that he was deliberately mocking Tibitus—a slight she would normally make him bleed for. She ground her teeth and fought for the next move. He was clearly trying to get her to react. He wanted her to fight him, and gods, how she was ready to rise to the bait.

The riders reached them and she spotted Faxon in manacles, looking the worse for wear. His left eye was swollen shut, dried blood was caked around his mouth, and his nose was sharply bent to the left, broken and unattended. Fury roiled through her, hot and intense, and for a blind moment she could do nothing more than gaze at the assassin.

He wants to fight you, Nelek's voice sounded in her head. *He's manipulating you.*

Trenna felt the bite of the reins in her hands and had to focus to loosen her grip. Carefully, utilizing every ounce of willpower she had, she met Faxon's good eye and held it.

"You let them shackle you?" she asked.

Faxon's mouth twisted with wry humor. "It amused me."

Trenna hummed low in her throat and focused on Gideon again. She had underestimated the man's anger, but she wouldn't make that mistake again. She wanted to take Faxon and leave, let Gideon run his army right into the fort just for the arrogant smirk he was sending her way. But her family needed this army and they needed it now. They had to have made it to Kiavana already, which meant they were under siege, which meant she had to help Gideon on his path.

She took a deep, steadying breath and resigned herself to the situation.

"There is an Eldur fort a little over a mile from here," she spoke to Gideon, forcing herself to sound calm and passive. "If you keep on this path you will run straight into it, and they will fight you to the last man before they let you pass."

"I do not know of any fort on this pass," Gideon said.

"Yes, well, you're inside Dyngannon borders now," Trenna said. "Unless you were Eldur you wouldn't know."

Gideon glanced at Faxon and then back at her, scowling in doubt. "You've been away from Dyngannon a long time, General," he said. "How do you know it wasn't abandoned?"

"Because I just came from there."

"Is that a fact?"

"Yes," Trenna said through her teeth.

By gods, he was irritating.

"Who mans it?" he asked.

Trenna shut her mouth, a knot of fear coiling in her gut. Gideon was too intelligent not to recognize the name of her old unit. He was plotting something, she could feel it, and whatever it was wouldn't be good.

"That doesn't matter," she said. "What matters is that the path is closed. You will need to head west through the forest. It'll delay you by half a day but at least your forces will remain intact."

Gideon laughed without humor and wiped sweat off the nape of his neck, squinting over at her with a sharp, cat-like gaze. "Well now, General, a half a day is too long. Kiavana's been under siege for a fortnight now. Duke Brenson needs us. So, I'll ask again... who mans the fort?"

She squinted back at him.

He wouldn't kill her, dearly as it seemed he wanted to, but he might kill Faxon. In fact, she had a feeling the only reason Faxon was still alive was because Gideon needed to exert some form of control over her. She gripped her reins hard and looked up at the mountain pass.

"The seventh cavalry," she said at last.

Gideon's eyebrows rose. "Your own men?"

"Those who have survived in my absence, yes."

Gideon chuckled. "And why would your men fight us?"

"Because they don't have a choice," Trenna explained, fighting hard to keep her temper. "Porrex is holding their families in ransom. They either fight or watch their loved ones die. So I am telling you, my lord, that to keep your army intact the best route is through the forest."

He gave her an ugly smile that chilled the blood in her veins. "Or," he said and moved his horse closer to hers. He stopped just beside her and shifted in his saddle. "Or we hold you ransom instead."

Trenna stared at him, clear unadulterated loathing surging through her. Gideon was nothing like his father. He was cruel and proud and she detested him like she had never detested a man before, Porrex included. He shamed the Mavon name and one day, when this war was over, she would tell him so.

"You really think my life will outweigh the lives of their kin?" she asked, unable to contain her mockery. "Half those men never served with me. The half that did have lived in constant threat since my exile. You are an absolute fool, Gideon Mavon, if you truly believe that would work."

"Oh, I don't know," Gideon said, smirking down at her with so much superiority she nearly punched him for it. "General Lana is far more than a leader. She's a symbol of Dyngannon's pride. I've even heard whispers that all the Eldur hopes are pinned on you. It doesn't matter what name you go by, General, you *are* the one they're all waiting for."

Trenna crushed the reins in her hands, battling to keep from striking him. A nice, quick punch to the throat would do, knock that superior grin off his face. She looked down at Faxon, saw again the extent of abuse that had been thrust upon him and took another slow, calculating breath.

To hell with diplomacy, she thought. Gideon was an idiot.

Faxon's brow rose in either concern or surprise, probably both, and he took a step closer to her horse. His guards stepped with him, every man suddenly tense and coiled, ready for a fight. He glanced at the two armed men flanking him and scowled, then met her gaze and held it.

"We don't have time for this, Trenna," Faxon said, each word slow and deliberate.

He meant a fight. They didn't have time for a fight, and Trenna blinked, surprised he had read her intentions so clearly. She carefully relaxed her grip on the reins and turned back to Gideon. The man had his hand on the pommel of his sword, ready and waiting for some kind of action on her part. Trenna huffed a humorless laugh and shook her head, focusing on the distant line of Gideon's army as it continued up the pass.

"Your father never stopped talking about you," she said to Gideon. "Not in the ten years I knew him."

"Talk is cheap," Gideon said. His upper lip curled into a sneer so disrespectful that Trenna had to count to ten before talking again.

"The only thing cheap here is your sense of honor," she said and dismounted her horse.

Faxon and the men scattered, their little circle of bodies jerking away from where she stood. Even the horses shuffled away, unsettled by the quick movement, and Trenna smirked. She held her wrists out in front of her, scanning the group of soldiers before glaring up at Gideon again.

"I imagine if you mean to ransom me, I ought to be properly shackled," she said.

Gideon met her gaze with an unsettled frown, staring at her like she was an unfamiliar creature, a beast he could not anticipate. She stared back, her arms still outstretched, and prayed he sensed just how disappointed she was in the man he'd turned out to be.

Gods knew Tibitus Mavon would have been.

Twenty-nine

Dell kept a brisk pace through the courtyards, pausing just long enough to snag helmets from a pair of retreating soldiers. These she thrust toward Kaden and Troy without explanation and Kaden took his, barely glancing at the wounded men passing them. The soft glow of coming dawn lessened some of the shadows but he still couldn't make out the features of the men around him.

That was just as well, he thought, settling the helmet on his head. There were plenty of other things to occupy his mind, such as the stink of oil burning in pits and the constant shouting between posts. The ground was muddy, making his feet slip as he hurried toward the tower.

"What are your names?" Dell asked over her shoulder.

He fell into step beside her. "Kaden, and this is my brother, Troy."

"All right Kaden, Troy," she said with a brief nod. "Welcome to the southwest tower."

She stepped into the tower and immediately swiveled to the side, allowing a boy with an empty bucket to rush past. Kaden mimicked her, pressing up against the wall to clear a path. The tower teemed with movement, many bodies hurrying through the space in a strangely chaotic, yet fluid dance of duties. Kaden was simultaneously impressed and worried as Dell plucked a bucket from the ground and tossed it to Troy.

Troy caught it with a frown.

"We passed the main well on our way in; do you remember?" Dell asked.

"Yes," Troy said.

"Your job is simple. You get the water, run it back here, douse whatever fires were started in your absence and run back for more. Got it?"

"Dousing fires," Troy said. "Yes, I've got it."

"Good. Go."

Troy glanced at Kaden, shrugged once, and then turned back through the door.

Dell's attention switched to Kaden and for an uncomfortable moment he endured her critical frown. If it weren't for the hair and the slightly taller frame, he might have mistaken her for his mother. Her mouth twisted, sharp features contorting into a look of indecision, just before she snatched up a discarded crossbow and shoved it into his arms. He gripped the heavy crossbow, noting with some asperity that she hadn't supplied any bolts to go with it.

"You'll be on the top of the wall," she said and headed for the circular stair.

"Bolts?" he asked, keeping close on her heels.

"We're running low, so make them count," Dell said and picked up her pace. "You'll be given ten to start with; after that you have to go on a collection run like everyone else."

"Collection run?"

They reached the top of the tower and Dell paused, one hand on the thick oak door leading outside. Muffled voices shouted on the other side and then several solid thuds resounded through the door. The hair on Kaden's arms prickled and a sudden suspicion niggled at him. Dell smirked, her full mouth looking wicked and sensual, and for a dazed moment Kaden forgot the danger.

"You didn't think we were the only ones shooting in this engagement, did you?" she asked with a wink and opened the door.

A confusing mix of cool night air and blazing fire swirled around Kaden as he followed her out. Dell ducked low and ran for a position on the far side of the tower. Kaden ducked and followed, noting the seven other bodies occupying the tower as he went. They were all dressed in similar fashion to Dell: dark clothes, helmets, and thick cloaks that made them look like bulbous shadows crouched next to the crenellations.

"Oy! Close the bloody door!" someone shouted.

"I'll get it!"

"Bloody hell, Adelle! Where'd you dredge up this one?"

Kaden ground his teeth together as Dell handed him his bolts, fully aware of whom they were discussing. He kicked himself for not closing the door, felt his face heat in embarrassment just before a sundry of bolts and arrows flew over the wall. Squashing tight against the crenellated wall, Kaden held back a curse and waited for the firing to stop.

It didn't take long. The chink and thunk of bolts hammering into stone and wood slowed and suddenly Dell was up, a crossbow in hand and a determined frown contorting her face. He watched her, momentarily stunned as she leaned over the parapet and fired. She ducked back down and the man beside her popped up to take aim while she reloaded.

The movements were swift and fluid, practiced, and Kaden couldn't help admiring them. Everyone on the tower seemed to know when and how to move, anticipating each other and the enemy below like some deadly dance.

"You waitin' for an invitation, boy?" the man just beside him asked with an obnoxious, toothy grin.

Kaden grimaced and hoisted his crossbow, turning to glare down at the army below. Darkness obscured his view, meshing possible targets with inanimate objects and he had to hunt to find an enemy soldier. He saw a flash of silver, squinted and fired, hoping it was someone holding a sword. He felt the line snap free, felt the bolt whiz away, and for half a heartbeat he wondered if he'd hit anything at all.

A hand on his shoulder dragged him back down and he had to press hard into the wall again as the enemy returned fire. His neighbor had moved closer and kept a firm grip on him as they waited out the bolts. Smoke and sweat reeked from him and Kaden imagined the man hadn't bathed in several days. His scraggly beard had soot in it and his big eyes looked as dark as the shadows surrounding them.

"You shoot, you duck back down. Dun dawdle or you're dead. Understand?" the man asked, then looked back to Dell. "Gods above, Dell. The boy's too green for the tower."

"Dun worry," Dell said, her hands busy reloading. "We'll all be spreading toward the wall soon anyway."

"What? And abandon the tower?" the boy beside Dell asked.

Dell paused as several flaming arrows hissed by, three of them sinking deep into the tower door. One of the men dashed from his post, yanking up a bucket of water to douse the flames. Dell seemed distracted by this, watching as the man opened the door and sprinted inside, kicking it closed behind him. Then she looked back to the boy beside her and nodded.

"Varren's moving his ladders to the center of the west wall. He can't take the tower by force but he just might be able to overwhelm us there," she said. "Four of you will stay here, maintain the tower. The rest of us will reinforce the wall before he can get there."

"How do you know he's going for the wall?" Kaden asked, earning him a few snickers from the men.

He frowned, busying his hands with reloading while he waited for her answer. It didn't seem like a funny question to him. He'd been with her since she left Faolan and hadn't heard anyone give her a report. She flashed him a brazen smile as she cocked her crossbow's line.

"Because it's what I would do," she said and promptly moved to take aim.

Several of the men chuckled, each of them going back to the work at hand. Kaden waited the space of three breaths and then shrugged. Apparently, that was all the answer he could expect, and really, his parents tended to respond the same way to such questions so he oughtn't be annoyed. He lifted his reloaded crossbow and turned back to the crenellation.

~ * ~

Nelek spared a glance at the southwest tower as he followed Brenson through the yard and tried hard not to think of Kaden in danger. Or Troy. Or even Liana, though she was two steps behind him and just as moody as ever. Taking a deep breath, he concentrated on Brenson's voice, sequestering his children into a distant corner of his mind.

If they were going to survive this, he needed to focus.

"They've been trying to build trebuchets," Brenson said with a scowl. "We've sent skirmishes out to stop them but lost more men than we could spare."

"That's why you sent spies out, right?" Liana asked.

"No, not just spies, assassins," Lodas Mylonas answered before Brenson could respond. He took up pace just beside Liana and smiled in a lecherous manner that nearly made Nelek stop in his tracks. Liana, however, was quick on her feet and switched to Nelek's left side, nimbly distancing herself from the man. Nelek relaxed at the sight.

Daylight made Lodas's features sharper somehow, and the lanky form that had been so thin in the tunnels looked gaunt. Nelek eyed Lodas, who either ignored him or just didn't notice, and wondered who the boy took after more: Cahira or Sprague. Both had been notorious criminals during his father's rule, but managed to keep well enough away from politics to maintain their safety.

Cahira, he decided.

If memory served him right, Sprague was a stout man, burly and barrel-chested. Lodas was fine boned, or would be in a few years. At the moment he looked a bit like an ungainly stork, but he moved with fluid precision and Nelek knew the young man could be dangerous.

"The spy goes first, actually," Brenson said. "Then the assassin goes in. We've managed to stall them by taking out their engineers, but it's only a matter of time before they either catch the spy or find a better way of hiding construction."

"If they haven't already," Faolan noted.

They crossed the inner gate and into the outer bailey and Nelek scowled. Men ran to and from their posts, several ducking into the soldier's hall to eat or rest before running back to the fight. More fire pits smoldered in the ground, each of them hosting a cauldron bubbling with tar, prepared to be tossed over the wall should the enemy come close enough. He could smell the pitch in the air, mingled with smoke and blood, and for a heartbeat wondered how they had come to this.

Not even when he'd removed his father from the Kiavanan throne had they come to such destruction.

Nelek flexed his fists as they came to a stop by the bailey wall. The hair on the back of his neck prickled and he stared at the stone structure. Brenson had brought him here for a reason and now Nelek wanted to run far away. But he clamped down on that impulse and leaned over, peering down into the dark of the well.

He couldn't see the bottom, but he knew what Brenson was going to say anyway.

"There's enough in here for three days, maybe four," Brenson said. "The inner bailey well is holding up, but I don't have to tell you the panic that will run through this place if this one runs dry."

They paused as a boy ran up to fill his bucket. He worked quickly, barely nodding a "milord" to them before dropping the bucket and line down the well. Within seconds he had the bucket up again, loosed it from the line, and charged off the way he'd come. Nelek watched him go and frowned.

"We should start moving people to the inner bailey," Nelek said.

"And abandon the outer defenses?" Faolan asked, clearly offended by the idea.

"You'll have to abandon them anyway," Liana said. She nodded toward the outer gate. "Fire will take them down once the water is gone. If we go now we'll save lives and be able to fortify the inner walls."

Nelek glanced at his daughter. "Exactly," he said. "We won't be spread as thin and we won't be wasting water on structures we know we're going to lose."

"But there's still water down there," Faolan protested.

"Water that we might need elsewhere," Brenson said with a frown. "We can start transporting what's left to the infirmary."

"What about food?" Nelek asked. He gazed over at the soldier's hall, caught the smell of cooked onions faint on the air. "We'll want to move that as well. Centralize everything."

"It'll take some time but we can do it," Brenson said, obviously agreeing with him.

"How much time?"

"Depends on how many men I can spare," Faolan said. He looked displeased but resigned and crossed his arms over his chest. "Which isn't many. You're looking at a day. Maybe two."

"You've got a day," Brenson said. "After that I want to start relocating men to the inner defenses."

Nelek exhaled slowly, gathering his concentration again. This was bad but not impossible. Help was on its way. All they needed to do was hold on until reinforcements arrived—reinforcements that, hopefully, carried Trenna with them.

His gut clenched at the thought of his wife.

Why hadn't she arrived yet?

Gods knew the woman was alive; she should be here by now.

Unless she had deliberately altered course, she should have arrived long before they'd made it to Kiavana. And the only reason he could think of for her to divert was that she planned on coming with the approaching army, which meant she'd gone to see Mavon's son.

He relaxed a bit, deciding that this was, in fact, what she must have done. It would have been difficult for her to break into Kiavana on her own, after all.

"Liana," Nelek said, turning to his daughter. She stood straighter, one expectant eyebrow quirking up at him. "Start organizing the cooks and food out here for the transfer. I'll send word when it's time to start moving."

Thirty

His manacles yanked him forward, jolting him down the road and rubbing his skin raw at the wrists. Faxon glared at the wagon master's back, but made no complaint. He had a set of lock-picks sewn into the hem of his vest and knew he could release himself whenever he damn pleased. And in fact, when he finally did release himself, he was going to make a special trip to see this wagon master in private.

Smiling to himself, Faxon narrowly avoided a large pile of horse dung and started listing the different ways he could kill the man. Quick and easy was best. He would need his blades, though.

His eyes drifted to the bundle at the back of the wagon. He'd seen them store his gear there before they'd started marching and felt confident he could get it all back without a fuss. It would have to be at night, of course, and the bundle would probably be moved when the army made camp, but it still wouldn't be a problem.

Trenna grunted and stumbled at his right, distracting him from his plans. She was shackled as well and scowled at the manacles holding her to the wagon. This was obviously not the reception she'd anticipated from Gideon Mavon, but she wasn't complaining either.

In fact, by the sharp glint to her eyes, Faxon would wager his best dagger that she had plans of her own.

He decided to test that theory.

"If Nelek could see you now he'd be very cross with you," he said.

Trenna glanced at him and flashed an annoyed smile. "Well, he'd be cross with somebody."

"I'm rather surprised you let them shackle you."

"It amused me," she said, mimicking his own dry tone.

Faxon chuckled low in his throat. "Yes, you look quite entertained."

She made a noncommittal noise and frowned up at the sky. The sun was inching its way toward the horizon, only barely warming the mountaintops surrounding them. Winter clung stubbornly to the terrain, patches of snow intruding where only rock and earth should be. But Faxon knew the terrain wasn't what she was looking at. She was gauging the time, probably calculating distances too.

Something was coming.

Faxon frowned and moved to walk closer to her. If he knew anything about Trenna, it was that she always had a plan.

"Mind telling me what we're waiting for?" he asked, keeping his voice low.

She eyed him again. "Just trying to figure out if we'll reach the fort tonight."

"And?"

"And what?" she asked. "It's a godsdamn fort, Faxon. Manned by my men. They won't let Gideon pass and they won't pay any sort of ransom. Unless Gideon sprouts a silver tongue between now and when we get there, we're going to find ourselves in a battle."

"So what do we do?" Faxon asked.

Leave it to Trenna to tell him things he was already aware of and still manage to make them sound new.

She smirked at him. "Hell if I know," she said.

The wagon jerked to a halt, forcing them both to stop. Faxon watched as Trenna hissed in pain, carefully rubbing her wrists. His own wrists hurt but he refused to give these men the satisfaction of seeing him nurse his wounds, so he focused instead on what had forced them to stop.

The wagon had not gotten stuck in a rut or mud or anything, so it wasn't anything to do with mundane travel issues. In fact, the army itself had stopped marching and Faxon began to wonder if they'd reached Trenna's fort.

He squinted up the mountain pass, following the long line of men as it snaked around hillock and road, but could see no structure ahead. Two peaks rose jagged and rough on either side of the road, their tops still frozen so that they made a snaggle-toothed impression against a pale blue sky. The storm had passed some time ago and the air subsequently plummeted to freezing levels that bit through his clothing.

Faxon pulled in a deep breath and summoned the last traces of Eldur blood in his system. He would need more soon, he realized, and sent another angry glare to the wagon. Mavon's men had been far too competent when they searched him for weapons. They'd found all six vials of Eldur blood he'd strapped to his person and summarily dismissed them as some form of alchemy.

Narrowing his eyes at the front of the procession, he focused on his vision, willing the blood to show him what was going on. Brigetta always spoke of a trade when working with magic; one thing must take the place of the other. An injury transferred to a healthy host and vice versa, but Faxon was not bound by those laws. He was Human, not Eldur, and could manipulate magic differently.

That's because your trade is far deeper than the average blood mage.

The voice startled him, buzzing through him like a sibilant hiss, and he shivered in response.

Faxon scowled, deliberately ignoring the ominous warning, and focused instead on the coming danger. Three men were riding fast in their direction, originating from the front of the line. He recognized two of them as Mavon's personal guards, but the third was Eldur.

"You're sure about that ransom bit?" he asked Trenna. "Because it looks like one of your men is heading our way."

Trenna straightened, obviously startled by the announcement. She stopped rubbing her wrists and peered up at the approaching riders. She muttered several choice words under her breath and rolled her shoulder, shifting closer to the wagon as though she were pacing, but the chains would not allow her to move very far, so she ended up right next to him again.

"This is good news, isn't it?" he asked Trenna. "Ransom means no fighting. And no fighting means we get to Kiavana faster."

"And it means that the families of all my men are dead," she snapped at him.

Faxon rocked back on his heels and hummed. "Oh, right. I forgot that part."

~ * ~

She recognized Bervam right away and willed herself into standing still. He reined his horse several steps from her and frowned, clearly displeased by her current state of imprisonment. The two guards Mavon had sent with him edged their horses closer, both holding tight to their weapons. Trenna took a slow breath and eyed Bervam.

"You used to follow orders better," she told him.

He flashed an unrepentant grin at her. "You can thank me later."

"I'll throttle you later, you bastard. Now tell me, what's going on?"

Bervam patted his horse's neck, soothing the restless creature before answering her. "Several of the boys and I decided Porrex would be daft to kill innocents in the name of our sins. Holster said as it would be political suicide and the Eldur as a whole wouldn't stand for it."

"They stood for it before," Trenna said, quelling an unsettled fury as it surged through her. "You know very well they did."

"Those were soldiers, not civilians. And besides..." Bervam met her gaze and held it. "Our families would rather know we fought with honor than see us live in continued cowardice."

"You can't speak for all of them, Bervam."

"What are you talking about?" Faxon hissed at her. "Of course he can."

Trenna glared at Faxon, who jangled his manacles as though to remind her that they were still shackled to the wagon. She ignored his noisome argument and turned back to Bervam, who watched Faxon with an expression of mingled humor and irritation. She could see faint traces of distaste, could sense Bervam's discomfort, and worried for a moment that she was fighting a lost cause.

It seemed the rift between Human and Eldur was as present as ever.

"No," Bervam said after a moment. "I can't speak for all of them, but I can speak for the eighty-five who broke ranks with me."

Her heart ached at his words.

Eight-five soldiers.

Countless family members at Porrex's mercy.

Gods help her, what if they lost? What if Porrex did kill civilians to maintain his authority?

She looked up at Bervam and shook her head. "The price is too high," she said.

"The price isn't yours to pay," he said and turned to the nearest guard. "Go back to His Lordship and inform him that we will not be moving until General Lana is released and returned to us."

Faxon cleared his throat and Bervam sent her a questioning glance. Trenna nodded, too annoyed at the situation to pay much attention. She'd almost hoped her men could get out of this mess unscathed. Now they were split, some fighting with her while the rest would be forced against her. It would have been so much easier if they'd protected their families.

Not much easier, but at least then she wouldn't have civilian blood on her hands.

And there was the other thing, she thought, as she shifted the manacles on her wrists.

Twenty years in exile, happily raising her children. Had she spent even an hour of that time thinking of the men she'd left behind?

Gods, she wanted to crawl into a dark hole and never come out.

But no, she thought, meeting Bervam's unwavering gaze. Hiding would only dishonor them.

Trenna straightened her shoulders and waited for her release.

Thirty-one

Troy sped up the curving staircase, his arm straining with the full bucket and his legs burning from too many trips through the tower. He'd been up and down so many times his body felt clumsy and thick with exhaustion, but he kept going. At first he'd been angry about being relegated to water duty, not liking the separation from Kaden, but now he had a newfound respect for Dell's leadership.

All her runners were lean and tall and he had a feeling she'd chosen him because his height could take the steps two at a time. Kaden was nearly as tall but not quite, so the choice had been obvious, in retrospect.

The top tower door swung open just as he reached it and Troy had to swerve aside to avoid another runner retreating with his own empty bucket. Water sloshed, some of it splashing over the side to douse his tunic, and Troy cursed, trying to steady the thing before he spilled it all. The other runner flashed him an apologetic grin before charging down the stairwell.

Scowling, Troy straightened and moved to the door again, pausing to listen for the hiss and thud of bolts and arrows as they made their marks. When it seemed the volley had passed he opened the door and slipped outside, ducking low.

Scanning first for open fires, Troy shut the door behind him and hurried to the closest wall. He spotted Kaden by a crenellation, his hands busy reloading a crossbow and a frown of concentration on his face. Troy felt the knot of worry in his gut loosen a bit and crouched beside a pair of archers to wait.

When the next volley came, he would douse whatever fires it brought, run back to the wall and then rotate to the southeast tower. The rotation was methodical, simple, and under normal circumstances would be easy: tower, tower, wall, yard, but with the added weight of the water bucket and the teeming mass of soldiers in the yard it could be tricky to navigate.

"How many shots left?" Dell's familiar voice called and the archers responded with various numbers between one and five. Troy found her a moment later, watched as she leaned around a crenellation to aim and fire before settling back on her haunches. "All right, after the next volley we've got a bolt run. Ray, Travis, you're up. And... you... pretty boy... what's your name again?"

Some of the men snickered and even Troy smiled as his friend answered, "Kaden."

"Right," Dell said. "Ray, Travis, Kaden. You're the runners. Give your bolts to the men on your left, leave the bows where they are, and get ready."

Troy had only the barest moment to wonder what this run consisted of, before a loud voice warned of the coming volley and everyone ducked, bodies squashing hard into the stone wall as though to disappear. Troy hunkered low, hugging the bucket to his chest as the whizz and thud of bolts soared overhead. Several aching seconds passed before the sounds stopped and he looked up again.

Many blazing arrows had hit deep in the wooden door and several others smoldered on the floorboards. Troy leapt to his feet, kicking the closest arrows toward the door before flinging his water onto them, dousing fires before they could catch. Several of the archers stomped similar flames out, cursing vehemently at them until all that was left was smoke.

"Dell!" A voice cried, just as she shouted, "Runners!"

"Dell! Look!"

She glanced over the crenellation and whirled back around, eyes wide. "Trebuchet!"

Troy's stomach plummeted and for an endless moment he just stood there, empty bucket in hand, eyes fixed on the airy space just over the wall. A massive chunk of stone hurled up and over the crenellated wall, looking heavy and ungainly and utterly deadly as it continued its path toward the tower. Troy stared, mouth agape, his mind barely registering the pepper of arrows that trailed the projectile and realized a heartbeat later that the trajectory was off.

Something tore into his left shoulder, pain blossoming into his awareness just as a body crashed into him, tugging him down. He hit the wall with a grunt and then lost his breath as whoever had tackled him landed with their elbow directly in his gut. Bright lights sparked in his vision, but even dazed he managed to see the stone as it passed overhead, nicking the side of the tower just enough to make it spin before starting its plummet down into the courtyard below.

"Bolt run now!" Dell shouted from on top of him, her voice painfully loud as he began to realize who had tackled him. "Everyone else cover!"

Bodies began moving, turning toward the crenellations again to take aim and fire. Troy spotted Kaden as he passed by, charging toward the wall behind two others to start their run. He hesitated for a fraction of a second, meeting Troy's gaze as though to ascertain that he was all right before turning his mind more fully to his task. Troy tried to smile at him but grimaced instead, Dell's weight shifting on his chest as she moved to fire again.

His shoulder ached and he turned to look, spying the bolt that had lodged itself just above his armpit. It was buried deep, he could see that much, and began to wonder why it only ached. Surely he should feel something more than the low throb of the injury. And then Dell turned to him, cursing softly as she gripped the bolt to push it through.

Agony pulsed through the injury, licking up and down his arm, making a sudden spike into his chest, and Troy screamed.

"You mighta warned him, Adelle," someone said from beside them.

"He saw it," was Dell's reply as she began tying something tightly around his shoulder.

Dizzy with pain, Troy bit down hard on his lower lip, smothering his voice before he could whimper or create more of a spectacle of himself. It hurt, but it had missed the major bits. He might even be able to move his arm if he needed to, and with the constant swirl of activity around them he had the feeling he would need to very soon.

Dell tightened a hard knot right over the entry wound, which sent an aching pulse right through him but Troy managed not to groan. Then she turned away, lifting herself just enough to peer over the crenellation again and hissed a few curse words. Troy watched her, trying to count his breaths the way his father had taught him to, forcing his mind away from the injury so that he could think better.

"James!" Dell hollered, finally reaching for her discarded crossbow.

Another figure slid into view, crouching low to avoid another volley as it flew overhead. Troy tried to concentrate on him but couldn't make out more than the bare essentials: thin to lankiness, limbs jutting out in odd proportion to the rest of him, and a thin, dark scruff of facial hair that said he was almost a man.

"What's the plan?" James asked, his voice hoarse and breathless.

"Get ready to take the wounded one down," Dell said and Troy grunted. They hadn't been rightly introduced, so he shouldn't be so bothered that she didn't know his name. "When the runners get back, they'll hold the position while we begin a retreat."

"We're abandoning the tower?" James asked, clearly shocked.

"We don't have a choice," Dell snapped at him. "It'll take two more tries before that trebuchet actually hits its mark and I don't imagine any of us wants to be here when that happens."

James stared at her for a moment and then, with the barest nod of his head, shouldered his crossbow. Troy struggled to sit up, not wanting to be any more of a burden than he already was. An unpleasant clamminess cooled the back of his neck and for a dazed moment he feared he might pass out, but he counted his breaths again and managed to get upright.

He realized a moment later that Dell and her company hadn't stopped working. Each man kept leaning over the wall, firing, ducking back down to reload, or stamping out the fires that each volley sent their way. Marveling at their focus, Troy propped himself against the wall and searched for the closest weapon.

Gods knew he couldn't fire the thing with any accuracy, but he could at least load it.

~ * ~

Liana rushed into the stable master's front room, eyes doing a quick scan for anything useful. Necessity had turned the two-story structure into a temporary barracks, allowing soldiers to catch bits of sleep before returning to their posts, but it was quickly clearing out. Abandoned cots littered the floor, most of them empty of blankets and bedrolls, but here and there she spotted a forgotten bit of fabric.

Sconces flickered dim light into the room, casting deep shadows against the walls, but she spotted one tapestry hanging above the dying hearth and paused. She didn't know precisely why she stopped, gods knew there was too much to do and she really shouldn't, but something inside her jerked at the sight of it.

Her mother had spoken of that tapestry once, she remembered. Deep greens and browns painted an autumnal forest across the fabric, and at the center stood a mother bear and her two cubs, each of them picking their way across fallen logs. Quite without thinking, Liana stepped over several cots and made her way closer to the tapestry, trying to make out the details more clearly.

Outside, the rush of soldiers and shouts of many men coordinating the retreat to the inner bailey called to her, but Liana still paused, transfixed. Letting out a slow breath she stared at the careful embroidery, remembering her mother's voice as she'd spoken of Sir Modig, the horse master of Kiavana, and the gentle spirit the man had possessed. It seemed altogether surreal to be standing there, in exactly the space her mother had talked about when telling tales of home and how she'd met their father.

This was where she'd come after Father had knighted her, Liana thought. She'd paced directly in front of this fire, staring at this tapestry, trying to figure out what to do about the great "Puffer Fish," as she'd called Nelek back then.

Liana felt the hair on the back of her neck prickle up and her heart gave a sudden, intense squeeze. "Gods, Mother," she whispered. "Where are you?"

"Well, she's certainly not *here*," said a masculine and annoyingly familiar voice.

Liana did not have to turn to know it was Lodas, the man from the tunnels; she could sense his unrepentant gaze on her back and had to suppress the desire to snap at him. Snapping at him would not help the situation, and she had the unsettling feeling he liked it. Glaring over her shoulder, she abandoned the tapestry and headed for the side stairwell, not dignifying him with a response.

She needed to check the top floor, make certain the building was, indeed, empty before continuing her work outside. Most of the servants and general populace had already relocated to the inner bailey, leaving her to deal with only the stragglers—boys busy hauling water to and from the walls, or wounded soldiers. She was also, however, hunting for any equipment that might come in useful, so when she reached the second floor and spotted the trunk in the master bedroom, she automatically rushed for it.

It was locked, of course, and heavy. Grabbing the iron lock with one hand, she scowled at it, willing the stupid thing to open. Then she abandoned the lock and felt the hinges, hoping that maybe she could open the thing another way, but it was solidly built. She let out a growl of frustration.

"She's not in there either," Lodas said from the doorway.

Giving in to her irritation, she turned her scowl on him. "If you don't have anything useful to say, kindly go away."

He chuckled low in his throat and she cursed herself for letting him get to her. Kaden never let people bother him like this, she thought. Kaden was always calm and collected, capable of smiling through his anger, and not for the first time in her life she wondered why she couldn't have been blessed with that talent. It seemed unfair that they could be related and yet so drastically different from each other.

She didn't hear Lodas move, but felt his approach and stiffened in response. A moment later he crouched beside her, smirking first at her and then at the lock.

"Are we looking for something in particular?" he asked.

Exasperated, she leaned back on her haunches. "Anything that might help once we're stuck over there."

Lodas clucked his tongue twice and reached into his sleeve. "Many people spend their whole lives wondering what the inner sanctum of Kiavana looks like," he said, procuring two thin bits of metal from somewhere in his shirtsleeves. Liana frowned and squinted at them, understanding lighting through her just before he began picking at the lock.

"Somehow, I doubt this was the way they wanted to visit," she said.

He hummed a non-committal reply and concentrated on his work. Liana watched him for a moment, her gaze taking in his particulars with what she hoped was cool indifference. Black hair made loose curls around his face, the bulk of it tied back in what she imagined was a fashionable knot at the back of his head, and he had a long nose that hooked just slightly at the end. Dark brows furrowed as he focused on his work and she caught the glint of amber in his eyes just as the lock clicked open and he removed it.

He smiled at her, holding the lock aloft. "Milady," he said with a mocking bow of his head.

Liana rolled her eyes and reached for the trunk, opening it quickly. Inside was an assortment of odd things and it took a moment for her to rifle through them. She pulled out a ratted, old tunic and tossed it aside, then pushed past a bound leather book that Lodas immediately took an interest in. She saw him take the volume, but didn't protest. Whosoever it was didn't need it right now, and by the looks of the room hadn't needed it in a while.

Her fingers brushed something cold and a sudden sense of dread overwhelmed her. Liana yanked back her hand with a small cry of alarm. The cold bit deep into her, lingering unnaturally in her fingertips and making a slow crawl up her arm. Confused, she scowled at her hand but nothing seemed wrong with it. The warmth was slowly leaking back into the limb, so it seemed there was no permanent damage, and yet...

And yet something had just happened.

"Liana?" Lodas asked from beside her. Oddly enough, he actually sounded concerned. "Liana?"

"I..." she said, not sure how to answer him.

Her gaze moved back to the trunk and she reached again, more cautious this time. She moved fabric aside, uncovering the very base of the trunk, where several rusty metal shards lay in a haphazard array. Frowning, she leaned further into the trunk, trying to make out its shape.

She spotted the distinct shape of a cross guard hilt and froze, all the breath leaving her at once.

"It cannot be..." she whispered.

Lodas peered over her shoulder. "And yet, I daresay it probably is..."

He sounded far too interested for her tastes, so Liana began covering it up again, careful not to touch it this time. The pieces made uncomfortable scratching sounds as they came together in the fabric and for a heartbeat Liana thought she heard whispers hissing out from it. She'd known just by looking that this was the infamous Ebony Blade, the sword her father had destroyed on the day he freed Kiavana, and while she wasn't sure it could be of any real use to them, she also didn't think they wanted the enemy to find it, either.

"Curious," Lodas said as she stood.

"Actually, it makes sense," Liana said, cradling the fabric like a sack. "Sir Modig was the most trusted knight in Kiavana when the blade was felled. Of course they would leave it to him for safe keeping."

"No," Lodas said, wide lips quirking in humor. "It's curious that *you* would find it."

Not entirely certain what he meant by that, Liana frowned and shook her head at him. She was about to ask him for clarification when a loud commotion outside stole her attention. People were shouting something she couldn't quite make out, but it sounded urgent. Lodas frowned at the small window, and then understanding lit his face. He grabbed her elbow and began hauling her toward the door.

"Trebuchet!" he shouted, just as something came crashing through the beams overhead.

Wood splintered and the deafening thud of something heavy slamming into the floor resounded through the room. The ground tilted and groaned and Liana lost her footing, but Lodas's grip on her held fast. He drew her out of the room and into the stairwell, his feet remarkably sure on the trembling steps. The walls shook around them, adding to the thunderous rattle of destruction, and for a dazed moment Liana feared they would be crushed.

They reached the ground floor and Lodas yanked her into a corner, covering her with his own body as bits of wall and ceiling came crashing down around them.

Thirty-two

Brigetta glared at the mess of stone and broken lumber that used to be the stable master's home. She'd sent Lodas after Evaliana and knew the two hadn't escaped before that wretched boulder had crashed into the building.

Dammit, she thought and abandoned the load of linens she'd been carrying to the inner gate. Dropping the would-be bandages to the side, she dashed toward the ruined building, praying the two were still alive.

If anything happened to Kaden, Liana was the next in line for the throne. And if anything happened to Lodas, Faxon would be angry. Lodas was his only nephew, after all, and since they had no children of their own, someone had to carry on the Mylonas name.

She raced across the yard, grateful for the borrowed trousers Brenson had seen to her rooms earlier. Battle was irritably difficult on its own; she didn't need to be tripping on skirts while she was at it.

Skidding to a halt in front of the mangled threshold, Bree searched frantically for a plan. The structure was too unstable and any movement could send it all crashing down. She couldn't lift every stone to dig through there and she couldn't crawl in herself.

"Brigetta!"

She ignored the familiar voice, concentrating on the problem instead.

No crawling, no lifting, and no asking others to do so either, because they would just cause more damage to the two inside.

"Bree!" Faolan said, reaching her side. "You need to get inner before we lose this area."

All mundane options were exhausted; it was time to think magic.

Bree took the dagger from her belt. She could just sense the faint pulse of Evaliana's blood on the air, could feel its prickle at the base of her neck, and took a deep breath to steady herself. Under normal circumstances Bree would have used it, but she wanted to leave it there, to use it like a trail to follow, so she took her dagger and slid it hard across the base of her thumb.

Blood welled at the injury, pooling into her outstretched palm, and Bree closed her eyes to listen.

Faolan said something low and hoarse beside her, but he knew better than to interrupt her now. Concentrating, she measured her breathing in time with Evaliana's pulse, trying to come into sync with it. The chaos of retreat that had been so prevalent before died away, drowned out by the constant beat of Evaliana's heart in time with her own.

Bree inhaled once, slowly, feeling out with magic. She could sense its confusion, knew it was waiting for a real command, but she held it there, let it hang in the air as Liana's situation became clearer. For endless seconds she allowed herself to merge with Liana, ignoring Noffi's warning voice in her head that this was dangerous, that there were so many things she was doing wrong at the moment.

Magic needed commands or it would take matters into its own hands; she wasn't supposed to just feel her way through this. Merging with another, even in an effort to locate or save her, could be deadly to both parties.

Still, Bree let the moment stretch until she could feel Liana's skin like it was her own. The girl was bleeding in several places, and Bree scowled. Another sensation at the side of her neck caught Bree's attention and she concentrated harder, pushing past the sudden wave of giddiness that throbbed into her temples.

Breath, she realized. She could feel Lodas's breath on Liana's neck.

Her mind made a clear map of where the two were, how they were positioned, and she went back to work.

"Alt ramoolessa nefarri duss," she murmured.

Magic snapped into action, following her commands. An instant later, Lodas and Evaliana collapsed into a heap just in front of Faolan, who let out a curse of surprise. Bree opened her eyes again and the world swam. She felt her body tilt to the side but strangely could not stop it. Faolan caught her, scooping her up, and for a bleary second she smiled at him before her vision darkened and she passed out.

~ * ~

Trenna battled an increasing sense of shame as she rode beside Bervam. Names filtered through her, each one a searing brand in her mind as she began to realize the depths of Porrex's treachery. The men around her sent smiles of encouragement, each of them obviously pleased by her sudden return, and that seemed even worse.

Twenty years, she thought again. Twenty years of peace on Vakeshmeer Island had cost more than just the prince's life. At the time, she'd imagined Ronan would have wanted her to stay away, to raise Kaden in peace, but the full brunt of her actions hit her now. Ronan was not the only casualty at his father's hands; he was just the first, and she'd left without even considering what Porrex would do next.

Clenching her jaw, Trenna glared at the trail in front of them and held tighter to her reins. Her horse shifted, apparently sensing her agitation, and she was forced to relax her grip. Giving the mottled brown creature a reassuring pat on the neck, she hummed something soft and low and the horse responded in kind, continuing their trek.

"I remember when you used to have Gregorn ease your horses," Bervam said from beside her. "It's nice to see you've learned a useful trick or two."

Trenna glanced at him, surprised out of her brooding. "There was a man in Kiavana who helped me learn," she said, remembering Sir Modig with a wave of fondness. And then, because it seemed better than riding in silence, hating herself for hiding away all these years, she explained. "When the barrier was up and I first crossed into Kiavana, my memory was taken from me. So, I had no idea what my mission had been or where I had come from. Noffi's magic made me look Human, so naturally I thought I was and… I wandered about for years not knowing what to do."

"Your swords weren't a dead giveaway?" Bervam asked with a wry smile of his own, but he was obviously interested.

She hadn't been able to explain what had happened the first time she'd left the company, and she imagined many of the men were curious. In fact, several horses were drifting closer to them already, her eighty-five true crowding up as close as they could get to hear. Not all of them could, of course, and she imagined the tale would be slightly warped by nightfall, but at least a few of them would have the truth of it. With a small sigh, she settled in her saddle and continued to explain.

"I didn't have any swords when I woke there," she said. "Hell, I didn't even have clothes. I woke up stark naked on the other side of the barrier with no swords, no memory, and only the barest notion of a name."

Bervam whistled low. "Naked? I'd have paid good money to see that."

A titter of amusement went through the men and Trenna eyed him, trying hard not to smile at the rakish grin he gave her. Then someone said they'd have paid good money just to see her unarmed and another ripple of laughter had her grinning in spite of herself. Shaking her head, she tried to find her place in the story again.

"I wandered through the woods until I found a remote cottage that, thankfully, had someone's laundry hanging out to dry. I stole some pants and a shirt and meant to keep going but…" She felt her cheeks heat as the next memory hit her, but she'd already started and couldn't stop now. "It turns out I'm not a great thief. Brockley, the owner of the clothing, had been sitting not five steps away from me while I burgled him and I didn't even notice."

Bervam laughed at this but otherwise made no comment.

"He was remarkably good humored about it, though. Said he figured I needed them more than he did, considering he'd gotten to see all of my freckles." Trenna smiled again, remembering Brock's entertainment that day, and then a tide of pain pulled that smile away.

"This is the man who became Sir Brockley Croften, right?" Bervam asked. "I heard a rumor about him. Said he was your brother?"

"Blood brother," she confirmed. "We made blood oaths that bound us about a year later. He was working to be a guardsman in Nelek's employ and I helped him train for it. Swordplay was the only thing I was any good at and he had opened his home to me, kept me sheltered, fed, and clothed during those first few months."

"But you were gone for several years that first time," someone said from the left. "You're saying you never got your memory back?"

Trenna tried to locate the soldier but there was too much movement, and by the flicker of doubt on several of the men's faces she could tell this was a sentiment held by many. It was best to be honest and clear.

"It's not like I hit my head or something," she said. "Auliere completely wiped my memory when I crossed the barrier. She used blood magic and said it was the price for crossing the barrier into Kiavana."

Trenna saw several men nod, new understanding lighting their faces. Blood magic was not something that could be controlled by general Eldur; it required a mage, and her years without memory could not be blamed on her. "I didn't remember who I was until Nelek and I came to Dyngannon and Noffi performed the ritual to reverse the magic that had made me look Human."

"I remember that day," Bervam said quietly. Trenna glanced at him, but he kept his eyes on the path in front of them and shook his head. "Most painful thing I've ever seen, watching all that magic turn you Eldur again. Nelek was mad as hell and tried to reach you... He didn't understand what was happening. None of us really did."

Trenna shivered, both from the early morning chill and the memory, and frowned up at the summit. There were days she was truly thankful she hadn't been born with an affinity for blood magic. As grateful as she that magic could help her men on the battlefield, there was something terribly brutal about it, something deep and dark that frightened her.

They rode in silence for several minutes, the clop of hooves and restless snorts of their animals breaking through the stillness of the forest. Great trees forced them to weave their horses here and there, and branches snagged at her cloak so many times she gave up trying to correct it. The world smelled of cold, laced with crushed pine and the musk of horse, and as the silence stretched, Trenna breathed it in, let it focus and awaken her.

Mavon's men rode a little to the right of their company, close enough that they could keep an eye on them. She didn't doubt the man had some of his own soldiers riding in the middle of hers, spying. That was fine. Spies were nothing new to her and she had nothing to hide.

Behind her, Faxon rode on his own horse, looking bored. Trenna ignored him too, confident that whatever was going on in his mind had little or nothing to do with her. He might try killing one of the Human company that had put him in shackles, but he certainly couldn't do that right now, and she imagined he was practical enough to wait until after they'd rescued Kiavana for such a thing.

"General," Bervam broke the silence again and by the hesitance in his voice she knew what was coming next. She met his gaze and held it, waiting for the question. "What happened with Prince Ronan?"

Yet another loss, she thought and took a slow breath. She knew the rumors Porrex had spread about that day, knew the man had framed her as the murderer of the Crown Prince, and in her grief she hadn't done enough to refute him. It was time now to fix that.

"Ronan brought Noffi to me in Cadabyr," she began, her voice suddenly hoarse and quiet. "I was pregnant and needed the blood mage and he provided good escort. No matter what you heard, she came of her own accord. The prince did not abduct her."

Bervam scowled. "Oh, aye. I know. It'd take a fool greater than me to think anyone could have abducted that woman."

Trenna nodded once, glad that at least one of Porrex's lies could be so easily refuted. Noffi had been one of the greatest blood mages Dyngannon had ever seen; the idea that anyone would want to risk such an abduction was preposterous.

"Ronan and I were returning to Cadabyr fortress when we heard a battle," she said. "We followed the sounds to find several Eldur soldiers attacking Mavon… Tibitus Mavon, not Gideon… and Porrex was commanding them."

She remembered with aching clarity the sound of Ronan's voice as he'd confronted his father, the way he'd stood there, sword drawn, creating a barrier between Porrex and Mavon. Heroic, she thought, and every inch the heir to the throne.

"Ronan…" Trenna had to pause to breathe, pushing back the memory of how helpless she had been. If she hadn't been pregnant she could have fought beside Ronan, could have kept him safe. Their combined forces would have easily overwhelmed the numbers Porrex had brought that day.

But she had been pregnant, very pregnant, and thus unable to stop the course of events.

"Ronan…" she began again, stronger this time. "Confronted the king, demanding an explanation as to why he would order the assassination of Nelek's child."

There was an intake of breath around her as the implications of what she'd just said hit their mark. Nobody expected a king to be flawless, but they did expect certain boundaries to exist. The Eldur throne was rife with politics and backstabbing and, yes, murder, but to attempt killing a child was irrefutably wrong. It sullied Porrex's honor so deeply that not even his position as king could shield him from the consequences.

"Your child?" Bervam asked, his voice so soft she almost didn't hear him. "Did... was... was the assassin successful?"

"No," Trenna said. She chose not to explain that the assassin had been her own mother, though she imagined the timeline and the death of her parents all those years ago would give it away. "The blood mage was able to save the child."

"Thank gods," Bervam breathed his praise and glanced at the sky, repeating it once more for good measure.

Trenna watched him, touched by the sincerity in his face, and then, because she knew the story had to be finished, she continued. "Porrex did not deny the accusation, nor did he explain. He called Ronan a traitor and... there was a fight." She flinched, the memory of Porrex's blade arching toward his son making her heart twist in pain. "And... Porrex killed him. I tried to call out a warning but I was too late. Ronan could have easily handled the other men but... he had not expected his own father to cut him down."

The truth settled hard around them, uncomfortable and heavy, and they rode in silence for a long time. She could sense the battle in her men and understood how difficult it must be for them. It had been difficult for her too, dealing with the depths of the king's dishonor. But then, she had not been forced into service to the crown as her men had. The dark threat of discovery had haunted her over the last several years in hiding, but her men had been treated far worse. It was not hard for them to accept this truth; it was just one more reason to rebel, and with a deep, careful breath, Trenna prayed that rebellion would be successful.

It was long past time for Dyngannon to have a new king.

Thirty-three

Kaden kept close to Travis's heels as they dashed across the yard. Ray cursed just beside him, and Kaden glanced in time to see the boy's ankle roll through a patch of mud, but he didn't fall. Stumbling a bit, Ray managed to correct himself and keep his stride. Kaden nodded once to him, mostly because he felt silly for checking on him, and Ray flashed a boyish grin back. Then, they both had to concentrate on the run.

The sack slung over Kaden's shoulder was alarmingly light considering they'd been rummaging everywhere for bolts and arrows and he shifted it, trying to run calculations in his mind. They'd been to every section of the outer bailey save the other walls and towers; those Travis had said needed the arrows just as much as they did, so they were left alone. The armory had been abandoned already, all of its stores taken to the inner bailey, and Travis had ordered them to move on. Which, considering the trebuchet and the general evacuation of the outer bailey, made sense.

They would need those arrows on the inner walls soon.

Kaden spotted Sir Faolan carrying Brigetta to the inner gate and nearly stopped in his tracks. Two other soldiers were dragging more wounded just beside him, but Kaden didn't have time to investigate further.

The blood mage would be all right and he had bigger problems to deal with.

Travis slid to a stop in front of a quickly disassembling infirmary. The makeshift linen walls were being torn down by a pair of soot-covered boys, and a regal woman with a tight frown gave distinct orders to each of them. She had sharp, angular features and keen blue eyes that seemed to assess everything in sight, and for a heartbeat Kaden thought she looked familiar. Black curly hair snaked out of the kerchief tied over her head and there were smears of dirt and blood over her forehead and chin, the evidence of long hours with wounded men.

Kaden saw Travis reach into a barrel and begin yanking out what little contents there were: several arrows and a scant few bolts. Scowling, Kaden rubbed his face and prayed it would be enough for however long they needed to hold that tower. He glanced up at the tower in question, battling down a sense of inadequacy and hopelessness.

There were so few of them and the enemy outside seemed countless. How could they possibly survive another day?

The hair on the back of his neck prickled up and he realized he was being watched. The regal woman's gaze had locked on him and wasn't moving. Kaden stared back, confused by the sudden attention, and listened to Travis reporting to Ray.

"That's it," Travis said. "It's time to head back up."

"It's not much, but it'll have to do," Ray said. "Leastwise until we can abandon that damn tower and regroup inner."

"You intend to go back up there?" the woman asked, but she wasn't addressing the other two.

No, her attention was still fastened on Kaden.

That odd familiarity niggled at him and he frowned, trying to place her, which was ridiculous since he'd never been in Kiavana before, much less Dyngannon, so she shouldn't be familiar at all. He saw Ray and Travis exchange confused looks. They knew she wasn't asking them either.

Ray glanced at the tower, his restlessness to continue moving apparent, but something about the woman kept him silent.

"Yes," Kaden answered at last and the woman's brow furrowed.

"That is too dangerous for you," she said.

Kaden's face grew hot. He could sense Ray and Travis's attention settle on him again with renewed interest, and he clenched his fists. How in blazes did this woman know who he was? And she had to know who he was; her clear blue eyes told him that much.

Bree, he thought. This woman must know Brigetta. She must have told her about Noffi's prophetic announcement about the throne, and now he was going to be yanked into the center of attention.

Frowning, Kaden glared at the woman. "It's no more dangerous for me than it is for all the others up there."

Her eyebrow quirked up and a small, amused smile twitched at her wide mouth. A mouth, he realized slowly, that looked quite a bit like his father's. And Liana's. He glanced at her ears, but they were covered by the kerchief.

Not Auliere, he thought. His grandmother was dead.

Then who?

"You are your mother's son," the woman said with a gesture of dismissal.

Travis and Ray took that dismissal immediately, both pivoting on their heels to start the run back for the tower. Kaden waited the space of a breath, his gaze caught on the woman's very blue eyes, before he turned to follow. Whoever she was, she could introduce herself later. Family or not, there was more to be done today and precious little time to do it in.

"What the hell was that about?" Travis asked as he shoved the tower door open. "How do you know her?"

"I don't," Kaden answered as he ducked inside. "Who is she?"

Ray and Travis shared another look. With a shrug and a shake of his head, Ray passed them both and charged up the tower stairs. Travis hesitated a moment, frowning up at the stairs before looking back at Kaden. The conflict was clear on his face and the unsettled feeling that had taken residence in Kaden's belly intensified.

"Rumor says she's royalty," Travis said at last. "But the duke hasn't made a formal announcement. One thing I do know... she's one of them mages for sure."

Travis started up the stairs, not bothering to elaborate further. Frustrated, Kaden followed. He'd figured she was part of the family, on his father's side, but that didn't narrow things down much. By all accounts the royal family of Dyngannon was large and wide-spread. He had cousins upon cousins and as many aunts and uncles to cover them. Reaching the top of the tower door, he paused as a thought caught at him.

Most of his extended family were Porrex supporters. Whoever this woman was, she was openly defying the king, and if his parents were right, there were fewer of those to be counted.

Royalty, he thought, his hand flat on the tower door.

"My gods," he murmured aloud and glanced back down the tower stairs. "It can't be."

But it could and he knew it. What better time for the king's long lost wife to come out of hiding than after Noffi's death? Trenna had often spoken of the woman's disappearance, the maelstrom it had caused in the Dyngannon court, and the subsequent degeneration of Porrex's rule. If his mother was right, then Noffi had been the only mage powerful enough to help hide the woman's presence from the court.

Rumors of royalty indeed, he thought again and pushed the tower door open.

He ducked low at someone's shout and shoved the door closed behind him, rushing to the nearest crenellation. The thunk and whoosh of many different arrows passing him by shoved his heart into a gallop. He struck the stone wall with his shoulder. Dull pain blossomed in his joints, but he ignored it, dropping the sack of bolts and arrows just beside the archer nearest him.

The archer turned out to be Dell, who nodded her thanks and kicked a crossbow in his direction. Kaden took the weapon and prepared to load, noticing as he did so that Troy was still there. His friend was scowling, reloading weapons for Dell as quickly as she could shoot them. The cloth wrapped tight around his shoulder had dark stains and he had the gray pallor of the sick.

Gods, why wasn't the man in the infirmary?

Kaden yanked back on the string of his crossbow, latching it into place, and shoved a bolt in place. Shifting to his knees, he peered over the side of the wall, found the first available target and pulled the trigger mechanism. The string slammed into the bolt, sending it careening toward its mark, but Kaden didn't pause to see if it hit home. Sliding back into position, he reached for another bolt and started to reload.

It became a rhythm: reload, shoot, reload, with the frequent need to take cover from enemy fire. His shoulders began to burn from the strain of pulling back on the string and he could feel the uncomfortable trail of sweat under his helmet, but he didn't stop. None of them stopped. Not even when Travis got nicked in the head, his body slumping suddenly beside Ray, who pushed his friend to safety and took up the position to fire.

Kaden saw someone tending to Travis's head, confirming he was still alive. That seemed impossible to Kaden, who was momentarily immobilized by the amount of blood spilling onto the wooden floor. Suppressing a shudder, he went back to his work, focusing on the orders Dell gave and the deadly dance they seemed to be engaged in with the archers below. Minutes blurred together, and after a while Kaden stopped trying to determine the time.

"Trebuchet!" Dell called.

Curling into a little ball, Kaden squashed himself close to the wall, instinct commanding him to stay still. He panted into his knees and prayed hard that the block would miss, that their luck would hold. The hard press of his crossbow's handle made an uncomfortable dent in his shoulder but he dared not move, not yet.

The tower lurched suddenly and a loud crack rent the air. Kaden loosened his grip on his legs and grabbed for the wall, seeking anything to steady himself. The floorboards rattled beneath him, several even seeming to slip under his knees, and for an endless second he wondered if the tower might collapse. Dell was shouting something but he couldn't make it out over the din of crumbling stone. Kaden stared at her, trying to read her lips, and then realized the order.

"Fire now!" she was saying. Then she leapt up, took aim, and let loose an arrow.

Kaden grabbed his crossbow again and, with shaky hands, tried to take aim below.

So close, he thought; that was so damn close.

Why weren't they abandoning yet?

It took him an extra second to find a target. Pulling the trigger again, he ducked just as another series of arrows whizzed overhead. Kaden looked to Troy, who was arguing with Dell while still loading her weapons. They were right next to him but he still couldn't hear; his heart was beating too hard and his breath came in harsh pants that drowned everything out.

"Adelle!" someone shouted from the tower door.

All eyes swerved to the newcomer.

It was a smaller girl, all bones and dark hair, no more than thirteen. She didn't wait for Dell to answer but shouted again, "Duke says to retreat inner now!"

Thank gods, Kaden thought.

Dell nodded once. "Pack up! Help the wounded..."

Her words were cut off as a large boulder hurled by, crashing into the tower roof. The tower shook, rumbling under the weight and velocity of the rock as it tore through the structure. Kaden's heart seized in horror. He pitched forward, shoving himself to his feet before he even knew what he was about.

The girl. He had to reach the girl.

He could feel the tremble of the tower under him, hear the telltale smack and *ssskt!* of every arrow and bolt that peppered around him, but kept his eyes locked on the little girl in the tower door. She'd fallen to the side at the initial impact, was on her hands and knees looking terrified and dazed.

Someone shouted something behind him and then the deep thudding of an arrow struck his back. Kaden staggered, pain licking through him, but he reached the girl and snagged her up, dragging her to the adjacent wall with a growl of anger and pain. They collapsed together, Kaden half on top of the slight creature.

Bright lights swam in his vision.

"Kaden!" Troy's voice called from somewhere very far away.

His eyelids drooped once and he fought to open them again. The little girl beneath him shuddered and cried, and he let his breath out in relief.

She was alive.

That was all he needed to know before he let the darkness take him.

Thirty-four

Nelek stood in his old room, watching as several people shifted furniture about, setting out cots and boarding up the window, preparing the spacious room as a temporary barracks for the men. It was uniquely positioned in the main tower of the inner bailey with a pentice that ran between his room and the old guard tower at the southwest corner. The private walkway had afforded him some privacy from his father, allowed him to move more freely all those years ago, and today he was even more grateful for the structure.

This would provide a modicum of safety for the men, and a place for much needed rest between shifts.

Everything felt so different now, he thought.

Home felt different, and not just because of the siege pounding away at Kiavana's walls.

All that he had fought for in his youth, all those things that had been so important back then: fighting his father for control, hunting for the Ebony Blade and his mother, it all seemed somehow lost to him. He'd known who he was back then, understood the duty that had been before him and never questioned it.

Nelek watched as a man began stoking the fire, shoving more wood into the giant hearth, and wondered where his surety had gone. The flames caught, roaring in triumph as more fuel was shoved into it, and he took a slow, deep breath. He was tied to this land, to these people, but he wasn't sure exactly what the tie meant anymore. Brenson was the duke now, not him. Brenson had seen them through twenty years and more, brought about a peace with the border lords that even Nelek had been unable to reach.

What bloody use was he anymore?

"My lord," Faolan stepped briskly through the door, sweeping a look through the room before focusing on Nelek. "Evaliana was in the stable when it was hit. She's been hurt."

Stiffening in surprise, Nelek turned from the room before he even knew he was moving and marched to the door. "How bad?" he asked and cursed himself for ever letting the girl out of his sight.

"They're checking her now," Faolan said and began following him out of the room. They shared a brisk pace through the small corridor to the granite stairwell and Faolan updated him as they walked. "Lodas was with her when it caved; he seems to have taken the brunt of it but she's unconscious."

"What was she doing in there?" It was a stupid question, he knew, but he was angry and he asked it anyway.

"Hunting for last minute supplies, I wager," Faolan said.

Blessing the man for not pointing out that Nelek himself had put her on that task, he hurried down the stairwell and into the main hall. The bodies of the wounded lay heaped across the floor, crowding the main hall to the point that it was hazardous to walk. Faolan took the lead, picking his way through the hall to a section near the entrance where a tall woman in a cap was bending over Liana, her features pinched with concern.

Nelek moved to kneel beside his daughter, heedless of the murmurs and discord his presence was bringing to the room. Gathering Liana's slender, calloused hand in his own, he pressed it to his chest and focused on her face. Dirt and blood smeared her forehead and left cheek, and there was a cut in her lower lip that glistened red in the brazier light. Her dark hair had come loose from the bun she'd been wearing earlier, making a chaotic mess of curly tresses around her head. His heart did a heavy thump in his chest and for a moment he couldn't breathe.

But then he did breathe, exhaling her name, "Liana."

He didn't care that his voice broke, or that the eyes of everyone around him were fastened on the scene. All of his might was concentrated on his daughter as he tried to will her eyes open.

"She will be all right, Nelek," a woman said from above him and he looked up.

For a heartbeat he thought it was his mother standing there, but that was impossible. Auliere Dyngannon had died over twenty years ago, just outside this very hall. He remembered it well: the way Brenson had cradled her weakened body, the way her black hair—so much like Liana's hair—had looked dull in the open air. And the way the curse of the Ebony Blade had made black webs under her too pale skin, crawling up her face and toward her temple until at last she had succumbed to it.

But no, this was not Auliere. She was too tall, for one. And she had broader cheekbones and a more prominent nose. Still elegant, as all Eldur were prone to be, but this woman was somewhat harder. Nelek stared, stunned into momentary silence as she knelt on the opposite side of Liana.

"She will be all right," the woman repeated, nodding down to Liana. "The wounds are superficial. She just took a solid whack to the head. She'll wake before the battle is over."

He imagined the words were meant to comfort, but Nelek barely registered them. A gnawing, angry worry had already begun weltering in his gut and it would not ease until Liana opened her eyes again. For a long moment he knelt there, cradling his daughter's hand and searching for what to do next.

People were staring.

Battle was waging outside.

Brenson would need him to do something, to help somewhere.

Slowly he gathered his wits, using the process of elimination to determine who the strange woman was. If not Auliere, she could only be one other person. "Hello, Grandmother," Nelek said, forcing his voice not to falter. "Brenson failed to mention you were here."

"He overlooks things sometimes," she said. "We must forgive him, given the battle."

At the mention of battle, Nelek glanced at Sir Faolan, who was closely monitoring a nurse as she saw to Lodas. The man's face was pinched with worry, dark brows furrowed into a tight knot over his eyes. He did not seem to notice Nelek's attention and Nelek debated disturbing the man's thoughts.

It was always so much easier if you were the one wounded, he thought. It is far more painful to watch the suffering of someone close to you, and far braver a task to stand beside them while they are hurting.

And yet, they did not have time to stand there.

"My lord!" A small, sweaty boy skidded to a halt in front of them, bobbing in the barest bow as Nelek and Faolan both snapped their attention to him. "My lord, the outer bailey has fallen."

"And the inner gates?" Faolan asked at the same time Nelek tried, "The archers on the towers?"

"Inner gates are holding, sir," the boy reported, glancing nervously between them. "All archers are accounted for. They're bringing the wounded now."

"How many wounded?" Nelek asked, his mind on Kaden and Troy.

"All," the boy said. "But most still stand."

The knot in Nelek's gut tightened. There was a commotion at the main doors as new wounded were brought in. Through the gloom of the space, Nelek could see several unfamiliar faces, many young men sagging against their friends as they were led into the hall for treatment. He spotted Troy, pale as a sheet and favoring his arm, and nearly breathed in relief. But Troy's gaze was fixed on another figure being carried by two others. Nelek stood up abruptly.

It was Kaden.

~ * ~

Brigetta waved off another blackish tincture that smelled heavily of onions and garlic and pressed a hand to her own forehead.

This wasn't the first time she'd overtaxed herself performing magic, but it was the first time she'd ever done so in public. No doubt the frightened little girl trying to force-feed her was as startled by Bree's sudden frailty as she was by the very magic that had caused it.

Noffi would not have pushed herself so far, she thought.

No, Noffi would have found some other way to free Liana and Lodas from that crushed building and kept the infallible appearance of the blood mages intact.

By gods, she was so stupid.

"They say you must drink this," the scarecrow of a girl murmured at her side. "They say you will be all right, if you drink this."

Bree glanced at her again, saw the earnestness in her wide hazel eyes underlined by fear, and took the proffered cup. Not bothering to ask who "they" were, Brigetta took a slow sip of the hot, salty substance and tried not to gag. It had a grainy texture to it and the scent of onions was so heavy it made her eyes water.

Returning the cup to the apprehensive little girl, Bree struggled onto her elbows to survey the room. Her head felt unnaturally heavy, like it was bobbing in water and quite out of her control, and there was a painful tingling sensation prickling all over her skin. She could almost hear Noffi's voice in her head, admonishing her for pushing too hard.

"Only the blood houses the magic, not the body. Do not be so foolish as to think the body has no limitation just because you can alter things as you like."

Scowling, Bree shoved the memory away, not even caring under which instance her former mentor had said those words. If Faxon were here he'd have likely said the same thing, just more gruffly and with the added emphasis of physical touch to make her listen. He was quite fond of grabbing her by the shoulders and growling in her face whenever he felt she'd taken too great a risk.

The thought of her husband made something squeeze in her chest and she wondered how much longer it would be before he reached them. He and the general couldn't be far now; they just had to hold out a little while longer.

The room took shape before her, dimly lit and populated by many moving shadows. The hushed murmur of various conversations seemed to blend together into a low, almost ominous hum. She was in an alcove in the great hall, her body situated on a rough blanket with two other wounded on either side of her. Bree spared them both a glance but neither was moving, both so deep in drugged and pained slumber that they likely wouldn't have known if the great hall were breeched and the enemy standing over them.

A querulous flutter took up residence in her gut and she sat up further, swaying a bit.

Coming to Kiavana might have been a mistake, but it was a mistake she could correct. All she needed was to find Kaden Dyngannon and magic the boy away. She couldn't depend on the idea that Faxon and the general would get here in time; she knew that now.

A commotion at the entrance drew her attention. Several more wounded were pouring in and the buzz of conversation grew like a mounting wave, crashing through the great hall with snippets of news that Bree began to make sense of.

"Outer bailey has fallen…"

"First his daughter, now his son…"

"We'll be invaded for sure…"

She saw a man rise abruptly and rush to the doors, his voice barely audible above the tumult of the crowd. "Kaden!"

Brigetta swallowed back a tide of fear and commanded her body to move, shoving herself to her feet in a hurry. She took three staggering steps forward and nearly collapsed, when a firm arm about her waist caught her up, easily taking her weight. Bree saw Faolan's scowling face a moment later and breathed in relief, relaxing into him.

"I must see," she said.

"Aye, I figured you would say something like that."

Under any other circumstance, she might have smiled at him but here and now she was too focused on getting to Kaden to manage it. Faolan swooped her up, cradling her body against his chest as he began the trek through the great hall. For a heartbeat she was reminded of who they'd once been: Sir Faolan Mylonas and Brigetta Chridhe, trusted members of Duke Brenson's council. He'd fancied her back then, she knew, and she'd be lying if she said she hadn't entertained thoughts of them together. But then the assassin had come for her, had come straight into her bedchambers during the small hours of the morning, and she'd been forced to make a deal just to stay alive.

She supposed some might see Faxon's decision to marry her rather than kill her as romantic, but at the time there'd been no joy to it.

No, she thought as Faolan carried her to where Kaden was being laid nearest the hearth. No, at the time she'd only mourned the loss her marriage represented. And it was not without its difficulty, shoving all hopes of a future with Faolan out of her mind, even after Noffi arrived and she began her training as a blood mage.

Chastising herself for thinking of it, Bree frowned and tried to focus on Kaden.

They'd laid the boy face down, allowing room for the broken shaft of an arrow imbedded in his back. Brigetta breathed a protest but didn't move until Faolan had set her feet to the ground again. Nelek crouched beside his unconscious son, his face pale with shock and terror, and beside him stood Troy, who was recounting the events in a hoarse voice.

"...He managed to save the girl..." Troy said, but Nelek did not seem to hear it.

Bree's heart stuttered in her chest and she came to kneel across from him, gently reaching a hand to touch Kaden's shoulder. She could feel the strong pulse of magic and blood in him, but the injury was substantial. The arrow had gone in at an angle and its head was buried somewhere under his left shoulder-blade.

Scowling, she imagined it could have been worse; it could have been his spine. But that thought was not comforting in the least.

Once the arrow was removed, there would be more tearing in the boy's flesh, more bleeding, and he would need a caretaker for some time. Bree did not have the strength to magic the boy and a nurse both to safety.

Gods help her, she'd failed.

Thirty-five

Faxon reined in his horse just beside Trenna, eyeing the approaching soldier with a mix of disdain and tolerance. If he weren't mistaken, this soldier had been the one to break his nose just prior to Trenna's arrival and for a moment Faxon tried to calculate how much force he would need to shove a blade through his eye socket. Not much, surely, the eye itself was soft. But behind it could be skull, which would require more pressure.

And then he wondered why he had never tried this experiment before and shifted in his saddle, squinting more at the oncoming soldier. But the man had news they needed to hear, and the partnership between Gideon's army and Trenna's eighty-five men was strained enough as it was. Like it or not, it was better to let the man live.

With a disgruntled frown, Faxon looked away. They'd probably all die in the next hour anyway.

"What news?" Trenna asked as the soldier came to a stop just before her.

"The outer bailey has fallen," the man reported with a wary glance at Faxon and Bervam. "There are two standards on the field, one for the Dyngannon main army and one we haven't seen before."

"The main army will be led by Navell, my half-brother," Trenna said. "Describe the other standard."

Faxon began picking at his teeth, which seemed to annoy the soldier because the spindly man gave him a frown before answering.

"It's a silver boar on a red background…"

Trenna cursed, low and heated, interrupting the man, who eyed her more keenly. He didn't have to ask if she knew who boasted such heraldry. Bervam made an annoyed sound as well but did not take up the explanation.

"That would be Varren Silvanus," she said. "My *real* brother."

"Lots of family on the field today," Faxon said, earning himself a green-eyed glare from the woman. He shrugged at her, unmoved by the silent threat. "What's the plan?"

"His Lordship Gideon," the soldier interrupted with a glare of his own, "instructs you to take up position against the boar while he takes on the main army."

Bervam shifted in his saddle and looked about to argue, but Trenna waved a hand, cutting off the protest.

"Very well," she said. "Where is the boar situated?"

"They're on the west side of the fortress, trying to relocate their trebuchet now that the main army is inside the first bailey."

"Very good, thank you," Trenna said and the man turned his horse, spurring off toward Gideon's army. When he was out of earshot she turned to Bervam. "Tell the men to get ready."

"Lana," Bervam said lowly. "Varren and his men are probably in the same position we were. They don't want to be here."

"I know," Trenna said. "Porrex likely has my nephews and nieces all tucked away in Curahadh or Varren wouldn't be here."

"How can you be so sure?" Faxon asked, garnering their attention again. He really hated when they forgot he was there. "I'm just saying he might hate you too. You're not that likable, Tren. And you have been gone for twenty years."

"Longer than that, really," Bervam said, shrugging when Trenna gave him a look. "I know because Varren retired ages ago," she said through her teeth. "He retired so he could get married. You can't be a soldier and married in the Eldur army, it isn't done. So the only way he is here is if Porrex forced his hand."

"Oh, right," Faxon said, his mind suddenly turning to Brigetta. "Eldur marriage and its side-effects."

He'd managed not to think of his wife stuck in Kiavana Fortress, surrounded by an army and likely wearing herself thin using too much magic. His grip tightened on the reins and the horse shuffled beneath him. Soothing the mare with a gentle pat, he began to calculate how much blood he would need for the battle. He'd kept his normal regimen of half a vial a day and still had two vials of Trenna's blood and one of Kaden's.

He felt a prickle at the base of his neck, the sense that he was being carefully watched, and frowned. The Entity was back.

No, the Entity had never left.

Reaching into his shirt, he pulled out a vial labeled with a small "T" and uncorked it. He would not consume Kaden's blood this close to battle; gods only knew what that might do to him. Trenna's blood was powerful, he knew this, and it was, he thought, made for battle.

Ignoring the wary gaze of his two companions, he drained the vial in one gulp, swallowing hard. The thick substance coated the back of his throat, leaving behind the taste of copper and salt, and the world changed again to silvery hues. He'd been expecting the color change this time but still found it fascinating. It had to signify something other than Trenna's noble family line; he just hadn't figure out what yet.

When this was all over, he was going to sit down and commit his whole mind to puzzling through the bloodlines and their meanings.

That was, if he survived.

"Inform the men that Varren's army will fight with everything they have," Trenna said, though her gaze was still fixed on Faxon and she was wearing possibly the most disturbed expression he'd ever seen. "Tell them to spare their lives if they can."

"That won't be easy," Bervam said.

"Battle never is," Trenna said, finally looking away from Faxon. She met Bervam's gaze, holding it a moment. "And tell them Varren's mine. If I can reach him, I might be able to convince him to stand down."

Bervam nodded once and turned his horse, galloping back toward the eighty-five just behind them. Faxon frowned, staring over at where Trenna was checking her weapons. With one hand she gripped her saddle bags and tossed them off the horse, letting them collapse to the ground with a heavy thud. Then she reached to pet the mare's neck, murmuring something low and soothing to the creature that he couldn't hear.

She didn't seem to notice or care that Faxon was watching her, so he continued, listening harder as she leaned over to bury her face in the horse's mane. He heard her then, or maybe it was the Entity purring the words in his ear, he couldn't be sure, but he heard the cadence of a familiar prayer and felt the hair on his arms stand stiff.

"Loran, God of War, I beseech you in this hour of my death. Let me fight well. Not for the sake of glory or victory, but for the men at my back and for all the men who have gone before me," she whispered, her fingers curling into the leather saddle until it creaked.

A wisp of silver light pulsed into view, moving to curl itself around Trenna's bent form. Faxon shifted in his saddle, certain no one else could see this and curious to know its meaning. He watched the light caress her, growing brighter and brighter as she began to recite names that he could only guess were fallen comrades.

"Ronan Dyngannon," she murmured and the silver strands of her hair shimmered in the fading daylight. "Gregorn Belcan... Veryl Sorely..."

Faxon saw Gideon's army in the distance as they moved off, heading down for the fight, and felt something tight squeeze around his chest. Behind them, moving horses and men became louder as the eighty-five checked their weapons and dropped anything unnecessary to the fight, but Trenna did not move. She remained as she was, whispering names into the ether, hands still gripping her saddle like a lifeline.

Faxon knew better than to speak, just as the soldiers behind them had gone silent. Bervam returned, his head bowed in solemn acknowledgement of Trenna's actions.

Is she your champion, then? Faxon wondered, testing the Entity. But there was no reply, only the silver swirling around her, floating out to touch Bervam, whose head remained low, his eyes closed. Faxon glanced back at the men, watching as tendrils of light curled and wisped between them, circling some and merely passing through others. None were aware of the spectacle, not on a conscious level, but he could see as one by one their shoulders straightened, their expressions turning to resignation and determination.

At last Trenna straightened in her saddle, her face set at grim, focused lines. She urged her horse forward and they all moved, melding into the forest, heading west.

~ * ~

Trenna felt the eyes of her eighty-five on her back, sensed the tension running through them, and took a slow breath. Varren's main camp nestled into forest before them, still far enough away that the tree line covered her, but close enough she could hear the hum of distant conversation. The scent of woodsmoke drifted through the air and the shuffle of hooves told her the army had their horses hobbled further west. Someone was hammering something too; several someones, by the sound of it.

If she knew her brother at all, he wouldn't be here. He would be down at the fortress, on the front lines, commanding his men. Unless, of course, he was visiting his wounded in the infirmary.

The gods could be so cruel sometimes, she thought and gave Bervam the first signal.

Bervam turned in his saddled and jerked his head to the west, sending two men off to secure the army's horses. Trenna watched them until they disappeared into the brush and finally slid from the saddle, landing beside her mount. Bervam frowned at her, clearly disliking the move, and she winked up at him. Cavalrymen were meant to stay mounted, she knew, but her job in this mess required a bit more stealth.

Not that Bervam really knew what her job was meant to be yet, but he would understand after everything was done.

Faxon dismounted beside her, moving to tether his horse with hers even though he didn't know the details either. Eyeing the Human, she thought about arguing, but they were out of time and there could be no conversation this close to battle. So she shrugged, accepting his company before signaling to Bervam once again.

The plan was relatively simple: secure the horses first, then advance in a pincher shape from the north and south, pushing the enemy toward the main battle at the fortress. Varren would get word, wherever he was, and order the attack to switch focus from Kiavana to the eighty-five.

At which point Trenna sincerely hoped Gideon's army would have engaged or ended the hostilities from the main army, because she didn't want Navell to see her take Varren alive. She had a sinking suspicion that any failure on Varren's part would culminate in the deaths of her sister-in-law and all their children.

It would work, she told herself again, rolling her shoulder back. She felt the tension as the joint rotated and took a steadying breath before giving the signal to Bervam to advance.

This had to work, she thought as she began moving into the campsite, because she refused to trade her brother's family for her own. They were all going to survive this.

Crouching low, Trenna slipped around several tents, mindful of her feet as she headed deeper into the camp. Faxon, bless him, was equally quiet behind her. They made it to the center of the site before someone finally shouted the alarm in the south. Bervam had been spotted, she thought, and had to duck behind a tree as several men burst into action.

As predicted, the main force was down at the fortress fighting, leaving only a few to guard the camp. Trenna watched them rush southward, waiting until they were several paces away before leaving cover. She hurried to the centermost tent and slipped inside, confident she had the right one.

She heard the tent flap close behind Faxon and concentrated on the dimly lit interior. Command tent, she breathed in, thankful, and scanned the space one more time, making sure they were alone.

There was a table in the center, just a bit of plywood held up by engineered sawhorses, but it looked sturdy enough. One bedroll lay haphazardly against the left wall, a rumpled pillow and tangled mess of blanket on top.

Varren never had been tidy. Worse yet, he kept his squire so busy that the boy couldn't keep things neat either.

Her brother's fingerprints were everywhere as she stepped deeper into the tent. A pile of clothes and armor that needed mending lay beside the bedroom, some of them stained with so much blood that it took her several seconds to breathe. Leaning against the table was a cracked shield bearing the scarlet and silver heraldry of the House of Silvanus. This she touched as she neared the table, feeling the familiar edge under her fingers, and for a heartbeat she prayed he was all right.

Gods, Varren, look at what they've done to us.

She could almost see her brother leaning over this very table, growling about men and supplies and how unnecessary this whole campaign was.

At least she hoped he thought it was unnecessary. She didn't want to imagine her brother believing in this war.

Faxon shifted by the tent's entrance and she glanced at him. He was studying her in the dimness, his eyes flashing feral gold, and Trenna suddenly felt open and vulnerable. She wasn't certain why and chose not to dwell on it, reaching instead for the map pinned to the table. It was, as she'd known it would be, a map of the battlefield with all the enemy forces and their positions clearly marked.

If there was one thing her big brother did well, it was organizing a map.

She scanned the map twice, locating the position of Varren's trebuchet and his main forces, and straightened. He had a lot of men, but he'd spread them out along the edge of the forest that bordered Kiavana Fortress. That seemed odd, she thought, and cut an invisible line down the center of his forces with her fingertip.

He wasn't expecting reinforcements. If he were, he would have concentrated more on centralizing everything.

That meant Navell wasn't sharing information.

"Interesting," she murmured, her voice swallowed by the empty tent.

Nearly empty. Faxon lowered himself to a crouch by the entrance, his form nearly completely disappearing into shadow.

Outside, Trenna could hear the distant battle, several men shouting the alarm for Varren to come, so she abandoned the map. Faxon rose to his feet as she approached, unfolding himself with predator-like fluidity and she nodded to him, not bothering to explain. He seemed content just to follow her as she pushed the flap open and stepped out into the campsite again.

Dawn was fast approaching, tinging the horizon with the first faint glow of light, but most of the forest was still dark. The areas not lit by campfire swarmed with restless shadows: men—hers and Varren's—doing their bloody work. Trenna inhaled sharp pine and musky smoke, then let her breath out slow as she calculated distances.

Less than half a mile to the main force. A little more than that for flanking positions.

She started moving, confident Bervam would reach her before long. He would be ordering the pincher shape to close already, overtaking the whole of the camp. She could hear them coming closer: men and horses and the clang of swords meeting.

If they pushed as soon as the formation closed, they might still have some cover when they reached Varren's forces.

Trenna picked up her pace, half jogging past the smaller tents and dead fire pits. Faxon kept right behind her, not questioning as they moved from campsite and into denser woods. If she had her bearings right, there would be a shallow ravine nearby. A creek ran through it, winding its way down to the fortress and near the gardens.

The hair on the back of her neck and arms stood stiff suddenly and she stopped, crouching low to listen. Faxon knelt beside her, his eyebrow quirked in question, half his face hidden by the dark. Shaking her head, she listened harder and tried to pinpoint what had her instincts on high alert. The battle behind them was coming to an end, so it wasn't anything there.

No, there was something off about the darkness in front of her, something that had an unpleasant tingle running down her spine.

They were being watched.

Trenna squinted, throwing all her senses into the shadows before them. Yes, they were definitely being watched, but from where?

Beside her, she felt Faxon stiffen and glanced at him. His gaze was trained on something to their left and his entire body had gone taut with surprise. Trenna followed his gaze, trying to spot whatever had his attention, when there was an explosion of movement just in front of her.

Trenna lurched back as something sleek and sharp made a diagonal slash at her midsection. Blade, she registered a heartbeat before it came again, arcing back toward her with deadly precision. She hit the ground with her back and rolled to the left, scrambling for her feet again.

Out of the corner of her eye she could see that Faxon was equally engaged with someone and then had to concentrate because the dagger-wielding man attacking her wasn't stopping. He rushed her, making no sound but a soft grunt of effort and the crunch of leaves underfoot.

Trenna slid her weapon from its sheath, catching the man's dagger at an angle that proved far more advantageous than she'd anticipated. The dagger flew away from them and the man cursed, reaching for his belt. He wore a hood, which seemed odd, and the part of his face not in shadow was covered by a dark beard, but he could only be Eldur.

Process of elimination told her that.

"I don't want to hurt you," she said and then, loudly, "On me!"

It was a familiar order, simple and affective. Her men would be there shortly.

"I mean it," she said to the man, still hesitating. "Don't force my hand."

Behind him, Faxon was a blur of shadow and limbs. She couldn't tell who was winning. The man in front of her drew his sword in one fluid motion, eleven inches of silver steel glinting with the light of coming dawn. Even at a distance and in the relative dark, the boar's head pommel was unmistakable, and Trenna's heart leapt in her chest as the blade swung at her.

Weaving aside at the last moment, she deflected the sword—her brother's unmistakable sword—and kicked out at him. Her foot caught the solid muscle of his right thigh and he staggered away.

"I know it's you," she said, hearing the approach of many men on horseback coming their way.

Her men, she hoped. But it could be Varren's men coming to support the camp.

"Varren…" she tried again, but he let out a guttural howl and came swinging that cursed sword with so much violence it could have taken her head clean off.

Trenna ducked and swerved away from him, scurrying to the left as fast as she could. But it wasn't quite fast enough. The bite of steel sliced into her right shoulder, tearing past her sleeve and burning a line of pain through her skin. She grunted and hurried back several paces, touching the wound with her free hand without taking her eyes from Varren.

Warm blood slicked over her fingertips, dread coiling in her gut as she stared over at her brother. There was more light now, a faint glow illuminating the forest bit by bit, giving her a somewhat clearer view of the man. His black hood hung low over his face but she recognized him anyway, saw the glint of green hidden under there and the thin line of his mouth just visible through the beard. Trenna watched as he straightened, lifting his blade in a purely antagonistic stance.

Gods help her, he wasn't stopping.

Thirty-six

Kaden was laid next to his sister, the broken shaft in his back forcing them to put him face down, but Nelek could still see his face. He was ashen and lax, his ear still rounded and Human and Nelek clenched his fists. He didn't know why but it felt wrong seeing his children as Human rather than Eldur. It hadn't bothered him this whole trip; why did it bother him now?

Was it so wrong that they should die looking Human? They were surrounded by Humans here. They were fighting alongside Humans, and Humans were bleeding with them. And in fact, it was the Eldur pounding at the walls right now, not Humankind.

So why did this trouble him so much? Was he himself harboring some prejudice against these people?

No, he thought, still staring at his son.

There was movement all around him, Bree and his grandmother working to save the lives of his children, and still Nelek stared. He wasn't even staring at Kaden anymore, not really. His gaze had locked on the space between his children, on the thrush covered floor right between their faces, so that he saw both of them and neither of them at the same time.

No, he thought again, he did not harbor ill feelings for Humanity. But that did not mean his children should die as anything less than their true selves.

"Turn us back," he said and Bree's head snapped up. He became aware of the conversation around him: Faolan telling him they had to go, the army was at the inner gates, his grandmother insisting she could take the wounds from Kaden, and Troy demanding to know what was to be done for Liana, but he held Brigetta's wide-eyed gaze and cut through it all. "Turn us back."

"It is too dangerous!" his grandmother protested, her hands reaching for Kaden in a protective manner. She had long, elegant fingers that shone ghostly white in the gloom of the hall. He watched as they clutched at Kaden's good shoulder and listened to the woman a moment longer. "You and Evaliana certainly, but the boy could die."

"We could all die, and very soon," Faolan said, his voice low and urgent. "Is this wise?"

Nelek slanted a glare at Faolan, who scowled and looked away. Whether it was wise or not, it was time to show Kiavana who was standing with them. Nelek turned back to Brigetta, who was watching him with a keen understanding that told him she could do this. It was going to hurt, but she could do this if they were willing. He nodded once to her, indicating that he was willing and therefore his children, unconscious though they were, would also be willing.

"Do it," he said and she produced a dagger from her belt.

"She's already stretched herself thin today, sire," Faolan said through his teeth. "She was unconscious up until a few moments ago."

"This will not strain me," Brigetta interrupted him, positioning the knife near Liana's hand. "Think of it like a ribbon that has been tied. All of my energy was spent tying the ribbons. Any one of them can tug the ribbon free on their own without affecting me at all."

"That is because the strain will be placed on their individual bodies," his grandmother said. She sounded peevish and reached for a dagger of her own, slicing through the palm of her hand with a hiss of displeasure. "And the boy at least is leaking strength as we speak."

Nelek faltered, frowning at his son.

"Kaden is stronger than you give him credit for," Brigetta said, eyeing the older woman. "And the transformation will heal what wounds he has already sustained without a subjugate to transfer them to. Nelek is right."

For a heartbeat he reconsidered, Kaden's still form causing a knot of panic to coil in his gut. Nelek had no working knowledge of blood magic. He only knew what Trenna had told him of it, and what he'd seen Brigetta perform. He looked to Bree, hoping for some kind of clarity or sign that the girl was as talented as she claimed to be. But this was the woman Kaden had thrown out of their party, a stranger they had met a little less than a month ago.

"We are out of time," Faolan said from beside him and Nelek took a deep breath.

Brigetta was also the woman who had helped free his mother thirty years ago. She may not have been given the opportunity to become acquainted with Nelek and Trenna, but she knew Brenson. And Brenson trusted her.

"Do it," he said again, drawing his own dagger.

Bree nodded once, gathered Liana's hand and stabbed it straight through with her blade. Liana twitched and exhaled a pained breath, eliciting a startled sound from Troy, who bent to kneel beside the girl. On the other side, Kaden's hand had likewise been skewered and all eyes fell to Nelek, who hesitated once more, shut his eyes and prayed he was doing the right thing.

He felt the bite of his dagger as it slid into his palm, tearing through skin and muscle and skidding between bones to pop out the other side. The dagger's hilt slammed into his palm with the force of the movement and pain rocketed through his hand and up his arm. He ground his teeth to keep from shouting something obscene, hearing the creak and crack of his jaw under strain but unable to let up.

Bree's voice became suddenly clear, chanting words he barely remembered. They were the same words she'd taught them at the first ritual, the one binding them as Humans, but that felt so far away now. Years ago, not mere weeks.

"Lorenessana et all acht tae," she said.

There was a sound, a kind of roaring, like holding a seashell to your ear, only it was growing in intensity: waves crashing against cliffs, against his own skull. And then it hit him, some invisible, unyielding wall smashing against him. He staggered. Someone grabbed his arm, helped him to his knees just as he felt his ears begin pulling upward, tearing up into their natural peaks with a wholly unnatural sensation that seemed to echo through his body.

Flame ignited in his center, pouring out of him to swirl and churn, burning every inch of his skin. He became aware of Liana and Kaden, both of them shouting their own agony nearby, and tried to concentrate on them, to see them beyond the flames. He found Kaden first. The silver streaks in his hair caught the light of fire all around them, making him easier to spot through the whirlwind.

Nelek swayed, grinding his teeth even more as he watched his son writhe on the dirty floor. The pain was lessening, the fire dimming down, sinking back into each of them bit by bit. He saw at last that his grandmother had, somehow, aided Kaden by taking one or two of the boy's more superficial wounds. The scrape he'd had on his forehead was now a red gash just over her right eye, and her lower lip was swollen with injury. But the larger wound, the more debilitating wound, had been removed by magic alone.

As the last of the flames receded, pooling back through their skin, Kaden sat up straight, panting and glaring.

"A little... godsdamn... warning... next time!" Kaden said between breaths.

"I feel like I was trampled by a score of angry, fat horses. Twice." Liana said with a low groan.

Troy chuckled and sat back, finally looking to Nelek, who let go of a shaky breath.

They'd survived. By gods, they'd survived.

"Right," Faolan said from beside him. The man looked a little shaken himself, but he managed to find a professional tone. "Now would be a good time to reinforce the bloody gate, sire."

Professional tone if not professional words, Nelek thought and looked to his children. They both looked bedraggled and a trifle green, but alive and unhurt. They wouldn't stay unhurt for long, but for now they had a fighting chance. Nelek pushed to his feet again, grimacing as his body flared to life with new aches and pains from the ritual.

Gods, blood magic was awful.

"Reinforcements have been spotted!" a woman's voice called from the entrance.

Nelek squinted over at her, recognizing her as Adelle Croften. She was half bandaged herself but still standing and for reasons he couldn't comprehend, the sight of her gave him hope, more hope than even the announcement that rocketed through the hall.

"Have they engaged yet?" Faolan called back.

"A large force to the east bearing Mavon's signature," Dell reported, glancing back out into the yard. "And something's driven off the boar in the west."

"What are the duke's orders?"

Dell flashed a grin that looked half joyful and half crazy. "Forward, sir. The duke's orders are to shove these bastards out of our home."

~ * ~

Pain bloomed in Trenna's side, shooting through her lower back and lower still, down her leg, making her stagger. Her foot caught on something in the uneven ground and she fell to her knee, leaving Varren's sword a clear path to her head. Cursing, she dove to the left, rolling over her shoulder and nearly losing grip of her sword.

Scrambling to her feet again, she caught sight of Bervam moving to support her and waved him off. He scowled at her and she pointed to Faxon, or at least in Faxon's general direction, before parrying yet another blow from her big brother.

Her favorite brother. The brother who had taught her how to handle a sword in the first place.

"Varren!" she said, scurrying back an extra step.

If she kept her distance maybe she could tire him out, and maybe he'd actually talk to her.

"Varren, there has to be another way..."

"Why in gods are you here?" he said and swung again.

Well, he's talking at least, she thought and prepared to evade him some more.

"It wasn't my choice," she said.

"The hell it wasn't!"

He feinted left and half turned, his sword making a tremendous whoosh as it sliced through the air just at her midsection. Trenna moved with him, avoiding the hit and again refraining from striking back. He was tiring; she could sense it. His blows were becoming staggered and his breath puffed out in heavy pants. But she was also breathing hard, her sword gaining in weight with every passing second.

She needed to end this and end it now.

"Varren..." she said again and he growled something incoherent at her, pivoting fast on his heel.

Steel glinted in sunlight, and she registered the dagger in his off hand a heartbeat before it was airborne. Someone called her name; she wasn't certain who because Varren was still moving. He was charging, in fact, closing the distance between them nearly as quickly as the dagger.

Swearing, Trenna swiveled leftward, trying to turn her body to avoid the dagger and secure her footing before Varren barreled into her, but it was too late. The dagger hit her left shoulder, its blade piercing the padded armor and straight into her skin. She felt it as a dull thud at first and then the joint ached to life seconds before Varren's body slammed full-length into her. His shoulder caught her at the eyebrow, the impact jolting through her as they toppled together to the ground.

Dazed, she was only distantly aware of hitting the side of a tree trunk, the scrape of bark biting into her scalp as they slid off and Varren's weight pinned her down. His hand was curled into a fist in her armor, yanking her up an inch off the dirt so he could bring them nose to nose.

"Navell has my son," he said and Trenna's heart stuttered.

Porrex might hesitate to kill a child, but Navell was a wholly different story. Their half-brother enjoyed tormenting them and always had; he would have no qualms about murdering his own nephew.

Gods, Varren had the right of it. There was no other way.

Varren yanked the dagger from her shoulder, sending a burst of agony pulsing through the joint, and she hissed just before the blade pressed to her throat. It was warm and slick with her blood. She froze. Varren's eyes were a hard green, the color of moss on stone, and for a heartbeat she swore he looked like he had when they were children. The gruff beard replaced with smooth skin, a short jaw with a slightly cleft chin, cheeks still clinging to baby fat, and laughter in his face. Oh gods, how her heart ached.

She blinked and the image was gone but the ache remained, lodged deep in her gut and more painful than ever—so painful it was an effort to breathe, let alone try to speak.

A sword leveled at Varren's throat and she heard Bervam's clear warning. "We've all got risks to take, milord."

Varren's brows drew together, his eyes narrowing into angry green slits. She had a feeling he was scowling, but couldn't see it beneath his beard. Trenna remained still as Bervam reached down to direct the dagger away from her throat, his sword never leaving Varren's neck. Varren reluctantly released the dagger and slid back onto his haunches, relieving her of his weight.

"You all right there, General?" Bervam asked without looking at her.

She kept her gaze on Varren's face and reached to grip the wound in her shoulder. It hurt and would be a hindrance in battle, but she thought it would be all right. Or at least she hoped it would.

Grimacing, she began to scoot away from Varren, holding tight to the wound because it was too damn deep and she would need a bandage before she could go further. Varren remained silent and still, but she could see he was clenching his jaw tight and there was still a debate going on in that head of his.

"Ouch," she said to him as she got a knee under her and began inspecting the wound more closely. "A little to the right and we'd be having a whole different sort of day, brother."

"Give the dagger back and let me try again," he said.

"Your family is weird, General," Bervam said and she smirked.

"You'll get no arguments from me there," she said, climbing to her feet.

Faxon was nearby, watching the conversation with a cool sort of indifference, but he had a bandage in his hand that was obviously meant for her. She nodded to him and he moved to inspect her shoulder, gingerly shifting aside her shirt and armor for a better view. Trenna let him, turning her attention again to her brother.

"If you fail, my nephew dies?" she asked.

He nodded once.

"If you die, my nephew still dies?"

He nodded again.

"Where are the rest of them? Cassiana and the girls?"

Varren glanced at Bervam, who still hadn't removed the weapon from his neck; then, with a slow, deep breath, he turned back to Trenna. "Curahadh," he said. "Porrex is keeping them as his personal guests in the palace."

"Of course," she said, mostly to herself.

Would Porrex truly kill all those families? Her eighty-five were betting he wouldn't. And really, with so many of them in defiance to his rule, he couldn't conceivably maintain his standing with the people if he did. Even his strongest supporters would abandon him if he committed such an act of genocide.

But he could make life awful for them. And he could, if he wanted Varren out of the way, simply kill Cassiana.

Faxon tore the sleeve of her shirt further, exposing the wound even more. Trenna saw him uncork a vial with his teeth and thought he meant to steal more of her blood, but then he upended the vial and a white, powdery substance poured over the gash in her shoulder. There was a smell like citrus and sea salt and a burning sensation overtook the wound. She jerked away, cursing, and reached to try brushing off whatever it was, but Faxon caught her hands to stop her.

"What the bloody hell, Faxon?"

The burning went deep, slithering through the wound, through her shoulder, making even her collarbone ache, and for a dizzy second she swayed. Faxon held her upright with one hand and with the other he pressed the bandage to the injury, making it clear that whatever he'd done, she wasn't meant to undo it.

"It's cauterizing the wound and cleaning it all at once," he said, looping the bandage under her armpit to secure it. "You can thank me later."

"What the hell is it?" she asked, but Faxon just winked at her. The ache began to recede, not by much, but enough that she was able to concentrate on her brother again.

Varren met her gaze, looking for all the world like the dignified nobleman he was even with the sword threatening his life. Trenna motioned to Bervam and the sword fell away, removing the immediate threat, but they all knew Varren wouldn't be going anywhere without permission.

In the distance she could hear battle, great cries of men and women down at the fortress, and for a moment she hesitated. She needed to get back to Nelek. She needed to find her own children and make sure they were all safe. Her skin seemed to itch with the need to see them all, but Varren's steady gaze stopped her.

He didn't say anything more, but then he didn't have to. She knew the stakes for them both and she knew what they needed to do. There was a flicker in his eyes, something like recognition, and his brow furrowed at her.

"All right then, brother. Let's go save your son," she said.

"Trenna," Faxon said, his voice low and quiet but she knew everyone else could hear him too. "Couldn't we do that after we make sure neither of us is about to die via our spouses?"

Bervam stiffened, glaring hard at Faxon as the implications hit. If Faxon had meant to keep his marriage to an Eldur a secret, it was certainly out now. Varren, on the other hand, kept his attention fixed on Trenna. There was no longer any animosity there, no blame or rage, and she could sense a confused hope radiating from her brother, which was almost insulting.

Did he really think she would ignore the threat against his family?

Trenna flexed her fists and concentrated on Bervam, ignoring Faxon for the moment. "Captain," she said, "Varren's men cannot appear to have slacked in their duties. They cannot in any way seem to be throwing the fight. And neither can we."

Bervam began to nod slowly. "So... your orders are to charge?"

"Yes," she said and eyed Varren again. "Though I suspect they are lying in wait for us down in the ravine. There will be a section of men guarding the trebuchet in the forest west of us, but the main force will be hiding to ambush you."

"I'd ask how you figured that out," Varren said, "but in truth, I don't care at the moment."

She winked at him, choosing not to elaborate further. He didn't need to know she'd snooped through his tent, or that his very presence alerted her as to where he'd placed his men. She'd been gone a very long time, but she did know her big brother.

"Subdue them at the ravine," she ordered Bervam. "There will be spies among them; you can count on it. Don't kill them if you don't have to, but bloody well make them go down any other way."

"And what exactly are you going to be doing?" Faxon asked.

He was irritated, she could tell, so she turned to face him. "Go with the captain. Use whatever magic you can to aid them and then break for the castle. Let Nelek know we've arrived."

"You didn't answer my question," he said.

"But I did," she said and stepped closer to Varren. "I'll be rescuing my nephew."

Thirty-seven

Nelek shoved his way through the throng of soldiers crowding the inner bailey gate, shouldering past men and women alike who were ready for the fight. The gate itself was set into a recess in the inner bailey wall, reinforced by iron grates over its large oak door. Brenson's men still had command of the inner wall, but by the shouting and rush of bodies up there, Nelek could tell they were near to being overrun.

He almost diverted for a ladder, intending to help, but spotted his brother's auburn hair nearer to the gate and pressed on. Nelek was able to see glimpses of Brenson the closer he came, taking note of the stained and torn tunic covering his chainmail. It sagged at the left, billowing dingy white in the morning breeze and obscuring the charge at the center of the fabric. Nelek's gaze caught on the lions sewn into the ivory linen, on the firm stances and the sharp curve of claws reaching toward the rose between them, and had to take a steadying breath.

Brenson was not a warrior, not really, but he looked every bit as fierce as the men surrounding him. Reddish stubble traced over his jaw and chin, and his mouth contorted into a ferocious scowl as he shouted his orders.

"Dump the oil!" he hollered, his voice clear over the tumult. Seconds later, Nelek heard the order repeated above them.

Just as he reached Brenson's side he heard the enemy screaming on the other side of the wall. A distinctly unpleasant smell followed and Nelek did his level best to ignore it. Rubbing his nose with a knuckle, he nodded to Brenson, who gave him a grim smile.

"I do believe your wife has arrived," Brenson said.

"Was she spotted?" Kaden asked from behind them and Nelek half turned to see him. Liana was just beside her brother, weapons out and ready.

"As a matter of fact, Levatto says she was fighting Varren Silvanus in the forest just outside the castle gardens," Brenson said.

"Well, she obviously won," Liana said.

"Perhaps," Brenson said and looked up toward the top of the wall.

Nelek followed his brother's gaze, spotting Adelle once again, her limber frame leaning over the wall to signal something down at them. Brenson nodded to her and she was off again, shouting something to the men that sounded a good deal like the portcullis was about to be raised. Brenson reached aside to where a young boy clutched a shield nearly as tall as the boy himself. He was a tiny thing, all angles and thin bones, but he did his duty and handed the shield over, disappearing through the crowd in the next second.

"Make ready!" Brenson shouted, drawing his sword.

Nelek unsheathed his longsword at the same moment, listening to a chorus of men as they repeated the order down the line. He saw Liana bouncing on her toes beside him, rolling her shoulders back and stretching as best she could. Kaden too was preparing himself and Nelek swallowed down a lump of fear.

Loran, God of War, we beseech you now, he prayed but his mind stumbled over the words.

Gripping his hilt tighter, he eyed the portcullis as it was raised, scowling at the still closed gate. This would not be the hour of their deaths, he told himself. He wouldn't allow it.

The gate slammed open and with a great cry they poured out, surging forward all at once so that Nelek was carried with them, pushed alongside his brother with the charge. They passed under the shadow of the gate and out into the sun, funneling through just to spread out into the bailey courtyard, where a sea of Eldur soldiers awaited them.

Many were already in combat. Others were dragging the wounded away, men still screaming and covered in steaming oil being shoved back behind the lines. Nelek took it all in with a glance, checked his brother at his side, and then his children. But Kaden and Liana had already moved off, Kaden leading the way and Liana on his heels for support.

Brenson charged toward the center of the formation, Faolan beside him, and Nelek hesitated for a heartbeat before turning to follow Kaden. Brenson would be all right, he told himself, and then he swung his sword, beating back the first Eldur he encountered. The soldier staggered aside, making room for the man behind him to thrust a pike toward Nelek's midsection.

Nelek swiveled to the right, felt the brush of the spike as it grazed over his chest, skidding off the leather of his vest, and then he launched for the pikeman. Barreling through the man, Nelek groped for the shaft of the pike, gripping it just in time to swing it at the first soldier, who had regained his footing and was coming at him once more. The soldier ran into the flat of the shaft, missing the pike end by a hairsbreadth, his weight and the force of the swing shuddering through the weapon.

Tightening his grip, Nelek pushed forward, ramming the shaft against the Eldur's midsection. A second Eldur, one who had been swinging for Kaden, got caught in the shaft's path, the spiked end skewering the man's left side. He grunted, his swing ran off course, and Kaden stabbed him firmly in the chest.

Nelek released the pike, letting it and the two Eldur collapse to the ground. There was mud underfoot, mud and oil and blood. Nelek registered it before turning back to the tide of soldiers, parrying several blows as the enemy attempted to advance. Everything smeared into movement: parrying, blocks, strikes, screaming men from both sides of the battle, the clash of metal on metal. For every man Nelek took down, there seemed to be two more, all faceless under their helmets, all hacking furiously with whatever weapon they had on hand.

Arrows flew by in swarms, sometimes volleying toward the enemy and sometimes toward their own men. Nelek was meshed in with the front of the line, relatively safe from arrows, and yet he ducked low, trying to keep himself as small a target as possible. Kaden and Liana did the same on either side of him.

Liana shouted suddenly, not in pain but in fury and Nelek shifted, slicing down one fellow so he could check on his daughter. She had sustained a cut to her upper left arm, but gained an extra weapon somewhere. He saw her kick the enemy closest to her, following with her sword to catch him at the throat. She pivoted on her heel, ducking low and spinning at the same time with her weapons out. Three unlucky men met the blades as she advanced in whirlwind fashion, each of them crying out as she passed.

With fluid agility she finished each of them off, swords blurring through the air one after the other until at last all three collapsed. Around them the line of men broke, backpedaling to allow for smaller pockets of fighting.

Someone in the enemy ranks had realized they were too closely grouped together.

"Nelek!"

He barely heard the voice over the clamor and retreated a step to scan the field. Up on the wall Adelle had rallied the men and made a valiant push against the enemy, toppling the siege ladders that had been peppering the outer wall. She was directing archers to take positions. The courtyard itself was a writhing mass, the deep greens and blacks of the Eldur uniforms clashing against the golds and reds of Kiavana. Everyone was moving, blurring together in his vision until he located who was calling for him.

It was Faolan.

Faolan's left arm dangled limply at his side, blood smeared his face and stained his uniform, and Nelek could see he was having a hard time fending off attacks. Beside him Brenson was in a similar state, bloodied and wounded but still hacking away at the ranks in front of him.

"Uncle Brenny could use some help," Liana said, heaving great breaths of air as she surveyed the situation.

"I dare you to call him that to his face," Kaden said, equally breathless.

Nelek scowled at the sight, glancing past Brenson to the Eldur surrounding the man. He was about to be flanked. The enemy was pressing in on all sides and there were a lot of them.

"Liana, take left. Kaden, take right. I'll meet you both in the middle," Nelek said.

He glanced at them both to make sure they'd heard him. Liana grinned at him, Kaden nodded, and Nelek turned to run for his brother's position. Sprinting across the courtyard as fast as he could, he ignored the rest of the battle: the whiz of arrows overhead and the shouts of men on all sides. He saw Liana and Kaden break off, rushing toward the fringes of the group bent on killing Brenson, and he saw the Eldur man who had managed to flank his brother moving in for the final blow.

Nelek ground his teeth, his feet pounding against the muddied ground, slipping so much that he feared he might lose his balance. But he didn't. He managed to reach Brenson, or more accurately, he reached the Eldur trying to murder his brother and struck out with his sword. He felt the blade pierce the soldier's back and shoved forward, knocking the man aside so he could reach Brenson.

Brenson backpedaled until he was side by side with him, panting and looking the worse for wear. He flashed a weary smile in Nelek's direction, his face a mess of mud and gore, and for a heartbeat Nelek couldn't breathe. But the blood on his brother's face did not seem to be his own and even if it were, he didn't have the time to dwell.

Another pike snapped into view, headed for Brenson once more, and Nelek beat it off, directing it toward the ground so that he could kick and snap the shaft in half. Reaching out, he grabbed Brenson's shoulder and shoved the man behind himself, taking up position beside the beleaguered Faolan. It was all blades and teeth now, the Eldur snarling at him, pressing the advantage, desperate for blood.

Something clicked off in the back of Nelek's mind and the sounds around him went suddenly mute, replaced by the frantic thrum of his own heartbeat. A primal, berserk shout tore out of him and he launched forward into the fray, swinging his sword wide. The closest Eldur was too stunned to react and he hacked downward, angling his blade to strike the man at the juncture between shoulder and neck. Nelek spun, muscling his sword away from the fallen Eldur to block a sword coming for his chest.

Diverting the blade, Nelek slid in close to his new attacker, so close he could feel the warmth of the man's breath on his cheek as he drove his fist into fleshy gut. The Eldur exhaled hard and staggered back a step, but Nelek followed, keeping in close and grabbing at the loose bit of fabric near the man's shoulder. Using the fistful of linen, Nelek yanked the soldier leftward, using him as a shield against yet another pikeman.

The pike hit the Eldur at midback and he cried out, his body bowing in agony just before Nelek released him to swing at the horrified pikeman.

Gods he hated pikes!

Pikes and spears with their damned six-foot-long reach.

Growling, Nelek slammed his hilt into the pikeman's face, felt and heard the crunch of bones as they snapped under his strike. Blood spurted from the pikeman's nose and he released his weapon, groping blindly at his face. Nelek took the opening, stabbing the man through the gut before he could recover.

He planted his feet and prepared for the next attack, but a shout of alarm drew his attention to the outer gate. More Eldur were pouring into the courtyard, running headlong for the battlefield. There was something different about them, and at first he thought they might be their reinforcements, but they were Eldur and began cutting down any Humans in their path.

Not reinforcements.

Not men from the boar either, as they had the same standard on their shields and chests as the rest of the men they were fighting.

He realized a moment later that they were shouting something to each other and after another moment he heard it clearly. "Blood mage! Make way for the blood mage!"

The hair on the back of Nelek's neck stood stiff and he squinted hard at the gate. A pocket of Eldur shuffled into the courtyard, their shields up in a cube-like fashion to protect the mage at their center. What Nelek could see through the tight ranks surrounding the man— at least he thought it was a man—was the flash of a metal chest plate and boots that rose to his knees.

There was a crack like thunder that shook the ground and the western wall lit up with fire, the sudden blaze racing through the men up there. Nelek gazed in horror as the fire enveloped the entirety of the wall, Kiavana's archers screaming, some of them leaping from the parapets to fall eighty feet through the air.

Adelle, he thought. Gods, Trenna would never forgive herself if Brock's daughter died before they could meet.

Another ground quaking crack rent the yard and the southwest tower burst into flame. Nelek's stomach dropped. Liana cursed beside him, then charged toward the cubed formation, her lithe form ducking around any Eldur who got in her way. Kaden was off a heartbeat later and Nelek, glancing back at a wide-eyed Brenson, turned to follow.

Gods help them, they had to get rid of that mage.

~ * ~

Faxon trailed Captain Bervam closely, his feet sliding through dirt and mud along the ravine's edge. He knew this place, had used it many times before as an escape route from the castle proper during his more illicit years in Kiavana, and therefore was quite familiar with the terrain. The creek that ran through here came from high up in the northern mountains and fed the castle gardens. Most of it was natural, but here and there ditches had been dug up to divert the stream, bringing water to the village just south of the castle itself.

If Varren had been a cleverer man, he would have diverted the flow to the castle foundations and flooded out the tunnel system hiding under there. But Faxon doubted the man had been aware of the system running underneath the fortress, and even if he had, he would have sought to use that information for something else, such as gaining entrance to the inner bailey.

The castle itself was in clear view here, its massive walls standing firm and tall on the other side of the ravine. There was a lot of movement going on up there, he could see that much, but he couldn't quite make out the particulars from where he stood.

Trees and brush obscured their view on all sides as Faxon splashed through the creek behind Bervam. Loose silt shifted underfoot and water seeped over the tops of his boots, soaking down his shins. It was irrational of him, he knew, but he truly hated it when his feet were wet. At least outside of a bath. He could handle it then, but when his footwear got cold and wet he wanted to strangle somebody.

His eyes caught on the line of Bervam's shoulders and he imagined, just briefly, what it would be like to garrote the man.

Faxon felt a pinching at the back of his neck, some instinctual warning, and he ducked a heartbeat before the war cry sounded from the other side of the ravine. The bushes along the far side of the creek burst to life, soldiers leaping out with their weapons drawn, and Faxon watched as they charged headlong toward him. The blood, Trenna's blood, came roaring to life in him, the silver edges of his vision smearing a bit, honing in on individual soldiers as they made their charge.

His heartbeat slowed, or maybe it was just that the world around him slowed; he couldn't be sure. What he did know was that the soldiers each had shadows to them, something unnatural in that they did not behave as shadows ought. Rather than following their owners, these shadows seemed to be leading, and Faxon realized an instant later what it was he was seeing: these shadows were showing him exactly what the soldiers were about to do.

He exhaled, slow and controlled, and grinned.

Rushing forward, Faxon followed each shadow, correctly anticipating its moves and cutting through the men quickly. One man meant to swipe at his head, but Faxon ducked and stabbed him just under the armpit, twisting the blade before yanking it back out to attack a man on his right, who was focused on an Eldur somewhere just behind Faxon. This man didn't even see the blow until after Faxon had already struck, his blade dragging straight over the soldier's jugular.

His heartbeat remained steady, a slow, peculiar *tha-thump* in his chest, and the chaos of the little ravine battle seemed razor sharp to him. He saw Bervam barreling his way through two men, could sense—and see—that the man had things well in hand.

By gods, was this the way Trenna saw battle?

He heard the Entity chuckling in the back of his mind and bristled, annoyed at being so clearly mocked, but the Entity gave no other answer.

Grinding his teeth, Faxon focused on the fight, slinking through the enemy ranks with confident strikes and fluid motions that caught him several startled stares from Bervam and his men. Faxon sent one of them a wink and a wicked grin just before turning to chop at the leg of an oncoming soldier. The soldier screamed and toppled forward, whereupon Bervam knocked the man upside the head, rendering him unconscious.

"We're supposed to be keeping them alive!" Bervam hissed at him.

Faxon glanced down at the mangled leg. "Oh, right. I forgot."

A thunderous crack rumbled from the direction of the castle, drawing their attention from the fight. Faxon looked up just as the fortress wall burst into flame. Only it wasn't natural flame; he saw that straight off. No, this was a conjured flame, a mix of orange and purple that sped over the length of the wall.

"By gods," Bervam said from beside him. "They've brought out their blood mage."

Thirty-eight

Trenna ducked behind a patch of bushes, holding her breath as several of Navell's men rushed by. They were on the outskirts of Navell's main company, who by all appearances were hurrying to battle. In fact, Trenna could see down the hillside where Gideon's army was converging on the forces laying siege to Kiavana. Navell had likely given orders to charge, and Gideon's men were meeting them head on.

Varren crouched just beside her, his taller frame bending low to keep from sight.

He always had taken after Father, she thought and flinched.

What had he been told about their parents' death? It was unlikely he was given any truth over the last twenty years. When this was all over, she would need to sit down with him and tell him everything.

"Quit looking at me like that," Varren muttered and peered around the brush.

"Like what?" Trenna asked and did the same, checking the rush of men.

Most had already run to formation at the base of the hill, but there were a few stragglers hurrying between tents, donning armor and weaponry. Orders were shouted for every man well enough to carry a sword to get moving. Trenna pinpointed the infirmary tents at the far side of the camp. They were set in a circular group of their own, one large tent surrounded by several smaller ones, all shrouded by old trees.

Why didn't Navell have them protected near the center of the camp?

"Like you regret leaving me to twenty years of hell," Varren said, his voice hushed.

Trenna looked at him. Shame knifed deep into her heart and she struggled for a response, but he cut her off before she could speak.

"Tell me what happened to Ronan," he said, glaring at her. "What *really* happened to Ronan."

"You seriously want to do this now?" she hissed at him.

Three more soldiers ran past their hiding space and she checked the infirmary tents again. Varren had said Drotan was assigned to one of the nurses there, safe enough from the fighting for Navell to use as a means of control and yet close enough to make the threat against the boy's life real. They would need to get closer to see inside, and closer still to steal the boy away.

"I deserve to know, Tray'Lana," Varren said when it was safe to speak again. "He was my friend."

"As he was mine." It was her turn to glare. "I cannot believe you think I would ever harm Ronan Dyngannon!"

She glanced around the brush and pushed to her feet. This was as clear a shot as they were likely to get and she sure as hell wasn't going to sit around letting her brother accuse her of murder anymore. He cursed behind her and there was a rustle of movement as he came to follow.

Slinking around abandoned campfires and bedrolls, they made quick work of the campsite, stopping behind a cluster of trees just beside the infirmary. These tents were green rather than the standard brownish shades the rest of the army used, and they connected in several places to allot for emergency surgeries. A blood mage was always preferable but when it came to the more dire wounds, most soldiers chose to undergo mundane medicines and take their chances.

They would rather risk it themselves than see a comrade take the pain for them.

Trenna felt the rough scrape of bark against her back and leaned around the tree to investigate further. One tent flap was open, allowing her a glimpse inside to where many men lay sprawled over bedrolls. Here and there a nurse slipped between the men to administer medicines or see about bandages, but she could not find Drotan.

She wasn't even certain she'd be able to recognize the boy if she did see him. Shame bit harder into her and she gripped her hilt. Gods, she'd been away too long.

"I do not believe you killed him," Varren whispered beside her and she stiffened.

"The hell you don't," she said.

"I don't," he said again, more firmly this time, so she looked at him. There was a resigned acceptance in his face and she relaxed just a little. "You and Ronan were too close for any enmity to get between you. But I still deserve to know what happened to him."

She let her breath out slow, turning back to watch the tent flap. Eventually the boy would have to wander by, she reasoned. She really had no other plan if he didn't.

"Porrex killed him," Trenna whispered.

"Porrex killed his own son?" Varren asked, but there was no disbelief in his tone. "Gods."

"Yes," she said and steeled herself for what she had to tell him next. "Ronan demanded that Porrex answer for the assassination attempt on Kaden's life."

"But Kaden…"

"Wasn't born yet, I know," she said, keeping her eyes on the tent. There was a younger man in there, she could see him, and by the shape of him she knew instinctually that it was Drotan. "It was a poison meant only to kill the infant."

"Gods, Lana…"

"Actually, I go by Trenna now," she said and nodded to the tent. "I see him."

All at once Varren stiffened, turning to peer around the trees and into the tent. He breathed a soft, thankful prayer when he spotted his son and slid back around to look at her again.

"What's the plan?" he asked.

"You really think I plan this shite?" she asked and rose to her feet. "Stay here. If they see you, the rest of your family is dead and we can't have that, now can we?"

"But..." he began and then cursed, low and heated, before hiding behind the trees again.

She smirked, listening to the hiss of obscenities behind her. Unsheathing her sword, she walked to the tent, diverting to slice through several of the anchors keeping the tent tethered to the ground. Some of the fabric sagged but otherwise the structure remained upright.

Her heart pounding in her chest, she felt the familiar contours of the weapon's grip against her palm, smelled the acrid sickroom smells trademark of an infirmary, and ducked inside.

Her eyes adjusted swiftly to the dimmer light and she caught sight of several wounded men who seemed to recognize her. They gave her open-mouthed stares as she continued through the tent, heading in Drotan's general direction. Several had bloody bandages wrapped around their heads, and still others had their arms strapped into slings across their chests. One or two were too weak to move, but they opened their eyes as their companions began murmuring to one another.

She caught snippets of what they were saying, mostly her name and "traitor" and questions about where Navell was.

As she approached Drotan—who looked like a scrawnier, baby-faced version of her brother—two men converged to intercept her. They were not among the wounded; she could see that straight off. Both unsheathed their weapons to stand shoulder to shoulder, barring her from Drotan.

Drotan, bless him, slid off to the side, his hazel-blue eyes darting between her and the two men. "Please don't hurt them," he said and it took her a moment to realize he was speaking to her.

"Shut it, boy," the bearded fellow on the right said and then sneered down at her. "We were expecting Varren. This is a fun surprise."

Trenna exhaled slowly and rolled her left shoulder, grimacing as the joint clenched tight, agony licking down her arm and across her chest. That was going to be a problem, she thought and concentrated on the room. There were three occupied beds in their vicinity: two left and one right, and a narrow walkway between. The path behind her was crowding with what wounded could stand on their own, she could feel them closing in, blocking the way to the exit, and took a slow, steadying breath.

The bearded fellow on the left licked his lips, nervously shifting his weight from foot to foot. Trenna cocked her head to the side, trying to count how many weapons were about to be used against her, but she couldn't quite remember how many she'd seen on the trek in.

"Haven't you got anything to say?" someone asked from behind her.

Her gaze caught on Drotan, who was no longer cowering in the corner but had fetched a weapon of his own and moved to support the bearded twins before her. He looked terrified but resolved and she wondered just how long it had been since Drotan and Varren had spoken.

Obviously too long, if he meant to fight her rather than come along like a good little rescued boy.

Gods, could nothing go right?

"Drotan, your father is dying," she said, seeing the flicker of pain cross the boy's face. "I've come to fetch you to say goodbye."

The rest of the tent's inhabitants seemed to breathe in unison, all aghast at this news, and for a heartbeat she regretted the lie. But if she could lie her way out of this, then that was the better plan, given that she was surrounded by already wounded men. She didn't relish the thought of kicking a man while he was down, and by and large everyone in this tent was down in some fashion or another.

"You're lying," Beard One said. He seemed to be the more vocal of the two. He also clearly disliked her, as proven by the scowl he kept on her.

"My troops overran Varren's position several minutes ago," she said, keeping her attention fixed on Drotan. Gesturing to her own bandaged shoulder she continued, "Your father did his best to kill me but I prevailed. And since I do hold true to my family obligations... I am here to make sure his last moments are spent with you."

"Bring him here," Drotan said, his fist clenched tight around the hilt of his sword.

"Moving him is unwise..."

"If he's dying anyway, then that doesn't matter!"

Trenna sighed and shook her head. This was not working. And she had a bigger battle to get to.

"Well, I tried," she muttered and leapt forward, slicing Beard Two clean across the thighs.

He howled in pain, swinging a heavy fist at her head, but she was already moving, sliding in close enough she could feel his breath on the back of her neck as she turned. His fist collided with Beard One, who had also turned and was attempting to grab at her wounded shoulder. Beard One grunted, grasping at his companion instead as the two toppled to the ground.

Trenna felt the swing of a weapon in front of her and stopped it with her sword, registering a heartbeat later that it was Drotan attacking her. She scowled, shoving his sword off to the side.

"You're going to feel very silly about this later," she told him.

Drotan swung again and she parried, backpedaling so she could check the crowd of wounded men surrounding them. They all seemed to be waiting, watching the fight but ready to jump in should the Bearded Twins fail. They stood in clusters, some leaning heavily on wooden crutches while still holding weapons, some near the tent's central pole, and still others hovering over their more wounded comrades as though to protect them.

Good men, she thought, and parried Drotan again.

He was red-faced, either from exertion or frustration, possibly both, and Trenna felt a familiar pinch of regret in her chest. She did hate being at odds with her own family. But if she could bring Drotan out of this safely, there was a chance her brother could forgive her. A slim chance, but a chance nonetheless.

Beard One pulled Beard Two out of the way, shoving him toward several of the wounded who began administering what aid they could to him. Trenna watched him from the corner of her eye as she continued evading Drotan's swings.

The boy was seriously lacking in the swordsmanship department. She would have to talk to Varren about that.

Beard One shouted something unintelligible at her and rushed toward them, his sword raking upward in a diagonal motion that threatened to take both her and Drotan down at the same time. Trenna spun, reaching with her off hand to snag Drotan's jerkin at the collar and drag him with her. Drotan, who'd been swinging down with his own weapon, caught the other sword with his own, sending Beard One's longsword crashing to the ground.

Drotan gasped, so alarmed that he might have accidently harmed his bodyguard that he reached a hand out as though to help the man. Trenna, still holding his jerkin, kicked the boy at the back of his knee and he collapsed with a grunt. Then, recognizing that he was going to be a lot easier to deal with unconscious, she snapped the pommel of her sword into the back of his head and he fell limp at her feet.

Beard One was scrambling for his sword, desperate to regain control of the situation. Trenna leapt over Drotan, her right foot slamming down onto Beard One's longsword, forcing him to release it once more. She saw something silver in his left hand a breath before he swiped the dagger at her midsection.

Swiveling left, then right, she avoided his attacks, feeling the whoosh of his heavy swings as they passed her. Sidestepping, she let him come at her twice more, estimating the distance between him and the cluster of men at the center pole. Praying she had it right, she parried again, felt the solid slide of her blade against his just before she twisted her blade around, burying its point in Beard One's shoulder.

He hissed in pain, backpedaling from her, but she pursued. With a shout of her own, she kicked him at his hips, sending him toppling backward. He collided with three of the wounded men by the center pole, who in turn collapsed against the pole.

For a moment she feared her gamble had failed, but then the pole tilted, the already loosened outer perimeter gave way and a cry of alarm rose up. Trenna dropped her sword and knelt, snagging the dagger from her boot with one hand and taking a firm hold of Drotan with the other. The tent billowed around them, drooping suddenly as the center pole collapsed. Several men shouted in pain, the fight forgotten, and then the heavy cover of fabric muffled them.

Trenna stabbed the linen with her dagger, muscling the blade through until it tore a good sized hole for her to escape. Pulling herself out, she dragged Drotan behind her, giving one last glance at the weltering mass in the center of the collapsed tent. It might have been comical, all that confused movement and heated swearing under there, but these were not healthy soldiers and she feared many of the more critical patients would be lost.

Shoving the dagger back into her boot, she hefted Drotan as best she could and hurried for Varren's tree. The boy was heavy in spite of his lankier frame and she grunted, half dragging his feet across the dirt. Varren left his hiding space to meet her halfway, taking his son from her in one fluid move to hoist him over his own shoulder.

"It was necessary to beat him?" Varren asked, glaring at her as they began their hurried retreat.

"He started it," she said, breathless. She became aware of a steady throbbing in her shoulder and grimaced, pressing her hand to the alarmingly moist bandage there without looking at it. She didn't need to see it to know it was bleeding again.

Thunder cracked through the air and down at the fortress she saw a tower burst into flame. A hard knot coiled in her belly and she breathed, "Nelek."

Forgetting the wound and Varren and his errant son, Trenna ran for the fortress.

~ * ~

Troy sprinted after Brigetta, following the blood mage up a stairwell and through a room crowded with soldiers. Orders were being shouted over the din of many bodies moving, everyone urgently rushing through the space, and he was forced to weave around pockets of men in his pursuit of the woman. Sweat and blood lay heavy on the air, almost more so here than in the makeshift infirmary three flights below.

He swallowed back the taste of copper, ducking out of the room and onto the eastern wall. He spotted several things at once: the southwest tower ablaze, several men screaming as they attempted to escape the inferno, the outer courtyard writhing with combat, and the squared formation of shields just inside the castle gates.

His shoulder ached but he reached for his weapon anyway, his gaze catching on Liana as she launched an attack at the cube of shields. He would know her form anywhere, all that lithe grace smacking past spears and swords alike, and for an instant he felt both proud and terrified. She managed to cut the legs of an Eldur, who promptly collapsed inside the formation and was swallowed up as the men closed ranks.

Gods, they were good.

Brigetta hummed, not a happy sound, and started off again. For a conflicted moment Troy considered abandoning the blood mage in favor of fighting, but he spotted Dell at the far end of the wall. She was fighting off a wave of Eldur that had managed to climb onto the battlements and what soldiers she had left on her side were flagging.

With one last glance at Liana and the others, he ran for Dell's position, passing Brigetta on the way. Shouting something unintelligible even to himself, Troy rammed his good shoulder into the body of the Eldur closing in on Dell. Pain jolted through him, his wound flaring to life, but Troy forced himself to concentrate around it. The Eldur staggered into the low part of the crenellations, teetering over the ledge, and Troy took the opportunity to kick him in the thigh, sending him screaming over the wall.

Nodding to Dell, Troy drew his sword and turned for the next soldier cresting the wall. But the Eldur's eyes went round under his helmet, his gaze caught on something just to the left of them. Troy didn't wait to check; he stabbed the man at the shoulder and the Eldur dropped his weapon, losing purchase with the ladder. Troy saw him fall several feet down before catching himself again, nearly colliding with another soldier below.

Gripping the ladder, Troy began pushing and shoving, trying to get the cursed thing off the wall. Gritting his teeth, he strained as several more soldiers began climbing, their added weight making the ladder that much more difficult to move.

"Bloody hell," Dell said from behind him but Troy still didn't look.

He became aware of a change in color, the quiet light of morning altering under something brighter, something hotter. The men down on the ladder stilled, almost as though they were waiting for something, and that gave him the moment he needed to shove the ladder away. It scratched over the stone wall, bumping over pits and grooves as it began a diagonal slide downward, crashing into another such ladder. The combined weight of both ladders was too much and they cracked near their centers, collapsing to the ground.

Panting, Troy straightened and looked up. Then he took a hasty step back, his gaze locking onto the large fireball that hovered just over the wall. It roiled and shifted, blazing bright orange and red just three feet overhead. Remarkably, it did not descend. Troy glanced over to where Brigetta stood, her arms outstretched, fingers clawed, her mouth moving to utter something none of them could hear.

An instant later the fireball burst, transforming in midair from hot flames to cool water. Troy ducked as the water poured over them, soaking him through. Dell cursed and shoved sodden hair from her face before shouting for everyone to guard the blood mage.

Several of Kiavana's soldiers began abandoning the wall, moving to converge on Brigetta, discarding their swords in favor of long range weapons and shields wherever they could. Troy glanced down at the courtyard, squinting to make out Kaden's silver-streaked hair in the melee. His friend was hacking at the squared formation alongside his sister, Nelek just on the other side of them. Together, they were slimming the enemy ranks as best they could, trying to beat their way to the mage protected within.

Troy's stomach clenched tight and he turned to run for Brigetta. As much as he hated to admit it, this was all about the mages now and there would be no chance for them if Bree fell.

Thirty-nine

Brigetta's body was waning. There was an ache between her shoulder blades that seemed to spike up and down her spine, a clear sign that her body had reached its limits. But she couldn't stop, not now. Not with all those men down there and that cursed mage trying to blast them all to pieces.

Not with Kaden and Liana in the fray.

This mage seemed to favor fire. He tried to send another ball of flame her way but she deflected, replacing his fire with a flock of very confused geese. Someone snorted a laugh at the squawking spectacle and she became aware of many bodies pressing in close to her. She couldn't risk pulling her attention from the ether to see, but she could sense their intentions were to protect.

Magic boiled through the ether, pulsing to life with every Eldur that fell. It pressed in on all sides, tingling over her skin, thrumming in time with her own wavering heartbeat. In the courtyard below, the mage was drawing on it again, she could sense the pull as magic rushed to answer his call and tried to prepare.

In the back of her mind she could hear Faxon's voice telling her to stop acting in defense and start fighting back. Defense never wins a fight, she remembered, especially with magic. She could try to wait for the mage to strain himself unconscious, but with her own weakened state it was more likely that she would fall first, leaving all of Kiavana to his destruction.

No, she needed to act and she needed to act now.

Scanning the yard for inspiration, she wondered what Noffi would do.

Noffi would do something big, something huge. Something that would have people talking about it for years to come.

She spotted Troy beside her, looking ashen and grim. He was holding a shield up, shoving back against an Eldur who had managed to reach them. Around him were several more Kiavanan soldiers, boxing her in like a Human wall that mimicked the formation around the enemy mage.

A wall, she thought and concentrated on magic.

"Loomaressa et all acht neevah," she said, pronouncing each word deliberately.

The ground rumbled, a low tremor at first but building and building until it was all she could do to stay upright. The soldiers around her gasped in alarm, steadying one another as the quake continued. Fighters in the courtyard staggered to and fro, several collapsing to their knees while still others managed to seize the opportunity and strike down their opponents.

Bree swayed, her vision of the yard smearing into bright colors. She could no longer make out who was where. Magic seared through her, her blood going hot—unbearably hot—as it waited for her next command. But her throat closed on the words, her tongue thick and clumsy in her mouth.

It was too much; she'd overreached herself.

Gods, what had she done?

Someone grabbed her, held her upright before she could fall over. She couldn't be sure if the ground was still shaking or if it was just her body giving out, seizing from the strain. Her jaw clamped shut, all of her muscles tightening against her will, and the view of the courtyard altered.

She saw Faxon at the gates, cutting his way through the Eldur with terrifying proficiency. Behind him were men in a different uniform, men who were quite obviously fighting on their side of the battle, and if she could have she would have breathed in relief.

All was not lost, not yet.

Faxon recoiled in pain, falling to his knee just as the Eldur in front of him attempted to hack him down. Faxon dropped to the side, rolling away from the danger, his face contorted into a fierce grimace that would have frightened her in any other circumstance.

She couldn't speak to him, couldn't let him know what was happening, couldn't apologize for failing him, and that was an agony all its own.

He writhed on the ground, every muscle in his arms taut, his fingers clawing through dirt as he tried to lift himself. She saw the strain on his face, the curl of his upper lip as he snarled and reached for his vest pocket.

Troy's voice was in her ear, calling her name over and over in a panic, but she couldn't see him. Her vision was still of Faxon, impossibly of Faxon, and she knew then that she was dying. Her heart fluttered in her chest, rapid and light. She tried to coach it into a steadier pace but she could only pull in a thread of air through her throat, which seemed to confirm her fear.

She really was dying.

Faxon pulled a vial from his vest, flicked the stopper open, and lifted it to his lips with a shaking hand. She saw him drink, saw the working of his throat as he swallowed hard, and then her eyelids drooped closed and she saw nothing else.

~ * ~

Trenna sprinted downhill, her feet sliding over muddied ground the closer she came to the fortress. Gideon's forces had shoved the Eldur west and her eighty-five—Gods, she hoped there were still eighty-five—had a clear shot for the gate. She could see them pushing forward, chopping and slicing their way through Navell's men. Navell, she noticed, wasn't anywhere in the fray.

She leapt over a jumble of bodies, her legs jolting as she hit the ground harder than anticipated. Agony flared through her shoulder and she hissed a curse, staggering to keep upright. Pressing the heel of her hand into the wound, she blinked around a wave of giddiness and shook her head.

"T-Trenna..."

The voice was familiar and she paused. Panting, Trenna searched for its owner. She found him a moment later, kneeling and clutching at the ground, a weird golden light shimmering around his body: Faxon.

Taking a step toward him, she felt the ground begin to shake, everything rumbling and trembling underfoot, and the light around Faxon grew brighter, more prominent. Trenna watched, perplexed, as Faxon was engulfed in blinding gold shades. She had the sense that he was changing somehow, that his body was elongating, morphing. His fingers stretched, curving into wicked claws, she saw that much until at last she could bare it no longer and was forced to look away.

Shielding her face, she wasn't prepared for the gust of heat and wind as it exploded out from Faxon's position. She lost her balance, tumbling backward into mud, rolling until she hit the body of some unfortunate soul nearby. Her shoulder ached, pain spiking down her arm and through her collarbone and she held it again, demanding the pain to stop somehow, to go away and let her continue.

When she opened her eyes, the rumbling had stopped. The light too was gone and where Faxon had been, there stood a creature she had never seen before. It was long, four legged like a reptile, with a jagged tail and a pointed snout. Large, sharp teeth as thick as her forearm curved out of its mouth and at its elbows were two more hooked bones protruding outside its skin.

Trenna gaped at it, stunned immobile as it turned to gaze at her with feral golden eyes. Faxon's eyes, she realized, and continued to stare.

It moved with a fluidity that proved it was a predator, turning to the gate and letting loose a horrible roar that rumbled through the ground. Launching forward with powerful haunches, it—he, she thought, this was still somehow Faxon—charged the gate, leaping over Captain Bervam's shocked form at the last moment.

Realizing she had to move, Trenna struggled to her feet, shoving one knee under her so she could push her aching body all the way up. She swayed, a wave of giddiness washing over her, and she nearly went back over, but a hand on her elbow kept her upright. Bervam was there, looking ashen and just as startled as she was.

"What in blazes is that thing?" he asked, gazing at where the creature's tail was disappearing through the gate.

"Not sure what it is now, but I know who it used to be," she said and started forward.

"Used to be?" Bervam echoed and followed her, but she didn't elaborate further.

Beyond the wall came the reverberating roar of the beast again and several screams rose up in answer. Trenna raced for the gate, Bervam on her heels as they sprinted into the courtyard. Together they burst into the chaos of battle, separating out to attack those soldiers not already in retreat.

She recognized the formation near the center of the courtyard and her stomach dropped. Blood mage, she thought. Somehow she'd held onto the belief that Brigetta would be the only mage on the battlefield today, but as a whirlwind of fire swept through the bailey, dread crawled up her spine.

The swirl of fire headed straight for the creature, catching up any unfortunate soldiers in its path. They screamed as their feet lost purchase with the ground, their bodies combusting into flame as they rose higher and higher. Faxon snarled at the fiery tornado, pounding his long, spiked tail into the ground so hard she could feel it through her feet.

A crack rent the ground where his tail struck, zigzagging its way toward the whirlwind. Seconds later the earth opened up with a thunderous rumble, revealing an enormous, gaping hole in the tornado's path. The whirlwind dropped inside, disappearing into the hole with a loud, hallow howl that filled the courtyard.

Well that was useful, she thought, glancing at Faxon as he leapt over the hole. He landed on all fours, curved claws scraping over the ground, his long tail swishing through the air behind him.

A glint of silver caught her eye and she turned, spotting Kaden as he rushed the cubed formation. Liana was beside him, ducking low to cut open the knees of the soldier closest to her. A hole opened in the formation as the soldier collapsed and Kaden, slippery as an eel, slid inside before it closed again.

Trenna's heart seized at the sight, pride and worry crashing into her. She ran hard for them, scanning the crowd for Nelek but not seeing him.

Gods, where was he?

She reached Liana's side just as another hole opened in the formation. Under the press of soldiers she could just see Kaden's face, his mouth contorted into a scowl and his eyes flashing fierce green.

"Mother!" Liana said beside her and Trenna paused just long enough to wink at her daughter before launching into battle.

The hole in the formation was taking longer to close this time, confused soldiers realizing the attack had come from behind them rather than in front, and she leapt inside. Something nicked her elbow, sharp and quick, and then the hole was closed, bodies sealing her in the center of the formation.

Kaden's eyes rounded in recognition when he saw her and he flashed a quick grin. "You're late," he said.

Trenna almost responded, but the formation had shrunk once more, allowing three of its outer ring to turn and face the threat inside. There was no inner ring, she noticed that straight off, which meant that Liana and Kaden and whoever else was out there had managed to thin the ranks quite a bit. It also meant that, aside from the three soldiers currently bearing down on them, the blood mage at the center had no real protection.

She could see the mage clearly now. He had his back to them, his arms were outstretched, and a wide cloak swept the ground at his feet. Just audible under the grunts and shouts of fighting, she could hear the familiar murmur of magic in use. The sound made the little hairs on her neck stand stiff, memories stirring in her that she'd long forgotten. Memories of battle, of formations just like this one; only in those memories she'd been part of the formation, protecting the mage at its center rather than attempting to murder him.

For a conflicted moment she hesitated, her sword poised to block the oncoming soldier.

Blood mages weren't merely a tool for battle, they were physicians and historians. To cut this man down would not only take out the immediate threat, it would devastate Dyngannon to its core. Even before her exile, Trenna had known there were not enough blood mages to care for the Eldur people.

How many innocent lives would she condemn to sickness and death by taking this man down?

Her sword met steel blade, metal scraping over metal as she deflected the first blow sent her way. She caught the soldier's hazel-blue glare from under his helmet, all the malice he had aimed directly at her, and Trenna wondered if she knew him. Their swords slipped apart and he came again, sweeping low and fast this time so she had to jerk back.

The pointed weapon breezed past her midsection, missing her by a hairsbreadth. Trenna lunged forward, trying to thrust her own sword into the man's chest, but her body was tiring and she wasn't fast enough. Worse yet, her arm was straining to keep the sword upright, her muscles had been pushed past their endurance, and she'd lost so much blood that giddy lights peppered her vision.

Gods help her, she was losing.

She could see Kaden at her right, fending off two men with youthful ease and the grace of a practiced swordsman, and suddenly felt her age.

On the other side of the formation she heard Faxon give a low, reptilian growl. The unnatural sound seemed to claw at the back of her neck, trailing down to the base of her spine. It had an effect on the soldiers too. She could see them all shrink back on the left side, huddling closer together, and knew that had to be where Faxon was. And in fact, she could see the spiked ridge of his spine towering above them just in her peripheral view.

Trenna had just enough time to wonder where his head was before the Eldur in front of her brought a hammering blow against her sword. She felt the leather grip fly from her hand and watched as the sword spun away from her, clattering to the ground. The man shoved his pommel toward her face and she made a labored attempt to swivel aside, to let it pass her, but again she was too slow.

He had a blunt, square pommel at the end of his hilt. The corner of it smashed into the side of her face with so much force she thought her cheekbone cracked. There was a sickening crunch and agony pulsed through her jaw and temple. Trenna staggered to the side, desperate to stay upright, to stay conscious. But her vision was dimming, everything turning fuzzy at the edges, and her foot caught on something.

She tilted and fell, which turned out to be a good thing because that cursed Eldur was still coming. His sword passed through the air where her head had been, and then her wounded shoulder crashed into solid earth. She made a weak attempt to kick him, to stave him off, but he anticipated the move, distancing himself just long enough for her foot to miss. Then he came back, stomping on her leg in one quick move.

Her knee bounced once, pain jolting up and down her thigh, and then he leaned his weight into it, pinning her there. Cool mud slicked over her face, soaking into her hair, and she could taste dirt and copper in her mouth. Dazed, she watched him angle his sword, gripping the hilt with two hands, preparing to stab it downward into her.

She tried rolling to the left and right, but his foot remained steadfast on her leg, the heel of his boot unrelenting at her knee, and she could not summon the strength to dislodge it. The sword dropped fast, heading straight for her, its point glinting in the sunlight. Trenna shouted something unintelligible and twisted to the left as fast as she could, curling her body in toward her pinned knee.

The sword sank into the ground inches from her back and the man above her swore. An instant later he yanked the weapon up, preparing to aim once more, this time with an inescapable, horizontal swing that would slice her straight across the middle.

Heart hammering in her chest, she tried again to pull her leg away. Her fingers slid through mud as she clawed for more leverage, desperate to drag herself out of the sword's path. She saw the downward swing, the sharp edge of the sword fast approaching, and raised her hands in a feeble attempt to block it.

A familiar voice shouted her name from the left and for a heartbeat she thought it was Kaden. Gods, her own son was to witness her death. That seemed unnaturally cruel. She flinched, both in anticipation of the blow and recognition of the pain Kaden was about to suffer. She closed her eyes and glanced away, not wanting to see this final moment, and thought of Nelek instead: Nelek who was fighting somewhere else, who was about to die with her. There was nothing she could do about it, not this time.

At least their souls would travel to the After together.

The resounding clang of metal on metal crashed together near enough to be deafening, but not so deafening she did not hear a breathless grunt from her would-be murderer. She had the sense of bodies colliding above her and the pressure on her knee abruptly let up.

Trenna opened her eyes, spotting Kaden above her. His sword was angled in such a way she knew he had stopped the killing blow from hitting her, and the breath left her in a rush. The Eldur soldier she'd been combating collapsed to the ground inches from her, whatever blow he'd just suffered knocking his helmet free of his head. He had copper streaked brown hair and a wide, flat nose, as though the nose guard of his helmet had shaped the poor man's face.

In a blur of movement another body fell atop the soldier, knees slamming so hard into his chest that Trenna could hear something crack in there. It took her several seconds to recognize Nelek, his face twisted in rage as he pounded the soldier's face repeatedly with his fists. Her heart squeezed tight at the sight of him and she stared, too stunned by the violence in her husband to move.

He kept striking the Eldur, over and over, his fists cracking into skull and cheekbones and jaw, splitting open skin to reveal the bloody tissue beneath. He might have kept going long after the soldier had gone limp under him, except that a frigid gust of wind roared over them, knocking him half off the unfortunate man.

Kaden staggered to a knee and she grabbed at him to keep him from falling further. A cry of alarm rose from the formation, several men trying to retreat while several others tried to keep the protective wall intact for the blood mage. Kaden's eyes grew wide and she followed his gaze, spotting the large, spiked tail as it barreled through the soldiers in front of the mage.

"Get down!" Nelek shouted.

Trenna snagged a fistful of Kaden's jerkin, yanking him down until he was prone just beside her. The tail came again, swiping through the formation with so much force it tossed men from their feet, opening a hole wide enough she could see the beast as it swung about, ready to charge. Trenna cringed, clutching at Kaden's shoulder and praying Faxon wouldn't pummel them in the process.

She needn't have worried.

Faxon rose up on his haunches, towering over the vulnerable blood mage. His head canted to the side and his snout curled up, revealing thick, sharp teeth. Dark gold scales glistened in the sunlight, trailing over the lean muscle of his torso and down his legs. Whatever he was now, she thought with no small amount of admiration, he looked quite magnificent.

As he came back down, forelegs rushing to the ground just in front of the mage, his mouth opened wide. In a blink, he snatched up the mage, his jaws snapping closed with a horrible crunching sound. The mage's scream cut short, gurgling off into a whimper that was lost in the next second as Faxon flung his broken body toward the western wall.

"Holy gods above," Kaden breathed beside her.

There was movement around them, orders being shouted that she had not heard in many years: retreat. The Eldur ranks had fallen and were fleeing the castle gates, stumbling over each other in their escape. In all her life, she had never seen a force so desperate to get away, and she felt at once relieved that the fighting was over, and ashamed.

This was what the Eldur Army had come to?

Faxon opened his mouth again, wicked teeth stained with blood, and roared. The sound of it carried across the courtyard, chasing after whatever soldiers had not already fled. She felt the sound in her chest, an uncomfortable vibration that seemed to challenge her, calling out to something deep inside her very being. She stared at him, at the graceful predator he had become, and wondered if this was just a trick of magic or something more permanent.

With a contemptuous snort at the quickly emptying gate, Faxon turned and loped for the eastern wall, taking the courtyard in three strides before leaping up and onto the crenellated wall. His clawed feet crushed the stone under him, making the wall itself seem to waver with his weight. And then he lowered his muzzle to nose at a small figure at the top of the wall.

Brigetta, she thought; he must be checking on Brigetta.

"Trenna?" Nelek's voice pulled her attention from the scene on the wall and she shifted to look up at him.

He was crouching beside her, his angular face lined with concern as he reached out to check the wound on her shoulder. He had a gash across his brow and another along his jaw. Both were bleeding, making smeared trails that framed his face and mingled with his hair. Trenna touched his cheek, then the stubble along his chin, and felt the burn of tears behind her eyes.

"I missed you," she said, her voice a trifle raspy.

His eyes met hers, impossibly blue and dancing with laughter and relief. He didn't respond, not in words, but leaned down to kiss her, his lips tasting of blood and dirt and battle. She rose a little to meet him, felt his hand slide behind her head, his fingers curling into her hair, and kissed him back.

Epilogue

Kaden stood in the doorway of the great hall, watching the comings and goings of people in the aftermath of battle. The hall itself was still being used as an infirmary and likely would be for several days to come. What he'd seen of his Uncle Brenson led him to believe the man would open up his private rooms for the wounded if need be, so there would be no relocating the ill for some time.

He could see Brenson on the far side of the hall lingering with Nelek, who refused to leave Trenna's side. His mother had taken a beating during the fight but it was evident to everyone that she would survive. Still, it was a comforting display of devotion on his father's part not to leave her, and Kaden couldn't help a small smile.

One day he hoped to have a love like that. A love that ran deep, that knit two souls together so completely their very identities were defined by it. Perhaps those of a more independent nature might balk at such an idea, but Kaden believed his parents were the better for their relationship. He knew both of them could exist outside of each other and yet, they were their best selves when together.

He imagined it was a kind of addiction, loving like that. But instead of ruining a life, as addictions were wont to do, this one built something special, something every person who knew them could recognize and yet not quite define. Something everyone yearned for.

"She got here just in time," Troy said from beside him.

Kaden half turned and smiled at his friend, reaching out to grip his good arm. Troy smiled back and nodded toward Trenna and Nelek.

"Don't you think?" Troy asked.

"Yes, she did," Kaden said, glancing out into the courtyard. "Though by most accounts we owe the victory to Faxon."

At the mention of the assassin, Troy squinted out into the yard as well. The cost of the battle was still prominent. Men were picking through the fallen, carefully removing them to somewhere outside the fortress walls. Near the northeast tower Faxon's form had not changed yet and he lay curled into a ball like a cat, his massive head resting over clawed feet. His eyes were closed and Kaden could see the gentle rise and fall of his breathing, signifying that the beast was fast asleep.

"Do you think he did that on purpose?" Troy asked, still eying the creature.

"I have no idea," Kaden said. "I wouldn't even know what to call... that."

"A wyrm," a voice said from behind them and Kaden turned around.

Brigetta stood there, her face ghastly pale as she leaned against the woman he'd come to recognize as his great-grandmother. He really ought to ask the woman her name, but at present he had other concerns. Such as the unwavering look in Bree's red-speckled eyes. She was here for her hour and she would not be deterred this time.

"A wyrm?" Troy asked. "What in blazes is a wyrm?"

She smiled at Troy, her expression turning sad as she glanced over at her husband. The creature stirred, lifting its head for just a moment to gaze over at them. The eyes were so clearly Faxon's that it left Kaden feeling uneasy. He drummed his pommel with his fingers, only slightly comforted by the weapon's nearness. He'd seen what Faxon could do against mere swords and knew there was little defense against such a creature.

"It's a transition," Bree said at last and Faxon put his head down again. His eyes, however, remained open and fastened on them. Or more accurately, on his wife, and Kaden realized with a jolt that the creature could hear them even at this distance. "I am uncertain what will become of him."

"He will become something new," his grandmother said.

With a deep breath, Kaden turned away from the creature and looked to Brigetta. The fate of Faxon Mylonas, as interesting as it sounded, could not delay the inevitable and in truth, Kaden was tired of avoiding it. Brigetta had manipulated his family, dragged him from his home, and forced him into battle, but he could no longer muster anger for the woman. Not anymore.

He wasn't certain exactly when it had happened, perhaps up on the tower with Dell and the archers or perhaps in the field fighting alongside his sister and father, but Kaden knew down in his bones that his fight wasn't over. The fight for Dyngannon, the fight for peace between Eldur and Human that his parents had begun all those years ago, it was in his blood. It called to him, had always called to him if he were honest with himself.

His gaze slipped past Brigetta and back into the hall. Trenna was sitting up and she was looking at him. Their eyes met and across the distance he could sense his mother's resignation. She'd fought so hard to give him the choice, to allow him a freedom no king before him had ever known: the right to walk away. But even she knew the choice to be a farce.

No man, no real man, could ever choose to walk away when people were in need. And these people were in dire need of peace. Somehow, Kaden would find a way to bring it to them.

With one small nod to his mother, Kaden took another breath and said, "I will do it. I will be king."

Meet A. J. Maguire

A.J. Maguire is a science fiction and fantasy junkie. She loves stories in all shapes and sizes, and believes that the answers to every question in life can be found in the tales we tell. A devoted parent, she enjoys sharing all her geekery with her son and intends to continue consuming and sharing stories long into her old age.

Works From The Pen Of
A J. Maguire

Sedition - War was coming. Years of conspiring with his brother, of hunting for his lost mother, and war was finally coming. With options and allies depleting, Nelek finds that his newest and brashest bodyguard, Trenna Croften, could be the key to everything he's been fighting for.

Sabateur - He'd promised to unite the land, to bring Eldur and Human together in peace, but Nelek Dyngannon never expected that peace to come at the cost of his wife. Together, Trenna and Nelek must battle past the demons of Trenna's past in order to forge a peaceful future.

Letter to Our Readers

Enjoy this book?

You can make a difference

As an independent publisher, Wings ePress, Inc. does not have the financial clout of the large New York Publishers. We can't afford large magazine spreads or subway posters to tell people about our quality books.

But, we do have something much more effective and powerful than ads. We have a large base of loyal readers.

Honest Reviews help bring the attention of new readers to our books.

If you enjoyed this book, we would appreciate it if you would spend a few minutes posting a review on the site where you purchased this book or on the Wings ePress, Inc. webpages at: https://wingsepress. com/

Visit Our Website

For The Full Inventory
Of Quality Books:

Wings ePress.Inc
https://wingsepress.com/

Quality trade paperbacks and downloads
in multiple formats,
in genres ranging from light romantic comedy
to general fiction and horror.
Wings has something for every reader's taste.
Visit the website, then bookmark it.
We add new titles each month!

Wings ePress Inc.
3000 N. Rock Road
Newton, KS 67114